Ivy Lane

Cathy Bramley

CORGI BOOKS

TRANSWORLD PUBLISHERS
61–63 Uxbridge Road, London W5 5SA
www.transworldbooks.co.uk

Transworld is part of the Penguin Random House group of companies whose
addresses can be found at global.penguinrandomhouse.com

Penguin
Random House
UK

First published in Great Britain as four separate ebooks
in 2014 by Transworld Digital
First published as one edition in 2015 by Corgi Books
an imprint of Transworld Publishers

A CIP catalogue record for this book
is available from the British Library.

ISBN 9780552171236

Typeset in 11½/13pt Garamond by Kestrel Data, Exeter, Devon.

**Penguin Random House is committed to a sustainable future for
our business, our readers and our planet. This book is made from
Forest Stewardship Council® certified paper.**

Printed and bound in Great Britain by Clays Ltd, Elcograf S.p.A.

For my mum, Sue

allotment

a-lot-ment

noun

1. a plot of land rented by an individual for growing vegetables or flowers, often occupied by a variety of delightful characters who also enjoy baking, gossiping and match-making.

synonyms: plot/garden/home

Spring

Chapter 1

I did up my coat, pulled on a woollen beret and wrapped an excessively long scarf around my neck until only my nose and eyes were left bare. Anyone would be forgiven for thinking that I was trying to exit my new little terraced house incognito. But I wasn't. There was no need; no one knew me anyway.

It was the thing I loved most about it. Apart from the original tiled fireplace in the front room. That was unexpectedly pretty.

Here in Kingsfield, a small market town on the edge of Derbyshire, I could start afresh. Although I had only moved a paltry twenty miles, the simple joy of not facing pitying smiles and awkward silences would make a huge improvement to my life, I was sure of it.

The front door was sweet, too, with its stained-glass panel. I hadn't noticed it when I came to view the house. That particular December day had whizzed by in a blur. I'd arrived for an interview at All Saints Nursery and Infant School with low expectations for my chance of success and somehow was offered the job on the spot. I called in to the local estate agent's on a whim and was shown details of a 'highly desirable property ideal for madam's needs'. Ten minutes later I was viewing it. The decor was dated, the kitchen was tiny and the bathroom tiles were held on with mildew, but it was only five minutes from school and I liked that it was such a clear, empty space. There had also been a leaflet poking out from the letterbox advertising vacant allotment plots, which was when inspiration had struck.

Serendipitous to say the least. I've probably spent longer choosing a takeaway.

As I held the front door open I steered my bicycle carefully over the front step, past the remaining packing cases, taking care not to further damage the hall wallpaper after yesterday's unfortunate accident with an anglepoise lamp, and stared at the sky.

If James was here . . .

My eyes welled up with instant tears and my step faltered. I really had to stop beginning my thoughts with that phrase, but as it was New Year's Day, I let myself off this once.

But if James *was* here, he would look up at the clouds and say, 'Ah Cumuly Cirruly (or something similar) – perfect conditions for a ten-mile stint up a hazardous mountain path.'

But as he wasn't here, I would have to settle for simply knowing that the sky was an encouraging shade of blue and the clouds the merest of gossamer wisps. As New Year's Days went, it was not bad at all.

I glanced back at the row of coat pegs in the hallway and decided against wearing my yellow hi-vis waistcoat. I would be home before it got dark and in all honesty, although my personal road safety was of paramount importance, it really did clash with my coat. I have some standards. My cycle helmet was a must, though, I decided, forcing it on over my beret.

I mounted the saddle, pocketed my front-door key and

pushed off, glad for once of the padding on my rear-end, the result of sitting on it for a year and feeling sorry for myself.

'Onwards and upwards, Tilly!' as my dear old mum would say.

Although I didn't quite have my bearings yet, I was pretty sure of the way; Ivy Lane allotments was less than a two-minute cycle from Wellington Street, where I lived. In fact, I could have walked. But these days I went everywhere I could by bike; I had learned that cycling past people with a cheery wave was far preferable to having to stop and chat.

Noon on the first of January and the streets were deserted. I didn't pass a single car or person along Wellington Street. Hardly surprising given that most of my new neighbours had welcomed in the New Year enthusiastically with fireworks, loud parties and even, sometime after two if I recall, an outdoor drunken conga. I turned into the next road, past a little arcade of shops; the newspaper shop was open and the pub on the corner had all its lights on, but the café, estate agent and other small businesses were closed. I cycled past my new school; a few days and I would be there. Working. The thought gave me the collywobbles and I cycled a bit faster.

Ivy Lane was very similar to Wellington Street: larger semi-detached houses at one end and terraces at the other. The allotments were well hidden and I had to cycle up and down the street twice before I spotted a gap in the terraced houses. I put out my hand, indicating to no one that I was turning right, and followed the driveway to the end.

'Thank you,' I murmured to the wooden noticeboard welcoming me to Ivy Lane allotments.

Imposing metal security gates with an enormous padlock on the inside formed the entrance to the site, which made me feel both safe and slightly nervous. I braked in front of them and took the manila envelope from my pocket. All my dealings with the allotment committee had been done by email prior to my arrival in town and this was my first visit. I had a welcome letter from a lady called Christine, allotment secretary, a key for the padlock and a map showing me how to find plot 16B, which was technically half a plot as someone else rented 16A.

Undoing a padlock that weighed more than a Shetland pony and was on the far side of the gate whilst simultaneously supporting a bike between my knees was a mistake, but by the time I realized this, both my trembling arms were through the bars and I was committed. After twenty seconds of fumbling, the padlock fell to the ground.

I was in. David Blaine, eat your heart out.

Flushed with exertion and success, I hauled myself and my trusty bike inside and re-locked the gate.

A tarmacked road, wide enough to take a car, curved through the middle of the allotments. Either side of it, the ground was divided into neat rectangles of earth, each separated from its neighbour by a wide grass border. My heart soared at its symmetry and order. I loved a nice right angle. Back gardens of the terraced houses on Ivy Lane formed one boundary of the site and a mixture of hedgerow and trees formed the other.

I began to wheel my bike along the road, keeping an eye on the wooden stakes at the end of each plot, indicating its number. I didn't see any As or Bs, though – how would I be able to tell which half of plot sixteen was mine?

The allotment site stretched further than my eye could see but I guessed there were around thirty plots. Surprisingly, there was a lot more to the place than just vegetable beds: nearly every plot had some sort of tree, bare now, of course, in the middle of winter, but I could imagine how lovely it would look in the summer. Sheds seemed to be very popular, from stylish little huts with net curtains at the windows to ramshackle affairs made from corrugated plastic and old doors. Greenhouses, patio furniture, picnic tables, water butts, even the odd barbecue . . . The place was certainly well used, by the look of it.

I paused in front of a low wooden building like a cricket pavilion in the centre of the site. There were no lights on and, like the rest of the allotment, it was completely deserted. A couple of Portaloo-style toilets and a garage completed what I assumed to be official headquarters.

Quashing the feeling that I was trespassing, I continued my explorations and soon found myself at plot sixteen.

Oh.

Despite my horror, I couldn't help a wry smile from escaping; I needn't have worried about establishing which half was mine.

The end nearest the road had a splendid display of green tufts, which I recognized as leeks, reminding me of my previous headmaster's dubious hair transplant, although his had been black, not green obviously. Behind them, I spotted fat red cabbages and huge green spikes – I squinted to focus my eyes. Sprouts! Goodness, I never knew sprouts grew on sticks like that! And right at the back was a complicated arrangement of canes and string, protecting what looked like bare twigs.

Beyond two trees and a neat wooden shed was my half. The contrast was, to put it mildly, shocking.

You know the story of Sleeping Beauty falling asleep for a hundred years and the forest outside the castle becoming overgrown and impassable?

That was my half.

13

I thought back to my collection of garden tools, which consisted of a pink hand fork, a trowel, matching gloves and a rake. Woefully inadequate. My gardening experience was limited to buying coriander by the pot and making cress egg-heads with my class two years ago. It had always been *James*'s dream to grow our own vegetables, whereas I had been more than happy with Birds Eye peas and a tin of sweetcorn.

I propped the bike up against a bench and tiptoed across the dewy grass towards my end for a closer inspection.

So this was to be my 'new interest'. Hands on hips, I surveyed the brambles, nettles, thistles, dock leaves and some other trailing weed and tried to conjure up positive thoughts.

Neglected, unloved, desolate . . .

Stop right there, thank you very much. Deep breaths, Tilly.

I blinked and stretched my eyes to send a clear message to the tears.

New Year's resolution number one: We are moving on.

OK, that was better.

I was here because I needed a fresh start, a fresh attitude and some fresh air, at least, that was what my counsellor had told me. And my mother had agreed, especially to the fresh air bit. Apparently I was beginning to acquire the complexion of Miss Havisham.

The undertaking of an allotment seemed an ideal way to tackle New Year's resolution number two: Keep busy.

That shouldn't be difficult; if I was to bring this patch of wilderness back to life, I would certainly have my hands full.

Plus, above all else, I craved peace and solitude, and what could be more peaceful than gardening? A bank holiday and this place was like a morgue! I shivered. Yes, I felt sure that New Year's resolution number three would be easy to stick to here: Keep myself to myself.

And as maudlin as it sounded, if I was entirely honest, I thought if James somehow knew that I was getting down and dirty with Mother Nature, he would in some small way be proud of me.

What do you think, James, can I make a go of it?

'Of course you can, love,' came the reply, close to my ear.

I screamed.

Chapter 2

My heart thumped. I clutched at my chest and lost my balance, slipping from the turf into a patch of thorns.

'Steady!' Two strong arms grabbed me from behind and yanked me to safety.

Miss Clumsy Oaf strikes again. And I still had my cycle helmet on. Great look, Tilly. Oh well, at least my scarf was covering the worst of my blushes.

I turned towards my assailant-cum-rescuer and bent to remove a prickly frond from my tights, buying time to get my breathing back under control. Assailant was perhaps a bit harsh. In front of me was a man, older than me, with close-cropped hair, blondish, and a very sheepish smile. Broad and beefy were the two words that instantly came to mind.

'I was going to say you'll fit right in here, you know, talking to yourself, but I guess I should apologize for frightening you. I came to introduce myself,' he said, his blue eyes creasing with concern.

I didn't know what was worse: the fact that I had been talking to myself or that I wasn't aware that I had spoken out loud. I made a mental note to watch out for this worrying development in future.

He fiddled with the sleeves of his thick woollen jumper and seemed to be waiting for me to speak but I was still panting and clutching my chest.

He cleared his throat and stuck out a hand. 'I'm Charlie. Pleased to meet you and, er, sorry again.'

I took my helmet off and shook his hand.

'Tilly.' My voice came out all rusty from disuse. Good. I couldn't have been talking that much, after all.

'So what are you up to today?' he said, eyeing up the tangle of weeds behind me. 'Clearing?'

Clearing. The very word filled me with panic. I couldn't possibly clear this patch of wasteland on my own. What had I been thinking? I wondered if it was too late to swap to another plot. Perhaps someone else would enjoy the challenge. Someone who owned a spade, for example.

'Um . . .'

'Gemma will be pleased to have someone her age sharing the plot. We've all been speculating who would take it over since the last lot got kicked off.'

Kicked off? I swallowed, wondering what misdemeanour warranted a 'kicking off'. If it was incompetence, I would probably soon be joining their ranks. A woman my age sounded promising, though. Unless she was as nosy as Charlie.

'You don't say much, do you? Not that I'm complaining. My ex never shut up. It used to do my head in. I love peace and quiet. That's why I'm down here now; I thought I'd be the only one without a hangover today. Looks like I got that wrong.' He grinned at me. 'Not that I'm complaining. Now I'm repeating myself. Oh, please say something, you're making me nervous.'

I laughed at that and he wiped his brow with mock relief. He was very sweet and was trying so hard to be friendly. It wasn't his fault that I had also chosen today to explore because I'd wanted to be alone.

'This visit is just a recce.' I straightened my beret and smoothed my elaborate side fishtail plait (the result of too many hours watching YouTube videos). 'To see what I have let myself in for.'

He raised his eyebrows.

I cringed. 'I wanted a challenge but . . .' My voice faded and I realized part of me was already planning on giving up.

Charlie stepped forward and kicked at the brambles with the toe of his boot. 'You wait, you'll soon lick this into shape. That's the miracle of gardening. As soon as spring comes, stuff wants to grow, it's nature, isn't it?' He shrugged.

He bent down and poked at the ground. 'Look.'

I crouched down at his side to see what he had found. He smelt of woodsmoke and earth. This was the closest I had been to a man in eons. There was a chance I was blushing.

Charlie pointed at a clump of green spikes just visible above ground. 'Green shoots. New life. No matter how badly this plot was treated last year, it still has hope, do you see? It's still going to try again.'

I stood up quickly. 'I see,' I mumbled.

'My plot's over there.' Charlie straightened up and pointed to the far side. 'The one with the creosoted shed.'

I nodded politely.

'I'll leave you to it for a bit. But come over later and I'll show you round.'

'Sure.'

As soon as he was out of sight I planned to make my exit. I belatedly remembered my manners and thanked him as he strode away.

Now, where was I? As well as the plot that time forgot, I had inherited a dilapidated compost bin made from old wooden pallets, a scruffy slabbed area that might once have had a shed on it, a flaking wrought-iron bench and a stumpy tree. It seems everything on plot 16B needed some TLC, I thought, sitting briefly on the bench until the cold penetrated my coat.

Join the club.

I coughed. 'Join the club.' I hadn't said it aloud the first time, I was sure of it. Phew.

Beyond my plot was the allotment boundary bordered by a swathe of trees. I wandered through them, brushing the low-hanging twigs back from my face. Ahead of me, two branches from neighbouring trees had entwined to form a natural archway and someone had placed a stone bench beneath them. I gasped. Even on a cold January day, it was totally enchanting and the romance of the setting brought unexpected tears to my eyes.

I turned hurriedly to retreat to the safety of plot sixteen and smacked straight into a wall of muscle encased in rough wool.

'Don't tell the committee, but I've had a key cut to the pavilion. Come on, I'll make you a cuppa, you're shivering.'

Jesus Christ. This chap was as stealthy as a ninja.

I stood my ground. 'Charlie, if we are going to be friends,' I instantly regretted my words as his face lit up, 'you have got to stop creeping up on me. I can barely tolerate other people's company at all, let alone surprise attacks.'

I shouldn't have said that; now he was crushed.

'Oh, go on then,' I said, softening. 'A hot drink would be lovely.'

*

The inside of the pavilion smelt of old socks and wet dog and it was only marginally warmer than outside, but it did have the major attraction of a kettle and as my feet had the onset of frostbite, I was glad to come inside. Apparently we had to sit in the dark, though.

'Half the committee live in that row of terraced houses over there.' Charlie nodded through a dirty window towards the back gardens facing on to the allotments. He lifted two chairs from a stack and set them next to the central table. 'One sign of life from this place and they'll be over like a shot with pitchforks and air rifles.'

Marvellous. Day One and I get attacked by an angry posse for breaking and entering. I could see the headlines already.

Charlie disappeared into the tiny kitchenette while I sat and waited. The room reminded me of a scout hut: wooden floorboards, lots of windows and zero insulation. I could imagine it all steamed-up during committee meetings. At one end of the room, above some cupboards, was a series of posters: rules (lots of), price lists (everything from Manure to Mars bars) and notices (AGM, contact details for the committee and social events). This allotment lark looked to be a full-time occupation for some, and I hoped that no one tried to rope me into social events. That was *so* not on my agenda.

Charlie handed me a mug of black coffee, added two heaped spoonfuls of sugar into his own and offered me a slug of brandy from his hipflask, which I declined.

He waggled his eyebrows playfully as he sloshed some in his own. 'Just a drop to warm the cockles. Shouldn't really; it plays havoc with my medication.' He crossed his eyes and stuck his tongue out to one side as if to reassure me he was joking and I couldn't help but laugh.

Sitting in the Palace of Pong with a complete stranger drinking the worst coffee of my life should have had me running a mile, but I was actually semi-happy. I felt proud of myself all of a sudden.

You're doing it, Tilly, you're actually moving on.

'So,' said Charlie, smacking his lips. 'I'm thirty-five, single, a fireman, moved to Kingsfield five years ago. Took up allotment gardening as a form of stress-relief. You?'

I took a deep breath. This was the bit I hated. 'I'm twenty-eight, new to Kingsfield, a teacher. Start a new job next Monday. I thought I'd start gardening to force myself out of the house, get away from marking books.' It was partly true. I cradled the mug in my hands and let the steam defrost my nose. Charlie was nodding; he was a very good listener.

I sighed. 'I'm a complete novice, though. Seriously, I don't know my cucumbers from my courgettes. Goodness knows how I'm going to cope.'

He jumped up, rummaged through the cupboards at the far end of the room and returned with a packet of biscuits. We slurped and dunked for several moments before Charlie set his mug down and touched me lightly on the arm.

'Don't worry about it. That's the beauty of this place. Everyone is so generous with their time and their knowledge.' He chuckled. 'Even their veg in the summer. There's no shortage of expertise here; even after three years, I'm still learning from others. You'll love it; we're like one big family.'

I spluttered and choked and sprayed a mouthful of hot coffee all over Charlie's face. We both jumped to our feet; my face red with embarrassment, Charlie's red from scalding liquid. I slammed down the mug, grabbed my cycle helmet and ran from the pavilion.

'What?' pleaded Charlie from behind me. 'What did I say?'

'Sorry,' I yelled over my shoulder. 'Got to go.'

Family. The tears streamed down my face as I cycled back home. I wasn't ready – might never be ready – for another family.

Chapter 3

It was six weeks before I dared show my face at Ivy Lane allotments again. I had been fully occupied with settling in to my new job and, much to my surprise, I was absolutely loving being back in the classroom. It was only three days a week, a job share with another teacher, but it had been fifteen months since I had last worked and even getting up in the morning at seven a.m. had taken some getting used to, let alone the lesson planning, marking and interaction with hordes of strangers, big and small. The weather had also provided me with a good excuse to stay away by snowing heavily and then freezing and finally flooding; definitely not conducive to gardening. And besides, I was putting off facing Charlie again.

But it was February half-term, my school work was up to date and my meagre possessions were all unpacked and neatly arranged at home, and I had completely run out of excuses not to come.

This time as I cycled slowly down the road towards my plot, I noticed several other people dotted around: in greenhouses, bent over crops, pushing loaded wheelbarrows, and there was a gentle sense of industriousness about the place. I felt my spirits lift and took large nosefuls of fresh air.

It was simply a matter of making my wilderness tidy and orderly, and growing things to eat, I supposed. No need to stress or panic over it.

I discarded my bike at the bench, marched on to plot sixteen and prepared to make a plan. Two things struck me instantly: behind the sprouts on plot 16A was a newly dug bed of soft black soil, hundreds of little white lumps protruding from the earth. Whoever owned this half of the plot was clearly a very hard worker. Secondly, there was music coming from the shed.

I hesitated.

There was a good chance that I would have to make polite conversation with said 'hard worker'. On the other hand, there was no time like the present for setting some ground rules. I would be polite but distant; on no account did I want to get embroiled in some ardent gardeners' discussion about the merits of manure versus leaf mulch.

I knocked on the shed door with, I felt, the perfect amount of force: assertive but not unfriendly. The music stopped, followed by a yelp and a tinkle of glass. I swallowed. What was I interrupting exactly? Perhaps I should tiptoe away and come back later . . .

The door opened a fraction and one big blue eye stared at me through the gap. I caught a flash of blonde hair and an over-powering blast of . . . nail polish?

'Heart attack dot com!' squealed whoever it was.

The door flew open and the shed's occupant grabbed me by the arm, hauled me inside and slammed the door shut. We both landed in deckchairs opposite one another.

'I thought you were my mother!'

She rolled her eyes skywards, fanned her face and retrieved a bottle of clear nail polish from behind a plant pot. Then, worryingly, she did a double-take and gasped. 'Oh gosh! You're not a homeless person, are you?'

I glanced down at my outfit: brown waterproof jacket (James's), grey jogging bottoms (James's), brown and green check shirt (you've guessed it – James's). Unflattering, yes. Baggy, certainly. Comforting sort of body armour, absolutely. But homeless?

'No,' I said, my voice aiming for casual. 'I'm Tilly, I've taken over the other half of this plot. These are just my gardening clothes.'

'Oh, you're Tilly.' My kidnapper smiled at me knowingly, nodding her head as if I had just solved a Sudoku puzzle for her. 'Right. I'm Gemma.'

Gemma was roughly my age, or maybe a little younger. She had short blonde curly hair swept off her face and pinned to one side with a satin pink rose. She wore a pale pink velour hoody and matching trousers. Her face appeared to be completely free of make-up but her skin was glowing, her bright eyes framed by long eyelashes and lovely eyebrows. I don't think I'd ever noticed anyone's eyebrows before. I bet she thought my face looked like an uncooked doughnut. But the most unusual thing about her – considering that she was sitting in a shed – was that she seemed to be in the final stages of a French manicure and was waving her nails in the air to dry them.

I didn't wish to cast aspersions, but she didn't look much like a gardener. And why was she worried about being caught by her mother at her age? I revised my motivations for knocking on the shed door; I was curious to know more and, anyway, Gemma didn't seem the type to discuss fertilizer options.

'Have you seen my mum?'

I shook my head. 'Don't think so. Who is she?'

Gemma grinned. 'Christine. Allotment secretary, rosy

face that looks like she scrubs it with Brillo pads and grey permed hair. I swear she's the last person in Britain to perm her hair. Soon folks will be travelling from the four corners of the earth to look at her crinkly head. Feels like that seaweed you get at the Chinese. I love her to bits, though.'

'Not yet,' I said. 'I'm meeting her this afternoon, to be officially welcomed to the allotments.'

'I'll warn you, though: she'll have you signed up to some sub-committee or working party before you can say—' Gemma looked at my feet, 'new wellies.'

I made a mental note to get my new boots dirty before going home. Nothing screamed 'newbie' like immaculately clean Cath Kidston wellingtons.

'Make yourself useful,' said Gemma, pointing towards a stubby thermos flask. 'Pour us a drink while these babies dry and you can tell me all about yourself.'

I did as I was bidden – it seemed easier – and gave the usual minimal details that I was now used to imparting before deflecting the conversation back to my new neighbour. The liquid in the flask was cranberry tea and utterly revolting.

'Unusual place to give yourself a manicure,' I said, raising an eyebrow and concentrating on not wincing at the taste of the tea.

The shed had two windows, shelves containing glass jars, tools, balls of string, plastic seed trays, a bottle of baby oil and nail varnish remover. Bigger tools were hung up on nails on the back wall and an open bag of compost sat in the corner. On the back of the door was a mirror.

'Yes, well, seeing as I'd finished planting the onions, I thought I'd treat myself,' said Gemma. 'Let's open the door, shall we?' She stood up, dropped her nail polish into her handbag and propped open the door with a watering can.

There was something a bit shifty about her answer but I decided not to pry.

'You've made a nice job of it,' I said instead, inspecting the pearly white tips of her short nails.

'I'm a beautician,' she said, dismissing her handiwork with a shrug.

If she wasn't a stereotypical gardener, she wasn't a stereotypical beautician either. Where was the orange make-up, the false eyelashes and the plunging neckline? I had a sudden urge to hold a forefinger over my eyebrows and another over my top lip. 'Ungroomed' – if there was such a state – didn't begin to cover it.

'But I firmly believe that beauty comes from within,' she continued with a sigh. 'That's why I do this.' She waved a hand over her allotment. 'Growing your own veg, eating healthily, getting out in the fresh air . . .'

Inhaling acetone in a closed shed, I added mentally.

'Talking of which, I should get on,' I said, getting to my feet reluctantly. (I could hardly believe it – I was actually quite enjoying our chat. The ground rules seemed to have gone out of the window.) 'I've got an incredibly bushy patch to sort out.'

'I can help with that,' said Gemma, following me out of the shed and past the trees, towards my half of the plot.

'No,' I said. Gemma flinched. I must have pulled my owl face. James used to say I was dead scary when I did that. 'Thank you,' I softened my voice, 'but I can manage.'

Gemma shrugged and showed no signs of leaving me alone. I gave her ten out of ten for persistence. 'OK, but if you change your mind, I'll do mates' rates. Fifteen quid for a bikini wax.'

I hooted with laughter. As if I would discuss my, er, lady garden issues in public.

'No. That bushy patch!' I said, pointing towards the bramble mountain of Kingsfield. 'Oh!'

How bizarre, the weeds had almost gone. The entire rectangular plot looked like it had been given a very bad haircut. All that remained was a scruffy covering of stubble. But what an improvement! I stared at the ground, my brain trying to work out what I was seeing.

Gemma's all-knowing smile was back.

'Did you—' I began.

She cut me off with a shake of her head. 'Charlie did it. He said he frightened you off when he met you and felt really bad about it. He borrowed a strimmer and cleared the weeds by way of apology.'

I felt my face go bright red. Poor Charlie. Other than try to be friendly, he had done nothing wrong.

'I thought at the time he was being very generous,' said Gemma, her lips twitching. 'It all makes sense now.'

I was saved further analysis of this turn of events by the appearance at the end of our plot of a small stout person of indiscriminate sex wearing a bobble hat, duffel coat and black wellingtons.

'Gemma, love, there you are!'

A woman then, judging by the voice, with a soft Irish accent. She marched closer and beamed when she saw me.

'You must be Tilly,' she cried, picking up speed. She flung her arms round my waist (I don't think she could have reached any higher) and squeezed me tightly, tickling the end of my nose with her bobble hat. 'I'm Christine. Allotment secretary. Delighted, delighted,' she said. 'And what a grand start you've made. Grand, grand.'

'Remember what I said. She's tricksy,' whispered Gemma.

I took a step backwards in a vain attempt to regain my personal space.

Christine turned to her daughter. 'I thought you could give me a hand with the last of the potatoes. Between us we could make short work of that today.'

'Sorry, Mum,' sighed Gemma, 'but I've been here hours already putting those onions in, my back's killing me. I don't think I could dig another spadeful.'

She placed her hands in the small of her back, stretched and pulled an ooh-the-pain face. I glanced down at her pink trousers: not a fleck of mud. Not one.

Christine tutted. 'Ah well, 'tis a lovely job you've made of it, lovely. No matter, I'll wait for your father.' She started to stomp off. It seemed she did everything at top speed.

'Christine,' I called to her retreating hobbit-like form.

'Yes, love?' She turned and raised her eyebrows until they disappeared under her hat.

'I think I'll need to borrow . . . equipment . . . of some sort, for the next stage of my plan.' I was out of my depth but loath to admit it after such a 'grand start'. As soon as I got home, I would start that book that I'd borrowed from the library on the subject.

'You will, you will.' Christine nodded vigorously. 'Meet me at the pavilion at six thirty this evening and I'll show you the equipment list before the AGM.'

AGM? No thanks.

'But can't I—' I pleaded.

'Good opportunity to meet folk, too.' Christine zoomed in on a sprig of green in Gemma's new onion bed and whipped it out. A weed, I presumed. I heard Gemma huff beside me.

The very thought sent shivers down my spine. I changed tack. 'I don't think I'm free—'

'My potatoes are calling, bye for now.' Christine was already at the roadside as she raised her hand.

'But, Christine?'

'See you later.' She was gone.

You can't say I didn't try.

'I don't want to go to the AGM,' I said with a sigh.

'Told you she was tricksy,' said Gemma, rubbing her hands together merrily. 'Anyway, I'm glad you're coming, you can keep me company, not to mention lowering the average age by fifty years.'

'Well, in that case, I can't wait,' I said with a grin. I zipped up my (James's) jacket. The cold really began to bite when you stood still for a while. 'Right, I'm off.'

'Already?' said Gemma, pouting. 'You haven't done anything yet!'

I stared at her perfect manicure pointedly and she tucked her hands under her armpits.

'I've got a date with a very thick book this afternoon,' I said airily.

'Ooh, is it dirty?'

'You could say that.' I pressed my lips together as her eyes lit up. '*Allotments for Dummies*. I'll see you later.'

As I cycled down the road and out of the gate, I could still hear Gemma's tinkling laugh. If I was in the market for a friend – I wasn't, but theoretically speaking, if I was – I could do a lot worse than Gemma.

Chapter 4

At six twenty I reluctantly left the warmth and solitude of home and cycled along the wet streets through the dark and drizzle to Ivy Lane allotments. The pavilion lights were on and despite my arriving early, there was already quite a crowd inside. My hands felt clammy as I padlocked my bike to the bench and took off my helmet, and I wondered for the umpteenth time how Christine had managed to talk me into coming.

Tricksy, I reminded myself. I would have to be on my guard or else by the end of the night I'd probably find myself elected to the committee.

I took a deep, calming breath and went inside, determined to stick to my plan: hire rotavator; mend fences with Charlie, if he was there; leave as soon as possible.

'You came!' Gemma leapt out in front of me, grabbed me round the neck, kissed my cheek and ushered me past a group of people to a spot by the radiator.

'Relief dot com! This is Mia.'

I followed her head-flick to a teenage girl who was sitting on the floor, knees up to her chin, completely absorbed in a mobile phone that appeared to be glued to the end of her nose. Judging by the slumped shoulders, the heavy frown and the thumbs stabbing at the screen, Mia was about as pleased to be here as I was.

Gemma leaned in closer. 'My daughter. Fourteen with an attitude that can strip nail varnish.'

'Crikey! You don't look old enough to have a teenage daughter!' I said, forcing a smile.

I'd thought she was like me, but she wasn't. She was a mother. I felt unjustifiably let down and the urge to get out of here as soon as possible pressed heavily on my heart.

I would just find Christine and get it over with. I glanced over Gemma's shoulder to seek her out.

Gemma shook her head. 'Looking for Charlie? Never seen him at a meeting. He doesn't like the aggro. Calls himself a pacifist.' She twinkled her eyes at me. 'Were you hoping he'd be here?'

The thing with Gemma was that she crammed so much information into every sentence that I was still reeling from the last revelation when she started again. So far she'd kissed my cheek, shocked me with her age (maybe I could get used to that cranberry tea after all) and seemed to think I was interested in Charlie. As yet, I hadn't uttered a single word.

'Not at all, I just need to thank him for—'

'I take it back. The man himself. Well, well, well.' She sucked her cheeks in and arched those lovely eyebrows. 'I'll get us a cup of tea. Oh and my mum wants to talk to you, she's over there.'

Charlie stood in the doorway in a dripping-wet coat, his face shiny with raindrops. The weather had obviously worsened in the last five minutes; I'd get soaked cycling home if I left now. He knocked his hood back and scanned the room and when his eyes found me, he waved and began to walk towards me. Eek! I hadn't planned what to say to him yet.

I spotted Christine sitting down with a laptop on her knee and sprinted towards her.

'Christine, have you got a minute?'

Without her bobble hat on, I was treated to a close-up of The Perm. The tight grey curls looked as if the rollers were still in and I could see her pink scalp between the gaps. She was wearing a fuchsia-pink jumper that matched her cheeks perfectly and jeans that were too short.

'Oh hello, love,' she said distractedly. 'This infernal machine.' She shook her head, bashed at the keyboard, tutted and sighed.

Gemma appeared at my side and handed me tea in a cup and saucer.

'I'll save you a seat,' she whispered and vanished.

'Christine, would it be all right if I hired the rotavator for the day? I've done a bit of digging . . .' I paused for Christine to appreciate my pun, but it fell on stony ground; she simply looked at me briefly before resuming her laptop abuse.

'I thought I'd use that to break the soil up and then,' I consulted the notes I'd written on the back of my hand, 'then fork the top layer into a fine tilth.'

'Good idea, love. You need to see Nigel about that.'

'But—'

'He's not here yet. Are you any good with computers?' She peered at me woefully and patted the empty seat beside her. Now, I might not have known much about growing vegetables but I did know my onions when it came to IT and it seemed a shame to see an older woman struggle with technology, so I sat.

She settled the laptop on my knee and began to explain her problem. I saw Gemma on the other side of the room trying to attract my attention but I couldn't possibly leave now, it would look rude.

By the time I had shown her the difference between the insert and delete button and that there was a template especially designed for recording the minutes of meetings, everyone had taken their seats and a rotund man with a comb-over and a tweed jacket had called the meeting to order.

'That's Peter, our chairman, lovely man, so dedicated,' sighed Christine. 'He's on the plot next to you and our Gemma. He's into some exotic stuff.'

I so hoped that that was some reference to vegetables and not . . . anything else.

I tried to stand up to make my getaway and replace the laptop on Christine's knee, but she barred my way with a surprisingly firm arm.

'Good of you to take the minutes, darlin', very good of you.'

I sank back down into my seat with a resigned huff. There was no point arguing; besides, judging by the drumming on the roof, the rain was now in full flow and I really did want to sort out the rotavator business before I left.

A middle-aged man dropped into the empty seat beside me, breathing heavily. His jeans, splatted with raindrops, had creases down the front and he had on a mustard-coloured shirt and tie under his V-necked sweater.

'That's Nigel,' whispered Christine.

Well, that was something. At least I'd be able to nab him at the end of the meeting easily enough. Now all I had to do was try to blend into the background and keep my head down . . .

'As you'll all know,' began the chairman, 'we finally managed to evict Frank Garton from plot 16B last year—'

There were a few jeers and mutterings at the mention of my predecessor. I wondered again what he'd done.

'And I'm pleased to welcome Tilly Parker to Ivy Lane allotments!' Peter extended an arm in my direction and around thirty pairs of eyes swivelled my way.

Cringe city.

'And bless her heart,' Christine piped up, 'she's an expert at the computer, so she's offered to take the minutes for our meetings.'

The room exploded with the sound of applause and I practically fainted with horror. Did she say meetings – plural? Not on her nelly. I glanced over to Gemma whose bemused expression and slow headshake said it all. Even Mia had looked up from her phone to smirk at me. And was it my imagination or did Nigel just emit a snort of mirth?

'On behalf of all of us, I'd like to welcome you to our little community,' said Peter with a bow. 'Perhaps you'd care to tell us a bit about yourself?'

The blood drained from my head, a giant lump formed in my throat and I felt my thighs tremble.

'Actually, Pete,' said a voice from further down my side of the room. It was Charlie. 'My shift starts at eight; do you think we could stick to the agenda? Sorry, don't mean to be rude.'

Peter cleared his throat. 'Of course. Righto. Item one . . .'

I sent Charlie a grateful smile and silently mouthed my thanks. He grinned back and gave me the thumbs-up.

Fence mended.

One out of three wasn't bad, I supposed, as I began to type the AGM notes furiously.

An hour later and it was all over bar the next round of tea. Everyone began to gravitate towards the kitchenette and a convivial buzz of conversation filled the pavilion.

'Well done, love,' said Christine, taking the laptop from

me. She inserted a USB stick deftly and made a copy of my document.

'No problem,' I said, making a mental note never to sit next to her again. I stood up, circled my aching shoulders and turned to my neighbour. 'Nigel, can I have a word?'

'You fell for that, hook, line and sinker,' said Gemma with a giggle as she approached and handed me yet more tea.

'Your mother has turned delegation into an art form,' agreed Nigel.

'I don't like to see people struggle,' I said.

Gemma choked on her tea. 'That one knows her way around a computer better than Mia. She's a PA!'

'To a chartered accountant,' added Nigel gloomily, 'but I didn't find that out until she had made me the treasurer. Anyway, how can I help?'

I repeated my plan to hire the rotavator and managed to drop in 'fine tilth' again. Nigel made a note in the official equipment-hire diary and we arranged that I would collect it on Saturday, weather permitting.

'I can help you with that,' said Charlie, materializing at my side.

'Thank you,' I said, feeling my cheeks get hot. 'But you've done enough already.'

A sturdy woman with a double chin and a crooked nose elbowed her way into the conversation. 'We women can manage on our own, Charlie. Not everyone is a damsel in distress, are they, Tilly?'

The rest of us watched as she tipped her tea into the saucer, blew on it and slurped it up through pursed lips. I was reminded of the time James and I were in Egypt on camels and his suddenly knelt down for a drink, nearly flinging him out of the saddle.

'Have you met Shazza?' asked Gemma, trying to keep a straight face. 'She's on the plot next to ours.'

Peter's wife, then. And presumably into the exotic too.

'Hi, Shazza.' It came out as a squeak and a second wave of heat tinged my cheeks.

'She'd love some help, Charlie,' said Gemma. 'I'd help myself, but I've got masseuse's shoulder at the moment.' She winced and rotated her shoulder to demonstrate. Shazza rolled her eyes in disgust.

I really did want to protest, but what was the point? I did need help. But as soon as the plot was dug over and I had soil the texture of breadcrumbs, I wanted to be left to my own devices. Easier said than done in this place, I thought, looking round at the sea of curious faces.

'Mum, time to go!' yelled Mia from the doorway.

'Oh, Mikey's here.' Gemma pulled a tin of Vaseline from her jeans pocket, dabbed a bit on her lips and fluffed up her hair. 'My husband. He's a car mechanic, so don't be surprised if his hands look a bit grubby. Come and meet him.' She took my arm and steered me towards the door before I had a chance to refuse.

Mia, although still scowling, had put her phone away and I was able to take in her features for the first time. Brown eyes and cappuccino-coloured skin, topped off with a cloud of tiny curls. Her skin-tight shiny leggings and trainers made her long legs look like golf clubs and as we got closer I noticed how much taller than Gemma she was. The only thing that she seemed to have inherited from her mother was the luscious long eyelashes. At a guess I'd say her dad was Afro-Caribbean. And very tall. Unlike the diminutive, ginger-haired Austin Powers lookalike standing next to Mia, jingling his car keys.

Five pounds says there was an interesting tale there.

I was introduced, kissed, hugged, glared at (Mia) and then they were gone.

Nobody was paying me any attention and it was the perfect time to slip away. I left the building without making eye contact and collected my bike. A sixth sense told me that someone was calling my name, but it was late and I'd had quite enough social contact for one day.

Cycling back through the dark streets I tried to make sense of the evening. I'd sorted out the equipment hire, made friends with Charlie again and managed to navigate the conversation without revealing too much about myself. All in all, a successful night. But why was it that despite my attempts to remain aloof, I felt as if this tight little community was pulling me in?

Chapter 5

As I walked through the gates of Ivy Lane allotments the following Saturday, I was treated to a sight of bums in the air, all shapes and sizes, as people bent over to tend their plots. It was a cloudy but mild day and without exception each and every one of them straightened up and gave me a cheery wave or called 'Good morning' as I passed by and then continued with their work – alone.

I wasn't sure where I was going wrong.

So far, allotment gardening (not that I had actually touched any soil yet) seemed anything but a solitary affair. And much as I was grateful for Charlie's offer of help, I couldn't help looking forward to today being over. I hadn't had so much as a minute to indulge in a bit of quiet contemplation, and that, after all, was what had attracted me to it in the first place. But surely once all the hard labour was done and my novelty value as the newbie had died down, everyone would leave me to my own devices? I could live in hope, I thought with a small sigh.

My bicycle was at home today on account of the fact that I had brought my rake with me and hadn't fancied cycling with a potentially lethal weapon dangling over my shoulder. I had also packed a bag with a flask of tea and a flask of coffee, a tin of biscuits and a tub of jelly babies. What I lacked in useful gardening tools, I hoped to make up for in superior elevenses.

I stopped to allow a scruffy-haired man to cross the road in front of me with his wheelbarrow. He was wearing a holey jumper and a papoose containing a sleeping baby with spiky black hair. We smiled at each other, he whispered something that sounded like 'rhubarb rhubarb' and I watched him as he went on his wobbly way.

No sooner had I resumed my wander along the road when a stout man with grizzly white hair and quiff-like eyebrows jumped out in front of me from behind a water butt. I gasped and reeled under the weight of my heavy bag and narrowly avoided knocking his block off with the rake.

'Sorry!' I yelped.

He scanned the road from left to right, keeping his body bent double like an elderly international spy. He gripped four cans of lager tightly under one arm.

'You never saw me,' he muttered, leaning close, one finger pressed to his lips. And then spouted a whole load of nonsense from which I managed to decipher 'heresy', 'chaser' and 'the King'. Before I had chance to retreat from his beery fumes, he'd scuttled off and disappeared between the pavilion and the toilet block.

The poor soul. Obviously delusional. I dithered between turning the requested blind eye and reporting him to the powers that be.

Out of the corner of my eye, I spotted Charlie, Gemma, Christine and Nigel awaiting me on plot 16B.

Nigel was pointing out things to Charlie on the rotavator, Christine was picking up stones from the earth and throwing them into the trees beyond and Gemma was applying hand cream. For once I was glad of the crowd.

'Has anyone seen an alcoholic round here?' I said, propping my rake up against Gemma's tree next to an assortment of implements.

'Why, love, have you lost one?' Christine tittered at her own joke. She stood up, nudged her bobble hat out of her eyes and plonked her hands on her hips. Her cheeks were red with exertion, or possibly wire wool, and she was breathless.

'Bushy eyebrows?' asked Gemma, slipping on a pair of white cotton gloves. Today her hair was clipped to one side with a giant diamanté spider.

I nodded, wondering anew how she managed to stay so pristine in this environment.

'Thick Northern Irish accent?'

That might explain why I couldn't understand him. 'Possibly,' I said.

Gemma rolled her eyes. 'That's my dad, Roy.'

'Oh no, he promised me he'd paint the outside lav at home today.' Christine grunted with exasperation. 'And I hid his Hennessy whisky on purpose till he'd finished it.'

That explained the heresy.

'Now he'll be sitting in Dougie King's shed drinking beer with whisky chasers all day. I'll kill him,' she muttered, sending a large stone whistling through the air with venom.

And that explained the rest. Good job I didn't call the police.

Nigel cleared his throat. 'It should be returned clean, undamaged and refuelled. That'll be ten pounds, please.' He held out his hand. 'I would stay and help but I'm rotating my compost bins today.'

Ten pounds for a perfect weed-free rectangle? Bargain. I handed over the cash willingly.

'And leave me at the mercy of three women?' said Charlie with a grin, not looking unhappy at the prospect.

'Four!' came a voice from Gemma's shed.

'Mia,' Gemma answered my questioning eyebrows. 'She's grounded.'

Charlie saluted at Nigel's retreating form.

In my head, this morning would run as follows: Charlie would operate the rotavator; I would perhaps have a little go, to show willing and because it looked fun; we would collect any big weeds and put them in my compost bin (goodness knows what Nigel's rotating one was, but I imagine it was a great deal fancier than my broken effort); then if I had any time and energy left, I would start turning the soil over with a fork. Oh yes, I was getting the hang of this gardening jargon.

'Right, the worst of the stones are out,' said Christine, handing me a garden fork. 'Gemma, get yours, love, and you, son. We need to get the big boys out by hand first.'

Gemma looked as horrified as I felt and Charlie gazed at his rotavator longingly.

'We can't just go mad with that machine,' tutted Christine, 'or all we'll be doing is chopping the roots of the weeds up into tiny pieces. In six weeks this plot will be ten times worse than it is now.'

There was no use arguing.

An hour later, my legs had seized up, my bum was aching and my wellies were well and truly christened.

'Tea break!' I announced, praying that Christine wouldn't overrule me.

'Thanks for all your help, everyone,' I said, settling down on to a plastic bag next to Charlie on the damp grass after finding us all a receptacle for a drink. Even Mia came out to join us and perched in the apple tree with the tub of jelly babies.

'I think I would have given up by now,' I admitted. 'It's quite daunting, tackling something like this on your own.'

It was true, I realized. It was one thing to potter amongst the vegetable beds sowing a few seeds and quite another to bring an overgrown plot back to life.

Charlie smacked his lips appreciatively and reached for another biscuit. 'No worries, that's what friends are for.'

My cheeks burned. Charlie and I were not friends; we knew nothing about each other, which was just the way I wanted to keep it. Try telling that to Gemma, though. I didn't meet her eye, but I could sense her nudging her mother and winking.

I jumped to my feet. 'Let's fire the rotavator up.'

Charlie was right behind me. 'One end to the other first, according to Nigel, then side to side.'

Gemma returned to her half of the plot with Christine and the two of them were soon tangled up in bamboo canes and string. Mia disappeared back into the shed, moaning about her homework and lack of wifi.

Charlie was soon into his stride and I flittered about, feeling a bit superfluous, moving weeds and kicking clods of earth off the path. Eventually, Charlie took a breather.

'You have to keep on top of weeds,' said Charlie, wiping his arm across his brow. 'I learned that the hard way.'

'Dig them out, you mean?' I said, noticing two men with their arms around each other's necks weaving unsteadily towards us like a geriatric version of The Monkees. One of them was the man with the eyebrows I'd seen earlier, the other a West Indian man with a wizened face, bandy legs, grey dreadlocks, and a nautical-style cap.

Charlie lowered his voice. 'That's Roy and Dougie. The Belfast meets Montego Bay Two Man Piss-up Club. This should be interesting.' And then more loudly, 'Hoeing is better, less disruption to the roots.'

I'd have to go invest in some new tools; the trusty rake alone wouldn't cut it. So far my shopping list consisted of spade and fork, which I kept referring to as spoon and fork accidentally, and now a hoe. I glanced across to see if Christine had spotted the return of her husband: steely glare, braced feet and crossed arms . . . I was guessing she had.

'Er, what about weedkiller, am I allowed to use that here?'

Charlie and I were making conversation to delay the eruption, which, judging by the metaphorical steam pumping from Christine's nostrils, was mere seconds away. He knew it. I knew it.

'Well, strictly speaking—'

'Yeah, Man, I use it all de time. Anytink for an eeeeasy life,' crooned Dougie in a lilting Caribbean accent. He waved one hand in front of him making gun fingers. 'Den I say "Die, ya bastard" and I fire. Dem weeds don't stand a chance.'

Charlie sucked in his breath, a low prehistoric moan emanated from Christine, and Gemma descended on Dougie like a small tornado.

She jabbed him in the chest. 'Irresponsible dot com.'

I pressed my lips together, trying not to laugh. We hadn't had a dot com explosion so far this morning and I'd forgotten how much fun it was.

'Don't you use that language around my daughter,' Gemma snapped, stamping on his toe with her pink wellingtons. 'She's at an impressionable age.'

Dougie cried out and hopped up and down whilst simultaneously squinting at me, looking confused.

Roy, who until this point had only muttered unintelligibly at the ground, let out an almighty belch, earning a prod in the backside with a bamboo cane from his wife.

'I know what a bastard is, Mum, we did it in history,' shouted Mia, poking her head out from the shed. 'It's when the mummy and the daddy aren't married and they have an ickle baby.' This said in an ickle-baby voice. 'And that,' she announced authoritatively, 'is how you get bastard hair.'

'Heir,' called Charlie, getting in there before me. 'The H is silent.'

Mia gave him a look that could have withered tomatoes on the vine and held up her ponytail for inspection. 'Mum's blonde curls mixed with my gay dad's afro? I think you'll find I was right first time.' And with a smirk she shut herself back in the shed.

'Bloody hell,' said Charlie quietly to me.

Gay dad?

Christine took another swipe at Roy for some reason. Meanwhile Gemma gasped, her face as red as her mother's.

Dougie seemed to find Mia's comment hilarious and let go of Roy to hold on to his sides as he doubled up with laughter, leaving Roy to fall headlong into my ramshackle compost heap.

'Whoa, steady on!' said Charlie. He hauled Roy back to his feet and with Gemma's help installed him on my rickety wrought-iron bench. Dougie used the commotion to retreat and moved off, seemingly to a reggae beat that only he could hear.

'Turn the rotavator back on,' I whispered to Charlie. He obliged, leaving Gemma and her family to recover from that particular load of publicly aired dirty laundry. Well, the women anyway; Roy was snoring raucously, mouth open, hands clasped across his beer belly. Gemma stomped off to the shed; I had the feeling Mia would be getting an extension to her grounding.

Another hour on and the earth was looking pretty good and fairly tilth-like, which was just as well because I had had enough for one day. I signalled to Charlie to turn off the motor when he got to the end of the far side and he gave me the thumbs-up.

'Tea break,' I yelled. Christine downed tools and Gemma emerged from the shed with a sullen Mia. I poured the dregs from the flasks and handed cups round.

'Phew, this is hot work,' said Charlie, peeling off his jacket. Underneath he was wearing a T-shirt, revealing a muscular chest, tanned arms and bulging biceps, one of which was adorned with a large tattoo of a dragon. There was an oestrogen-filled moment of gawping while we got an eyeful. All the man needed was a can of Diet Coke to complete the look.

'Wow,' whispered Mia in hallowed tones.

Gemma and I exchanged looks.

'Nothing wrong with checking out the menu,' murmured Gemma with a sly wink, 'even if I am married. What about you?'

She glanced at my left hand and I felt my face heat up.

'Single,' I said quietly. 'And happy to stay that way,' I added hurriedly as Gemma started to interrupt. 'Anyway.' I handed round the biscuits, smiling as Charlie took three. Time to change the subject. 'Let's talk tools. What, where and how much?'

'If you'd got a shed,' said Charlie, with a sidelong glance at Gemma, 'I'd say spend as much as you can afford. But otherwise just get the basics.'

'I've only got the basics,' said Gemma, looking a bit pink. 'Cheapo stuff. I borrow if I need anything special.'

I'd seen Gemma's selection of gardening tools – they looked brand new. 'You must look after yours very well, Gemma, they're spotless.'

'Well, I—'

A gravelly voice joined in the debate. 'Look after your tools and they'll look after you. That's my motto.' A silver-haired man with impressive ear-hair rocked backwards and forwards on his heels with his hands clasped behind his back on the path between my plot and the next. He was swiftly introduced as Alf and offered a biscuit.

Roy snorted in his sleep and woke himself up. 'Any chance of a drink?'

'I think I'd have to disagree with you there, Alf,' said Christine, yanking Roy to his feet roughly. 'I've been looking after this tool for nearly forty years and I'm still waiting for my end of the bargain. Come on, you great lummox.'

We watched Christine march a contrite Roy off towards the allotment gates. Charlie shook the drips from his cup and placed it back on the flask. 'I'll help you clean up and then I'll make a move.'

'Thanks again, Charlie,' I said once we had scraped the worst of the mud off the rotavator and given it a wash. 'If I can repay the favour, please let me know. As long as it doesn't require any gardening skills.'

'I'm sure I'll think of something,' he said, waggling his eyebrows and wiping the smile off my face. 'I'll return this for you, shall I? Bye then, ladies.'

Gemma and I watched as Charlie manfully manhandled the rotavator back along the road towards the pavilion.

'I'm sorry you heard all that, you know, earlier, about Mia's dad,' said Gemma, twisting her sleeve round and round her finger until it threatened to cut off her circulation. 'It sounds much worse than it is and I want you to think well of me. I want us to be friends.'

'So do I,' I said, patting her arm and chuckling at the way her smile immediately sparkled to match the spider in her hair. And the weird thing was, I meant it.

Chapter 6

My good intentions to heed Charlie's advice and 'keep on top of the weeds' had gone out of the window and it was two weeks before I made it back to Ivy Lane. Not entirely my fault; apparently, although I was doing a job share, according to my head teacher I didn't have to share the task of writing twenty-nine mid-year school reports, I could do them all myself. Lucky me!

It was probably for the best. My job-share colleague was counting down the hours to retirement and was highly suspicious of the school's online reporting system. In fact, she hadn't got to grips with any of the wonderful technology we teachers had at our fingertips; I regularly spent the first twenty minutes of my week resetting the interactive whiteboard after she'd been using it.

Anyway, doing the reports not only earned me Brownie points with the head, but the job kept me busy during the dark evenings, which prevented me from Dwelling On The Past. I did that a lot if I wasn't careful.

Two weeks would appear to be a long time in growing terms. The allotment had really begun to come alive in my absence: there were more people in evidence, newly dug vegetable beds aplenty and an underlying feeling of vitality and hope.

Or that could just have been me, of course; I was having a Good Day.

I still had my share of bad days when I could achieve nothing more taxing than lying prostrate on the sofa wearing one of James's old jumpers, watching *One Day* on a loop with only a bag of peanut puffs for company. But the ratio of good days to bad was on the increase. Today was such a day and I could go for . . . ooh . . . at least an hour without thinking about my old life, the one I had so carelessly let slip through my fingers.

I was even dressed in all my own clothes: jeans, gilet, hoody and wellies. I thought about taking a 'selfie' to send to my counsellor, but I was carrying my new hoe (cheapo as per Gemma's advice) and for safety reasons, decided against it.

Plot 16A was deserted. Phew. She was a lovely girl, but I had been hoping for half an hour to myself in the fresh air. I took a moment to marvel at Gemma's luscious leeks, the impressive onions and feathery carrot tops. I had to hand it to her – she ran her own business, looked after Mike and Mia and still found time to keep her allotment and herself in tip-top condition.

My plot, on the other hand, I noticed with a plummeting heart, whilst an enormous improvement on New Year's Day, was already starting to sprout weeds again and I still hadn't decided what to grow. If I didn't hurry up and plant something soon, Mother Nature would decide for me and I would have several square metres of chickweed, fat hen, couch grass and horsetail, and while their names sounded quite fun, I didn't imagine that eradicating them would be.

I retrieved my rake from behind the stumpy tree and

spent a few minutes of quiet contemplation alternating between hoeing and raking and trying to remember which vegetables I used to like.

'A shed. You'll be wanting a little shed,' Christine called as she waved at me from the road through Gemma's trees. The bobble hat was off. Spring must be on its way.

The square of slabs left by the previous occupant was crying out for a shed. I hadn't wanted to commit to the allotment, preferring to leave my options open, but in all honesty, it would be nice to have somewhere to keep stuff, not to mention a place to hide in when unwanted visitors came to call.

I waved back. 'You're right. I might ask for one for my birthday . . .' Hell. I could have bitten my tongue off. I hadn't wanted anyone to know. Now there would be balloons up everywhere, a cake with candles and sparklers, possible even a fly-by from the Red Arrows spraying 'happy birthday' in coloured smoke . . .

'Your birthday, is it?' said Christine, bustling over. Her eyes were already darting with excitement and she was nibbling on her lip. I could almost see her brain whirring with birthday plans.

I leant on my hoe and wagged a finger at her firmly. 'No fuss.'

'How about a drink in the pavilion, I've got some elderflower wine wants using up?'

I clamped my lips together and shook my head. 'Don't drink.'

'Cake then, tea and cake?'

She was relentless, but on this matter, so was I. I decided to throw myself on my sword. 'If you promise not to breathe another word about my birthday, I'll take the minutes at the committee meeting on Monday. Deal?'

'Deal,' said Christine with a brisk nod. 'I'll leave you to it.' She turned to go. Her jeans had escaped from her ankle-length wellies, and she bent to tuck them in, bum in the air, causing her gilet and sweatshirt to ride up. I was distracted from the view of her beige high-waisted knickers by the realization that we were identically dressed. Except I had a hood. A hood had to knock at least twenty years off, didn't it?

'Oh, see if Charlie is all right, will you?' she panted from her bent position. 'I just walked past him and he barely noticed me.'

I agreed, although I wondered whether that was just a smart move on his part. If I'd have done that, maybe I wouldn't be spending next Monday evening in Wetdogsville.

It was my first visit to Charlie's plot. It boasted a small tatty greenhouse, several panes of which were missing, the creosoted shed he'd pointed out to me before and two water butts. There didn't seem to be much growing except a large bed of greenery that to my uninitiated eye looked like weeds.

Charlie was miles away; leaning on his spade staring into space.

'You'll take root if you stand like that much longer,' I said.

He whirled round to face me and for a split second his face looked so full of anger that it took my breath away.

'Tilly! Am I pleased to see you!'

Heavens, from one extreme to the other! Now he was grinning like Dougie after four cans of Red Stripe. Perhaps I had imagined it. Either way, I felt awkward.

'So.' I jammed my hands in my gilet and made a show of inspecting his plot. 'What are you up to today?'

He smiled a forlorn little smile and sighed. 'Supposedly

digging in green manure, but my heart's not in it.'

Urgh! I felt my breakfast make a bid for freedom. I wondered what sort of animal produced green manure and whether I would have to do that on my plot. I was hoping to get away with horse at the very worst; the smell of that was bad enough.

'I'm not surprised!' I said.

Charlie grinned and shook his head. I didn't know what was so funny, but at least I'd cheered him up.

'You ought to try it on part of yours,' he said, lifting his spade up and throwing it javelin-style into his compost bin. 'It would help control the weeds until you know what you want to grow.'

I pulled a face. 'I don't know where to start. I don't even really eat vegetables.'

He laughed and held my gaze with his cornflower-blue eyes until I had to look away. He folded his arms, shifted his weight from foot to foot and seemed to be suffering from some sort of inner turmoil.

'Anyway . . .' I began.

'Tilly,' he said at the same time.

'Go on,' we said together and both laughed.

I nodded for him to continue.

He puffed his cheeks out and stared at the ground. 'I've had a shit time at work,' he mumbled. 'We were responding to an emergency call this week and one of the men got his face blown off. A factory on an industrial estate. No one's fault but . . .'

His shoulders sagged and he pinched his eyebrows together with his eyes shut tight. It would have been so easy to step over to him and hug him. It was what he needed; some simple human kindness. But I couldn't do it. Instead, I reached out and touched his arm.

'Sounds rough.'

His hand closed over mine and my heart started to beat frantically. I was itching to pull my hand away but it seemed churlish and unfriendly.

'Tilly,' he said, meeting my eyes. This time I didn't look away. 'You know what you said about returning the favour?'

I felt myself stiffen, but managed a nod.

'I could really use some company today. How do you fancy coming for some lunch with me? Just as friends. There's a café on Shenton Road does the best-ever jacket potatoes with leeks and bacon.'

Just as friends. That was how James and I started out.

Charlie must have sensed my reluctance. 'Please,' he said. 'You'll be saving me from a lousy fish-finger sandwich at home in front of *Loose Women*.'

That was one of my post-James favourites. On white bread obviously, with plenty of ketchup. My stomach rumbled.

'Just friends?' I asked, narrowing my eyes.

'Scouts' honour,' he said, holding up three fingers. 'And we'll sort out what veggies you should grow.'

'Deal,' I said for the second time that morning.

Charlie was right; the café did serve a mean jacket potato as well as piping-hot tea in chunky no-nonsense mugs. All I had to do was concentrate on eating and drinking and not the fact that this was the first time I had eaten out since being without James.

'So I was thinking,' I began, watching Charlie tip a small pile of salt on to the edge of his plate, 'there's no point going to all that bother of growing vegetables that are as cheap as chips to buy.'

'Like spuds?' Charlie flicked his salad garnish out of the way and scooped up a forkful of steaming potato.

'Exactly.' I loaded my fork with lettuce leaves in an attempt to look healthy. 'Or carrots and onions. Much better to focus on the expensive stuff. Things that I'm likely to enjoy eating.'

I chose to ignore the fact that this would also involve cooking. Let's just say my cooking skills were a bit rusty.

'I see,' said Charlie, his head low and his voice muffled by a large mouthful.

He was trying not to laugh. I realized I'd put my foot in it.

'Oh. Is that what you grow? Sorry.'

'It's fine.' He held his hands up, grinning at me. 'Go on, hit me with your fancy tastes.'

'OK. Well. Just a thought, but how about asparagus, mushrooms, artichokes and broad beans?'

He snorted, choked and gulped at his tea. I waited for him to get his voice under control. His cheeks were red and contorted with the effort of keeping his face straight; he would be giving himself terrible indigestion.

'I take it that's a no?'

He nodded furiously, coughing and banging his chest. 'Broad beans. Great idea.'

I wasn't going to ask why not the rest of them; I already looked like a numpty. 'All right, what else, then?'

'Do you like sweetcorn?'

I shrugged. Everyone likes sweetcorn; that's why you can buy it so easily in tins.

'Stick the cobs straight on the barbecue, a bit of herb butter. Delicious,' Charlie said, kissing his fingertips.

That *did* sound good.

'What else?'

'Onions. Now, don't look like that,' said Charlie, pointing a finger at my bottom lip. 'They look after themselves and you'll need all the help you can get. Anyway, I'm sure you can find some fancy variety if you try. You probably only want one more crop for now. It's too early for all your courgettes and whatnot.'

'But not asparagus?' I said sadly.

I'd really had my heart set on that. We had been in Spain once and spotted an old man walking down a country lane carrying a handful of it. James had leapt over the hedge, dragging me with him, and eventually found it growing wild at the side of a river. We'd taken some back to our apartment and fed each other stalks of it dripping with butter. It was probably the most romantic food I had ever tasted.

'It's not a beginner's crop,' said Charlie gently. 'Perhaps you could work up to it.'

'Fair dos,' I sighed, scraping up the last of my buttery potato. 'Shall we have pudding?'

'It's done me the world of good, talking to you today. The lads are great, but we don't really discuss things. Sometimes only a woman's company will do,' said Charlie as he walked me back to his car a few minutes later.

There had been a small tussle over the bill, with him trying to pay for it and me insisting that we go Dutch.

I won. Thankfully.

'Glad to help.' Charlie unlocked the passenger door but I shook my head. 'I'll walk home, if you don't mind.'

I rarely travelled by car if I could help it and the journey here was more than enough for one day.

He nodded thoughtfully and rested a hand casually on my arm. I held my breath.

Uh oh. Please don't blow it. Don't ruin a lovely lunch.

'Tilly, I'm not looking for anyone right now,' he said, his eyes flicking up to look at me and darting away again. 'But I do need a friend. Can we be friends?'

I took a step to the side to dislodge his hand as subtly as possible.

'Suits me.'

We smiled at each other and I walked away. He tooted his horn as he drove past and I waved. I must admit, contrary madam that I was, I was a teeny bit insulted. But overall, I decided, it was music to my ears. He was a fireman. He saved lives. And if he was happy for our friendship to be platonic, then I was happy to have him around. I just hoped he didn't change his mind.

Chapter 7

It was a Saturday morning and the world and his wife – or, to be more politically correct, partner – were toiling away at Ivy Lane. I was biding my time, waiting for an exciting delivery; my brand-new shed with two windows, a stable door and a pitched roof was due any moment. I didn't yet have anything to plant but I had done the weekly 'hoe down' as I liked to call it across my little patch to rein in the galloping weeds and I was now busy repainting the wrought-iron bench in Heritage Cream. This bench would be where I sat in summer, under the shade of my stumpy tree, now identified by Peter as an apple tree.

Gemma, I suspected, was in her shed. I hadn't seen hide nor hair of her but I'd heard music as well as odd grunts and ripping noises. She was probably giving herself a facial or something equally unhorticultural. I hadn't disturbed her because last weekend when I'd been removing the flaking paint from the bench with a wire brush, she had distracted me with tales about When Botox Goes Wrong and I'd ended up with a huge shard of rusty old paint under my thumb nail.

As luck would have it, Karen, the woman who shared the plot next door with 'camel-lips' Shazza, was a nurse and had cleaned it up and stuck a plaster on it for me. I'd got a bit confused regarding who was with who, but it turned out Peter, our other plot neighbour, had nothing to do with Shazza. He was married and apparently his wife didn't like gardening but did like cooking his exotic vegetables. I had been very glad to tie up that loose end.

Of course, the thumb had to go septic and I'd had a devil of a job ringing the bell on my bike with a huge bandage on my thumb all week.

My birthday in the middle of the week had been perfect despite my injury: a non-event that passed completely without incident. Unless you counted the argument with my mother. That had been a bit of a low point.

Mum had telephoned to wish me a happy birthday and offered to come down on the train from the genteel spa town of Harrogate, where she lived, and meet me at Selfridges for lunch followed by shopping to buy me a present. She wasn't at all surprised when I declined – I'd pretty much refused any sort of social outing for the last eighteen months – but she was taken aback when I asked for a shed for the allotment for my birthday.

'Darling, that's wonderful! So glad the allotment is working its magic and you are getting over that awful business with James. It's time, darling, it really is.'

Oh, was it *really*? My allocation of misery had been used up, had it? Grief-o-meter pointed to 'Get over it', did it? Sympathy, apparently, was now officially withdrawn.

I'd cried and ranted and said some awful unHarrogate-like things and slammed the phone down.

It was all right for her, I'd railed to myself, or possibly out loud, as I stomped round the house moving items pointlessly from place to place. She and Dad had had more than thirty blissful years together, I'd muttered, rearranging my jumper drawer in an attempt to get my emotions back under control.

I rang her back, of course, and apologized with a promise to visit before Easter.

That was the latest I could go; after that I would be busy planting. The thought made my shoulders wiggle with delight.

I couldn't wait.

I had spent an entertaining hour earlier this morning with Alfred (the man who looked after his tools), Peter the committee chairman and Dougie, with a cup of tea and a seed catalogue in the pavilion. It had been impossible not to share their enthusiasm for growing things and we had settled on sweetcorn, broad beans, shallots and a miniature variety of carrots for my first crops. Peter had suggested sowing seeds for green manure in the bit I wasn't going to be using for now. You simply sowed seeds and hoed them into the ground once they had sprouted, no green animal poo involved at all, I had been relieved to learn.

I was only halfway along the bench seat with my paintbrush when I heard the rumble and hiss of a lorry on the road.

'Delivery for Parker?' yelled the driver through his open cab window. A second man, chewing gum, stared gormlessly at me from the passenger seat.

I waved, replaced the lid on my paint tin and hurried over to where the driver was holding out a clipboard and pen for my signature. The assistant was already at the back of the lorry.

'Where do you want it?' shouted Gormless.

I joined him at the rear of the flatbed. I'd cleared the slabs in readiness; it would simply be a matter of lifting it into place.

'At the end, next to the . . . Oh!'

Drat, they'd messed up the delivery. There was only a pile of wood in the back. What a let-down.

'I think there's been a mistake,' I said, 'I ordered a shed.'

''Tis a shed. Comes flat-packed,' said the driver.

'Very clear on the website,' said his mate.

Buggeration. I watched them struggle with the huge timber panels towards my end of plot sixteen, dreams of sitting in my shed by lunchtime fluttering away like blossom on the breeze.

I stared mournfully at the departing truck, my brain scrabbling to form a new plan, when Shazza emerged, like a mirage from the cloud of dust kicked up by the truck's tyres, thundering in my direction. She had a drill in one hand, a lump hammer in the other.

I was a bit scared of Shazza.

She came to a halt in front of me, raised the drill above her head and pulled the trigger.

'Fancy learning how to use one of these?' she said with a beaming smile.

Fear clutched at my heart, but the impact of her words was immediately dissipated as Gemma's shed door opened and a young man of about twenty in a navy cagoule backed out of the shed looking very pleased with himself. He cupped his balls – *his balls!* – and I distinctly heard him say, 'These will be sore for the rest of the day.'

I watched the young lothario as he hobbled, bandy-legged, down the road and stopped at the plot next to Charlie's.

I recognized him now: he shared a plot with an older woman. A mother-and-son combo I'd assumed, but maybe not. Maybe he was a cub to her cougar. Whatever rings your bell.

Gemma had appeared and was daintily pulling up leeks

61

and arranging them in a wicker basket. She looked over and waved.

'New shed? Lovely!' she called.

I smiled but I couldn't think of a word to say. I turned my back on her to hide my confusion and tuned into Shazza's monologue about suffragettes and battery-operated power tools.

An hour later, the shed floor was in position and all the panels were laid out in situ. Shazza was still cracking on, and I was dying for a drink but didn't dare say anything.

'Right,' she said, revving up her drill again, 'let's get the rear panel up first. Ever used one of these?'

No, funnily enough. My DIY experience began and ended with assembling an Ikea bookcase with an Allen key. No batteries required.

I shook my head; my mouth was too dry to speak. Partly nerves, partly tea-deficiency.

She placed the drill in my hands. 'We'll have a dry run,' she said, picking up a spare bit of wood and a screw.

'Now, all you do is . . .' She wrapped her arms round me from behind and covered my hands with hers. I heard what could have been a cough, or more likely a snort of enjoyment from Gemma, and squeezed my eyes shut. How had I ended up in this position?

'And then squeeze the trigger, gently at first . . .'

'SHAZZA!'

Shazza leapt away from me as if she'd been burned. I let out a sigh of relief and we both turned to see Karen on the path behind us, a mug in each hand. Two pink spots coloured the nurse's cheeks and she looked like she was about to cry.

'I've brought you both a drink, but I can see you're otherwise engaged,' Karen said in a wavering, high-pitched voice.

'I was only helping the lass out, love. No need to upset yourself.' Shazza was at Karen's side in an instant, stroking her hair.

Realization dawned; I'd assumed they were friends or sisters. Not . . . more.

I looked over to Gemma for assistance and caught her eye. No help from that quarter, she was wetting herself laughing.

I strode over and gave her my teacher stare and got straight to the point. 'What's the deal with the shed shenanigans?'

Her face went pale, as well it might.

'Who told you?' she muttered.

I rolled my eyes. 'It was pretty obvious, you weren't exactly discreet about it.'

'Oh.' She seemed disappointed at that. 'Well, if I'd known you were coming, I wouldn't have done it.'

I groaned at her. Unbelievable. 'This is not about me, Gemma, what about Mike?'

'He was in on it. In fact, the whole family was in on it at one stage.'

Wait, what?

'Anyway, I'd earned it.' She jammed her hands on her hips and stared right at me, her blue eyes a picture of defiance. Her hair was held back with a thin pink Alice band today. She looked about twelve. 'After all that man put me through.'

'Who, Mike?'

'No, that awful Frank Garton.'

'Gemma, you've lost me completely.'

'Dumping stuff on my allotment. Always having dodgy meetings in the shed. We had the police round here every week before he was arrested.'

'So when he got kicked off the site, Mike, me, Mum and

Dad nicked his shed. Your shed.' She chewed on her lip and looked at me from under a furrowed brow.

A few moments of silence went by as realization slowly dawned.

'I wasn't talking about that! I meant that boy, last seen holding his privates, leaving your shed.'

'Oh, for goodness' sake, Tilly!' Her face broke into a wide smile. 'Why didn't you say?' She grabbed my arm and dragged me into her shed. There was a beach towel on the floor and I tried not to put my muddy boots on it.

'You swear you won't tell anyone?'

Like I had anyone to tell. 'Swear.'

She leaned towards me with a cheeky grin. 'That was Colin. He has a plot over the other side with his mum.'

I nodded, not sure where she was heading with this.

'He's a male glamour model. But his mum doesn't know.'

I opened my mouth to say that he didn't look like one, but frankly, what did I know? And I still didn't like the sound of where this was going.

'In return for services rendered, he does most of my digging and planting. Don't tell my mum.' She wagged a finger at me. 'See?' She held up a carrier bag and showed me its contents: several used wax strips covered in short and curlies. 'Back, sack and crack.'

I covered my gaping mouth with my hand. The mere thought brought tears to my eyes.

'Mum wanted me to have an allotment and don't get me wrong, I do love all the fresh veg and stuff and it is good to show Mia where food comes from and all that jazz. But when it comes down to it, I can't be arsed. Plus the fact no one wants a beautician to have skanky nails.'

She looked at me solemnly, waiting for my reaction. I laughed and I laughed and she joined in and I can honestly say it was my happiest moment for months. Finally we wiped the tears away from our eyes and I gave her a hug. She smelt of flowers and coconut oil.

'You're brilliant, Gemma,' I said.

'You don't mind about the shed?'

I shook my head. 'No, my new one is much nicer. No offence.'

She shrugged good-naturedly. 'None taken.'

Through the shed window I caught a glimpse of Shazza and Karen, poring over the instruction leaflet for the shed. With any luck, they'd do it for me if I stayed out of the way for a long enough.

'Hey, Gem?' I said, settling into her spare deckchair. 'Will you do me a manicure?'

She clapped her hands with delight and reached for the nail file.

Emmeline Pankhurst would be turning in her grave.

Chapter 8

The late-March sunshine flooded my new pied-à-terre with shards of sparkling light, which made tacking the curtains up more like a game of Russian roulette with a hammer than DIY.

Finished.

I stood back with an audible 'Ta dah!' and admired my handiwork. The flowery fabric I had found in a charity shop gave the perfect finishing touch to the shed and together with the old shelf unit and the plastic patio chair the place looked quite homely. I stepped outside to admire the exterior view.

It had been painted an uplifting shade of Wedgwood blue – a gift from Gemma (via Roy who she'd coerced into doing the actual painting) for stealing the shed that Mr Garton had left.

The overall effect was magical; I may have been biased, but mine was surely the most beautiful shed at Ivy Lane allotments.

Doing up the shed was the first step to making my plot look loved and doing it had given me, unexpectedly, an enormous sense of well-being.

I missed home-making, I realized. My rented accommodation was quite adequate, but a little soulless. After selling our old house, I didn't have the heart to make another home, so I got rid of most of the knick-knacks, the cushions and the pictures that I'd enjoyed collecting over the years. And although the place had seemed bare at first, it had been less painful not to be constantly surrounded by reminders of happier times. Maybe now was the time to do something to make the house mine, paint a room perhaps.

Today, though, I was content to work on my allotment. It was a beautiful spring morning, I had a list of jobs to do here and then I was off to see Mum for the weekend. It was only a week until the Easter holidays and I had survived school for nearly a term. I smiled contentedly to myself; there was quite a lot to be happy about.

Sitting in a tin on the shelf was a batch of homemade peanut flapjacks. I wasn't the best baker in the world, but one thing I'd learned about allotment life was that most things could be traded. I had a box of teeny shallot sets to plant and I was hoping for some top tips and maybe even an offer of help.

Flapjacks in hand, I went in search of willing volunteers.

Neither of the neighbouring plots were manned today and the first person I spotted was Nigel in his greenhouse at a table constructed out of an old kitchen worktop. He was wrist-deep in velvety black soil, wiggling his bottom and singing 'Copacabana' by Barry Manilow. It seemed I wasn't the only one with spring fever this morning. I cleared my throat and waited for him to notice me.

Nigel's plot was somewhat aspirational to a novice like me; a study in military precision – hardly surprising given that he was a retired army captain: raised beds, straight paths, a series of pristine compost bins and weeds strictly forbidden.

'Tilly!' He looked completely unabashed at being caught

out singing the 'Who shot who' line in an American accent at full volume and I liked him all the more for it. 'Good morning, just potting up my runner beans.'

I'd opted for broad beans myself and they were already sown; a double row of wrinkly old beans that I'd plopped into a narrow trench and covered back over with soil. I had great hopes for them; they were the beans for beginners, I had been told. Foolproof, apparently. It had taken me hours, all that raking and whatnot, but it had been so easy that I was convinced I'd done something wrong. In fact, the hardest bit had been marking out the rows with canes and string. I was from the Nigel school of gardening; wobbly lines were strictly prohibited.

'Flapjack?'

Nigel whipped off his gardening gloves and selected the largest piece.

'My wife was an excellent cook,' he sighed. 'I do miss home-baking.'

Poor Nigel. I knew from Christine, the font of all knowledge, that he'd lost his wife a couple of years ago. The allotment had been their joint passion. How lovely to have shared an interest like that. I racked my brains to think whether James and I had shared a hobby, but all I could come up with was tequila slammers. That would hardly have been a suitable pastime to take with us into old age, would it? I didn't even drink these days.

'Take another piece for later,' I said. He helped himself and set it aside on a clean bit of his workbench.

'I'm planting shallots today, any tips?' I said, mesmerized by an oaty lump stuck to his jumper.

Nigel paused from his chewing and frowned. *Come on, Nigel*, I urged silently, there was no such thing as a free flapjack. He swallowed his mouthful.

'Ah. Yes,' he said, finally. 'Leave the tips showing.'

He shovelled the rest of the flapjack into his mouth and raised a hand. 'Thanks for that.'

Dismissed.

I turned ninety degrees, marched off and resisted the urge to salute.

The plot opposite Nigel was occupied by an elderly woman; I'd never seen her close up, but had noticed her pottering about on several occasions wearing a furry hat with earflaps and a shapeless chunky cardigan. Her shed had lace curtains at the window and was flanked by an array of terracotta pots, currently brimming with tulips and pansies. The plot was neatly dug and dominated by a large polytunnel in the centre, but I couldn't see any evidence of vegetables or the woman herself today, come to that.

Up ahead there were four children running round on the plot next to Nigel's, all pre-schoolers – just as well seeing as it was a school day. A woman emerged from the shed: long red hair, red lipstick and a black polo-neck jumper. 'Hiya!' she yelled at me. Amazing that I hadn't met this in-yer-face woman before now; she was completely unmissable.

No point asking her for help; she already had her hands full, but I was in happy mode and could do sociable if the situation required. I walked up the path and the children immediately crowded round her for protection. Or perhaps a look in my cake tin. You could never be sure with small children, pre-programmed as they were for survival.

I introduced myself and quickly learned that Brenda normally came to the allotment early in the morning before work – she had her own catering business – but her van was in for repair, so she had taken the day off; she only wore black, not because she was in mourning but because it made life easier, and she had three children. I say 'quickly

69

learned' because she spoke like a machine gun and barely stopped to draw breath.

'This lot,' she said, taking two pieces of flapjack, breaking them in half and placing them into eager little hands, 'are my grandchildren. I've got eight altogether.'

I scanned round the allotment nervously. I had only cut the flapjack into nine squares.

She grinned at me and ruffled the hair of the smallest two. 'So what are you growing, then?'

I filled her in on my endeavours to date, which as well as the broad beans consisted of twelve pots of sweetcorn sitting on my spare bedroom window sill (the sunniest spot in the house) and a thick row of carrot seeds next to the beans.

Secretly, carrots (even if they were a miniature variety, like mine) fell into the 'pointless because of price' category, but so many people had told me to give them a whirl that in the end, I'd capitulated. I'd chosen to ignore Charlie's advice, though.

'Make sure you get rid of all the stones. If a baby carrot hits a stone, it'll split in two and grow legs,' he had warned.

I didn't mind that; novelty carrots would be infinitely more interesting. Besides which, stone-removal seemed like ridiculously hard work for a bunch of carrots. Digging the ground over with my new fork had taken enough effort. In fact, the reason I was looking for help with the shallots was that my bum still ached from all the squatting I'd been doing recently.

'I grow potatoes,' said Brenda, pointing to a few straggly plants, which was all she seemed to be cultivating.

Just potatoes? I was so glad I hadn't shared my 'cheap as chips' philosophy.

'Planting season starts on Good Friday, so I'll have my

hands full then,' she said. Her nails were long and painted a dark red; Gemma would have been impressed.

'Although I'm not so bothered about earlies; I concentrate on main crops. Took me a while to sort that out, though. The first season I was here, I grew these tiny little spuds. You could have put 'em up your nostrils,' she mimed the action for me with her forefingers, just in case I couldn't imagine it for myself, 'and still have drawn breath.' She mimed that too.

I said goodbye and approached the plot opposite Brenda where a silky-haired girl in denim dungarees was hoeing between rows of an oriental-looking cabbagey thing. She had a papoose strapped to her front. I had seen that baby before, but this time it was awake and its two dark brown eyes gazed at me between the straps. My step faltered and my breath caught in my throat; what a beautiful face. It was such a perfect little thing, completely content in its snug surroundings. I ached to touch that velvety skin. The woman – mid twenties, I'd say – looked up, smiled and then resumed hoeing. If pressed, I would hazard a guess that she was Chinese.

'Gorgeous baby,' I said. 'Boy or girl?'

'Girl.'

Clearly not one for small talk. Which was fine.

'Would you like a flapjack?' I held out the tin in her direction.

She looked at me through her dark fringe and shook her head. 'We don't eat sugar.' And after a second's pause, added, 'Thank you.'

'OK, bye then.' I shrugged and turned to walk away.

There was a 'H-hum,' behind me followed by a quiet, 'I do.'

I turned to see the lady I'd thought was elderly smiling

shyly at me from the edge of her plot. Today she was hatless and obviously no more than fifty at most. She was slight, had shoulder-length greyish-blonde hair and the body language of a mouse.

'Eat sugar, that is,' she said.

Hurrah, an ally in unhealthy food! I held the tin out but she had her hands full with pots and gestured for me to follow her into the polytunnel.

Inside was very warm and heaving with greenery.

'Flowers,' she said, waving a proud arm across the polytunnel. 'My plot is entirely devoted to flowers. No point growing veg, I don't eat much. Except cake. And my flowers bring me great joy.'

'What are these?' I pointed to a cardboard box marked 'swaps' filled with small pots of plants, all different as far as I could tell.

'They're for Seedling Swap Sunday.'

I'd seen the poster outside the pavilion. From what I could gather, plot holders with a surplus of seedlings could swap them with each other. I hadn't paid it much attention; it seemed a little advanced for me. Nice idea, though, if you were into community events.

I swapped names with Liz, handed her a flapjack and pressed onwards to the far corner of the allotment. I'd never really been up here and I could see Alf sitting on a chair scraping mud off a trowel.

'Roasted.' Alf's answer when I asked for shallot tips. 'Like garlic, in whole with the meat. Delicious.'

Not exactly what I had in mind, but he did offer me some produce in exchange for a flapjack. The sun was warm for March, so I slipped off my gilet and counted my blessings. Where else could you get lungfuls of fresh air, friendly banter and a free armful of curly kale on a Friday morning?

I skipped merrily back to plot 16B with my complimentary greens, resigned to planting my own shallots. It was like the story of the little red hen. Except that the analogy didn't really work because I couldn't, in all honesty, see a horde of people queuing up to get their hands on my shallots in summer.

There were a few weeds beginning to creep up on my path and I decided to deal with them first before getting stuck into planting. Very carefully, I sprayed each one with weedkiller, taking my time to ensure I didn't spray anything important. There was no breeze, so the spray shouldn't have drifted down to anyone else's plot, but I wasn't taking any chances.

The shallot was an odd crop to grow; it hardly seemed worth it, I thought, running my hands through the small brown bulbs in my shed a few minutes later. Why not simply eat them now? I was pretty sure that when I came to harvest them they would look exactly the same as they did now. I did a bit of raking to show willing and started pushing them part way into the ground. I hadn't been planting long when I sensed Gemma's presence behind me.

'You could offer to help, you know,' I said, without turning round.

'I would, obvs, but I've got to give a full body massage this afternoon and I need to conserve my energy. Ask Colin.'

'No thanks. Not if it means handling his privates.'

Gemma giggled and I turned round to waggle my eyebrows at her.

'Offer him something else.'

'Like help him make an Easter card for his mum?' I tutted. A teacher's services might not be quite as useful as a beautician's to a glamour model. It wasn't as if I even had a cane he could borrow. I shook my head to banish the image of a young, smooth-skinned Colin draped over a desk and wielding a whip.

'You never know,' she said and then squealed. 'Look, Tills!' She was pointing at my carrot bed.

I would have to have a word with her about that. Trust Gemma to make a nickname from my nickname. Rolling my eyes, I stood up to see what she had found.

I clapped an oniony hand over my mouth and gasped.

Gemma put an arm round my waist and gave me a squeeze. 'Well done, babe.'

'How's that for beginner's luck!' I don't think my smile could have been any wider.

I'd done it! My carrot seeds had actually started to sprout. I had planted seeds and they were coming up to greet me. It was only a few seeds, a few spiky shoots appearing above ground, it wasn't as if I'd invented a time machine or won the lottery or found a cure for bad breath (my pet hate). But at that moment my happiness knew no bounds; I felt so proud of my achievement.

If I compared myself to this time last year, well, there simply was no comparison. I stared down at the bright green carrot tops and felt my eyes blur with tears.

It was really happening, plot 16B was coming back to life. And as I returned Gemma's hug, it occurred to me that perhaps I was too.

Chapter 9

As soon as my work at the allotment was done I'd dashed off to the train station.

I had a lovely time in Harrogate with Mum; we weren't close like Gemma and her parents but that didn't mean we didn't enjoy each other's company once in a while. We browsed for hours in the shops on Montpellier Hill (she bought lacy knickers, which I chose not to question, and I bought a scarf from Oxfam), had an indulgent afternoon tea in Betty's Tea Rooms and spent the evening in companionable comfort snuggled up in front of the TV with the *Downton Abbey* boxset and a slab of milk chocolate.

Over the course of the weekend I filled her in on my new life in Kingsfield: funny stories about the children in my class, tales of triumph at the allotment and I even embellished my role as minute-taker at the committee meetings to reinforce just how well I was integrating back into society. It all sounded very positive, even to my ears. It did the job, too: Mum only mentioned the lovely young single man from the local history association twice and thankfully kept her comments about the telephone calls she had had from James's parents to a minimum. I missed them both dearly, but I wasn't ready to get in touch – not quite yet.

She waved me off on the Sunday-afternoon train with a promise that as soon as I had a bed for the spare room, she would come and visit. She might love her only daughter but clearly wasn't prepared to compromise on comfort.

No sooner had the train pulled out of the station than my ears started to burn, my head began to throb and by the time I was back in Kingsfield I was running a fever.

I woke on Monday morning bathed in sweat and could barely speak to phone in to school to report my absence. Three whole days passed in a fog of sleep, pain and paracetamol but by Wednesday the worst was over and I made it back into school for the end of term, much to the relief of my job-share partner who hadn't done a full week's work since 1999.

The fallout of this unexpected turn of events was that it was Saturday morning, the first day of the Easter holidays, before the thought of my allotment even entered my head. Goodness only knew how big my carrots were going to be by the time I got round there! The beans were bound to be up by now and even the shallots would have thrown up their first little shoots.

I switched off the TV, shed my pyjamas and packed a hasty snack-bag of Pringles and orange juice. It was only as I picked up my bag, wheeled my bike over the front step and prepared to lock the door that I remembered what I had forgotten to remember.

Eek, the sweetcorn!

Those poor little pots in the spare room hadn't been watered since before I'd left for Harrogate. I dropped my bike and dashed upstairs fearing the worst.

There they were; twelve white plastic cups that I'd filched from the staff room at school. Abandoned. Ruined.

The compost had completely dried out and shrunk away

from the sides of the cups. Ten of the seeds had germinated but I almost felt glad for the two that hadn't. All ten little seedlings were dead; shrivelled and crispy.

I gathered them up and carried them downstairs to put in the dustbin. I was cross with myself. And disappointed. Now I would have to sow some more. What a waste of time and effort.

I was still reeling from the effects of my illness, hence my over-reaction to a few withered seedlings. But I could sense the signs; it didn't take much to send me into a spiral of gloom these days and I needed to nip this setback in the bud before it took hold.

I cycled off to Ivy Lane, pep-talking to myself all the way. This was a blip, a classic beginner's mistake, no need to beat myself up over it, plus there was always tinned sweetcorn in an emergency.

'Morning, Tilly,' called Dougie, from the picnic bench outside the pavilion as I rode past. 'Nice to see a bit o' sun, after all the rain this week!'

'Absolutely!' I called back. Had it rained? I'd been in no fit state to notice. Rain was a good thing, though, at least the rest of my crops wouldn't have failed from water-shortage in my absence. I couldn't wait to inspect them.

Christine flagged me down with both arms as I passed her plot and I dismounted reluctantly.

'Seedling Swap Sunday tomorrow, Tilly,' she said in such a tone that implied my presence was a given.

I shook my head. 'Maybe next year. I wouldn't insult any-one by offering them any of my plants!'

'Community, Tilly; it's the spirit in which it's given that counts.'

I made vague noises about seeing how the carrots had turned out which satisfied her and pushed my bike onwards. Charlie was loitering at the end of his plot, arms folded. Even though I was cryogenically storing my emotions for the foreseeable future, I must admit to casting an appreciative eye from his chunky boots, past his multi-pocketed army trousers and up to his white T-shirt, stretched tantalizingly across his broad chest. The petulant facial expression sort of ruined it, though.

'You're back, then.' He turned and stomped off to his greenhouse.

I was never going to make it to my own plot at this rate, I thought with a sigh, and followed Mr Sulky Pants up the path.

'Wow!' I said to break the ice. 'You've been busy!'

Every surface, every shelf and all the available floor space was crammed with seed trays brimming with bushy baby plants. I'd never really given greenhouses much thought, considering them only useful for growing tomatoes. If I was still here next year, I might get one.

'I thought we were friends,' said Charlie, not looking at me. He picked up a tray of seedlings and started transferring them one at a time into individual pots.

'Ah,' I said, nudging him teasingly, 'we are friends. Have you missed me?'

'I haven't seen you for weeks.'

'I've been ill.'

He stared right at me then, his eyes like searchlights checking my face for the truth as if he didn't believe me. I felt the hairs stand up on the back of neck; he was making me feel uncomfortable.

'That's all right then.' He suddenly grinned, and instantly he was back to friendly Charlie, the one with the twinkly eyes and the cheeky smile. I felt myself relax a bit and changed the subject.

'They look healthy little chaps,' I said, nodding at his seedlings.

'Broad beans,' he replied. 'I've got tons, I might donate some tomorrow.'

So that's what mine would look like with any luck. It struck me belatedly that he had sown his indoors, in the safety of his greenhouse. I had a pang of worry for my double row, left to battle with the elements.

'Do they suffer from the rain if you plant them straight in the ground?' I asked, unsure that I wanted to hear the answer.

He flicked a bean from a pile of unplanted seeds towards me and I picked it up. 'Mice. That's the main problem. A seed is like a golden nugget to them.'

'They eat them?' I swallowed. I didn't think I could cope with another loss so soon after the sweetcorn fiasco.

'Yep.'

I fled.

There was no sign of life on Gemma's half – human, that is – though the plot itself was burgeoning: her raspberries were starting to sprout leaves, plump onions protruded from the soil and a variety of greenery poked through a sheet of netting.

One glance at my half confirmed that my fears had been valid.

This was a nightmare, after all my hard work. I had been so happy with my modest success and everything was ruined. Instead of an immaculate double row of broad bean shoots, there was just bare earth, punctuated by mouse-sized holes. Not a speck of greenery in sight. I ran to unlock the shed and grabbed my trowel. The path was dotted with dead patches; the weeds had gone, but so had half the grass. I must have trodden in the weedkiller and walked it up the path.

With a sinking heart I dropped to my knees and began to dig, hoping to prove myself wrong. Maybe they simply hadn't germinated yet, or were just on the cusp of pushing their way skywards.

I had to hand it to the mice; they were thorough. I skimmed the earth with my trowel from one side of the plot to the other and didn't find a single bean.

I sat back on my heels, knees caked in mud, panting with exertion, and tried to hold back the tears.

Only then did I notice the shallots, or rather lack thereof. I must have planted a hundred, easily. Now there were . . . I did a rough count . . . no more than fifteen left.

I didn't understand. Why had everything gone wrong? I felt my fragile layer of happiness tear and peel away like the papery skin of a bulb.

All that remained were the carrots. Bloody stupid carrots. There were lots of them, their feathery fronds battling for space with their neighbours. Except for the end nearest the path, which was bare; presumably I had somehow managed to douse them with weedkiller too.

Maybe it was because I was still low from my illness, but suddenly I felt drained and weak. Disappointment flooded through me and I had an overwhelming urge to lie down and give myself over to a good cry.

'Looks like the birds have had your shallots.' I recognized Charlie's voice but I couldn't bear to answer him. I shut my eyes in a vain attempt to block the tears. 'I was worried about you when you ran off.'

Go away. Leave me alone.

'Lol!'

Oh no. That was Gemma's unmistakable voice. 'So much for the old beginner's luck!' she added with a chuckle.

Since losing James I had kept everything bottled up. No

matter how awful I felt, I had been determined that no one would be able to tell. Now all my emotions came rushing to the surface.

I wiped a hand across my face, adding mud to the tear tracks, and stood up. My legs were shaking, my lungs on the verge of collapse and my head felt like concrete. I was a complete and utter failure.

'I give up. I can't do it,' I sobbed. 'I can't even grow easy stuff. Everything I touch just dies.'

Gemma lurched towards me, her face crumpled with horror. 'I was only joking . . . I didn't mean—'

'You don't understand,' I said, shaking my head like a loon. 'I've failed. I've failed again. Why can't I keep anything alive?'

I pushed past them, tears blinding my eyes.

'Tills?'

'Don't call me that,' I shouted. I wanted to go home, shut myself away and hide.

'What about your shed?' called Charlie.

'What about it?' I shouted. 'I don't care. I'm not coming back.'

What was the point? What was the bloody point?

I lay awake most of the night, taunted by my failure as a gardener, and finally fell asleep around dawn. Barely five minutes later, or so it seemed, I was rudely awakened by someone knocking loudly at my front door. Someone who clearly had a death wish.

I clomped down the stairs. My head was pounding, my eyes were sore from scrubbing at them with toilet paper and I had toffee popcorn stuck in my teeth. I flung open the door and prepared to let rip.

A short stout man with a ready smile, which only wavered

momentarily as he took in my appearance, greeted me from a safe distance up my path. It was drizzling and he had his shoulders hunched up to his ears.

'H'llo,' said Christine's husband.

'Morning, Roy.'

Even though it wasn't Christine in person, I knew I had to be on my guard. I had no intention of going to the allotment, community spirit or not.

'C'n-I-c'me-in?'

I stood aside to let him in.

Drunk, I had no chance of understanding him; sober, I still struggled. The trick, I had found, was to imagine I had a UN translator in my head, slowing his words down and adding in the missing vowels.

'Let me take your wet coat.'

He shrugged off his coat and I hung it over the banister and nodded towards the kitchen. He climbed up on a bar stool while I put the kettle on.

'That was Christine's chat-up line, thirty-odd years ago,' he said wistfully.

'Really?' Hard to imagine Christine doing the chatting up. On the other hand, once she had made up her mind that Roy was the one . . .

'I was driving to work, the back of the car full of half-used paint tins. It wasn't a van, just a car I'd ripped the back seats out of. Anyhow, I looked down at my diary to check the address of the job and next thing I knew I'd hit a lamppost. Twelve gallon tins of paint came flying down the length of the car, blew their tops and covered me head to toe in emulsion. Now this was the seventies. None of your neutrals: mustard, avocado, brown . . . I staggered out of the car, dripping with paint, and knocked on the nearest door for help.

'Christine answered wearing this flowery nightie. A vision, she was.' He looked off into the distance and I had to stop myself from tittering. '"Let's get you out of these wet clothes," she said, all forceful. I couldn't believe my luck. We were married six months later.'

'That's a lovely story, Roy,' I said, placing a mug of coffee in front of him. And the longest speech I had ever heard him make.

'Never said it to me again, mind you.' He took a sip of coffee and winced. 'Got any whisky?'

'No.'

He shifted awkwardly in his seat. 'So it just goes to show.'

He was working up to something. 'What does?' I asked.

'Sometimes bad things happen for a reason. Like you having a bit of bad luck on the allotment.'

'Do you really think so?' My eyes filled with tears and I stared down at my mug. It was so sweet of him to come and cheer me up.

'Don't let it get you down. All gardeners lose a few crops now and again, it's a steep learning curve and—'

'Roy,' I held a hand up, 'I lost everything except the carrots. Why did I have to learn the hard way?'

'Ha!' He jabbed a finger at me. 'You see, you've learned. You make a mistake, you move on.' He paused and then added softly, 'Same in life.'

I couldn't respond to that. My throat felt tight and I hugged my mug to my chest for comfort. I couldn't bear it when people were kind; it made it so much more difficult to control my feelings.

'Come to Swapsies Day, or whatever the hell it's called,' said Roy.

My mouth twitched with a tiny smile at that, but I shook

my head. 'No. I don't belong, I've got nothing to swap and I embarrassed myself yesterday.'

'Heavens above, don't I embarrass myself every day of the week?' He flapped a hand at me. 'And you're one of us now, Tilly; course you belong. And if you'll accept them, I've half a dozen pots of sweet peas you can have.'

His kindness was too much and big happy tears filled my eyes. I put my mug down smartly before I changed my mind. 'Go on then,' I said bravely. 'Let's go.'

'You might want to get out of your pyjamas first,' said Roy with one bushy eyebrow aloft.

'Good point.'

We grinned at each other.

I handed him his coat. 'Thanks, Roy.'

'See you in an hour. Don't be late.'

Chapter 10

The rain had dried up and there was a festival atmosphere at Ivy Lane allotments. Long trestle tables had been arranged outside the pavilion, some with plants, one with second-hand gardening books (I might have a browse there later) and another with refreshments. At the roadside end of most plots were small tables laden with plants and handmade signs indicating the varieties. People were milling about, wandering on to each other's plots, swapping notes, exchanging plants and generally having a good old chinwag.

Despite my mood, I was charmed by it. A chink of hope appeared in my veil of misery and for an anxious moment I thought I might let out a hiccuppy sob. Thank goodness Roy had persuaded me to come; this was so much better than flopping around ankle-deep in self-pity at home.

I had brought a nice tin of biscuits with me that I'd bought from Betty's in Harrogate. Not exactly the same as swapping a seedling, but it was better than nothing.

At the end of mine and Gemma's plot I found six pots with several plants in each. A piece of paper was tucked underneath them and 'Sweet Peas' was scribbled on it in pencil.

My heart contracted with gratitude. Over on their plot, I caught sight of Roy and waved. He waved back, held his newspaper up and disappeared into the shed. No doubt there would be a can of beer with his name on it somewhere in there. Good for him.

A cheery voice broke through my reverie.

'You get first dibs on my beans, Tilly.'

It was Charlie carrying a large tray of healthy, uneaten broad bean plants. My cheeks burned with shame and I took a deep breath. Better get the worst bit over with and move on.

'I'm sorry about yesterday.'

'No worries. I know what you women are like. My ex was always losing her rag. "Emotional", she used to call it.' He smiled and his eyes twinkled at me. 'Come on, let's get these plants in.'

He strode on to my half of the plot purposefully and I followed. I wasn't sure I wanted to be compared to his ex, but at least he didn't seem to be holding a grudge. It appeared to be a regular thing in our friendship: me apologizing to him.

Charlie paused outside the shed and nodded towards the pocket of his tight jeans, his hands still full with the tray. 'I've got your shed key in my pocket, help yourself.'

Was it me or had it gone incredibly warm all of a sudden?

He burst out laughing and held his hand out with my key in it. 'Only kidding, you should have seen your face!'

I let out a breath and laughed with relief. Good job Gemma wasn't here, I'd never have lived it down.

'Pass me a trowel and I'll put them in for you now.'

I opened the shed and found him a trowel, but when he asked for bonemeal, my face must have gone blank because he rolled his eyes and jogged back to his own shed to fetch some.

I went over to examine my remaining shallots while I waited, but I soon had a visitor.

'Callaloo,' sang Dougie, producing a tray of spindly green shoots from behind his back, 'a taste of Jamaica. Better than all your boring English rubbish.'

'Thank you,' I said, taking the tray from him. Whatever callaloo was. 'Can I swap you for some sweet peas?'

'No, but you can swap them for a kiss,' he said, pushing his cap up and leaning in, lips already puckered.

'Biscuit?' I pressed the tin towards him to ward him off.

'Spoilsport,' he said with a wink, but took a biscuit anyway. 'Keep them warm till the weather heats up,' he called over his shoulder. 'Callaloo likes it hot, like me.' He sauntered off, cackling to himself.

Next to appear was Liz, hovering nervously on the path holding a pot. Her hair was pulled back into a rough ponytail and I could see her grey roots growing though the blonde highlights. She took a piece of shortbread from the tin and nibbled the edge.

'I've brought you marigolds.' She was so quietly spoken that I had to strain to hear her. 'For companion planting. Put them near your carrots, they'll ward off pests and help with pollination.'

It was very kind of her. I handed her a pot of sweet peas, which she declared to be delightful and of a variety she didn't have. She was just leaving as Charlie returned, and when he said hello, she seemed to shrink into herself and tiptoed away as fast as she could.

He frowned as he watched her leave. 'Something I said?'

'Perhaps she's allergic to testosterone,' I said with a wry smile.

He seemed to like that. I left him chuckling away, planting the broad beans while I took some sweet peas to Shazza and Karen next door and came back with a handful of onions to supplement my meagre shallot crop.

Charlie's method of planting was diametrically opposed to mine; no string and no straight lines, in fact, it was more of a patch than a row. I itched to intervene, but in the interests of inter-plot relations, I opted to fetch us both tea from the refreshment stall instead.

Peter was in charge of the teapot and poured me two mugs of builder-strength brew. He smoothed the flap of hair across his balding head and coughed.

'As chair of the committee, it grieves me to see new plot holders suffering any setbacks,' he whispered gruffly.

I murmured my thanks as I spooned sugar into Charlie's tea, my cheeks flaming. It seemed news of yesterday's meltdown had spread further than I'd imagined.

'Plenty of lettuces going spare in my greenhouse, Tilly. I've done you a little tray, please help yourself.'

Peter's plot was on the other side of ours, although I'd rarely seen him do anything, he was always in the pavilion sorting out everyone else's problems. People were so kind, I thought, as I weaved my way through the crowd back to Charlie, with a clump of radishes from Nigel in a bag looped over one arm and a full mug in each hand.

By the time I got back the broad beans were in, as were the new onions, and my plot was looking a whole lot better than it had twenty-four hours previously, if slightly more chaotic. I felt a bubble of happiness rise in my stomach; maybe I had been a bit hasty to give up yesterday.

Charlie downed his tea and tipped out the dregs. 'Can you be left on your own for five minutes, while I swap the rest of these beans?'

'Sounds like a line from a pantomime,' I said. 'What are you hoping for – a cow?'

He rolled his eyes, hugged me to him briefly and left before I had chance to react. I felt my head lurch and my throat grow tight; how long had it been since I'd had a man's arm around me like that? I sank down heavily on my bench and tried to ignore the tingling sensation that his touch had left on my body.

Don't panic, Tilly, he's just a friend.

'Hiya!'

Brenda, with her red hair and matching lipstick, stood before me, her arms straining under the weight of a hessian sack.

'Miles away, you were. I've got a proposition for you.'

Implausible as it seemed, Brenda was even more persuasive than Christine. By the time she left, I'd agreed that she could commandeer part of my plot to grow potatoes in exchange for a share of the crop. Apparently she was 'going for gold' this year and needed more space. Just what I'd always dreamed of – potatoes . . . However, given my track record so far it seemed like a good plan; the less space I had, the fewer mistakes I could make.

I didn't feel confident enough to wander around other people's plots with my biscuits and sweet peas, so I stayed put and kept a beady eye trained on my broad beans in case the mouse burglar returned. Visitors came thick and fast and I rarely had a moment alone: pak choi from the Chinese-hippy-sugar-free mum, a spare piece of netting from Alfred who helped me make a broad bean prison with it, and some pots of herbs from Vicky who had the plot nearest the gate.

My favourite visitor was Colin. He waited until his mum was taking a turn manning the book stall and crept up bearing a gift of pea plants.

'Can you keep a secret?' he asked, glancing furtively over his shoulder. His check shirt hung off sloping shoulders either side of a concave chest and I couldn't help but compare his with Charlie's muscular physique.

'I know about the modelling,' I hissed, at the same time hoping he wasn't about to reveal anything too risqué. It wasn't that I was a prude, I was just, well, a little rusty in that department.

'I'm not gay!' he declared, pulling himself up tall.

I was startled. That hadn't entered my head. Until now.

'Gemma says you're a teacher.'

I nodded, praying she hadn't mentioned anything about the Easter card.

'Would you help me with my reading in return for a bit of help with your allotment?'

I had to stop myself from crushing him to my chest, I felt so sorry for him. I'd volunteered at an adult learning centre as a student; developing literacy skills in people who had struggled to cope with normal everyday tasks had been a massively humbling experience.

Colin was waiting for my reply, chewing his nails and fidgeting from trainer to trainer. Designer. Modelling must pay well.

'I'd be delighted,' I said, meaning it from the bottom of my heart.

He beamed at me and puffed out his chest. 'Planting, weeding, anything; I don't mind.'

I sent him on his way with a bourbon biscuit, both of us richer from our chat.

By lunchtime all the swapping was over. I sat down on the bench and cast an eye over my haul. My fellow plot holders had donated enough vegetable plants to stock a small supermarket and I still had four pots of sweet peas in my possession. It seemed word of my epic failure to cultivate had got round. Everyone was falling over themselves to come to my aid and wouldn't take anything from me in return.

But as well as donations, everyone had offered help with the planting, given me tips on protecting the young plants from predators and shared a story or two about their own disasters. Losing the odd row of seed to birds, mice and squirrels were so commonplace that I felt a bit of a diva for my strop yesterday.

A surge of warmth infused my whole body. I felt overcome all of a sudden by the community's generosity. People had been so kind and helpful and I couldn't for the life of me work out what I had done to earn it. I would give it another go. We could do it, me and my plot. We might be battered and damaged, but we could start again and hopefully come back stronger.

I took a deep calming breath.

Gemma's plot was still deserted. I missed my friend. *My friend.* My eyes filled with stupid tears and I tilted my head back to blink them away.

The bench rocked precariously as a second bottom plonked itself down at my side. Christine patted my leg.

'Where's Gemma today?' I sniffed, blotting the tears with my sleeve.

'Shopping.'

I was surprised; I would have thought that a social event like this would have been right up her street. Even if only as an opportunity to sell facials to the weather-beaten plot holders.

'Would you say you were a cat or a dog person?' said Christine, apropos of nothing.

I thought hard about my answer, not least because,

knowing Christine, it could be a trick question. Back in the 'let's buy a cottage in the countryside, have lots of babies and live happily ever after days' with James, we had always dreamed about completing our perfect life with a golden retriever. Without that fantasy to fall back on I wasn't sure what sort of person I was. And I wasn't just referring to the pet preference.

'Don't know.' I shrugged.

'A dog is your best friend,' said Christine, picking up the tray of pea seedlings and pinching a few bits off. 'It's loyal, it depends on you. Greets you when you come in, shares your emotions. Whereas a cat is much more of a free spirit, far less needy and more of a taker.'

'A cat person then, probably,' I said.

Christine tucked my hand through her arm. 'Come with me. I've got something to swap with you. Bring the biscuits.'

Why did I get the feeling I'd walked right into another one of her traps?

She led me to her shed, pushed me inside and waited at the door. Roy was sleeping peacefully, head lolling on his chest. Curled up on his lap were two tiny kittens; grey stripy balls of fluff and utterly adorable.

'Strays,' said Christine. She took a handkerchief out of her pocket and blew her nose. 'We found them wandering around last night. No sign of the mother. Poor little mites.'

I scooped up one of the sleeping kittens and held it to my face. Its heart was beating fast and furiously against its fragile ribcage. It woke up and pressed a miniature paw to my cheek.

'Gemma's taking one,' said Christine, helping herself to a biscuit. 'She's out getting collars and bowls as we speak. Mia's chuffed to bits.'

No way. I could see where this was going. I deposited the kitten back on Roy's lap. 'And you're having the other,' I said firmly, meeting Christine's eye.

She dabbed at her nose. 'I'm allergic, else I would. Mike has agreed to one, but won't take both because of the vet bills.'

'Have you asked around? Maybe they're just lost.'

Christine shrugged. 'Perhaps. But in the meantime they need homes.' She paused and laid a hand on my shoulder. 'Animals bring out the best in people, I always think. They find a way into even the most resistant heart. And you'd be doing me a big favour.' She sniffed dramatically.

A pet. During the past week, I'd struggled to look after myself and failed dismally to keep even a few plants alive. I wasn't sure I was fit to take on the responsibility of another life.

Roy opened his eyes and grinned. He was so wide awake suddenly that I suspected he had been listening all along.

'So, Tilly, which one are you having?'

I smiled at him, remembering his earlier words. *You make a mistake, you move on.* If it hadn't been for him and Christine, I'd still be moping around in my pyjamas. But what an unexpectedly successful day it had been instead; a replenished allotment, a willing assistant and new literacy student, and now it seemed a new member of the Parker family. Before I had chance to change my mind I scooped up the kitten again.

'Hello, little one. I'm your new mummy,' I said, rolling my eyes as Christine and Roy exchanged smiles and my new kitten snuggled into my neck.

Chapter 11

From my spot at the picnic bench outside the pavilion, nursing a mug of tea, I was in a prime position to enjoy the sun on my face and the heated debate between Nigel and Peter, who were in the throes of organizing this morning's Easter Egg Hunt for the children. The doors to the pavilion were open and the old-fashioned curtains flapped in the breeze. The table in the centre of the room was heaving with chocolate; we had all donated small chocolate eggs to be won as prizes and the committee had supplied a giant egg for the overall winner.

I sipped my tea and chuckled to myself at our esteemed chairman and treasurer squabbling over everything from where to hide the clues to who was going to explain the rules.

I was ready for a drink after an hour on my plot; I'd hoed diligently between the vegetables to remove the weeds and checked the netting for infiltrators. A week after Seedling Swap Sunday and, touch wood, everything was still alive. The straight lines and right angles that I had envisaged had all but disappeared, but I was getting used to the pretty patchwork effect created by small quantities of each variety. Anyway, there was only one mouth to feed in my house, large crops would probably just have gone to waste and I couldn't imagine the kitten would want to join me in a bowl of lettuce.

A check-up at the vets had revealed that it was a male, in rude health and about eight weeks old. I'd called him Cally, after Dougie's callaloo, because he adored the heat and had quickly located all the warmest spots in the house; from my recently vacated chair to the box I'd lined for him under the kitchen radiator. He had only been in residence for one week and already had me completely besotted.

I glanced at the gates looking out for Gemma; she was due to meet me here any minute and I couldn't wait to compare notes about our new arrivals.

It looked as if the Easter Egg Hunt would be well attended; Peter's wife, a glamorous granny with long hair twisted into a bun, heavy mascara and several gold rings on each finger, had brought their three grandchildren who were currently climbing trees with Shazza and Karen's two nephews. All of Brenda's eight grandchildren were here too. Brenda was looking a little frazzled; she reminded me of the woman who lived in the shoe today, constantly herding children from other people's plots and trying to find them all jobs to do. She had been down to the pavilion twice already and asked Nigel rather desperately if he could hurry up and start the game.

Gemma arrived then, wearing a very Eastery yellow tunic with huge white buttons over navy leggings, instantly making me feel frumpy in my jeans and check shirt. She was just in time to witness Peter blowing a very loud whistle and announcing that the fun would commence as soon as the rules had been explained.

'About as much fun as a maths test, if they've got anything to do with it,' she muttered, kissing my cheek. She poured herself a cranberry tea from a flask in her bag and settled next to me on the bench.

A crowd of children quickly gathered in front of the pavilion steps and bounced on their toes. They looked hyperactive before they had consumed half their body weight in chocolate, which didn't bode well for the future.

At the last second they were joined by Liz, with two dainty toddlers by her side.

'My neighbour's children, such a blessing,' she whispered to Gemma and me, and the hippy, pak choi, no-sugar family complete with papoose.

Two thoughts struck me: I must make an effort to learn their names, it was getting ridiculous; and why were they entering an Easter Egg Hunt when the baby was too small and too unlucky in the parent department to eat chocolate?

Peter set up a flipchart on the steps of the pavilion and Nigel handed out clipboards and crayons.

Gemma and I exchanged looks; it appeared to be very complicated. The children fell silent as Nigel, regularly interrupted by Peter, explained that hidden around the allotment were wooden clues (the news elicited groans; I grinned, imagining that the children were poised for a cocoa-solids blowout without anyone noticing), they were to take a rubbing (Gemma snorted at this) from each shape and jot down the letter written on the shape, which would join together to make a word at the end. Then they should follow the clue to the next one. There then ensued a litany of rules as to what constituted cheating and the children, somewhat less bouncy, ambled off to start the hunt.

'I thought your mum would be here today, overseeing the men?'

'She and Dad go to church on Easter Sunday. Mum will be here later, to hand out the prizes. She doesn't trust the

Chuckle Brothers to do it properly. Oh, and she says we're to wait here until she comes because she's got an announcement.'

'Exciting!' I said, arching an eyebrow.

'Possibly,' said Gemma, sighing so emphatically that I felt her breath on my face.

'What's up with you, you seem down?'

'Mia is spending Easter with her dad. I miss her.'

Which reminded me, I still hadn't heard the story of Mia's conception. It didn't seem right to pry when I was so aloof about my own history.

'You've got Mike,' I said, nudging her playfully.

'Yeah but he was off working at the crack of dawn this morning. I feel like I've been doing a sponsored silence.'

On Easter Sunday? He had to be the hardest working mechanic I'd ever known. No wonder Gemma was lonely. 'Never Knowingly Quiet' would be an apt motto in her case.

'Hey!' She whirled to face me, suddenly perky again. 'Join us for lunch!'

My natural response was to refuse. I had a perfectly decent lunch of spaghetti hoops on toast lined up with no conversation required.

She sensed my hesitation and pounced. 'It's roast lamb.'

I did love lamb and the nearest I came to a roast dinner these days was a frozen ready meal.

She smiled a smile that could only be described as triumphant and upped the ante. 'You can bring the kitten.'

Well, I couldn't refuse that, could I? Denying Cally an opportunity to play with his sibling would have been selfish.

'Go on then, I'd love to. So, kitten news,' I said, already looking forward to a good gossip now that the area was empty again.

'Aw.' Gemma's face went all gooey. 'Fur ball dot com! It's a boy and we all love him to bits.'

'Same here!' I said.

'Even Mia puts her phone down occasionally now, except when she's posting pictures of him on Instagram.'

'Name?'

'We can't agree. I want Smudge, Mike wants McQueen and Mia says if he isn't called Odell after her current pop crush, she's phoning ChildLine.'

We were still laughing about the indignation of youth when a boy, Brenda's eldest grandson, reappeared with his clipboard and a very disgruntled face.

'We can't find any of the clues,' he shouted in to the pavilion, slapping the clipboard down on the table and sitting down in protest. Other children trailed behind, several on the verge of tears.

Nigel and Peter appeared hastily with mugs and mouthfuls of food.

'What? You can't give up that easily,' said Nigel. 'If it was too easy it wouldn't be a hunt, would it?'

Liz materialized beside me. 'It's true,' she said, chewing on her lip. 'I don't want to be a nuisance but—'

'Fix!' shouted one of the older girls.

The hippy family returned too. 'Might be a bit of a mix-up with the clues,' said the dad, raising his hand.

'And we're desperate for chocolate,' said his wife. 'We gave up sugar for Lent.'

'That's Helen and Graham and baby Honey,' whispered Gemma. *Vegetarians*, she mouthed, raising her eyebrows knowingly as if that explained everything.

Peter and Nigel put their heads together, muttering in strained tones. There seemed to be a lot of finger-pointing at each other going on and the children were getting mutinous.

I sensed a busman's holiday coming on . . .

'Who's ready for a drink of orange juice?' I cried, jumping from my seat, unbalancing the bench and sending Gemma lurching backwards.

Yells of 'Me please!' filled the air and the men, shooting me looks of pure gratitude, disappeared behind the pavilion, presumably to solve The Case of the Missing Clues.

Between us, we managed to cobble together some refreshments for the children: I had the remains of my Betty's biscuits, Liz (randomly) had half a Victoria sponge and Dougie, who I'd found asleep in the pavilion, ransacked the cupboard in the kitchenette for the committee's emergency stash of custard creams.

By the time the men came back, Peter's comb-over now dangling in long sections over his ear and Nigel running a frantic finger round his collar, I had the situation under control.

Nigel held his hands up to attract the children's attention. 'Er, there seems to be a cross-mogrification in the clues.'

'What?' said Brenda's eldest, looking like he wished he'd stayed at home with his Xbox.

'It means, they've cocked it up,' cried Dougie from the pavilion steps, hooting with laughter.

'Right,' I said, turning to a clean page in Peter's flipchart. 'Who wants to play name the kitten? The winning name gets a massive Easter egg.'

I left Dougie in charge of the marker pen and the children taking it in turns to write down kitten names while I organized the rest of the assembled adults. 'Has anyone got a basket?'

A motley assortment of bowls, buckets, baskets and trugs was assembled in minutes and distributed amongst the children, while Nigel, Peter and Gemma ran round the entire allotment site hiding all the small chocolate eggs.

'Play nicely, help the younger ones and don't eat too much chocolate,' I said, declaring the Easter Egg Hunt back on. 'Don't come back until you've found them all!' I added.

The children charged off and we all sighed with relief. Gemma and I resumed our seats.

'Now, where were we?' I said, closing my eyes and tilting my face up to the sun. 'This is nice.'

'You were amazing,' said Gemma. Even with closed eyes I could sense she was staring at me. 'You came from nowhere and just . . . Mia will love the name Jake for the kitten. She's mad about Jake Bugg.'

'Good.'

'You remind me of an onion,' she said.

I opened one eye and snorted at her. 'I'm listening. This is going to be a compliment, I take it?'

'Just when I think I've got to know you, another layer peels off and I learn something new. There are still more layers, though, aren't there, Tilly Parker?'

'Do I make your eyes water?' I said, trying to make light of her observations. Gemma's probing was making me uncomfortable. I was happy to listen, not so happy to reveal my own secrets. I hoped that that would be enough for her for now.

'Mmm,' said Gemma and presumably closed her eyes too because she went quiet for a few seconds.

'Happy Easter.' I opened my eyes to find Charlie by our bench. He handed me a box of truffles in an egg-shaped box and Gemma a bunch of daffodils.

It was the only Easter present I'd received and I was very touched. They looked expensive, the daffodils by comparison were without packaging and, at a guess, I'd say he had just swiped them from his plot.

'How come I don't get chocolates?' Gemma pouted with a sly sideways grin at me.

I was thinking the same thing; Charlie and I were meant to be friends, the last thing I needed right now was to be singled out for special attention. My face, already pink from the sun, felt like it was sizzling.

'I was just thinking of your figure,' he said, holding out his arms, his face a picture of mock-innocence.

'I'll thank you not to think of my body at all, Charlie, I'm a married woman.'

Thirty minutes later all that was left of the Easter Egg Hunt was discarded silver foil and sticky faces. Christine had arrived and herded all of us to the pavilion steps.

Peter began a speech about the successful start to the year, the forthcoming events and one or two housekeeping notices and I found myself drifting off in the sunshine.

Easter already. Spring was flying by; it would be summer before too long and then I'd be kept busy on the allotment! I thought back to New Year's Day and how daunted I had felt on that first visit to Ivy Lane. So much had changed for me since then. My counsellor had been right; moving to Kingsfield, taking on the plot . . . A fresh start had been exactly what I had needed. And although it had taken time, I had also adopted a fresh attitude: letting people get close to me again; making friends like Gemma and Charlie (although the latest Easter gift development was a bit of a worry). I was a part of this community now, whether I liked it or not. I opened my eyes and glanced round the assembled crowd, and actually, I realized, I did like it. And as long as I could continue to remain in the background, gradually gaining confidence, that would suit me just fine.

I tuned back into the speeches as Christine took centre stage.

'Let's give a round of applause to Nigel and Peter for organizing the Easter Egg Hunt. Another successful event.'

Everyone clapped politely. I caught Gemma's eye and shook my head as I saw a 'But' form on her lips. No public recognition for me, thank you very much. She rolled her eyes and folded her arms in a huff.

'And now to our exciting news.' Christine's eyes sparkled; she was quivering so much she could barely pull the envelope from her handbag. 'We've had a letter from the BBC! They are going to film an allotment special for the *Green Fingers* programme and they have chosen to feature Ivy Lane. Suzanna Merryweather, the TV gardening celebrity, will be joining us here in Kingsfield.'

There was a collective gasp; shoulders were straightened, hair patted and lots of oohs and ahhs. I was grinning at how strong Christine's Irish accent became when she was excited until Gemma squeaked and gripped my arm so tightly that I cried out in pain. Christine flapped her hands at us to be quiet.

'We'll all be in it, of course,' she said, her eyes searching me out in the crowd. 'But they specially want to follow someone's first year on the allotment.'

She took a deep breath to deliver her pièce de résistance, but I had already guessed what was coming. I shrank down in my seat and prepared for my summer, and possibly my entire life, to be changed beyond recognition.

'Tilly, you're going to be a TV star!'

The applause resumed, this time even louder, and everyone stared. I felt like an escapee caught in a searchlight.

'But . . .' I gawped at Gemma for help.

She looked at me and grinned. 'Told you she was tricksy.'

I smiled weakly at her as a new version of the summer flashed in front of me, followed swiftly by a cold wave of fear that sent shivers down my spine.

A TV crew at Ivy Lane. Filming me. Journalists had a way of wheedling secrets out of people. It was their job. One sniff of a story and they were like dogs after bones, the more sensational the better.

And right now keeping my secret was possibly more precious than life itself.

Summer

Chapter 12

It was a warm Saturday at the beginning of May and as I sailed through the gates of Ivy Lane allotments I could see that the place was alive with activity. It might have been busy at this time of year anyway as far as I knew, this being my first season, but there seemed to be an additional frenzy to the hoeing, weeding and planting this morning. I suspected that the root of this extra 'effort with a touch of hysteria' was the forthcoming visit from the *Green Fingers* TV show. It was all anyone could talk about.

It was a revelation to me; so far all I had witnessed from my fellow plot-holders was the therapeutic side to cultivating your own vegetables (and the social side in the case of Roy and Dougie – now that Dougie's homemade scrumpy had matured, they spent most of their time serenading us with a medley of Daniel O'Donnell and Bob Marley songs).

'Morning, Tilly,' called Christine from the steps of the pavilion as I cycled past. She was overseeing the erection of five colourful hanging baskets along the covered porch that ran the length of the building. 'What do you think – grand or what?'

'Beautiful,' I replied, winking at Nigel and Alfred who were balancing on stepladders and rotating the baskets to

Her Ladyship's satisfaction, looking like their arms were about to snap off.

I waved and wobbled past the other plot holders and dismounted at my half of plot sixteen. Gemma's shed was open. Hurrah, that meant I would have the pleasure of her company while I worked. And my apple tree was in blossom, double hurrah.

'Ivy Lane allotments will look like a film set by June,' I said, parking the bike next to my shed and heading over to see her.

'They all think they're going on flippin' *X Factor*,' grumbled Gemma from her deckchair. '*Green Fingers* will be looking for quirky characters not perfect plots.'

She rolled up her pink capri pants and stretched her legs out for maximum UV exposure.

'I, on the other hand, shall be cultivating nothing more strenuous than a tan,' she added, leaning back and tilting her face to the sun.

Today her hair was clipped back with a pink ladybird and I eyed her summery outfit enviously, wishing I had the confidence to strip off. I *was* wearing a T-shirt and my arms, exposed for the first time in yonks, were already turning pink but my legs, clad in skinny jeans, were sweltering.

'I swear, Mum, if you make me be here when they're filming I'm going to go and live with Dad,' said Mia, without looking up from her phone.

Grounded again, presumably. She was sprawled out on the grass next to Gemma, wearing barely decent denim shorts and a T-shirt.

Probably just as well my legs weren't on display, I thought, noticing how toned and golden Mia's teenage limbs were.

'I'd rather die than be seen on a gardening programme.

They'd probably make me stand up in assembly at school and talk about it,' she continued with a shudder.

I smothered a smile; poor girl, her mother would relish the limelight, but I was with Mia on this one and remembered how much I'd yearned to blend into the background at her age. Still did, come to that.

I was feeling pretty excited today. Not because of the TV thing – the mere thought of that had the same effect on my stomach as the smell of Shazza's mushroom compost. My good mood was down to an imminent event: the harvesting of my first crop. Yippee!

After a catastrophic start to my allotment career in which I nearly threw in the trowel, the plot that I shared with Gemma had come on in leaps and bounds over the last month and my radishes, I had been reliably informed by Nigel, were ready for harvesting.

'OK, drumroll please,' I announced, willing my crop not to let me down.

'Get a picture of this on your phone, Mia,' said Gemma, leaning forward in her deckchair. 'This is history in the making.'

I knelt down gingerly on the edge of the path near what I referred to as my salad patch, delved down into the roots with my pink hand fork and lifted the first fruits of my labour.

Four pinky-red spheres with tiny white roots twinkled at me through the crumbly soil. Mia zoomed in close – to be honest, they were quite small – and took a photograph.

'Look at these beauties,' I said, holding them high as if I'd won an Oscar. 'Like little rubies.'

Radishes. I couldn't even remember buying radishes before and now I had grown my own. With Nigel's help, but even so.

'Ah, look at you, beaming with pride!' Gemma got to her feet and I yielded to her rib-crushing hug.

It was ridiculous but tears sprang to my eyes. Gemma was right, my heart was singing with joy and I sent my counsellor a silent message of thanks for encouraging me to take on the allotment as a way of getting my life back on track.

A few minutes later I had a little pile of radishes on the path. A few had grown too big and spongy and several were too small to bother with, but on the whole I was flushed with success.

'We ought to try some,' said Gemma. 'Go and give them a wash under the tap, Tills. Whoops, sorry!' She cringed at me. 'Tilly.'

While I fetched a basket from the shed to put them in, Gemma began extolling the virtues of the radish to Mia from the grass path at the edge of my plot.

'Packed with vitamin C, love,' she said, 'and very low in calories.'

'I don't think Mia has to worry about her weight,' I said, pinching the tops off the radishes and dropping them into my basket.

'Huh!' said Gemma. 'Maybe not now, but when she first hit puberty she ballooned like—'

'I'll wash those,' said Mia, snatching the basket out of my hand and sprinting off to the tap.

'This allotment is largely for her benefit,' whispered Gemma, although Mia was out of earshot by now. Gemma did make me laugh; she had a habit of being discreet only when there was no one else around. 'It's hard work but it's worth it . . .'

That was debatable; she palmed off all the hard jobs to Colin.

'Teaching her about eating healthy food is one of the best gifts I can give her.'

I touched her arm gently and she patted my hand. Underneath that bubbly, carefree exterior she was a great mum. The sort I would have given my right arm to be. My heart pitched suddenly, but Gemma, as usual, brought it straight back up again by snorting with laughter.

'Besides which,' she said mischievously, plonking down in her chair again, 'I've met Mia's grandmother. That woman's butt has probably got its own postcode.'

I joined in the laughter and glanced over to the tap. Mia had turned the water on full blast and had soaked herself and Liz, who was waiting in turn to use it. I had two minutes at most.

I cleared my throat. 'Can I ask you a personal question?'

'Of course you can!' She looked at me in surprise. 'We're mates. My life is an open book.'

A wave of something close to nausea washed over me. Mine was more like a secret diary that required a special key to open it. A key that was currently in hiding.

I took a deep breath, forced a smile and carried on. 'Who is Mia's dad?'

Gemma rolled her eyes as if the story of Mia's parentage was so old hat. 'A tall, dark and handsome hairdresser called Kevin from Birmingham who I met on an experimental colour course in London when I was eighteen.'

'You were a hairdresser?'

'Trainee. Although, to be honest, I wasn't cut out to do hair. No one ever wants what will suit them.' The glance she flicked over my straggly locks didn't go unnoticed. I dreaded going to the hairdresser's. Such inquisitive types.

Moving on.

'So what happened?'

'We were staying in a hotel and let's just say we ended up experimenting with more than hair colour. Both virgins we were. A few weeks later I found out I was pregnant and he came out as gay. You can imagine what that did to my sexual confidence. I mean, just how bad in the sack do you have to be to turn a man gay?' Her huge blue eyes searched mine and for a moment I thought she genuinely wanted an answer.

'Are you still in touch with him?'

'Yeah. Kevin's not a bad dad, actually; Mia sees him every month and he's quite handy for free haircuts. Anyway, after I had Mia, I decided to retrain as a beautician.' She sighed and pinched her thumbs and forefingers together. 'I see myself as a holistic healer focusing on the outside of the body. Healing people is my gift.'

I studied Gemma's face with affection as she lay back, closed her eyes and soaked up the early-summer sun. I had only known her four months, but already she had brought some much needed fun into my life. I hadn't made many friends in Kingsfield, but she, like her name, was a gem. A gift.

'I've been meaning to ask you,' I said, giving up all pretence of gardening and setting up a chair next to hers. 'I thought grounding a teenager meant not allowing them out. But Mia is – very regularly, I notice – allowed to come with you.'

'Ha!' said Gemma. 'How little you understand of Planet Teenager. Firstly, Mia has got a very cunning streak—'

'Oh, I can't imagine where she gets that from,' I said, wide-eyed.

Gemma arched her perfect eyebrows at me innocently.

'At fourteen she thinks her job is to push the boundaries twenty-four/seven. It's my job to keep the boundaries intact.'

'Yes, but isn't the punishment meant to be being grounded at home?'

'What, lolling around in her bedroom with unlimited wifi?' She scoffed. 'That's not punishment, it's heaven. Whereas here I can embarrass her and she gets hardly any phone signal. Both of those things are murder for Mia.'

I nodded, it all made sense now.

'You'll see,' she said with a brisk nod, 'when you have kids.'

I swallowed hard, momentarily at a loss for words. As if that was going to happen any time soon.

Mia was on her way back from the tap, swinging the basket, her arm fully rotating like the sails on a windmill. Goodness knows what state the radishes would be in. Caught unawares, Mia seemed much younger and Gemma and I exchanged indulgent smiles.

'Besides which – don't tell her – I like having her near me. A few more years and she'll be gone. Flown off to start her own life.'

I looked at her sharply, worried that she was going to get all tearful on me. That was usually my domain. But her eyes twinkled. 'That's when phase two of Gemma's beauty empire will commence.' She sat up tall in her seat and held out her hand for the basket. 'Come on, Mia, let's have a taste then.'

The radishes were a triumph. By that I mean crunchy and peppery and exactly as a fresh radish should be. To me they tasted of success and accomplishment and of the start of a new era in my life. Quite a lot really for one small vegetable.

'Ooh, have one of these, Mia,' said Gemma, pursing her lips, 'they're like sweets.'

I wouldn't have gone that far.

Mia tried one and declared it as bad as earwax. I wouldn't have gone that far either.

'So what are you grounded for this time, Mia, if it's not too personal?' I had given up trying to be cool around Mia. While I still thought of myself as young, I suspected she thought I had one foot in the grave already.

Mia sighed with all the pathos she could muster. 'My phone bill.'

Gemma glared at her daughter and shook her head at me. 'Fifty quid! Texting her new boyfriend, apparently.'

I thought Mia might blush, but she smiled dreamily. Perhaps she was more like her mother than I'd given her credit for. She also didn't seem particularly repentant.

Gemma tutted. 'That's three legs I have to wax to earn fifty quid.'

The mind boggled.

'Talking of which . . .' she added, jumping out of her seat and running to her shed. She returned with a wodge of leaflets and handed one to me. 'My new price list. So if you fancy getting *your* legs done . . .' She looked pointedly at my jeans.

I drew my feet underneath me protectively. 'No thanks.'

Ivy Lane wasn't ready for these legs just yet.

Alf, pushing a wheelbarrow, grunted his way to the edge of our plot. He rested his hands on his hips and puffed out his cheeks. He looked like a scarecrow in his battered straw hat and moth-eaten shirt.

'Would either of you two ladies like some strawberry plants?' he said, pointing to his barrow. 'I potted up my runners last year and I've got too many now.'

Gemma declined the offer, saying she didn't have room. Neither did I really, but I did like the idea of strawberries.

'Dig up the lettuces, then you can make your salad patch

into a strawberry patch,' Gemma suggested. 'We'll help you eat the strawberries if you like.'

I grinned at her, noting the word 'eat' as opposed to 'plant'. 'But the lettuces are only tiny, they're not ready yet.'

'True,' said Gemma, 'but the baby leaves will be tender and sweet. We'll have some, won't we, Mia? Fancy a salad for tea?'

'Oh, not more sweets,' said Mia, rolling her eyes and patting her stomach. 'You're spoiling me today, Mother.'

I swapped the strawberry plants for half of my radishes. Alf was chuffed and I was happy to pass them on (you could have too much of a good thing) and I set the little pots down next to my shed.

Before I was able to plan my next move, Colin swaggered down the path towards me in a pair of low-slung jeans.

'Seeing as our plot could win gold at Chelsea, and my mother has gone home a happy woman, I'm here to offer my services,' said Colin, wearing a cheeky grin. 'Do those strawberries want planting?'

I hesitated. The idea was that I tended my own plot: exercise, fresh air, a sense of achievement . . .

'Oh, go on then. Thanks, Colin,' I said, opting to enjoy the sunshine from the comfort of my chair instead of at ground level, as soon as I'd shown him where to put them.

'Still OK to do another chapter today?' he muttered as we went into the shed to fetch some tools.

'Of course,' I said and smiled.

It had become obvious that Colin was dyslexic when we'd started reading together at Easter and I couldn't believe that it hadn't been picked up before now. I'd pointed him in the direction of an adult literacy course that was due to start soon but in the meantime, whenever he managed to escape from his mother's clutches, I was helping him with his reading practice. We were halfway through *Killing Mum*. His choice. I didn't question it.

Colin's droopy jeans retreated even further as he bent down and I was treated to an eyeful of his underwear. I didn't want to damage his self-esteem but I was sorely tempted to let on that, actually, women didn't find grey boxer shorts particularly exciting. Then I caught Mia staring at his bum with undisguised appreciation. Maybe just *old* women, then. I turned away and tried not to feel ancient.

'Got any mulch?' Colin asked, tapping the base of the pots sharply to free the small strawberry plants.

I shrugged. I was still getting to grips with the allotment jargon. I might have had mulch, and then again I might not. It depended what it was.

'Straw,' he explained. 'To protect the base of the plants.'

'No, but I can soon sort that out,' I said. The allotment shop was open and I strode off to pick some up.

The shop was less retail emporium and more converted garage with double doors and shelves full of odd things like Epsom salts, seaweed extract and vermiculite. I found Christine in charge. She was sitting on a bag of John Innes Compost No. 1 and gazing into the distance like a lovestruck teenager. In fact, she wore an identical expression to Mia's not five minutes ago. I had never seen her so still, she normally moved like an industrious ant on a mission.

'Aidan Whitby,' she said. 'Doesn't the very name of him make you want to swoon?'

'Mmm,' I said vaguely, handing over a fiver for a bag of straw.

Aidan did nothing for me and Whitby made me think of crabs, donkeys and Dracula. Nothing swoon-worthy about that list. I wondered what she was on about.

'Our director,' she clarified. 'I've received a letter from

him today confirming the time of our meeting.' She widened her eyes. 'A TV director coming to Ivy Lane.' She sighed.

'That will be exciting, won't it?' I said, wishing I meant it. I seemed to be the only person who wasn't thrilled about it.

'I've pinned the notice up on the board. Spread the word please, Tilly love, we need everyone there.'

'Sure,' I said, picking up my straw.

'And I'm counting on you to be our shining star, promoting allotment gardening for beginners and the younger generation. It'll do wonders for our profile, wonders.'

I gave her a tight smile and made my exit, my heart pounding with dread. Christine was going to be sorely disappointed, I thought.

Chapter 13

I shook the box of cat biscuits and listened.

Nothing.

Even this small act of defiance on the part of my kitten was almost too much to bear tonight.

Last May I didn't get out of bed all month. This year was a definite improvement on that: I had dragged myself into school each day, but by evening I'd had enough and right now the urge to dive under the covers and succumb to the misery that the month brought was almost overpowering.

Maybe next May would be even better and I wouldn't Dwell On The Past at all.

I took a deep breath. *Keep telling yourself that, Tilly, and it will come true.*

I played a quick game of Things To Be Thankful For to cheer myself up (Supernoodles, Ant and Dec, and Lycra) while I cleared away my dinner things and stowed them in my tiny galley kitchen.

There. No one would ever know I'd been.

Despite coming on in leaps and bounds at the allotment, making friends and putting my stamp on my half-plot, I still didn't feel ready to put down roots on the home-front. I didn't especially want to examine why this was but part of me suspected I was still hoping to wake up and find the last eighteen months had been a dream. A bad dream.

I sighed and shook the box again.

Cally at four months old was fast becoming a stroppy teenager in cat years; slinking to his own tune and completely ignoring my calls when it was time to shut him in the kitchen before I left the house. Eventually I heard the soft thump as he jumped down from my bedroom windowsill and the tinkle of his collar signalling his descent down the stairs. He brushed his stripy grey body against my legs and sat neatly by the back door.

'Sorry,' I said, bending to ruffle his chin. 'You're not allowed out on your own yet.'

My spirits took a nosedive as I glanced at the clock. I should go. I didn't want to but I would, I decided, scooping up four pots labelled 'sweetcorn mark two' into a carrier bag. My pumpkin seedlings could wait another few days, but these really needed to be in the ground. If I was quick, there would be just enough time to plant them before the extraordinary meeting in the pavilion.

I strapped on my helmet and hi-vis waistcoat and cycled off.

My part of Kingsfield had virtually no greenery except a few scrappy grass verges and a handful of melancholy poplar trees and somehow this made the arrival at Ivy Lane allotments extra magical: up Wellington Street I rode, left along Shenton Road by the shops, right into All Saints Road past my school and finally a left turn into Ivy Lane, where, between the ends of two rows of terraced houses, a driveway led Narnia-like to a lush green world, an oasis of serenity amidst the chaos of suburbia.

Although perhaps not right now, I thought, as I approached the pavilion.

Roy, shielding his eyes from the evening sun, looked up at Christine who was on a stepladder on the pavilion porch, hammer in hand and a tangled string of bunting trailing over her shoulder.

'For heaven's sake, Chris,' snapped Roy, 'you'd think it was a visit from the Royal Bloody Family.' He caught my eye and shook his head in exasperation.

I dismounted to find out what was going on.

'He farts like the rest of us, you know,' he added.

'Not like you, I hope. You stinkin' great warthog.'

Roy swiped a hand through the air irritably and turned away. 'I'm surprised you've not had us lined up on the road waving flags,' he shouted over his shoulder.

Christine froze and you could almost see the cogs in her brain clunking as her eyes darted to and fro: where will I get thirty Union Jacks in Kingsfield on a Monday night?

I would quite like to have watched the drama unfold but as I was limited for time I pressed on to plot sixteen.

Gemma's shed door was open again and I shouted hello as I went by.

'Evening, Tilly,' she replied. Gemma must have come straight from work; she was dressed in her white beautician's tunic and black trousers, and her hair was gripped back with an ordinary hairclip. Her tongue poked out from between her lips and she appeared to be drawing something on a large piece of cardboard. I mentally crossed my fingers that it wouldn't be a sign to hold up during the meeting, like those sequin-covered messages of adoration that you saw at gigs.

I gathered what I needed for planting: watering can, compost, trowel and bonemeal and made my way over the vegetable beds to see how my young plants were doing.

Although I hadn't been much of a cook lately, the

abundance of fresh food springing up all around me and the satisfaction of picking something I had grown myself was beginning to tempt me back into the kitchen. Last night I found myself dreaming about a primavera risotto that James and I had once had in Rome, all unctuous and creamy and I planned to recreate it using my own shallots, broad beans and peapods – strictly speaking it should have been mangetout but there couldn't be too much difference, surely? – and beg a bit of asparagus from Vicky-near-the-gate.

I might even push the boat out and invite someone round to share it with me. How about that for progress?

I bent down and held my breath as I inspected the little patch of peas, pak choi and callaloo; nibbled but no worse than last week. Hurrah, one nil to me in the slug wars. Far from only having myself to feed, last week I'd discovered I was, in fact, feeding an army of slugs who, as soon as my back was turned, marched through my juicy plants leaving nothing but bare stalks.

It had been a setback, but such, I had come to understand, was the nature of gardening. I'd bought some slug pellets and, thankfully, they seemed to be working.

Planting my sweetcorn was the work of a few moments so I tidied away my things, called for Gemma and the two of us ambled towards the pavilion, me rather more reluctantly than her.

'If they ask for people to have main roles,' said Gemma, linking her arm through mine, 'I'm going to put my hand up.'

'Really?' I grinned at her. 'I'd never have guessed.'

'Ooh, he's here, look!'

Gemma pointed to a white transit van adorned with the *Green Fingers* logo. There was a man inside with a mobile phone pressed to his ear. Christine and Peter were on the pavilion steps as welcoming committee, poised to pounce on the poor man as soon as he emerged. Christine had changed into a dress and cardigan. The buttons bulged across her tummy slightly and the orange flowers clashed with her pink cheeks but I didn't think I'd ever seen her look so radiant.

'Wellingtons, Mother!' hissed Gemma as we passed her on our way in.

'Wha—' Christine looked at her feet, thrust her hands through her steely grey curls and darted into the little office.

We pushed our way into the pavilion. It was heaving; even more people had turned up than for the AGM in February. The room had been arranged lecture-style with assorted chairs facing a top table nearest the door. We squeezed past Dougie in the front row and found spare seats near the back.

'Ladies and gentleman,' boomed Peter as he and Christine led a tall dark-haired man into the pavilion and took their places at the top table. The room fell silent immediately. 'Allow me to introduce Aidan Whitby, TV director for the *Green Fingers* show.'

Aidan raised a hand and smiled self-consciously. Some people clapped. Gemma included. I huffed to myself; he would have to do more than simply climb out of his van to impress me.

'Where's the girl?' said Dougie, straining his neck to look out of the open door.

At that moment Charlie and Alf arrived together and everyone laughed. I pointed to the empty seat next to me and Alf's eyes lit up, but Charlie barged past everyone and dropped into it before he had taken a step. Poor Alf. I heard Gemma snigger beside me.

'Hi,' he whispered in my ear.

We were a bit squashed and the heat radiating from Charlie's thigh was so intense that I wondered whether he had come straight from a fire.

Aidan Whitby stood up and cleared his throat. 'Hello, everyone, and, er, thank you for coming.'

The laughter died down, the audience straightened up and several bosoms heaved. He was slim, had a broad nose, which somehow made him look quite friendly, and thick wavy hair, which grew in a circle like the whorl of a fingerprint. Even from the back of the room I could see his brown eyes taking us all in, scanning our faces.

He's in the media, I reminded myself, be on your guard at all times.

'He looks very intelligent,' I heard Colin's mother Rosemary whisper to Liz.

I glanced at Gemma to roll my eyes but she was gazing at Aidan, transfixed.

For heaven's sake.

'Suzanna sends her apologies, she's at the Chelsea Flower Show filming the pre-show build-up,' said Aidan, hunching his shoulders in a can't-be-helped manner. Cue gasps from an over-excited audience.

'So I'm afraid you're stuck with me tonight,' he continued with a self-deprecating smile.

'Sorry to go on about this,' said Dougie, a chewed pencil hovering over an old envelope, 'but what dates will the lovely Suzanna be here? Exactly.'

'Er . . .' Aidan hesitated and caught Peter's warning glance. 'I can't confirm that at the moment. Depends on her filming schedule.'

Dougie sank back into his chair gloomily.

Aidan explained that filming would begin in June. For

most of the time, it would be just him and a cameraman. They wanted to follow us over the summer with the climax of the episode being the Ivy Lane allotments annual show in August. I'd heard about the show from Christine. It was a highly competitive affair with an official judge and prizes up for grabs for every type of vegetable under the sun.

Suzanna Merryweather and possibly a make-up artist would apparently be here only intermittently.

'I hope you don't expect us to wear make-up?' said Nigel, flaring his nostrils.

'Hear hear,' said Roy, folding his arms.

Aidan had one arm wrapped across his body and his other hand across his mouth. I suspected he was smothering a chuckle. 'The make-up artist would be purely for Suzanna. Whether you wear cosmetics is your choice. We're looking for real lives, real people, not made-up for the camera, or glamorous. Dress exactly as you would normally, the scruffier the better.' He looked round the room and beamed at us.

'Phew,' said Christine, looking pointedly at her husband.

'Charming,' said Gemma, patting her curls.

'Sorry,' stammered Aidan, waving his arms like an apologetic octopus. 'That came out all wrong. What I mean is. . .' He took a deep breath. 'We think this episode of *Green Fingers* will be very special; a true celebration of British allotments.' He paused to smile at the committee.

'He defo uses hair wax,' hissed Gemma. 'No one gets a tousled look like that without putting some effort in. I admire that in a man.'

'We don't want boffins who've studied at – I dunno – Kew Gardens,' he went on. 'Or word-perfect actors who don't know one end of a wheelbarrow from the other. We want people with passion; we want grass-roots experience

– any little hints and tips you may have, skills that have been passed on from father to son,' he looked around suddenly, 'or mother to daughter, obviously, or even father to daughter . . .'

'Oh, I don't know,' I replied in a whisper as Aidan paused and ran an anxious hand through his hair repeatedly until it stuck up in peaks.

'Anyway, you get my drift,' he said. 'The point is that we want to find out about the real people at Ivy Lane and what makes it so unique.' He exhaled with relief.

His speech had done the trick; he seemed to have got everyone back on side and there were happy faces all round.

'And rest assured, if you're being filmed, it'll be obvious,' said Aidan. 'There'll be no hidden cameras spying on you. Except that one. Ha-ha.' He pointed up at the ceiling where a red light winked from the motion sensor for the burglar alarm.

The entire audience shifted in their seats as one and Liz even yelped.

'Joke, joke, sorry,' he said, holding his hands up with a grimace. 'Moving on.'

He took a piece of paper from his pocket. 'I have a list of plot holders who have been nominated by the committee to be interviewed.'

He forced his sleeves up over his elbows as if he was getting ready to get stuck in. His slate-grey shirt had epaulettes at the shoulders. A smattering of chest hair was just visible at the open neck.

James hadn't had chest hair, he was completely smooth. I wondered how different it would be lying skin to skin, my cheek resting on a hairy chest.

I sat up straight with a jolt, startled by my own train of thought, and fanned my face.

'I know!' whispered Gemma with a wink. 'He is rather attractive, isn't he?'

'No, no, it's not that.' I wasn't sure what it was. Other than quite a shock to be thinking about bare chests.

'He's not an object, you know,' tutted Charlie.

'Tilly Parker?' Aidan's brown eyes searched the room.

My entire body went on red alert.

'Here!' shouted Gemma, pointing out my puce-coloured face to the TV director. I cringed as everyone turned to stare.

Aidan glanced at me, then at Charlie – who chose that moment to stretch his arm along the back of my chair – and back to me. He held my eyes for a second and my heart thumped anxiously. He pressed his lips together and – so fractionally that I almost missed it – raised his eyebrows.

What? What was that supposed to mean?

'Who else is on the list?' yelled Gemma.

Christine jumped up from her seat and snatched the piece of paper out of Aidan's hand, glancing nervously in my direction, or maybe Gemma's, it was hard to tell when her eyes were so glossy with adulation. 'We'll go over this another time.'

'Right,' said Aidan, leaning away from her. 'That's it, I think. Oh, one final point. We really want you to enjoy having us here, just be yourselves, relax and act natural.' He nodded to signal the end of his speech and exhaled as if he was glad to get that over with.

We all clapped, even me. I'd liked him more than I thought I would. Except for the 'we want to find out about the real people' part.

Peter closed the meeting, thanking everyone for coming, and we made a bid for freedom and fresh air.

Aidan had been cornered up against the noticeboard by

Brenda and as I passed him he caught my eye and grinned. I couldn't help chuckling at his please-rescue-me face and I was about to go to his aid when Charlie tapped me on the shoulder.

'Fancy going for a drink?' he said loudly.

He probably meant just as mates, but I flinched, besides which he had practically shouted down my ear.

'No,' I answered sharply, softening as his face drooped, 'not on a school night.'

'Right,' said Gemma. 'I'd better dash.'

Before I could question her, she ran off. I said goodbye to Charlie and by the time I had asked Vicky about her asparagus and made it back to the plot to collect my bike, Gemma had stuck a cardboard sign on the outside of her shed, offering *Green Finger Specials*, including hair, make-up, nails, waxing and even men's haircuts for five pounds. She tapped the sign as I went past.

'This is my big break, Tilly, I can feel it. Isn't it exciting?' She fluttered her eyelashes and shimmied and I smiled back, wishing I shared her joy.

I must admit, I had been reassured to some degree by Aidan's words, but still, I'd much rather be left alone. I had been so looking forward to a peaceful summer; warm afternoons spent within this community that had welcomed me with such generous arms. Everyone was so excited about being on TV but I couldn't shake the feeling that our gentle equilibrium would somehow be disturbed by the TV crew's presence.

With a heavy heart I wheeled the bike on to the road and headed for home. My allotment had suddenly lost a little of its magic, and I wasn't sure if it would come back.

Chapter 14

I was crouching carefully in between my broad beans and pak choi, trying not to squash anything. Thanks to Charlie's rather wonky planting, there was a wedge-shaped space that I reckoned I could squeeze Christine's courgette plant into. I turned the soil over with my hand fork and peered over my shoulder.

I was literally keeping a low profile.

The *Green Fingers* crew had arrived on site for the first time and Peter was doing the rounds, showing Aidan and a cameraman the highlights of the allotment. When I arrived they were in the shop and as far as I could make out they were doing a slow circuit of the whole site, plot by plot. They hadn't got as far as sixteen yet. I was hoping to barricade myself in my shed when they did.

It was only ten o'clock but the sun was already warm on my back and I wished I'd tied my hair up before leaving the house. Every time I bent forward wisps of it tickled my face and my neck felt a bit sweaty. I pulled a piece of string out of my pocket left over from tying up the peas and twisted my hair into a messy ponytail.

'I've got a gap before my next treatment, Tilly,' shouted Gemma. 'Do you want me to sort those eyebrows out?'

Gemma had been here for two hours and had had a steady stream of clients all morning. Upper lip waxes mainly, I was told. The worst job so far had been trimming Alf's ear tufts.

'Shush!' I hissed, dropping to my knees. 'No thanks, they're fine.'

'Huh,' said Gemma, thankfully at lower volume. 'They look like two slugs kissing. The George Clooney look might work for . . . George Clooney, but to be honest—'

'All right.' I stabbed my fork in the ground, brushed the mud from my jeans and rolled my eyes. Gemma squealed with delight and skipped back to her shed in her pink Crocs. In the six months I had known her, she had tried to make me submit to her ministrations on numerous occasions and I knew this would make her day.

I sat down in her makeshift salon. 'Just do the bit in the middle above my nose, that'll be enough for now.'

She gave me a hand mirror and pointed to the hairs she planned to relieve me of.

'I could tweeze them, but I haven't got all day so it'll have to be a wax strip,' she said.

Sitting in an allotment shed surrounded by gardening paraphernalia was not how I envisaged my first ever wax, but if Gemma managed to denude Colin's intimate areas here, I was sure my monobrow was in safe hands.

'What a glorious summer's day,' she sighed. 'The sun's out, the sky is blue and you and I are about to make our TV debut!'

I grunted, not wanting to risk speech in case it threw the wax strip off course and I ended up browless like James had done on his stag weekend. His hadn't been a whole brow luckily and the pencilled-in section had been undetectable on the wedding photos, but his mum hadn't been amused.

Gemma was very quick; a couple of sharp intakes of breath and it was all over.

'There you go.' She stood back, satisfied.

I checked my reflection. Gemma had been right. That was much better, or at least it would be when the redness had gone down. My expression had lost that annoyed look.

'In fact, would you shape my eyebrows too, Gemma, while I'm here?'

Gemma gave me a beatific smile. 'With pleasure. And why don't we do your legs, too? Then you can get them out for a change.'

I tried to shake my head, but she had it firmly clamped. 'I'd rather not. Besides, the TV crew could be here any minute and I don't want them to find me in your shed stripped to my knickers.'

'Oh, I do,' she said with a cheeky grin. 'It would do wonders for my beauty business.'

'You do know they're making a programme about gardening, don't you?' I said, wincing as her tweezers tweaked and plucked at speed across my left eyebrow.

'Quiet!' Gemma straightened up and looked out of the window. 'They're here. They're on plot fifteen. Come on.'

She flung open the shed door and darted down the path to greet Peter and the *Green Fingers* crew.

I remained in her stripy deckchair, momentarily stunned, staring in the hand mirror. My left brow was a work of art, my right brow still left something to be desired.

Ten seconds later, Gemma stomped back in, her lips pressed together in fury.

'I'm fuming,' she spat superfluously, throwing her beauty tools back into her case. 'Aidan said I'm not on his list! They're not filming me. I don't believe it. Passed over for fame by my own mother!' She stared at me, her blue eyes glittering with indignation. 'Well,' she said, folding her arms. 'That's the last time I trim her corns for free.'

There was a sudden commotion outside. Dougie and Alf were running – actually running – along the road, collecting the other plot holders en route.

'It's Suzanna! Suzanna Merryweather is here,' shouted Dougie, beckoning to us to join him. 'Come on!'

Gemma shrugged. 'Might as well, seeing as I'm surplus to requirements.'

I pointed at my unfinished eyebrow and pulled a 'you've got to be joking' face.

Gemma hesitated for a millisecond and darted off to join the stampede, pushing past Peter and his visitors who were by now hovering at the end of our plot. Aidan was shaking his head and chuckling and a man in his forties in jeans and a baseball cap, and a large camera balanced on one shoulder, was openly laughing.

I guessed this was not the 'act natural' they were hoping for.

'Tilly,' called Peter, his consonants sounding crisper than usual, 'please can I introduce Aidan and Jeff from the *Green Fingers* show?'

Great. By the time I had emerged from Gemma's shed, Aidan and Jeff were already on my plot. Peter had been waylaid by Rosemary and I could see him itching to get away.

'This is very nice,' said Aidan, once we had shaken hands.

'Thank you,' I said, aware that I was fiddling with my hair. My skin was tingling from all that waxing and plucking and I was probably all red and blotchy.

I decided to act busy so that: a) they would leave me alone and b) I wouldn't have to maintain eye contact thus revealing my odd eyebrow arrangement. I grabbed my little courgette plant and settled myself back in the space in front of the broad beans.

'OK if we watch for a minute?' asked Aidan.

'Sure,' I said with a shrug as I dug a deep hole and sprinkled in some fertilizer.

Aidan sauntered up towards the shed and rested a Converse trainer on my bench. He was wearing a sand-coloured shirt with sleeves rolled up and combat trousers with lots of pockets. He would look more at home on safari than filming in suburbia.

'What are you up to today?' he asked casually.

I glanced over to him.

My Wedgwood-blue shed, flanked by pots of Roy's sweet peas and colourful herbs, was like a page from a Cath Kidston catalogue. I would take a picture of that and frame it so that I could look at it yearningly all through winter. I would wait until he'd gone, though, even if he did add a certain focal point to the scene.

'Planting out my courgette,' I said politely.

I was vaguely aware of Jeff edging along the path, but chose not to look. At least he wasn't talking.

'Just the one?'

'You only need one plant on a plot this size; it might look small now but it will yield up to five kilos of courgettes all by itself,' I said, sounding for all the world as if I knew what I was talking about. 'That's quite enough for one person.'

'I see.'

Something in his tone made me look up again. His dark eyes met mine and I felt my heart flip like a pancake.

He was making me so nervous.

I pressed the earth in around the base of the plant and jumped up to fetch the watering can. I'd filled it earlier and it was very heavy. Water slopped on to my jeans and I tutted.

'Wow. That's a lot of water,' he chuckled, after I had virtually drowned it.

He was right, I'd overdone it really, not that I was about to admit that.

'Courgettes are very thirsty plants,' I said airily, hoping that the poor little thing could swim. 'And the ground is very dry at the moment. We've had barely any rain for weeks. There.' I stood up, hoping to convey that the job and our conversation were over.

'Nice carrots,' he said.

As far as Aidan was concerned it clearly wasn't over.

'Thank you.' There was an edge to my voice that I hope didn't go unnoticed.

'This is your first year on the allotment, isn't it? Aren't carrots supposed to be difficult to grow?'

'I am pleased with them, I must admit,' I laughed. It was probably belated beginner's luck — I certainly hadn't had much luck to start with — but they had turned out well.

'I covered the shoots with a ridge of topsoil to keep carrot fly away early on,' I said, smiling to myself, remembering all the carroty wisdom that Nigel had fallen over himself to impart. 'I'm hoping for a bumper crop in time for the annual show.'

'What is it about being on the allotment that you enjoy most?'

I stared at him and gave him a look that Mia would have been proud of. 'The peace and quiet,' I said.

There was a snort of laughter from Jeff. Oh, Jeff! I had completely forgotten about him and . . . he had his camera focused on me. Did that mean . . . ? Hell's bells!

'That was great, Tilly,' Aidan said enthusiastically, rubbing his hands together. 'Really good. We'll leave it there for now.' He nodded to Jeff. 'Perhaps next time you

133

can tell us about some of your other crops. And more tips like how to avoid carrot fly. That was exactly what we want.'

'But!' I said, wading towards him through the callaloo.

He began to stride down the path. 'Sorry, we've got an awful lot to get through today,' he said, smiling apologetically over his shoulder.

I stood open-mouthed. Such gentle questioning, I hadn't thought for a moment that I was being filmed . . . Oh, he was good. He was very good.

'Peter,' I heard him call. 'Did you say there was a lady who specializes in flowers?'

'Perfect, that was,' said Jeff with a wink, lowering the camera to his side. 'Really natural.'

As I looked down at my wet and muddy jeans, the piece of string slipped from my hair. And then I remembered my one bushy eyebrow complete with shiny red waxed patches. Natural wasn't the word I'd use.

The TV crew seemed to be here for the duration. At various times during the day I spotted Aidan chatting to different people; laughing with Dougie inside his shed (I suspected alcohol was involved), nodding earnestly as Liz gave him a guided tour of her flower beds and later I saw him sitting in a deckchair, mug in hand, listening patiently to one of Alf's stories.

He seemed to make time for everyone and to be genuinely interested in what we were growing and all the quirky little inventions people had for watering or keeping pests at bay.

Perhaps I'd overreacted; having the *Green Fingers* crew here seemed to pose no threat to my private life at all. For which I was mightily relieved. Because quite unexpectedly, Aidan Whitby was growing on me.

Gemma had recovered from her earlier snub and had

declared Suzanna to be an angel and even more beautiful in the flesh. She did all her own hair and make-up for the programme apparently, but Gemma had offered her services just in case. Suzanna had actually asked Gemma what moisturizer she used on her face to keep it looking so young and had even taken one of her leaflets!

I hadn't spoken to our resident celebrity. She seemed to spend most of her time in front of the pavilion talking to the camera, interviewing the committee or fending off amorous advances from Dougie.

'When all this is over,' said Gemma to me in her shed when she finally got round to sorting out my other eyebrow, 'I'm going to start looking for premises. My own salon. I can't wait. We've been saving up for years. That's why Mikey works such long hours, to build me up some capital. Bless him.'

'How exciting!' I said, trying to keep still. 'You deserve it too. He's a lovely man, your husband.'

I took a deep breath and concentrated on not being envious.

'When me and Mike got married we thought we'd have kids, you know, complete the family. But it never happened. Mike adores Mia, but I'd have loved to have given him a baby of his own. Still, I got one chance at being a mum and I'm grateful for that.'

I felt my chest tighten and my breath quicken. Perhaps some people only got one chance at motherhood. Perhaps I would never feel the warmth of my own baby in my arms. I pressed my eyes tighter shut.

'Sorry, Tilly, is this making your eyes water?' Gemma giggled.

I nodded.

'So anyway, we've put all thoughts of babies behind us

now,' she continued. 'No use worrying about a life you can't have. All my energies will be going into building a business, that's where my future lies.'

She stood up straight and passed me a mirror. 'How's that?'

'Tilly!' she gasped as I threw my arms around her and squeezed her tight. 'I know, I'm a miracle worker, right!'

Was that what I should do, stop worrying about the life I can't have? And if so what sort of future did I want?

Chapter 15

It was mid-June and the *Green Fingers* team were here again. They seemed to be here every time I was: Aidan making notes, or on the phone; Jeff with his camera permanently attached like an extra limb and occasionally Suzanna, breezing through like a ray of sunshine and chatting to all and sundry. I was doing my best to carry on as normal, although I noticed that everyone else seemed to be rather smarter these days with ironed shirts, rip-free trousers and lashings of lipstick. I felt quite dowdy today in my cream T-shirt and khaki linen trousers.

I was sitting in my shed having a restorative cup of tea. I'd just been filmed again. I'd known about it this time and on balance I think I preferred *not* knowing.

As soon as I'd arrived this morning, Aidan had pounced and, in that gentle but highly persuasive tone of his, talked me into 'doing a piece to camera'.

So I'd picked some peas and talked about how I'd already harvested some early pods for a risotto. But I'd been so nervous that when Aidan asked me to split open a pod for a close-up, my thumb had gone all rubbery and the peas leapt out and bounced off the camera lens.

And my voice! I'd come over all Princess Anne for some reason. All highly embarrassing although Aidan had seemed pleased.

Anyway, they had gone now, thank goodness. Jeff was filming Peter next door harvesting his globe artichokes and Aidan was, well, hovering at the end of my plot.

I tried to ignore him and turned to the morning's job list. Firstly, inspection time.

Weeds, lots of. Orange carrot tips peeked up through the ground – that was a good sign; the sweet peas were weaving their tendrils nicely up the bamboo canes and my pumpkin plant was beginning to meander merrily through the onions. Not bad, Tilly, not bad at all . . .

My next job was to sort out the broad beans, which were in dire need of some support. I'd mistakenly thought that if I put a few sticks in the ground the beans would throw out tendrils and cling on. But they hadn't. Wrong type of bean, apparently. And my in-depth research (a look at Charlie's plot) revealed that I needed to construct a broad bean corridor, which looked like a giant version of a game I used to play at school called Cat's Cradle.

Easy peasy.

Fifteen minutes later, my temper was wearing thin. I'd tripped over the bamboo canes four times and broken two of them, tied myself in knots, snapped three plants and lost the scissors. The ground was too hard to push the canes in far enough and every time I pulled the string tight, the canes just fell over. I would have no flowers left on the plants at this rate.

This was not a job for one person.

I was out of puff and cross and about to bundle the lot back into the shed when I noticed Aidan approach, hands in his pockets, whistling tunelessly.

I took a deep breath. Please don't ask to record this fiasco on celluloid.

'Want a hand?'

I could have cried. 'Yes please.'

I must have looked desperate because he grinned and took the bamboo canes out of my hand.

'What are you actually trying to do?'

I blew my hair off my face and pointed at the peas. 'Peas throw out clever little tendrils and climb up, clinging on to anything that comes close enough, so they don't need much support. See?'

Aidan bent down and peered at them dutifully. 'I see.'

'Whereas broad beans, well, broad beans aren't anywhere near as clever,' I said, trying not to sound petulant. 'They'll grow at least a metre tall and if they don't have proper support the stems will snap. I need canes all around the edge of the plants so that I can thread string across in a zigzag pattern.'

'I see,' Aidan said again. He laid the pile of canes down and one at a time, using all his weight, began to drive them down firmly in the ground along the edge of the bean patch.

I watched, feeling weak and feeble.

'What do you do for a living?' he asked when he'd made his way to the far end, making the job look easy.

I narrowed my eyes. Here we go. He was digging for personal details.

'Off the record?' I asked.

He stood up, ran a hand through his hair and chuckled. 'Yes. Off the record.'

Hmm, I bet that was what they all said. 'I'm a teacher.' No harm in telling him that much.

He nodded. 'That makes sense. You're good at explaining

things, you're very clear and concise and that's probably what makes you so natural in front of the camera.'

'Am I? Thank you.' I was ridiculously pleased with the compliment and felt I should return it. 'You're good, too. At directing. You put people at ease.' Like me, for instance. God, that sounded pathetic.

'Thanks.' He waggled his dark eyebrows at me. Gemma would have a field day with those. 'Well, you can direct me now. What's next?' he said, straightening up and resting his hands on his hips.

I handed him the ball of string and we stood opposite each other, threading it backwards and forwards and tying it around each cane as we went. His knots involved clever sliding loops, I noticed. Mine were more from the 'left over right and under' school of knots.

'Do you enjoy teaching, then?' he asked. His fingers brushed against mine as he passed me the string and I felt my knees weaken. Apart from Charlie, I rarely had any contact with men my own age, I realized, and certainly no physical contact. Even the staff at school were all women except the elderly caretaker. I felt all my nerve-endings spring into life and prayed that my cheeks didn't give me away.

I swallowed hard and nodded. 'Yes. There's something life-affirming about working with children. They see the world with such innocence, such curiosity.'

'Interesting.'

'Really?'

We had reached the end of the row and were standing almost toe to toe. He stared at me for a few seconds. 'Yes, very. I've had an idea—'

He broke off as Gemma came bustling towards us, with Mia trailing behind her.

'Ooh, you two look cosy,' she called, waving a hand as she dumped her bag on the grass between our half-plots.

We leapt apart and I busied myself collecting up the left-over bamboo canes while Aidan took out his phone.

'Now's your chance, Mia,' said Gemma, nudging her daughter. 'Aidan, would you mind having a chat with Mia about Media Studies, she's got a careers day coming up?'

'Oh God. Bit embarrassing. I did Zoology,' murmured Aidan, pulling a face at me. 'Of course,' he replied good-naturedly and strode off to talk to a glum-faced Mia.

I sat on my bench in the sunshine and sipped at a bottle of water. I wasn't on my own for long.

'Have I aged since the last time you saw me?' demanded Gemma as she dropped down beside me. 'That girl will be the death of me,' she continued without waiting for an answer.

'Not noticeably,' I said. 'Why, what has she done?'

I glanced over at Mia and Aidan. He was sitting on the grass beside her, his long legs stretched out in front of him. They were both laughing. He certainly had a gift for drawing even the most reluctant people out of their shell.

'Bunked off school. Only caught a bus to the flippin' airport with her friends because there was a rumour about One Direction landing by helicopter. I got a call from school. Did I know where she was? Can you imagine? Talk about panic dot com.' Gemma huffed and rolled her eyes. 'She's grounded for life now, I think.'

'That was brave.' I'd never have had the guts to do that at Mia's age. 'And did she get to see One Direction?'

Gemma tutted at me. 'Whose side are you on?'

I shrugged apologetically.

'Here's Mum; wait till she hears about this.'

Christine had arrived and was chatting to Aidan and

Mia. After a few seconds, Aidan left with a cheery wave and the other two walked slowly towards us. Mia's arms waved indignantly and then folded abruptly.

'She's told you, then,' said Gemma to her mum, shaking her head. 'I was worried sick, anything could have happened.'

'But it didn't,' said Christine diplomatically, 'thank the good Lord.' She wrapped her arm round Mia's waist and reached up to kiss her cheek.

Gemma frowned and obviously didn't want to let it go. 'No, but—'

'I bunked off once, myself,' said Christine with a cheeky smile.

'Mother!'

'Grandma, you bunked off?' The delight on Mia's face said it all.

'Yes.' She nodded proudly. 'The Beatles were putting on a matinee performance at the Hippodrome. So me, Maureen, Pauline and Eileen . . .'

I loved this story already. Obviously your name had to end in 'een' to be in Christine's gang.

'We worked out that if we could scrape together fifty-two shillings, we could have a box to ourselves and be nearer the stage.'

'And were you?' said Gemma, interested despite herself. 'Did you get close?'

'Right. Above. The stage.' Christine said dreamily, squeezing on to the bench beside Gemma. She stared into space. 'I could see the sweat on John Lennon's shirt. The actual sweat of him. And then the best thing happened.'

'Go on,' I said. I was right there with her at the Hippodrome.

'Well, I wrote "I love you" on a scrap of paper, tucked

it into my powder compact and threw it on stage. And then . . .' Christine's eyes filled with tears, she pressed a hand to her chest and gulped at the air.

I was filling up myself and I didn't even particularly like The Beatles.

'Paul McCartney picked it up,' Christine whispered. Mia gasped and dropped to her knees, although I was pretty sure she didn't have a clue who he was.

'He read the note and looked up at the four of us and waved. Mostly at me, I think,' she said earnestly. 'Well, we screamed our heads off. And then he started singing "Love Me Do" and looking at us girls and we cried all the way through it. I could have done with that bloody compact back by the end of it, I can tell you.'

Christine wiped the tears from her rosy cheeks and smiled.

'Unfortunately, the matinee was on a Friday and Mother Superior phoned up all our mothers saying that we had not been in school. I got three hours at the mangle for punishment. Worth every minute.' She sighed and Gemma and I exchanged incredulous glances.

'Well, I must say, Mum, you're not exactly backing me up here. I'm trying to set Mia a good example.'

'Oh, lighten up, Gemma, didn't you do the very same thing yourself?' muttered Christine out of the side of her mouth.

Gemma stretched her eyes wide. 'Absolutely not.'

'Elton John . . . ?' Christine raised an eyebrow at her daughter.

Colour flooded Gemma's face and her mouth was doing a fantastic goldfish impression. I pressed my lips together and tried to hide my mirth. Elton John? No wonder she was reluctant to come clean.

'Obsessed with that *Lion King* song, she was,' said Christine, addressing Mia. 'Knew all the words. So she bunked off school to queue up for tickets to Elton's concert.'

'Mum!' gasped Mia. 'You hypocrite. You bunked off school too.'

Gemma was shaking her head incredulously. 'How do you—'

'Saw you,' said Christine, cutting her off. 'I'd come to treat you to a ticket, knowing how much you loved him. You were walking away from the box office arm in arm with your friends. So I went home.'

'You never said a word,' said Gemma.

Mia's smirk was a work of art: lips pushed out like a duck, eyebrows practically at her hairline and her chin tilted at a confident jut.

'So there you go, we've all done it.' Christine pulled both her girls in close and whereas up until then I had felt part of the conversation, I suddenly felt like a voyeur, empty-armed and excluded.

'Part of me was proud of you.' She kissed Gemma's cheek. 'You've always had an independent streak and I wanted to encourage that.'

Gemma laughed softly.

'And Mia's got that same determination,' said Christine.

Mia and Gemma eyed each other and finally linked fingers.

'Besides, you saved me forty quid.' Christine exhaled a breath. 'Outrageous price for a ticket.'

'All right,' said Gemma sheepishly, 'I'm busted. But please, Mia, next time you go tearing off to meet your idols, tell me first, OK? Shall we call it quits?'

Mia made a show of considering the offer and Gemma

laughed. 'Come on, I'll treat you to McDonald's for lunch. Just this once.'

'Encouraging me to eat junk food, Mother! Tut tut.'

They walked away, arms around each other's waists and I smiled, thinking that it was amazing what the simple art of communication could achieve.

Christine caught my eye and squashed up to me on the bench. 'I'm a lucky woman.'

I nodded, not trusting myself to speak. A hole seemed to have opened up in my life all of a sudden.

'I love having my girls so near.'

The peaceful smile on Christine's face made tears rise to my eyes. I swallowed and managed a smile. Gemma had said something similar recently.

Love.

That was what was missing from my life. The realization hit me in the face as bluntly as a blow from a shovel.

I had taken on the allotment to fill a space in my heart, but now I wasn't sure it was enough. My little plot was well-cared for, blooming, healthy, but my relationships with other people were still sadly lacking.

Compared to Gemma my life was hollow. I only had a small family – just me and Mum – and I knew I was loved. But did I give love back? Did I make room for other people in my heart? Or did it have more padlocks than Dougie's shed?

James had been close to his parents. And they had happily absorbed me into their little family too, adopting me as the daughter they had never had. I had such happy memories of us all: family get-togethers, help with DIY when we bought our first home, Christmases spent at theirs and even a week in Cornwall together once. I'd lost contact now, of course. It had seemed less painful simply

145

to close the door on that part of my life than suffer the risk of rejection.

But now, after seeing the family bonds that tied these three together in love, I wondered if perhaps I had made a mistake.

'If you love someone, do you think a part of you will always love them, regardless of what happens?' I asked.

Christine patted my knee and didn't answer straight away.

'You know the answer to that,' she said softly.

I laid my head on her shoulder and let the tears fall. We sat in silence. Goodness only knows what Christine must have thought, but she didn't say a word. I would ring my mum when I got in. And then I would write to James's parents.

It was time I let people back in to my heart.

Chapter 16

The July air was hot, humid and still and in true British style, we did nothing but moan about it. There was also a tense atmosphere today and whilst I couldn't put my finger on what it was, it felt like we were all waiting for something.

I hoped it would be a nice something.

Gemma, dressed in a strappy sundress, was sitting on my bench watching me pick broad beans whilst filing her nails.

'My runner beans will take some beating this year,' she said. 'I've worked really hard on them.'

She must have seen my mouth twitch. 'Well, OK, Colin and I have.'

Her runner beans were impressive, I had to admit. They were over six feet tall and smothered with scarlet flowers. I'd just shoved a couple of dwarf beans in with my sweet peas. They were growing nicely, but I wouldn't do pots again; the watering was never-ending. And this flipping hosepipe ban wasn't helping.

'We dug a trench, lined it with newspapers and—'

'I know,' I said, 'I was here when Colin did it.'

'Are you going to have Cally's nuts off?'

'What?' I was used to Gemma dipping from one topic to

another like a cucumber stick at a buffet, but that was a leap too far. 'Gosh, I hadn't thought about it.'

'It stops them fighting and spraying everywhere,' she said, holding up her left hand for inspection.

'Seems a bit harsh, though, chopping off their testicles . . .'

'Oh, I don't know.' She mimed a slicing action with her nail file. 'Most men I know could do with a bit less testosterone. Talking of which,' she nodded towards the path, 'testosterone dot com.'

I turned to see that Aidan, wearing a soft cotton shirt and an easy smile, had materialized right behind me.

I felt the heat rise to my cheeks and prayed he hadn't heard my last comment. Or Gemma's.

'We should be out of your way after today until your annual show.'

He was leaving. I felt an instant pang. And then I felt startled. I hadn't felt a pang for a long time.

'Ahh,' said Gemma, her face falling. 'We'll miss you round the place. Won't we, Tills?'

I nodded, too overwhelmed to pick her up on her un-authorized use of 'Tills'.

I must have been the colour of Gemma's runner bean flowers – absolutely scarlet. He would be back, though, in a few weeks, which would give me time to ponder the pang. Good. I took a deep breath.

'Tilly, if it's OK with you, we want to film you walking down the road with a basket of produce.'

I had been filmed about half a dozen times in total and was now quite relaxed about matters. The *Green Fingers* van simply turned up without warning, filmed for a while and then disappeared. You'd have thought I'd have been pre-pared for an impromptu filming session by now.

So what on earth had possessed me to wear a pink

push-up bra under a white vest top to the allotment? A vest top that was currently sticking to my clammy body. It had looked quirky and cute in the mirror this morning, now it was verging on the tarty side. At least I was wearing long trousers. I glanced at Gemma, whose shoulders had fallen the way of her face. Dejected dot com. She had far more flesh on display than me.

I hatched a hasty plan.

'Only if Gemma's in the shot with me,' I said.

Without waiting for Aidan's response, she squealed with delight, plucked a handful of my sweet peas and threaded her arm through mine. 'You're the best,' she said, plonking a smacker of a kiss on my cheek.

Jeff, camera poised, was waiting for us on the road at the end of our plot. I'd never seen him without his hat on before, I hoped he'd rubbed suncream on to his head; there was no hair there to protect his scalp at all.

'Just chat casually,' said Aidan, 'as you were before I arrived.'

We shot complicit glances at each other. Not cat's testicles.

With baskets and arms looped *Wizard of Oz*-style, we began to walk as directed but it got off to a bad start when Gemma made a casual remark about the size of Peter's plums. We both collapsed in a fit of giggles and it went downhill from there. Suddenly everything we said sounded rude and even Jeff was struggling to hold the camera straight. Poor Aidan was doing his best to remain professional but the final straw came when Brenda tapped him on the shoulder and asked him if he'd like a close-up of her unearthing her Fiannas.

Gemma and I lost the plot and fell all over each other, laughing until our cheeks ached and our sides hurt, while

149

Aidan dispatched a bewildered Brenda with a promise to put her potatoes on his list for later.

'Right,' said Aidan, pulling his phone out of his pocket. 'This is your last chance. I mean it, ladies. I'm really pushed for time today.'

Gemma and I nodded, desperately trying to get our faces under control.

We trudged back up the road, followed by Jeff. Aidan rubbed a tired hand across his face and took a long swig from a water bottle. 'OK, let's go again.'

'Mmm, I'm not sure what to talk about,' I said.

'Just say something about community spirit,' said Jeff. I wondered if he knew how pink his head had gone and whether I should tell him. I decided against it, he might be touchy about his baldness.

'Such a nice bunch,' I said. 'Lovely people. There's a real sense of community at Ivy Lane.'

'Yeah . . .' Gemma nodded. 'And there's always someone to help you out if you need it.'

'Excuse me.'

Aidan growled and shouted, 'Cut.'

Rosemary, arms folded militantly, stood at the end of her plot, dressed in a Mother of the Bride outfit. She had not been shy with the face powder and her lips were lined with pencil at least five shades darker than her lipstick. Colin was just visible, the elastic of his underpants on show above their strawberry patch.

'There's more to Ivy Lane than just these two, you know.'

'Whoops,' muttered Jeff, 'natives are getting restless.'

Aidan pulled an apologetic face. 'That was great, thanks. We just need one more piece on your plot, Tilly. Five minutes?'

'OK.' I nodded as he walked away to pacify Rosemary.

'Thanks, Tilly, that was so exciting. I need a wee now,' said Gemma, kissing my cheek before dashing to the loo.

Aidan was very good with people, I thought as I walked back to my plot, very diplomatic. And although I hated to admit being wrong, being part of the documentary had been great fun and the highlight of my summer so far. I wiped a hand across my forehead, feeling a sheen of perspiration. I really ought to get out of the sun for a while.

I waved at Charlie as I passed the end of his plot. He was kneeling between a row of cabbages. He was red-faced and looked all grouchy in the heat.

He waved back. 'I'll be glad when this hot weather breaks,' he said. 'It's too much to be gardening in this heat.'

'We British are useless in the warm weather, aren't we!' I laughed and continued along the road.

I'd only had time to grab a quick drink when Aidan appeared with Jeff.

'We're going to have to make this brief,' he said apologetically. 'But I wanted you to do a piece that'll lead nicely into the annual show – you know, what's special about Ivy Lane, what categories you're going to enter, that sort of thing. Is that OK?'

'No problem,' I said confidently. *Help!* I racked my brains while Jeff got into position and Aidan gestured for me to stand under my apple tree. I hadn't really given the annual show categories much thought apart from my miniature carrots. I wasn't a particularly competitive person and, hand on heart, didn't really think I had grown anything worthy of a prize.

'So,' said Aidan, giving me his usual pointers, 'it's your first year, perhaps you could start by telling us what being part of the Ivy Lane community means to you.'

'Well . . .' *Everything. Being here means the world to me. I feel part of a family again.* I swallowed and felt tears prick at my eyes. 'Um . . .'

'Tilly?' Aidan rushed to my side in an instant and Jeff lowered his camera.

'Gosh, silly me,' I twittered, feeling completely idiotic. 'Must be the heat. Ignore me, I'm fine. Let's go again. Jeff, are you OK?'

Despite the sun, he had gone very pale all of a sudden. 'Bit of a headache, to be honest,' he said, rubbing the back of his neck.

'OK, let's start again, if you're sure, Tilly?' Aidan's brown eyes were full of concern and for one moment I thought he was going to put his arms round me. I wished he would; I was in desperate need of a hug.

I nodded and cleared my throat. 'Being here, away from the stresses and strains of the day, gives me space to breathe and,' my chest heaved as I gulped at the air, 'quite simply, I've fallen in love with life again.'

I could see Aidan nodding out of the corner of my eye. I turned to meet his gaze and his smile lit me up from the inside.

An electronic beep interrupted the moment.

'Oh damn,' said Aidan, looking at his phone. 'I was supposed to call the office an hour ago. Excuse me, Tilly, I need to get back to the van first to collect my notes.'

He dashed off and Jeff, looking a bit wobbly, set off for a sit-down in the pavilion. I began collecting my tools and stowing them in the shed and was suddenly aware of a dramatic change above me; a thick wall of grey cloud dissected the sky and the temperature had dropped by several degrees.

There was a storm coming, I was sure of it. I shivered and decided to dash to the pavilion to take cover in comfort.

As I passed the *Green Fingers* van, I caught sight of Aidan on his phone and smiled to myself. When he wasn't directing or interviewing, that man had a phone permanently glued to his ear. His laughter wafted through the open window and I slowed to enjoy it. OK – to eavesdrop.

'I can't wait to get on that plane to Peru,' he said with a groan. 'Get away from all these humans and their inflated bloody egos. It's the politics and one-upmanship I can't bear. Give me wildlife any day.'

I clapped a hand to my mouth and pressed my body against the back of the van out of sight.

Me? Did he mean me, or the Ivy Lane community generally? Had I displayed an inflated bloody ego? He had seemed so pleasant, so genuinely interested in us. He had coaxed us with his gentle questions, pretended to listen to our stories. But all along he was simply doing his job. And back then, not five minutes ago, I'd really felt as though he cared. About me.

My shoulders lowered a full four inches as I registered a crushing disappointment.

I ducked my head and ran into the pavilion just as a tremendous clap of thunder filled the air and made my ears ring.

The atmosphere inside the pavilion was no less stormy; Peter and Christine were under attack from mutinous plot holders.

'I spent weeks making that fertilizer from chicken droppings,' said Graham indignantly. 'That would definitely have added a quirkiness to the programme. But not a glimmer.' He threw a look of disdain in my direction.

'And I've grown purple carrots,' said Shazza, shaking her head incredulously. 'How can they not have been interested in purple carrots?'

There was an exasperated huff from the corner of the room where Karen, who by the look of it had heard quite enough about Shazza's purple carrots, had a hand pressed to Jeff's forehead. Gemma, on the other side of him, held his hand. He really didn't look well.

Further along, Roy sat chortling with Dougie, enjoying all the action.

'I'm more concerned about the hosepipe ban,' declared Vicky. 'Those marrows are such guzzlers and it's killing my back walking all the way to the gate with watering cans.'

As if by divine intervention, there was another enormous roll of thunder and the sky unleashed the most forceful rainfall I had ever heard. Water hammered against the corrugated roof of the pavilion and the noise was deafening.

'I think the hosepipe ban might be lifted as of tomorrow,' shouted Peter over the din.

The door banged opened and Aidan appeared, his soaked shirt clinging to his skin. 'The equipment,' he yelled. 'Jeff, all our equipment is outside by the toilets!'

Jeff's face had gone as grey as the sky. His body lurched forward, juddering like a man possessed, eyeballs out on stalks, and with a violent groan he threw up all over Karen's T-shirt.

'Sunstroke,' she said matter-of-factly. How could she not scream at being vomited on? 'He needs to get to bed.'

Aidan had his arms out in front of him, as if he was balancing on a tightrope, not sure what or who to rescue first.

'The shop,' I yelled, putting my own hurt feelings to one side for the time being. 'Let's get all your equipment in to the shop. That will be the quickest place.'

Aidan, Peter, Graham and I dashed back out into the storm and started pulling all the mysterious black cases into the shop. Goodness knows what they needed all that clobber for; I'd only seen them use one camera and a clipboard. The storm was in full flow now, with lightning flashes illuminating the dark sky and cracks of thunder that rattled my teeth. My clothes and hair were soaked and I tried not to think about my pink bra peeking jauntily through my white vest.

We finished the job as quickly as we could and dashed back, dripping and shivering, into the pavilion.

'Thanks, Tilly.' Aidan smiled at me, rubbing his hair with one of the towels that Shazza was passing round.

I flashed him a cool glare. 'Well, despite my *inflated bloody ego*, I thought I'd help you out.'

'What?' He frowned. 'Oh . . . no, you don't understand.'

'You need to get this man home,' said Karen, pushing between us. She had cleaned Jeff up and found herself an old T-shirt to change into.

'You get him home,' said Peter. Jeff looked dead on his feet and his head was lolling on his shoulders. Aidan had to virtually carry him to the door. 'I'll make sure the shop is secure before I leave tonight,' Peter added.

'Thanks for your help, everyone,' said Aidan, staring at me. 'We'll have to come back tomorrow and finish off.' He sighed. 'The bosses won't be happy.'

How could I have thought he enjoyed our company? He obviously didn't want to spend even one more day with us. I turned to Gemma, suddenly anxious to share all my woes.

'Shall we go back to your shed and have a cuppa?' I said. 'Gemma?'

Her face was a perfect match with Jeff's and she had a hand clamped across her mouth. 'I don't think I'll ever re-cover from seeing that man puke,' she mumbled. 'I think I'm going to be sick myself. Dad, can you take me home?'

Once all the invalids had departed I felt at a bit of a loose end. Although the worst of the storm had passed, the rain was still pelting down and I didn't fancy cycling home. I decided to go back to my own shed and wait for the rain to stop.

The constant sunshine over the last few weeks had turned the earth to concrete. I kept my head down and waded through the puddles. I felt Charlie's eyes on me from his sheltered position in the greenhouse, but I didn't meet his stare. I'd had enough of men for one day.

I set to with cleaning my tools and rearranging my shelves and was just beginning to get bored when Colin's face appeared at the window.

'Can I come in?' he shouted. 'I've got a new book. It's called *Heroes*.'

I had developed a soft spot for Colin, especially now that I'd felt the wrath of Rosemary. I grinned and opened the shed door.

We settled into plastic chairs and he produced the book from inside his jacket.

'Out of curiosity,' I asked, 'what does Rosemary think you do for a living?'

'Security guard,' he said with a crooked smile.

'Oh?' I concentrated on keeping my features neutral. He didn't seem robust enough to stand up to his mother let alone intruders.

He nodded as he thumbed through the pages to find his place. 'Yeah, I got the uniform from a shoot I did once. I sewed up the Velcro panels on the trousers and stick it in the wash every week. She's never questioned it.'

He shrugged his shoulders and we giggled. I was so glad he had come. De-stressing with a book was the perfect antidote to the dramas of the last hour.

I spoke too soon as the door to my shed was prised open by an outraged Rosemary.

'What on earth are you doing with my son?' she gasped.

'Mum! For God's sake, I'm nineteen,' he said, rolling his eyes.

And only reading a sodding book, I added mentally.

'Exactly,' she said, glaring at me. 'Too young to be locked in a shed with Tilly. Why can't you find a girl your own age?'

'I'm not *that* old,' I retorted.

My shed door, still flapping, was flung back again, this time by Charlie.

'What's going on?' he demanded, arms folded, looking every inch the Victorian father, although I wasn't sure by now which one of us was supposed to need protecting.

I'd had enough of this. 'Colin and I were reading. Now out, both of you!'

I snatched the book out of Colin's hand and waved it in front of their faces.

'Colin?' Rosemary pressed a hand to her mouth. 'You never read books.'

I rolled my eyes as she reached out to touch her son.

'Sorry about this, Tilly,' muttered Colin. 'Come on, Mum,' he said as he led Rosemary away, 'I've got something to tell you.'

Hallelujah, not before time.

I turned my gaze to Charlie. 'What was all that about?'

Charlie shifted uncomfortably and scratched his head. 'I saw Rosemary barge in and thought . . . you and him.'

I sighed. 'Well, we weren't,' I said, sinking down on to a chair, suddenly desperate for today to end.

'And I was jealous, I suppose,' he muttered.

'Charlie, I'm disappointed in you,' I said wearily. 'We're supposed to be friends.' I met his eye. 'Just friends.'

He backed towards the door and bowed his head. 'Fine,' he said eventually. He strode away and the empty silence suddenly felt deafening. I let out a breath and squeezed my eyes shut.

What was it I liked about the allotment again? Oh yes, that was it. Peace and quiet.

Chapter 17

The next day dawned fresh and crisp, as if the air conditioning had been left on all night. What a relief after the sauna of yesterday. I hadn't planned to go to the allotment today, I was supposed to be replenishing my meagre wardrobe with a dress – yes, a dress – to wear to the annual show, but after the events of the previous day there was no chance of me staying away.

I gave Cally his breakfast, tucked a large bottle of water and a cereal bar in my bag and cycled off.

The gates to Ivy Lane were already open and I sailed through, feasting my eyes on the rainbow shades of the allotments. Yesterday's rain seemed to have turned up the contrast and our fruit and vegetables appeared brighter and more vivid than ever. Winter had been brown, spring had turned the world green and summer . . . summer filled every tiny corner with colour. From bold reds to plumptious purples, vibrant yellows to playful pinks, the whole place hummed with vitality and harmony.

There was no sign of the *Green Fingers* crew and Charlie's car wasn't in the car park either, so with any luck I might be in for a peaceful morning. Although not entirely quiet; a pink bottom poked up behind a row of carrots on Gemma's half of plot sixteen.

'Are you OK?' I called, parking my bike and dropping my bag down on the bench.

'Yes,' said Gemma, swallowing whatever was in her mouth. 'I chucked up in Dad's car and then as soon as I got home I was fine again.'

'What are you eating now?'

'Spinach. Straight from the ground. Irony and bitter.' She stooped to gather another handful of leaves and popped them straight in. 'Have you seen your present?'

I followed her nodding head towards the door of my shed. Someone had left two jars of jam with little gingham caps on with a card wedged between them.

The gift was from Rosemary. I read the card out loud to Gemma . . .

Dear Tilly,

I can neither thank you nor apologize enough. The progress you have made with Colin's reading puts me to shame, as does my behaviour yesterday. I hope you can forgive me.

Fond regards,
Rosemary

'Oh, that is so sweet. Of course I forgive her.'

'Thank God she didn't barge in on Colin when he was in my shed,' said Gemma. 'Can you imagine! I'd be getting death threats, not jam. Hello, Alf.' She waved over my shoulder and I turned around to greet him.

Alf was making a slow beeline towards us. He seemed older and thinner. I'd always thought of him as sprightly but today he was leaning on a stick and breathing heavily.

'I don't suppose either of you youngsters could help an

old codger out for a few minutes, could you?'

I didn't have much to do so I willingly volunteered. He took my arm and we meandered up towards his plot.

'The gooseberries want picking,' he said. 'They're too ripe really, they're much easier to pick when they're firmer. My fingers are stiff today and I keep popping the buggers.'

'Do you know,' I said, 'I don't think I've ever eaten a gooseberry.'

He chuckled. 'You're in for a treat, lass.'

We went into the shed to find a suitable receptacle for the fruit.

'We had good times here, me and our Celia,' he said, waving a gnarled hand towards a series of curled-up old photographs tacked to the shed wall with drawing pins. I stepped closer to study them and my breath caught in my throat.

'Oh, Alf, what lovely memories.'

Taken from the same spot each time, the pictures showed the couple hand in hand outside the greenhouse, one from as far back as the seventies, judging by Celia's dress, the pair of them getting older and more stooped as the years went by. The most recent picture was just of Alf. Alone.

'Look at your jet-black hair!' I said, tapping a finger on the oldest picture and trying to keep the wobble from my voice.

'It hasn't been that colour for twenty years,' he said, handing me a basket.

'The two of you look very happy together.'

He nodded and turned away. 'We were,' he said gruffly. 'Life's not got its sparkle without her.'

How did that work then, I wondered, following him out to the gooseberries bushes: growing old with someone? It was one thing to love a person when their body was toned, their eyes had twenty-twenty vision and their tufty hair was still russetty and golden, when they were full of dreams of preserving the natural landscape of England and making a family of their own. I acknowledged that at some point the list had ceased to be generic – but it was quite another to carry that love to the end of life, when bits of your loved one had been replaced or dropped off or stopped working, when ambitions had been replaced by a mix of achievement and regret. How would that feel?

My eyes had misted up with tears and I blinked them away.

'What will you do with all these?' I said, dropping a fistful of plump fruit into the basket.

Alf wiped a hand covered in gooseberry juice on his trousers and sighed.

'Celia loved them,' he said, lowering himself into a deck-chair parked at the end of the row of fruit bushes. 'Pies, jam, crumble . . . gooseberry fool was her favourite.' He shrugged. 'Give 'em away, I expect. That's all I ever do now, give stuff away. Help yourself if you want some.'

I could have kissed him; he seemed so defeated.

'I'll make you a gooseberry fool,' I said, giving him a deliberately bright smile. I'd never tasted it, let alone made it, but that was what Google was for.

'Fire!' shouted a male voice, Nigel perhaps, pulling us out of our reverie. 'The shop's on fire!'

Alf and I stared at each other, I dropped the basket, grabbed hold of his arm and we headed towards the shop as fast as he could go.

Ahead of us, a fat cloud of grey smoke rose above the pavilion. The shop was tucked behind it, out of sight. Everyone was leaving their plots and running in the same direction. Shazza and Karen had grabbed buckets, Liz had got her watering can and Peter was fixing the hoses on to the taps. Brenda and three of her grandchildren stayed well back with Helen and the baby, but the rest of us formed a group in the car park.

'Has someone rung the fire brigade?' said Rosemary breathlessly, shooting me a timid smile.

'Mum's doing it now,' said Gemma, pointing to Christine, who had a finger blocking one ear and a mobile phone pressed to the other. Her elbows stuck out at right angles and she was pacing round in circles like a demented lioness.

Charlie appeared from the direction of the shop. His face was red and he was gasping for breath.

'OK, we need hoses, buckets, everything you've got,' he shouted.

'The hoses are on,' yelled Peter, jogging towards him. He paused briefly to fold his comb-over back into position.

'Fire service is on their way, so they are,' announced Christine. 'Five minutes, they reckon.'

Charlie grabbed the hose out of Peter's hand and ran off towards the shop.

'Turn it on full,' he shouted over his shoulder. 'Will any of the other hosepipes reach this far?'

'I'll check,' said Peter, scurrying to do as he was told.

Nigel followed Charlie. 'What can I do?' he yelled.

'Turn off the power to the shop. We don't know what started the fire. We need the electricity off in there.'

Unsure what to do, the rest of us huddled together, gradually edging closer and closer to the shop. Thank goodness Charlie knew what he was doing. Liz had set her watering can down, but Shazza and Karen started flinging buckets of water at the sides of the shop building. Thick smoke was streaming from the gaps around the double doors and even cracks in the roof. The air was heavy with the acrid stench of burning chemicals and soon we were all spluttering and holding our clothes across our mouths.

Peter pushed his way through the crowd with another hosepipe and aimed it at the shop doors.

Charlie turned towards us, his face pouring with sweat from the heat. 'I've doused the doors and the roof, I'm going to break the doors down now. Stand back, everyone, the smoke will be ten times worse once they're open.'

'Charlie, wait,' I cried. 'Is there petrol in there, could it explode? I know you're a professional, but what about protective clothing?'

Charlie, his mouth set in a grim line, glanced at me. 'It's all right; I know what I'm doing.' Then he smiled briefly as if to say thank you for caring and I smiled back nervously.

'No petrol,' said Peter, 'lots of chemicals. Is Roundup flammable, does anyone know? But . . . Oh bloody hell! The *Green Fingers* equipment!' He groaned and despite the intense heat, his face went grey.

Charlie kicked the door open; more smoke gushed from the gap and I stepped backwards instinctively.

Charlie pulled his T-shirt off, soaked it in water and tied it across his face.

Wow. There was something about a man being brave, while shirtless, that did something to my insides. Gemma slid her arm through mine and we exchanged glances.

Not just *my* insides, then.

'Who's got Aidan's number?'

Everyone looked at me for some reason so I went bright red even though I didn't have it.

'I have,' said Christine, scrolling through her phone. 'Damn. Voicemail,' she announced seconds later, slipping the phone into her pocket.

Charlie grabbed the other hose from Peter and aimed

both of them into the shop. 'Now, fill buckets and throw the water in,' he shouted.

In the distance I could just make out the harsh sound of sirens. Within seconds it seemed the sound had amplified and I felt a sob of relief well up through my body.

As the fire service sprang into action, unloading equipment in a slick and practised manoeuvre, a transit van pulled up in front of the pavilion.

A pale-faced Aidan, a pink-faced Jeff and a wide-eyed Suzanna joined the crowd wordlessly.

Five minutes later the fire was out and all that remained was the putrid smell and the smouldering shell of a building. The firefighters, with Charlie assisting, began to stow their equipment away again.

'Come on, everyone,' called Christine, clapping her hands. 'Let's all away in to the pavilion for a cup of tea.'

I felt so sorry for the *Green Fingers* team, watching them troop after Christine. This had to be an unmitigated disaster for the documentary. Aidan slumped against a wall and punched numbers into his phone, a hand constantly raking through his hair. Jeff sank into a chair and gazed at the floor and Suzanna shook her head as Gemma filled her in on the details. All that equipment, if not gone up in smoke then certainly damaged, possibly beyond repair. All that work. Wasted.

With an aching sadness, I went and helped Christine with the refreshments. As I went back in with a tray of mugs, Peter arrived and called us to attention.

'I've just had a word with the fire service,' he announced formally.

We all gathered to listen.

'As we weren't broken into, it doesn't look like arson. He guesses most likely it was an electrical fire.'

He put a fatherly arm around Charlie's shoulders. 'Three cheers for Charlie for his excellent command of the situation. If you hadn't been there, son, the consequences could have been much worse.'

I joined the others in a round of applause.

'Sorry about your filming equipment, lads,' said Charlie with a shrug, shooting Aidan a regretful look. 'I tried to rescue it, but I guess most of it will be ruined.'

Suzanna pushed through the crowd and pulled him towards her. Her long curly hair was tied up in a thick ponytail and her white dress was still white. She looked fresh and perky. I felt like a smoked mackerel by comparison.

'You're a star, Charlie; thank you,' she said, kissing his cheek.

'Let's have a picture of Suzanna and Charlie,' said Gemma, pulling her phone out of her pocket. 'We can send it to the *Kingsfield Mail*. Local hero comes to the rescue!'

'I helped too,' cried Dougie, squeezing in beside Suzanna and tapping his cheek for a kiss.

Aidan leaned across and shook Charlie's hand. 'I owe you one, mate,' he said. 'Luckily, these days all our filming is digital and uploaded straight away, so we haven't lost any footage. Thank God.'

'Oh, really? Well, pleased to hear it.' Charlie grinned, clapping Aidan firmly on his back.

My eyebrows flexed automatically; he had changed his tune. It seemed all was well in Charlie's world now that he had saved the day.

I poured some milk into a black coffee and went and sat down. Within seconds Charlie joined me. He smelt of smoke and earth and sweat and it took me back to when we first met in January. He couldn't keep the smile from his face; he was so pleased with himself. I smiled back. An overprotective, but definitely useful man to have around.

I wanted to add my congratulations to Suzanna's but I felt awkward. Yesterday he had tested our friendship sorely and I wasn't sure where we stood any more.

'Friends?' he said quietly into my ear.

I took a deep breath and stared at him, wondering what exactly he wanted from me. Was he really content to remain just friends?

'Friends,' I replied with a laugh. I bumped his shoulder with mine playfully and he spilt his tea into the saucer. I'd decided I was going to start letting people in, I couldn't change my mind as soon as things got tricky.

'Hey, who's this?' he said, sticking his lips out and exaggerating a long slurp straight from the saucer.

'Shazza!' I squeaked with delight.

'Keep your voice down,' he whispered, stretching his eyes wide, and we giggled like a pair of kids.

Chapter 18

Despite being visually unappealing, my gooseberry fool made with Greek yogurt was a triumph. In fact, I thought, licking the spoon one more time, if I ate any more I might not fit in to my dress. That was the problem with experimenting with recipes when you lived alone, you ended up eating every bit. I popped the bowl into the fridge to present to Alf later on and ran upstairs to get ready.

My new dress was hanging on the wardrobe door.

This would set tongues wagging. I'd lost count of the number of times people had told me to get my legs out on the allotment over the last few months.

I flung my T-shirt and leggings off and slipped the soft jersey fabric over my head. Round necked, short sleeves and hemline just below the knee; on anyone else this dress would be demure, but it was the most revealing outfit I had worn in . . . I did a mental calculation . . . almost two years.

I took a step back to get the full effect in the mirror and felt tiny bubbles of nerves fizz away in my stomach.

It was time.

At Easter Gemma had compared me rather unflatteringly to an onion, with layers and secrets as yet still unrevealed.

I preferred to see myself as a flower unfurling under the nurturing care of the Ivy Lane community. And today I was finally ready to turn my face to the sun.

It was the first Sunday in August and the day of the annual show, the climax to what had been a tense few weeks and a chance for everyone to show off their produce. It was the highlight of Ivy Lane's social calendar, so Christine informed me; the gates would be thrown open to the public and people from all over Kingsfield would be coming to visit.

And so would Aidan.

Four weeks had passed since the fire in the shop, when the *Green Fingers* team had last been on site. A professional company had been hired to clean up the fire damage, new doors fitted and the committee was awaiting an insurance pay-out to arrive before replenishing the stock. The fire was well and truly over.

However, there was still a tiny flame burning. Not brightly, or fiercely, but nonetheless, it was there. And it brought heat to my face every time I thought about Aidan.

The trouble was that I appeared to have developed a bit of a crush on a man who plainly wasn't interested. Someone who had simply been doing his job. I couldn't get that last filming session out of my head; he had truly seemed to care. And when I'd confronted him, he claimed I didn't understand. I was confused and needed Gemma's advice. Hence the dress, which would be the catalyst for a major heart-to-heart. Goodness only knows what she would make of all my news.

I glanced at my watch: eleven a.m. Only one hour left for any exhibits to be entered. I needed to get my skates on. My stomach performed a double somersault as I took a last look at my legs in the mirror and then, collecting an old-fashioned soda bottle, a tin of cakes and a slate cheeseboard, I set off for Ivy Lane.

It was a glorious day and the pavilion looked beautiful: bunting, hanging baskets and pots of trailing petunias adorned the porch and end-to-end tables covered with gingham cloths formed a huge track on the grass in front of it. Two gazebos housed refreshments, the raffle, and a bottle stall as well as an assortment of jams, preserves and cakes for sale.

Peter, at a makeshift desk on one of the picnic tables, had a queue of people already submitting their entries. Christine was directing plot holders to the judging tables with their produce and Nigel was erecting a barricade of cones and striped tape around the tables as if it was a crime scene. There was a tangible buzz in the air, like the hours before a wedding; anticipation, nerves and happiness all rolled into one.

The *Green Fingers* van was parked up. Aidan was here. I spotted him straight away as I walked past the pavilion but I forced myself to focus on Suzanna first. She was on the pavilion steps interviewing a well-turned-out man who I hadn't seen before and Jeff was filming, so I hovered nearby.

You know when you leave your best birthday present until last? That.

I took a big calming breath and glanced over at Aidan.

He hadn't shaved, his linen shirt was crumpled and his hair was sticking up in peaks at the back. I caught a whiff of his scent, spicy and masculine, and it sparked off a fluttering sensation in the pit of my stomach. My face felt like it was on fire. What started off this morning as a 'bit of a crush' was rapidly getting out of hand.

My pulse ramped up a notch and my lips took on a

numbness normally associated with a spell in the dentist's chair.

And breathe. In and out. Tilly Parker, has Aidan given you so much as one iota of encouragement? No, he hasn't. Stop being ridiculous.

I lifted my eyes to his face.

He was looking right at me with a boyish friendly smile, both eyebrows raised, creasing his forehead comically.

Around us I was vaguely aware of lots of activity: pushing and shoving at the only sink, an argument between Nigel and Graham about the authenticity of Graham's parsnips – 'It's simply not cricket,' I heard Nigel say, prodding Graham in the chest – and Liz scampering round like the white rabbit in *Alice in Wonderland* accusing everyone of stealing her scissors. But I kept my eyes trained on Aidan, soaking up every detail of his face, his body as he stepped towards me.

I'd missed him.

'You look lovely today, Tilly.' He held my gaze shyly.

That was the nicest thing he had ever said to me.

A sudden insistent thudding noise filled my ears and it took a moment to realize that it was my heartbeat.

I could have smiled beguilingly and walked on head held high. But no. This was Tilly Parker we were talking about.

'I thought you preferred the natural look,' I said. 'Old T-shirts and scruffy trousers?'

'Hmm.' Aidan tapped a pen on his cheek and pretended to ponder. 'It is a lovely dress, although I had been referring to your smile, but now you mention it, I did particularly like the white T-shirt you wore in that storm.'

The one that went completely see-through with the pink bra underneath. The one as pink as my face. He liked that? I didn't know where to look.

'Thirty minutes more!' shouted Peter officiously, earning disapproving stares from Suzanna and Jeff. 'Then the window for submissions is closed.'

'I'd better . . . er.' I dipped my boiled-beetroot-coloured head and made a dash for my plot.

Speaking to Gemma was my priority. I hadn't told her anything about James. She was going to freak out when she saw me in a dress. And then I would tell her. The thought of getting everything out in the open once and for all sent shudders down my spine.

Gemma was there, head bent over a table she had set up outside her shed. Dishes and plates of fruit and vegetables were piled precariously all over it.

'Ta dah!' I gave her a twirl and smiled nervously. This was it. My heart was banging away on my ribcage. I waited.

She lifted her head for a fraction of a second and gave me a vacant stare. I had to stop myself from gasping. Her hair was greasy and plastered to her head, her normally expressive eyes were dull and her skin pallid and grey.

'Very nice,' she mumbled and went back to doing something with her onions.

If she hadn't looked so awful I might have been offended, but as it was, I was worried. This wasn't like Gemma at all. I took a step closer.

'It's no use!' she screamed, sending me leaping into the air with fright. She hurled an onion with a grunt at her apple tree and it ricocheted off, sending a shower of juice in all directions. 'None of my onions match and I can't tie the raffia properly around the tops.'

Wow. I hadn't realized she would be taking the show seriously too.

I elbowed her out of the way and deftly tied the protruding onion tops with raffia to decorate them, sending a silent thank-you to my mother for all those hours she made me spend at the Women's Institute flower-arranging classes.

There.

'Gemma—' I began.

'Later,' she said, piling all her exhibits into wicker baskets. It might have been the strength of the onions, or the stress of the competition, I wasn't sure, but it looked as if her red eyes were a result of recent tears. 'I'll talk to you later,' she said and then hurried off in the direction of the pavilion.

Oh, I thought, watching her departing body weaving from side to side under the weight of the baskets. With a disappointed sigh I opened my shed.

I was only entering three categories: carrots, sweet peas and cupcakes. The cakes were in my basket but I still had work to do. I dug up half my carrots to find three of similar size, snipped a fat bunch of sweet peas and made it to the judging area with five minutes to spare.

Peter grabbed hold of my shoulders and kissed my cheek. 'My dear girl, I'd almost given up hope of you joining in,' he said, lifting the red tape over my head for me to enter.

'So had I,' I replied with a wry smile.

I laid three miniature carrots on my slate cheeseboard. The black contrasted beautifully with the bright orange roots and frilly green leaves. I set the slate down in between some purple carrots that must belong to Shazza and some huge ones that would have fed the entire cast of *Watership Down* for a week.

I arranged the sweet peas in the bottle and then hopped up the steps into the pavilion to pile my six cupcakes on to a cardboard cake stand. Each one was decorated with a different vegetable fashioned from fondant icing. To be honest, they weren't great; the carrot, courgette and parsnip looked like worms and the tomato, apple and strawberry weren't much more than coloured balls.

But I had made an effort, that was the main thing.

I slipped back under the stripy tape just as Charlie arrived, out of breath and carrying a box of produce.

'You're cutting it fine, lad,' said Peter, shaking his head.

'Sorry,' said Charlie, grinning in my direction. 'Just had to make a few last-minute changes.'

I rolled my eyes. A man could be too obsessed about the length of his runner beans.

Peter welcomed the man I had seen earlier as the judge and the judging commenced. The *Green Fingers* crew joined him in the cordoned-off arena and there was a noticeable lift in the atmosphere as the competitors relaxed while they waited for the results to be announced.

Gemma. I was so desperate to talk to her that I thought I would burst. I scanned the crowd gathered around the pavilion, but she was nowhere to be seen.

'Gone home to get changed,' Christine informed me when I questioned her. She shook her head. Her curls were in particularly rigid rows today and not a wisp of it moved. 'I don't know what's got into that girl today.'

Hmm. Me neither. And as much as I was worried about Gemma, selfishly I had been looking forward to a good chat about my rampant crush.

I spent the next hour keeping away from Aidan, unsure what I would even say to him. I returned to my plot instead and by the time I'd tidied Gemma's table and sorted out my abandoned carrots, the judging was over.

I smoothed my dress down over my hips and made my way back to the pavilion. The gates were open and a steady stream of visitors flocked through Ivy Lane allotments.

The stripy tape had been removed and cards marked

first, second and third had been slipped under the winning entries. The crowd surged towards the tables and I noticed Jeff hovering, camera poised and ready to capture the emotions of the ecstatic winners and sore losers.

It didn't take long for results to emerge: Shazza's hollers of joy at the carrot table could only mean one thing and judging by the audible gnashing of Nigel's teeth, it appeared Graham had pipped him to the post on the parsnip front. I hung back at first; I wasn't competitive by nature and anyway, I had low expectations for my first ever show.

Gemma slipped in beside me and put her arm through mine.

'Feeling better?' I said, scanning her face for any telltale signs. She had showered and changed and was much more like the old Gemma; clean curls, summer dress and a ready smile. Still very pale, though.

'Much better now I've seen this,' she said, squeezing my arm. 'Look! I've got first prize for my onions!'

We laughed and moved round the table. I'd come second with my sweet peas. Fantastic! But nowhere with my carrots. Unsurprising, given the competition.

I took a deep breath and turned to Gemma. 'Can we have a chat later, somewhere quiet?'

For a fleeting moment, she looked terrified and cast her eyes downwards. Then she licked her lips and smiled. 'Sure. Later on, yeah?'

I smiled at her, already wondering where we'd find somewhere quiet in this place.

'Bloody hell, Tills!' squealed Gemma, shaking my arm and pointing to a paper plate of green apples. 'You've got first place for your apples!'

I peered at the apples. Sure enough my name was on the winning entry. Odd. Very odd.

Suzanna materialized smoothly beside me and from the other side of the table, Jeff zoomed a lens right up to my face. Further investigation revealed that I'd also come third with my peas and second in the courgette category. Neither of which I'd entered.

'A glowing start to your first year on the allotment,' said Suzanna. 'Congratulations! How do you feel?'

'I'm amazed,' I laughed. 'Absolutely amazed. It's so unexpected.'

Which was rather an understatement, given the circumstances.

Chapter 19

After maintaining my expression of surprise mixed with delight, as opposed to pure shock, I broke away from Gemma and Suzanna as soon as I could and cornered Peter in the tiny pavilion office.

He was sitting at an ancient computer pecking away furiously at the keyboard with two fingers. He lowered his reading glasses and held up a hand. 'Confidential, I'm afraid. I'm totting up everyone's points to see who our overall winner is.'

Well, it wouldn't be me, that was for sure. Not if I had anything to do with it.

'Peter, sorry to interrupt.' I chewed my lip, not quite sure how to break it to him, he already looked busy enough. 'There's a bit of a problem with my prizes.'

'Now, Tilly, don't worry that you didn't get more first prizes, you did really well for a beginner,' he chuckled.

'No, that's just it, I've won prizes in categories that I didn't submit entries for!' I gave him an apologetic smile.

Peter gazed at me vacantly and then consulted the judge's sheet in front of him. He looked at me again. 'Well, how did that happen?'

I shrugged my shoulders. 'You tell me.'

He smoothed his collar and tie and frowned. 'Well, I can't imagine that the judge made a mistake.'

I had a sudden flashback to the moment I'd arrived with my entries. Peter had said he'd almost given up on me joining in. This had something to do with the *Green Fingers* show, I was convinced. I narrowed my eyes, folded my arms and gave him my best teacher stare. 'Peter, tell me the truth, did the committee enter on my behalf for the benefit of the cameras in case I let you down?'

A purple-red flush tinged his face. He did not like that one bit. 'What!' he said with a snort. I felt droplets of his spittle on my face and I took a step back.

'You knew it would be recorded and you wanted a feel-good ending to my first year on the allotment for the *Green Fingers* show.' The more I thought about it, the more insulted I was. It was as if they'd assumed my own entries wouldn't be good enough.

Peter pushed his chair back, stood up and tilted his chin. 'Preposterous.'

'I agree,' I said. 'And now I feel like a fraud.'

'I can assure you, the committee did no such thing. And frankly, I'm quite hurt. And they've filmed it now, have they?'

I nodded. Less sure of myself and my accusations all of a sudden. If not the committee then who? And why? It didn't make sense.

Peter was scratching his chin and shaking his head. 'What a mess. Do you actually grow all these things?' He consulted his list. 'Peas, courgettes, apples?'

'Yes, but—'

'So in theory you could have entered those categories?'

'Well, in theory—'

'It would be an awful bind to have to re-judge at this late stage.'

'But I don't deserve the prizes.' My head was spinning. I'd just accused a fine, upstanding member of this community of cheating and if he wasn't guilty, presumably I owed him a big fat apology. 'Peter, I—'

'The deed is done now.' Peter sat down again and pulled the keyboard towards him. 'And the film is in the can, as the saying goes. So we'll say no more about it.'

Dismissed like a disobedient schoolgirl by the headmaster.

How humiliating! I sloped off, back out into the sunshine, feeling all hot and bothered. And to make matters worse, I supposed I couldn't tell anyone about my dilemma, could I? Word would get round and the place would be in uproar; I'd already seen Vicky and Liz have a barbed conversation about each other's dahlias. No, I'd have to keep quiet about the whole bizarre episode.

I decided to escape to the toilets for a few seconds' peace. I rounded the corner of the pavilion, still huffing to myself, and ran smack-bang into Charlie's muscular chest.

'Whoa!' He caught me by my arms and laughed. 'What's that face for? I thought you'd be chuffed winning first prize for those apples!'

His hands were cool on my skin and had the much needed effect of calming me down for a moment. Even so, I wasn't in the mood for company. I wriggled out of his grasp and then froze, realizing what he had just said.

'Charlie?' I narrowed my eyes.

And then before I could react he pulled me into him and kissed me lightly on the lips. I gasped and sprang away.

'Charlie!'

His face split into a wide grin and he laughed. 'I entered

179

your stuff. Nearly missed the deadline, too. I thought you'd never finish digging up those bloody carrots!' He rolled his eyes.

'You?' An excruciating image of Peter's appalled face popped into my head. I stared at Charlie. 'But I didn't want to enter peas or apples or courgettes.'

He shook his head gently and smiled. 'You're so modest.'

'Modesty has nothing to do with it. I don't grow vegetables for prizes. I'm not interested in competitions. I'm just here for the simple pleasure of growing my own food and being in the company of my friends.'

Even as I said this, my heart seemed to swell and I felt tears prick at my eyes. If that wasn't my original intention when I took on the allotment, it certainly was now. Being with people like Gemma and Christine and Roy and even Charlie (when he wasn't dropping me in it) was now even more important to me than gardening.

'I know,' he said, taking hold of my arms again, so softly this time that I didn't push him away. 'You're an angel.' He pressed his lips to my forehead. 'My angel.'

Uh oh.

'Charlie, I—'

He hushed me with a finger at my lips. I glanced round, hoping that someone else would need the loo soon. Where were all the weak bladders when you needed them?

'You're so good; helping us all. Me, Colin, Alf and Gemma. I've watched you putting others first, and I wanted to do something for you.'

'That's very kind, Charlie, but there's no need.' I smiled and edged my feet backwards. This outpouring of affection was sweet, but it made me uncomfortable too.

Charlie's eyes were blazing at me, with an intensity that made my cheeks flush and my chest pound. 'There's every need,' he said. 'Because since you came into my life I've changed. You've made me a better person.'

'Charlie, I'm flattered, really I am—'

'You've given me hope,' he continued, his thumbs stroking my upper arms. 'I never thought I'd find anyone to love again. My ex-wife did a right number on me.' A flash of sadness clouded his eyes and my heart flipped over. Poor guy. 'I was a mess after we split up. I'm telling you this because I want you to know all there is about me.'

He wasn't the only one to think they would never love again. I simply hadn't been interested in men since James. But unfortunately it wasn't Charlie who'd broken the spell. It was Aidan.

'I'm your friend, Charlie, and your friendship means an awful lot to me. Really.' I reached out and took his hands. 'But only that.'

'Tilly, I've got history, I admit it. An ex-wife and a son.'

Charlie was a father? I had known him for eight months and he had only just told me? I loosened my grasp on his hands.

'But that needn't be a problem,' he continued. 'I only see him once a month, and sometimes not even that if she's being awkward.'

'What?' I couldn't believe what I was hearing. He looked at me blankly. Obviously I hadn't given him the response he had anticipated.

I straightened up and took a step away from him. My breath caught in my throat as my words tumbled out, all jerky and rough. 'You've got a family? A child? Do you not know how precious that is? What a privilege? I didn't know you when you were married but if you have changed for the better you would want that boy in your life. What parent wouldn't?'

181

He frowned and took a deep breath. He'd better not try to tell me I was overreacting. Quite frankly, I didn't care what he thought, I'd heard enough. I turned and walked away.

I walked as fast as I could without drawing attention to myself, up the road, along the path past my own plot, through the trees until I came to the stone bench out of sight from prying eyes. I sat down and drew long shuddering breaths.

The branches forming the arch above the bench were thickly wrapped in ivy and ribbons of it brushed softly against my hair. I pulled my knees up to my chin and pressed the heels of my hands into my eye sockets.

What was I most upset about: Charlie being a dad, Charlie being an absent dad, Charlie attempting to woo me, Charlie making me make a fool of myself in front of Peter? I sighed. Whichever way I looked at it, Charlie was involved.

I pulled my hands away from my eyes and smoothed the fabric of my dress. I ran my fingers down my shins, feeling the tight shiny skin of the scars that spanned from my knees to my ankles. I made a noise, somewhere between a laugh and a self-pitying sob. I'd been so self-conscious coming out with my legs showing this morning and absolutely no one had commented; all too wrapped up in their own problems to notice.

'Is that you, Tills? Flippin' 'eck!' Gemma grunted as she pushed through the trees. 'Jungle dot com in this place.'

'Hey,' I said, swinging my legs off the far side of the bench.

She plonked herself down, facing the opposite way to me, and nudged me with her arm. 'What's up, misery chops? Sulking 'cos your carrots didn't win?'

I shook my head and swallowed. My throat felt so tight I thought the words might not even be able to squeeze their way out. I *so* needed a hug.

'I've had a terrible fight with Charlie.'

She huffed. 'The silly sod. What's he done now?'

'He and his wife had a baby, Gem.' I blinked to ward off the tears. 'Charlie is a father and he barely sees his son. What sort of person does that make him?'

I leaned forward anticipating Gemma's arms to open up and give me a much needed cuddle. Or at the very least a scandalized gasp. But what I got was entirely different.

'A terrible one,' she wailed. 'A dreadful person who doesn't deserve any happiness.'

She dropped her face down into her lap and bawled. I watched in horror as her body convulsed with bigger and bigger sobs and a shiver ran down my spine. I pressed a shaking hand to my mouth and took several deep breaths as Gemma's recent behaviour stacked up like the clues in an episode of *Murder She Wrote*. The tetchiness, the sickness, the spinach-fest . . . Oh my God!

'You're pregnant.' I reached over and placed a hand gently on her back.

She looked up at me through bulging red eyes and nodded. 'I've been feeling weird for days and then I found myself out in our back yard pressing my tongue against the bricks of the house. And then I knew.'

'That's good news, isn't it?' I was aware of my heart thumping wildly against my ribcage.

'I don't know, Tilly.' She sniffed and wiped her arm across her nose. 'This was *so* not on the cards.'

'But Gemma . . . a baby,' I swallowed. 'You said you always wanted to give Mike a child of his own?'

I felt terrified all of a sudden. Before long Gemma would

have a baby. Could I cope with that? Would I still want to be her friend?

She reached across and took my hands. 'I did. For years . . . But not now. Not when I was just getting my life back. Mike will be delighted. And part of me is so happy for him, truly. And Mia'll be over the moon, I'm sure of it.'

I chewed on my lip. We would have even less in common. She might give up the allotment anyway, perhaps that would be for the best.

'What about my hopes and dreams? I'll tell you what. Back burner, that's what. Probably never to get to the forefront again. By the time this one is ready to fly the nest I'll be a grandmother. I'm nearly old enough to be a grandmother now, come to that.'

She edged towards me and we wrapped our arms around each other.

'I'll be fine. I'll come to terms with it, I'll change my plans and everything will be fine. I just needed this,' she said, lifting her head and gazing at me. 'A bit of time to get my head together.'

I looked at Gemma's stricken face. The story of me and James would have to wait. This wasn't the time after all. I leaned my head on her shoulder and let my own tears come. I was crying for her and her baby, for Charlie and his estranged family and for myself and the family that had so far eluded me.

We stayed like that until our faces were hot and our eyes were red.

Gemma pulled away first. 'I'm so ashamed of the way I'm feeling,' she said, handing me a tissue and dabbing one on her own face. 'I know people who would give anything to have a baby.'

How I didn't cry again, I'll never know. I managed a pathetic smile instead.

'Thank you for letting me confide in you.'

'That's OK,' I said, 'that's what friends are for.'

And as I said those words I wondered whether witnessing the next few months would be too much for my fragile heart to bear. But I stood up and offered her a hand, and we made our way slowly back to the pavilion.

Chapter 20

It was nearly four o'clock and the crowd had started to thin out. As we approached the pavilion, I spotted the *Green Fingers* crew talking inside and realized with a jolt that this was it. Filming was over. After today, I would probably never set eyes on Aidan again. My thoughts were falling over each other in their haste to take centre stage and I hadn't quite got to grips with how I truly felt when Peter clapped his hands to attract our attention.

'Mike's here,' hissed Gemma, clutching at my arm. 'Over there by Dad.'

We both waved and Roy and Mike waved back from their position at the edge of the road near the car park.

'Can everyone gather round,' Peter called.

Gemma sighed as we shuffled forward dutifully. 'He'll be a great dad.'

I shoved her gently with my shoulder. 'And so will you, be a great mum I mean.'

'A baby is a blessing, isn't it?' She searched my eyes nervously. I swallowed and nodded. 'Do you mind if I . . . ?' She tilted her head towards her husband.

No, don't leave me on my own.

'Of course not!' I laughed as I extricated myself from her grasp and flapped at her to go.

That performance was enough to earn me a place at RADA, I thought, watching her skip over to Mike and thread her arms round his waist.

With any luck by the time Peter had finished his speech, my breathing would be back to normal.

'Thank you to everyone who took part in our annual show,' said Peter. 'The standards were, dare I say, even higher than usual and the prizes in each category were very well deserved.'

Some less so than others, I thought, not knowing where to look; I had Charlie in my line of vision by the depleted cake stall and Peter on the pavilion steps in front of me. I stared at the ground, feeling my cheeks practically pulsating with embarrassment.

'Now, as you know, we have had some special guests here over the summer and as chairman of the committee, I should like to thank everyone at Ivy Lane for their co-operation during the filming of what I am sure will be an entertaining and riveting documentary.'

I thought I could detect a bit of harrumphing and bosom rearranging going on around me and once again cast my eyes downwards. As far as I knew, neither Rosemary's herb parterre nor Brenda's heritage potatoes had made it into the final cut.

'Today is their last day here with us,' continued Peter. 'We've had plenty of drama along the way,' he chuckled, 'and I for one have thoroughly enjoyed the experience. Let's give the *Green Fingers* crew a big Ivy Lane round of applause!'

Peter beckoned Suzanna, Jeff and Aidan to the front

of the pavilion and Nigel appeared with a bouquet of flowers for Suzanna. Jeff and Aidan raised their hands self-consciously and then melted away into the audience.

'Thank you so much, everybody,' said Suzanna, after kissing Nigel and Peter on the cheek. 'It has been an honour for *Green Fingers* to follow you over the last couple of months. You have been an inspiration and I've learned a lot. Graham,' she said, seeking him out and addressing him directly, 'the aroma of your special fertilizer will remain with me for some time.'

'You're lucky,' shouted Alf, 'it'll remain with us for ever!'

Graham blushed as we all laughed and Helen wrapped her arm around her husband proudly.

'And Dougie,' continued Suzanna, wagging a finger at him. 'I'll never forget the time we spent together in your shed.'

Charlie wolf-whistled and Peter and Nigel exchanged frowns from the sidelines. Dougie hooted with laughter and blew her a kiss. 'Any time, darlin'!' he called.

'You've made me, Jeff and Aidan so welcome and it has been a pleasure getting to know you all. Even those of you who were a little camera-shy to start with have made an enormous contribution to the programme. I'll miss you all.'

As we gave Suzanna another round of applause, my eyes drifted towards Aidan. He was standing sideways to me and I gazed at his profile. I barely knew him at all, I realized. Apart from the fact he appeared to be good at his job, stayed calm in a crisis and managed to put even the most resistant plot holders (i.e. me) at ease during filming, I knew nothing about 'Aidan the man'.

But what I did know was that he had awakened a place deep inside me that I had given up hope of reaching again. I was, purely and simply, attracted to him. I only had to look at him, as I was doing now, to feel all fluttery some-where beneath my ribcage.

The poor man; little did he know that when he said I looked lovely this morning, he had released this raging surge of hormones in me. It was perhaps just as well that *Green Fingers* had finished filming; another couple of days and I'd be launching myself at him. I smiled to myself. I had no intention of doing anything about these new feel-ings, but I was grateful for them nonetheless.

I felt . . . alive . . . like a woman again.

He turned suddenly and met my eyes as if I had shouted his name. I was still mid-smile, which was embarrassing enough and then my mouth went dry and my lips stuck to my teeth. I probably looked like a dog baring its teeth. But he smiled back.

'Nice lad,' said a gravelly voice in my ear. 'Single, you know.' I turned to see Alf standing at my shoulder. Despite the heat of the day he was wearing a tweedy cardigan frayed at both elbows.

'Who?' I asked nonchalantly.

He nodded towards Aidan, his eyes twinkling at me. Had I been staring gormlessly? Had everyone seen? I flicked a glance left and right, but no one seemed to be paying me any attention.

'Very talented,' he whispered in my ear and I caught a whiff of pear drops. 'I've spent some time chatting to him this summer. This is his first stint with *Green Fingers*. He works on wildlife documentaries normally. He's won awards.'

'Really?' I raised an eyebrow at Alf. I wondered if we were better to work with than animals or worse.

'And now we are going to draw the raffle,' announced Nigel. 'Suzanna, would you do the honours please?' He picked up a large plastic tub and gave it a shake.

People perked up, rooting through bags and pockets for their tickets and edging towards the trestle table displaying all the prizes.

'Suzanna reckons he's the best director she has ever worked with,' continued Alf.

I smoothed out the pink strip of tickets I had tucked into my dress pocket earlier. I had my eye on either the Jamie Oliver cookbook or the set of three hand creams; gardening had played havoc with my nails this summer.

The first ticket drawn out of the tub was Gemma's. She squealed, kissed Nigel and Suzanna effusively and returned somewhat subdued with a bottle of red wine. She caught my amused expression and raised her eyebrows heavenwards.

'Although he's a bit of a firebrand, according to Jeff. Always at war with his bosses. Apparently, he can't stand all the politics and backstabbing.'

I stared at Alf, seeing him in a different light. I'd always had Christine pegged as the font of all knowledge around here. I had clearly underestimated him.

'What did he call them now?' Alf scratched his head and stared up at the sky. 'Oh yes. Bureaucratic desk-wallahs with inflated egos,' he recited. 'Brave talk, I thought.'

Humans and their inflated bloody egos . . . Politics and one-upmanship.

So Aidan hadn't been talking about us at all. My heart sang and it was all I could do not to jump up and down on the spot. It hadn't all been an act. Aidan genuinely did like us. I was so relieved.

'I'm off home, I think,' Alf said with a sniff. 'My knee is giving me gyp and I never win at bloomin' raffles.'

I tucked my arm through his. 'Talking of brave, do you fancy coming back to my house to try my gooseberry fool?'

His eyes lit up so I scrunched up my raffle tickets and

with one last look at Aidan Whitby, I led Alf out of Ivy Lane.

Two hours later, after Alf had eaten nearly every scrap of food in the house and departed for home, I was weighing up the merits of the *Game of Thrones* box set versus a candle-lit bath and an early night when there was a frantic knocking at the door.

I ran to open it and found Aidan staggering under the weight of a very heavy-looking sundial.

His transit van with its distinct *Green Fingers* logo was parked on the street and already several neighbours had come out of their houses to stare.

'You won this in the raffle,' he panted.

'Oh.' Where was my perfectly adequate vocabulary when I needed it?

'Christine gave me your address. She said you didn't have a car and would I mind dropping it round.'

Numerous things went whizzing through my brain, like thank goodness I wasn't in the bath and who won the Jamie Oliver cookery book and was Christine doing a bit of unsubtle match-making . . .

'Kind of you.' Was what I managed to mutter.

I couldn't say I'd ever wanted a sundial but it did look quite attractive. The top dial bit was made of cast-iron and set into a concrete plinth – or maybe cement, I always got those two muddled up.

'It is very heavy,' he gasped.

'Oops, sorry!'

The poor man was breaking his back here while I contemplated the difference between building materials.

Now what? Should I tell him to put it down there on the step to save his spine? In which case it could well be stolen by the morning and I would have zero chance of moving it myself. Or should I ask him to carry it through to the back yard?

He answered my dilemma himself. 'Do you want it in the back garden?'

I nodded and waved him into the house. He had gone an uncomfortable-looking shade of aubergine. I ran ahead of him opening the back door and scooped the cat up into my arms just as he was about to weave through Aidan's legs.

'Anywhere will do,' I said, hugging Cally to my chest while I watched Aidan stagger down the two steps into the back yard.

He groaned as he finally set the sundial down and grinned at me while he caught his breath, leaning his hands against his thighs.

'Water?'

He nodded.

I handed him a glass and ushered him towards my plastic patio furniture. Aidan sat, took a long drink and looked at his surroundings. Cally immediately jumped on to his lap. I took that to be a sign of feline approval.

Aidan and me. Me and Aidan. In my garden. Just the two of us.

My back yard was a bit grim really, I thought, looking at it with fresh eyes: paving slabs, plastic furniture and now a sundial. At least I didn't have my washing hanging up.

'So,' I said, twiddling the ends of my hair between my fingers. 'You're off to Peru?'

He nodded. 'For eight weeks, once I've done the editing for this *Green Fingers* episode. Back to nature. Can't wait.'

There you go. Not interested in you, Tilly. He can't wait to get away.

I smiled with relief and shook my head when Aidan

looked at me quizzically. It was one thing to have a silly crush on him, it would have been quite another to act on it, i.e. a huge mistake.

James had felt very close by today. Not in an ominous way. But there. And now I realized why. They were very similar in some ways, Aidan and James: their love of the natural world, although Aidan was more into wildlife than landscape; their resistance to authority – James had once resigned from a job after a difference of opinion with management.

But in other ways they were very different: James had been the joker, happiest in the middle of the action, whereas Aidan seemed to prefer to put others in the limelight. In the looks department they were a million miles apart too. Aidan could pass for Mediterranean with his dark features, dark shiny hair and tanned skin. The only nationality James could pass for other than English was Scottish; he had the stereotypical complexion of a redhead and in sunny weather turned from blue to pink and back again with alarming speed.

'What are you filming this time?'

'Bears. There's a type of bear found most commonly in Peru.'

I nodded.

He looked impressed. 'You're up on your bear species?' He smiled and set his glass on the ground.

I went bright red, realizing that I'd been thinking of Paddington Bear with his duffel coat and marmalade sandwiches. Occupational hazard of being a primary school teacher.

'Not really,' I said, scrunching up my face, trying to look intelligent. I crossed my fingers and hoped he didn't test me.

'Look, I'd better go.' He sighed and pushed himself up, the chair legs grated horribly on the slabs and he grimaced apologetically. 'I've got to drive back to London tonight.' He lifted Cally down and gave him a last stroke.

'Is that where you live, London? That's a trek after a long day,' I said, walking ahead of him through the kitchen and back into the hall. I was aware that my voice dipped a bit with disappointment as I spoke. How uncool. How unsubtle.

'Early meeting in the morning, unfortunately.'

He lived in London. Another reason not to get involved. Get involved? Who mentioned anything about *getting involved*? I just liked him, that was all. Honestly, all the man did was say I looked nice this morning, and I've practically got our future all mapped out. He drops off my raffle prize as a favour to Christine and I'm working out when his eight weeks abroad will be up. Just before October half-term. In case I was bothered. Which I wasn't.

I was starting to panic and I wasn't listening to a word Aidan was saying. He could live in the Outer Hebrides now for all I knew.

I put my hand on the front-door handle and paused. This was it then. This was definitely, actually goodbye.

We looked at each other and he laughed softly. I hoped this was because he felt as awkward as me and not because I'd ignored a question or something.

He was within touching distance. In all the weeks and months that we had been near each other, we had never been alone and never this close.

My entire body was tingling. Did he feel it too or was my imagination simply playing silly buggers? And was it allowed? Was I entitled to be getting all flustered about another man? This was such unknown territory for me. I felt terrified all of a sudden. And completely out of breath.

He seemed huge. A huge presence in my tiny hall. He lifted a hand and for a split second I thought he was going to touch my face, but he ran it through his hair and then twisted his fingers through the belt loops of his trousers. 'Tilly . . . ?'

What should I say if he asked for my number? He was going to Peru. He lived miles away. But he smelt really nice and I was dying to touch his hair. And I was really, really going to miss him. Besides, I was supposed to moving on, wasn't I? What was the harm in giving him my number?

'Yes!' I gasped, all proud of myself.

'Can I kiss you?' he continued.

And then my hands *were* in his hair and his hands were cupping my face and we inched so close to each other that I could feel his heart thumping against my chest, although I suppose it could have been my heart beating against his chest.

I, Tilly Parker, was kissing a man.

I closed my eyes and I let my whole body melt against him. My legs and arms ceased to feel like part of me and I gave myself up to the exquisite surprise of his mouth on mine.

And I didn't stop to think about whether it was right or not, whether this was somehow being unfaithful to James, or what was going to happen tomorrow when Aidan was in London or next month when he was on his way to deepest, darkest Peru. And as our kiss deepened and he wove his fingers into my hair and down to my ticklish spot at the nape of my neck, I felt my body waking up after a very, very long sleep and I was acutely aware of the pinging sound of my erogenous zones.

It didn't last, of course. Moments later I felt bloody awful.

'I'm sorry,' whispered Aidan, his thumbs caressing my cheeks. 'I appear to have made you cry.' He lowered his head and gently kissed the tears away.

'Don't worry,' I said, arranging my mouth into a smile. 'Tears of joy.'

Well done, Tilly. Hardly the most complimentary way to acknowledge someone's kissing technique.

He shifted his weight awkwardly. *Now* he was going to ask for my number. Or maybe he felt as mortified as me and was dying for the next thirty seconds to be over. Like me.

Poor man. He only came to deliver a sundial.

I wrestled with the door, which had decided to stick for the first time ever, dammit.

The door finally gave up its struggle and I stood back to let him through.

'Aidan . . .'

'Tilly . . .'

'Go on,' I said.

He blotted a rogue tear that had made it all the way to my chin and blinked at me. 'I know that with me going away the timing of . . . this . . .' he waved a finger from me to him and back again, '. . . isn't ideal. But I would really like to see you again. Can I call you?' He looked at me questioningly and waited.

Was timing the problem? If he hadn't been going away would I have felt better, more inclined to see him again?

I wasn't sure.

It had all happened so quickly and so unexpectedly that my brain hadn't quite caught up with my heart and kissing Aidan – kissing *anyone* – suddenly felt like a massive deal. And whilst I couldn't deny that what I had done was the most magical, intoxicating and enlivening thing that I had done for a long time, I wasn't sure I was ready for anything else. Not yet.

I shook my head.

'I don't think so,' I whispered. 'I'm sorry. Good luck with the editing of our episode of *Green Fingers* and good luck in Peru.'

He looked at me for a long moment and I held my breath. He looked so disappointed that I almost changed my mind. I wasn't used to this. He took his wallet out of his pocket and extracted a card. 'Here's my number. If you change your mind, give me a ring.'

I tried to take the business card from him but his fingers covered mine and he held my gaze for five heartbeats. 'I hope you do change your mind,' he said, letting his hand fall away.

I let my breath out slowly. Of course. It wasn't now or never. I could keep his card and think about it. See how I felt in a few weeks. What a relief.

Finally, he planted a soft kiss on my lips and stepped past me only to stop on the front step and turn back.

'Thank you, Aidan.' He looked as if he didn't quite believe me. 'Really,' I added.

At the last second, I lunged forward and hugged him tightly, imprinting the feel of his stubble on my cheek, the metal of his belt buckle digging into my stomach.

And then I let him go.

Chapter 21

I had kissed a man.

The smile on my face when I woke up the next morning assured me that this was actually a good thing. Yesterday's doubts seemed to have faded in the night and I was left with an overwhelming feeling of happiness.

I had kissed Aidan.

I stretched my arms above my head, yawned and patted the covers to find Cally. He rolled over obligingly and purred while I stroked his dappled silver tummy.

Aidan Whitby. I chuckled, remembering Christine's words months ago. *Doesn't the very name of him make you want to swoon?*

Mmm, it did rather.

Last night's event had opened up a world of possibilities, showed me that maybe I wouldn't have to spend the rest of my life with microwave meals for one and a half of the bed permanently cold and unwrinkled. Maybe I would see Aidan again and maybe not. But I was coming alive, and my ability to give love was slowly returning.

He had scratched an itch I hadn't realized needed scratching. No, that sounded too much like fleas. He had awakened urges in me that I had forgotten I had. Too Mills & Boon.

For goodness' sake, Tilly. You snogged the face off him and you enjoyed every minute. Just admit it.

I squealed and waggled my legs furiously under the duvet.

I had kissed Aidan Whitby and my man-abstinence was officially over. OK, so afterwards I cried and sent him off without a glimmer of encouragement for the future, but that was fine. I had his number, he knew my address. If it was meant to be, it would be.

No need to stress or dissect it endlessly. The important thing was – the absolutely incredibly mind-blowing thing was – that parts of my body that had gone into an extended hibernation were awake and raring to go and rather than feeling that this was a betrayal of everything that James and I had shared, it felt fantastic.

I tugged open my bedside drawer and took out the latest letter I had received from James's mum.

You will always be part of this family, Tilly, remember that. There's a bed here for you any time you fancy a visit. You can even bring a friend if you like.

Maybe I would go and stay before the end of the school holidays, let them see how well I was doing, let them know that I still loved them.

I tucked the letter back in its envelope and sighed happily.

Time to get up.

Ivy Lane allotments was still recovering from the annual show and the committee had asked for volunteers to take down the gazebos, the bunting and the trestle tables and to have a general tidy-up after having so many visitors on site yesterday.

Work had already started by the time I got there. Christine had marshalled her family into action, Nigel and

Liz were dismantling tables ready to take them back to the church hall and Brenda was bagging up unclaimed raffle prizes.

'Here she is. Our sundial winner. Did you have a good evening, Tilly?' said Christine, poking her head out from under the canvas as she, Roy and Mia grappled with a gazebo. Gemma was wandering round picking up the various poles and pegs and stuffing them in a box.

Was it me or was everyone grinning at me? Why was everyone grinning at me?

And looking over my shoulder as if they were expecting someone.

Oh . . . did they think . . . ?

I picked up a show programme from yesterday and fanned my face. 'Aidan very kindly left it in the garden and then drove back home to London.'

'Are you sure?' said Roy, grunting as he pulled the pegs from the ground. Was I too young for a hot flush? And would they all please stop looking at me.

'He doesn't live in London,' said Christine, rolling her eyes. I hoped my face wasn't as pink as hers. 'He's a local lad. That's why *Green Fingers* chose Ivy Lane. His suggestion.'

Mia appeared next from under the gazebo. She was wielding a long metal pole and I hurried over to help before she maimed anyone.

She instantly dropped the pole and threw her arms round me. 'What do you think of our news? I'm going to be a sister.'

'It's fantastic,' I said, hugging her back. So Gemma had been right, Mia was delighted; I'd never seen her so animated.

She pressed her lips to my ear and whispered so softly

that it tickled. 'I thought Mum had sent Mike gay as well and they were just putting a brave face on it.'

I snorted at that.

'I'm going to help Mum with the business when I'm not at school,' she continued loudly, earning herself proud smiles from her grandparents. 'Set up the massage table, carry all the heavy bags, fill bowls with water and stuff.'

Gemma set the box down and wandered over to a stack of cake tins. 'Only because I've offered to pay her,' she said, popping a piece of left-over cake into her mouth.

'And I'm going to help decorate the spare room for the baby.'

'By spare room, she means treatment room, where I usually do my beauty. But needs must, and all that,' said Gemma with a sigh, but I could see she was secretly happy. She was blooming already. And suddenly very obviously pregnant.

I sidled up to her and put my arm round her shoulders. 'Gemma, how far gone are you exactly?' I asked, unable to tear my eyes from her surprisingly round belly.

'I feel such an idiot,' she hissed. 'I've been putting on weight for months and just put it down to lack of exercise. I reckon there'll be a baby in the house by Christmas!' She lifted another piece of cake to her lips and thought better of it, dropping it back in the tin.

'Doctor's for you this week, madam,' said Christine, taking her daughter's hand and leading her to a bench. 'Now no more lifting. At least you've got Colin to help you on the allotment, so I don't have to worry about that.'

She winked at me as Gemma's mouth fell open. Gemma looked at me and pulled a how-did-she-know face. It was the first time I'd seen her speechless.

Christine set a box of silver trophies on the table in front of Gemma. 'This will keep you occupied,' she said, taking a seat beside her and handing her a duster.

A little car pulled into the car park and Alf climbed out.

'It was a good show yesterday, the committee did us proud,' he said, waving to me. He looked healthy enough; my cooking couldn't have been too bad.

He lifted up his flat cap and scratched his head. 'That'll probably be my last show,' he said with a sigh. 'Getting too much for me, this gardening business.'

Christine swiped at him with a duster. 'Get away, Alfred, you've been saying that since Mia was in nappies and now Gemma has another one on the way. You'll see the lot of us off, I imagine.'

I picked up a silver trophy from the box and examined it.

'The awards,' said Christine, gesturing at them. 'We collect them in from last year's winners and then hand them out at the Christmas party to the new winners.'

Which reminded me . . .

I ran up the pavilion steps to the office. 'Peter, can I have a word?'

He bristled initially but accepted my apology for accusing him of entering the show on my behalf.

'Give my points to Alf, he came second in the apples. And it's not like I did anything to the apple tree to deserve the win. Whereas Alf prunes his tree and feeds it. So by rights . . .'

'Tilly, altering the winners' points now would cause all sorts of problems.' Peter glanced over his shoulder and then shut the door. 'Between you and me, Alf is already our overall winner,' he whispered. 'He'll get the big trophy and he'll be delighted with that.'

I was delighted with that result too and as the produce that Charlie had secretly entered had been grown on my

202

plot there seemed very little point in banging on about it.

Outside, Brenda and Christine, armed with silver wool and dusters, had sandwiched Gemma between them and were telling her how lucky she was to be giving birth now instead of thirty years ago. Judging by her glazed expression, I don't think she was appreciating their anecdotes.

'I'm off to peruse my pumpkins,' I said, offering Gemma my arm. 'Do you think you can waddle that far or shall I call for a wheelchair?'

'Don't you start,' she hissed, springing up from her seat.

We walked down towards plot sixteen arm in arm and I listened to Gemma rabbit on about her plans for the nursery and how she was hoping to scale back on work but to keep going as long as she could until the birth. Twenty-four hours on and what a difference; from confused dot com to over-the-moon dot com and despite a tiny niggle of envy – I was only human – I was happy for her.

Phew. Thank goodness I hadn't confided in her yesterday.

For a whole year after James went, I had people constantly asking me if I wanted to talk about it. It would make me feel better, they informed me confidently. But it never *had* made me feel better. In fact, it made matters worse, because all of a sudden the people who had encouraged me to talk about it didn't know what to say or how to react. A problem shared inevitably turned out to be a problem doubled; their sadness joined forces with mine until eventually everyone in my circle was miserable. In Kingsfield I was a woman of mystery with my hidden onion-like layers, but at least I wasn't a woman of woe.

I could so easily have ruined this exciting time for Gemma by sharing my past. Now at least by keeping everything to myself, she didn't have to feel what I was feeling. At least, what I *had* been feeling.

Gemma plonked herself down on my bench and I nipped off to the tap to fill the watering can. A water butt would be a must for next year. All this fetching and carrying water was a pain. I returned with a full can and began dousing my pumpkin plant. It was huge now and spread the entire width of the plot. Tiny pumpkins had started to grow and I was hopeful for plenty to take in to school for Halloween.

Gemma slipped her flip-flops off and flexed her toes in the grass.

'So come on, then.' She grinned at me. 'The truth. Is there something going on between you two?'

I thought about playing it cool, but my cheeks had other ideas and when I met her inquisitive stare she squealed and clapped her hands over her mouth.

'Tilly! That's so exciting! You and Charlie. Oh! An allotment romance!'

'Shush!' I shook my head and huffed at her. 'No, not Charlie. He's just a friend.'

Gemma scrunched up her face. 'Then . . . ?'

I felt very coy suddenly. 'Aidan,' I said in a small voice. Me and Aidan. 'I kissed Aidan last night.'

I dropped the watering can and went to join Gemma on the bench. Her mouth was hanging open. 'Please breathe,' I said, lifting her lower jaw up gently with my fingertip.

'Aidan Whitby.' She sighed, grabbing my hands and gazing off into the distance. 'Oh God, your life will change completely.' Her eyes snapped round to glitter at me. 'It will be a social whirl of premieres and red carpets. You'll need a stylist – me, obviously – and—' She gasped and pressed a hand to her chest. 'You might even meet Peter Andre!'

I frowned. 'You've lost me there.'

204

'Aidan does documentaries; he's bound to know Peter Andre.'

'Well, all that is highly unlikely because he asked me out and I said no.'

'What? Are you mad?' She stared at me open-mouthed again.

'He gave me his number,' I said airily. 'I might phone him when he's back from Peru. Or I might not. Who knows? I might even be going out with someone else by then.'

That was a lie, obviously. But I smiled serenely and kept quiet because I knew that if I closed my eyes a picture appeared of a handsome man with thick wavy hair and eyes the colour of conkers and a gentle smile. And that was enough for now.

Gemma gazed at me incredulously and then flinched. 'Hello, have we met? I'm seeing a whole new Tilly Parker today.'

I giggled at that. I felt a bit different too and I quite liked the new me. 'Anyway, I've got a busy summer coming up too. Loads still to do at Ivy Lane, obviously. Plus I'm off to spend a week in a holiday cottage with Mum in the Lake District next weekend. Pottering around stately homes, hilly walks and lots of cake no doubt. Can't wait.'

'Ah, that's nice.' Gemma nodded and then flinched. 'Bugger. I need the loo. I'm sure my bladder has shrunk to the size of one of your puny pumpkins.'

I pretended to be insulted. 'Urine is good for the garden, could you squat over the compost bin for me, do you think?'

She glanced from the compost heap to me and back.

'Joke,' I said, pulling her to her feet.

We linked arms and giggled all the way back to the pavilion. Life was great. My best friend was having a baby, there were still four more weeks of the school holidays and I had had my first snog in nearly two years. I felt full of hope and happiness and couldn't wait to see what autumn would bring.

Ahead, just outside the pavilion, a thick-set man in a grey suit was talking to Peter. He had his hands clasped behind his back and looked very out of place at the Ivy Lane allotments in his work clothes.

Both men turned to face us as we approached.

I stopped abruptly as if an invisible forcefield had sprung up in front of us and the smile melted from my face.

I knew that man.

A bolt of fear shot through me from my stomach to my head and ricocheted round my skull, its vibrations making my head spin. For a second I thought I would faint. I gulped at the air and leaned against Gemma for support.

The man's eyes narrowed and then widened as he realized who I was.

'Ah, these lovely ladies are two of our plot holders,' said Peter, blithely unaware of my sudden paralysis. He extended an arm towards us. 'Ladies, may I introduce Mr Cohen from the Probation Service?'

Some faces were instantly forgettable. But some, for the most obvious reasons, haunted you for ever.

'Tilly, are you all right?' said Gemma. 'You look like you've seen a ghost.'

'I'm fine.' My voice came out as little more than a croak and she held on tight to my arm. I looked into Gemma's eyes and saw her concern reflected back at me.

Whatever life was about to throw at me, I was going to need her support now more than ever.

Autumn

Chapter 22

It was mid-September. The new school term was well under way, the six-week summer holiday was already a distant memory and I had had barely a moment free to spend at Ivy Lane. But today I was determined to plant my cabbage seedlings.

I finished the weeding and dabbed my nose with a tissue. The air was nippy this morning, as if summer had packed its bags overnight without warning, leaving a brisk autumn to take up the reins. My hands were brittle with cold and I wished I'd brought some gloves.

I went into my shed to put away the hoe and blew on my fingers to warm them up. When I came back out, I'd got a visitor.

'Shall I tell you my guilty secret?' Gemma sank gracefully on to my cream wrought-iron bench and stroked her belly with a serene smile.

'Gemma! How lovely to see you!' I dropped a kiss on her cheek and tried not to stare at her tummy.

She was huge.

I had only seen her at the end of August, which was . . . I did a quick mental count . . . two weeks ago! To be fair, Roy had warned me that she was 'swelling up nicely' in the same proud voice he used for his swedes. Apparently, he'd said as much to his daughter and she had burst in to tears.

Best avoid all mention of hugeness.

I processed her question but didn't answer straight away and focused instead on the instructions on the box of fertilizer I had bought from the newly stocked allotment shop. I wrinkled my nose; it didn't smell very nice and the fact that it was called 'Hoof and Horn' wasn't helping.

Gemma scooped up an apple from the ground and crunched into it.

'You can pick a fresh one from the tree, if you like,' I said.

My stumpy little tree had come into its own this month and the branches were trembling under the weight of their ripe, crisp apples. They were 'Newton Wonders' according to Vicky's apple book and I was now officially an apple devotee; I couldn't imagine eating a supermarket apple ever again.

I stepped back on to the bare earth and sprinkled the fertilizer liberally across the soil where the spring cabbages were about to go and dug it in with my fork. The summer plants had all finished cropping and despite my best efforts with the hoe, my plot looked a bit scruffy and I was longing to get something new in the ground.

'Nah. The dirtier the better. A bit of morning dew, the tang of mud: perfect,' said Gemma. She poked her toe at a tray of sturdy little cabbage plants. 'To tell you the truth,' she said in between noisy mouthfuls, 'I could even eat one of those. Soil and all.'

Gemma's cravings had ceased to surprise me: bricks, pickled eggs, chalk and now, evidently, soil.

'Please don't. It's taken me two weeks to acclimatize those darlings for planting,' I said, pushing a strand of hair out of my eyes.

'Oh, come and sit down and talk to me,' she said, patting the bench. 'I've haven't seen you since you went back to school.'

I abandoned my cabbage patch, grabbed my flask from the shed and poured us two mugs of hot water. Wiping my hands on my jeans, I added a cranberry teabag to mine (it had taken me six months to get used to the taste and now I actually quite liked it) and picked a huge sprig of fresh mint from my pot for hers.

'So,' I said, enjoying the steam from my mug on my face, 'your guilty secret.'

Gemma chewed on her bottom lip and pulled her pashmina across her chest. I resisted a smirk at this pale blue one. Since finding out that her baby was due in December she had adopted a new dress code of loose-fitting smocks and long scarves frequently worn over her head and had, on more than one occasion, compared herself to the Virgin Mary.

Although I was prepared to bet that the mother of Jesus didn't hold her curls back with a cat-ears headband.

'Peanut butter,' she said, leaning in to me conspiratorially. She took a sip of her tea, pulled a face and helped herself to another handful of mint leaves. It looked more like a floral arrangement than a beverage. 'By the tablespoonful. Can't help myself. Every time I pass the cupboard I'm like this . . .' She pulled a face like a squirrel with cheeks full of nuts. 'I won't fit in my shed soon, let alone any clothes.'

'Can't fault you,' I said. 'I adore the stuff too.'

How a woman could be pregnant for six months without anyone, including herself, realizing was one of life's mysteries, but according to her midwife, not uncommon. Now Gemma did know, however, she was sharing every intimate detail of her pregnancy with me – from haemorrhoids to heartburn – and every so often, being privy to the changes in her body got a little too much. If I was honest, that was partly why she hadn't seen me lately; I had been picking my moments to come to Ivy Lane when I thought she wouldn't be there. Twinge of shame.

She lifted up her feet and started to give me a rundown of her new symptoms, pointing out her swollen ankles and a new varicose vein, and demonstrated how difficult it was already to touch her toes. I smiled and tuned out, sipping my tea and nodding intermittently.

I wish my guilty secret was as simple as hers.

The problem was that Gemma just thought I was a single saddo with nothing more sinister in the closet than a pitiful love life, a slack attitude to cooking and a penchant for privacy.

I had a 365-page calendar in the kitchen with a thought for the day on each page. Today's thought was from a deceased Scottish author called George MacDonald: 'Few delights can equal the presence of one whom we trust utterly.'

The words ran over and over in my head as I half-listened to her.

Gemma trusted me; she told me everything. And not only did I trust her, but I loved her company too, and yet I still hadn't entrusted her with the truth about *me*. About how I came to be in Kingsfield at almost thirty with no apparent baggage. And while this was initially a self-preservation thing, now I felt a bit grubby for keeping my skeletons under lock and key and the longer it continued, the more gargantuan the prospect of spilling the beans became.

There had been a moment in August, that day when the probation officer, Mr Cohen, turned up out of nowhere, when I had nearly blurted out the whole thing. I had been so convinced that he had come to see me.

As if the whole world revolved around Tilly Parker.

But then I realized there was another reason for his visit, unconnected with me, so I changed my mind and kept my secrets to myself.

He was coming again next week to host a meeting in the pavilion.

Our harmonious little haven, it seemed, was to be joined by a group of young offenders who were coming to do community service on the allotment. Mr Cohen would be available in the pavilion to answer questions and, according to Peter, assuage any concerns.

I wished him luck with that.

At the moment, nobody except me and the committee knew. And I only knew because Mr Cohen and I had history and he had taken me to one side and told me confidentially. Out of concern for my welfare, he'd said.

My gut feeling was that the Ivy Lane community would be horrified.

Part of me wanted to stay away and keep out of the inevitable hoo-ha about allowing these youngsters into Ivy Lane. Unfortunately, the nosy part of me was more dominant. Even though my stomach flipped at the mere thought of seeing Mr Cohen again, I knew I had to go. With back-up, preferably.

'Gemma,' I said suddenly, interrupting her monologue about the number of times she got up for a wee last night, 'will you come to the meeting tomorrow in the pavilion?'

She looked at me and frowned. 'I wasn't going to. I've more or less given up on the allotment now. With Mum and Colin doing all the work, there's no point.'

I gripped her hand and forced her to look at me. 'Please.'

My expression must have convinced her and she sighed. 'All right. Seeing as you asked me nicely. Oh no, look who it isn't!' she muttered.

I glanced up to see Helen the hippie walking slowly towards us hand-in-hand with her daughter Honey who had grown into a teetering toddler.

It had taken me a while to warm to Helen. We had got off to a shaky start in spring when she had spurned my flapjacks; and spurned me, for that matter. She dressed like a scarecrow (not that I was one to talk on that score) and – I was mortally ashamed of admitting this – had a beautiful baby girl. However, a few weeks ago I had been stuck in the allotment loo and had been shouting for help for what seemed like hours when she arrived to set me free with a screwdriver.

It turned out that as well as being painfully shy (hence not being great at small talk) she was doing a research piece for a newspaper about frugal living for a year (hence the allotment and the second-hand clothes) and once she got going, was very interesting to listen to.

'She is so vegetarian, she makes me want to eat raw steak in front of her and I don't even eat red meat,' Gemma hissed.

Just bricks and soil, I thought.

'It's not like you to be jealous!' I said, stifling a giggle at Gemma's grimace. 'What has she done to rattle your cage?'

'Oh, she's so wholesome and healthy,' grumbled Gemma, folding her arms and resting them on her bump. 'And gorgeous – with her smooth complexion, swishy hair and perfect figure. Well, what you can see of it under those baggy clothes.' She lowered her voice. 'And I'm such a blob these days I look awful.'

I stared at her open-mouthed. 'Gem, you have nothing

to be jealous about. You are the most beautiful woman I know.'

'Really?' She turned her massive blue eyes to mine.

I nodded.

'I'm filling up.' She blinked and hugged me.

'I'm sorry to interrupt,' said a soft silky voice.

We sat up straight to see Helen standing in front of us with two plastic bottles and cups. Today's outfit consisted of army trousers, rolled up at the ankle, and a voluminous black jumper. Did she specifically frequent a charity shop for giants, I wondered, or was it simply a comfort thing?

'Hello, Honey,' said Gemma, all smiles again. She twinkled her fingers at the little girl.

Honey instantly made a wobbly dash for safety behind her mum and peered at us from between Helen's legs, two tiny pigtails protruding either side of her calves.

'You look radiant, Gemma,' said Helen, smiling shyly.

Gemma ran a hand through her curls and wriggled in her seat. 'Thank you, so do you,' she said graciously.

'I've made some juices and wondered if you would mind testing them for me?' said Helen.

We happily agreed and Helen poured us a cup of juice the colour of sunshine.

'Well, it looks delicious,' I said, raising the cup to my lips. I took a generous sip and my eyebrows shot skywards.

Ginger. Not my favourite flavour by a long chalk.

Gemma tilted her cup up and drank it down in one. She wiped the back of her hand across her mouth and moaned with pleasure. 'What is in that?'

Helen beamed and held out the bottle to top up Gemma's cup, thus letting me off the hook nicely. 'Carrot, apple and ginger.'

'Delicious dot com,' squealed Gemma, wide-eyed and

wondrous. 'Ginger, that's my new favourite flavour. I need more!'

She grabbed the bottle out of Helen's hand and put it to her lips.

Helen looked a bit shocked. But in a good way.

'Mmm. Very fresh,' I said diplomatically. 'What's in the other one?'

'Blackberry, apple and beetroot,' said Helen, proffering the second bottle.

I gulped and held up my cup; I had been with her until the beetroot.

The juice was a beautiful rich red. I consoled myself with the prospect of having consumed my five-a-day for the entire week in one go and took a tentative sip.

'Lovely,' I said, sort-of meaning it. I would probably in all honesty stick to my Tropicana. Call me old-fashioned, but I much preferred my beetroot pickled and sliced on a cheddar cheese sandwich.

'I'm thinking of going into business so I can work around Honey. Open a little juice bar. Graham thinks it's a great idea, but I'm still a bit nervous.'

'Well, I'm a convert for starters,' said Gemma. She had a bottle-top-shaped orange ring around her mouth. 'Who's your target market? Where are you going to sell? What's your price point?'

'Er . . .' Helen shifted awkwardly and tucked her hair behind her ears. 'I've been concentrating on getting the recipes right first.'

Suddenly Gemma wrinkled up her nose, then pegged it with two fingers.

'Sorry,' she said, sounding like a rail platform announcer. 'Very sensitive olfactory organs at the moment.' She pointed to Honey.

The toddler had adopted the stance of a sumo wrestler, arms and legs akimbo, knees slightly bent, her face set in studied concentration.

'Whoops,' said Helen, scooping up her daughter. 'Nappy time. Thanks for the feedback.'

'Going into business?' hissed Gemma, releasing her nose as soon as Helen was out of earshot. 'She's away with the fairies, that one.'

'She needs advice from a successful businesswoman,' I said, nudging her with a well-intended elbow. 'A mentor.'

Gemma's eyes lit up. 'You're right.' She stood up, pressed a hand to the small of her back and hurried off. 'Helen! Wait for me.'

'Tomorrow at the pavilion,' I called to her retreating form. 'Don't forget!'

She gave me a thumbs-up and I let out a long breath.

I had to be there to find out exactly what Ivy Lane was letting itself in for, and she had to be there to catch me if I fell.

Chapter 23

'Criminals!' gasped Liz, pulling the lapels of her cardigan up to her neck as if she was in danger of being ravished any moment.

'At Ivy Lane!' wailed Rosemary, clamping a hand over her mouth. 'Oh no. Colin is at such an impressionable age. I won't have him led astray.'

Breathe, Tilly. In and out.

I was a bag of nerves. Just being in the same room as Mr Cohen again brought back all sorts of memories that I'd rather forget. Every time a voice was raised my leg shot up like James's used to do when he was watching *Match of the Day* and his team had a clear shot at the goal.

Roaring, high-pitched indignation, outrage . . . All types of raised voices had been aired so far and I was as tightly coiled as a well-laden mule in Buckaroo.

The last time we had gathered in the pavilion like this was in May to meet the director from the *Green Fingers* TV show.

Despite my current state of nervousness, the memory brought a flutter to my stomach and a flush to my cheeks. Then my fellow plot-holders had been buzzing with excitement at the prospect of being filmed for the allotment documentary. I, however, had been totally unimpressed by Aidan and hadn't wanted anything to do with him or his TV show, when in fact he was a perfect gentleman, talented, thoughtful and an excellent kisser . . .

Now I was definitely blushing.

This evening was a very different bunch of bananas. The layout of the room was the same: a top table with Peter, Christine and Nigel representing the committee and Mr Cohen from the probation service – looking as staid, steely and starchy as ever – but that was where the similarity ended.

There was more than a hint of hostility in the air, with most of the plot-holders in uproar and the committee members endeavouring to keep order. Mr Cohen, meanwhile, looked as if he had seen it all before a million times. Which, of course, he probably had.

Nigel was speaking and waving his arms a lot. Something about people less fortunate than ourselves. For a second I wondered if I was back in Harrogate at Sunday school. The chairs had been uncomfortable there, too, and I had always been watching the clock until it was time to escape. I tried to focus and flicked a glance at Gemma. She rolled her eyes and feigned a yawn.

'Why us? What has our little community done to deserve this?' demanded Shazza, her lower chin wobbling indignantly. Karen patted her leg and Shazza gripped on to her partner's hand, shooting her a grateful smile.

'They will only be here for six weeks, starting from the last week in September and they will be supervised, I assure you,' said Mr Cohen, in the calm, unflappable voice that had made me want to punch him two years ago.

Shazza sniffed. 'One foot,' she said, pointing a finger at Peter, 'they set so much as one foot on our plot and I won't be responsible for my actions.'

Peter, who at the start of the meeting had been quietly confident, was now sporting a sheen of perspiration over his bald head, a flush to his neck and a twitch in one shoulder.

Helen raised her hand. 'Mr Cohen, I bring my baby to Ivy Lane with me most of the time, what sort of criminals are we talking about? Will it be safe to bring Honey?'

Mr Cohen stared at Helen and consulted his notes before answering. 'Let me reassure you. These people are not criminals, they are young offenders. I can't go into specifics, but there are some misdemeanours for which the court feels that community service is a more appropriate punishment than a custodial sentence.'

I bet that came straight from a press release.

'We call it Community Payback these days,' he continued, flashing her the ghost of a smile. 'Giving the offenders the chance to make reparation within the community they're from.'

As if a few hours digging weeds was enough to make amends. For anything.

A sudden sharp pain made me look down at my hands; my fists had been so tightly clenched that my palms were crossed with fingernail marks.

'Such as?' said Brenda. 'Nothing too dangerous, I hope? Murder, manslaughter, anything of a . . .' she mouthed the next bit theatrically, '. . . sexual nature?'

We all stared at Mr Cohen. He took a deep breath and raised his eyes to the ceiling and then continued, wafting his hands in a traffic-calming motion. 'Not at all,' he confirmed with a curt shake of the head.

'Oh, good,' she said, pressing a hand to her chest.

Was it me or did she look a tad disappointed?

'Well, I hope the committee will be providing us with

adequate protection,' said Vicky, shaking her head in disgust. 'High-security padlocks for everyone's sheds at the very least.'

Christine got to her feet with an exasperated huff. 'Look, we have two plots that have become so neglected that no one has wanted to take them on,' she said, her glance falling upon me. My leg bounced up and kicked the chair in front by accident.

'And whilst Tilly had assistance to clear her plot after Frank Garton left,' she continued, 'no one has volunteered to clear these two.'

Heads swivelled. First to Charlie and then to me. Rather awkward. I didn't know where to look.

'Working with the probation service kills two birds with one stone,' continued Christine firmly. 'The plots will be worked on this autumn ready to be let next spring and a group of young people will learn a new skill. Not to mention benefiting from the community spirit that we pride ourselves on in Ivy Lane. Don't we?' Christine nodded vigorously around the room, her grey curls bobbing, cheeks aflame. 'Don't we?' She continued to nod until someone joined in.

Alf did.

He got to his feet unsteadily and linked his hands behind his back.

I'd not seen him for a few weeks and I was a bit shocked. He looked droopy and a bit sad and not unlike my courgette plant, which had seen better days.

He cleared his throat. 'I was a bit of a tearaway when I was a kid. My mother was at her wits' end until my granddad gave me my own vegetable bed. First bit of responsibility I'd ever had. I learned to respect the ground, to grow my own food and to understand the seasons.' He stopped and rubbed his nose in a slow circular motion. I tried to imagine Alf as a teenager. Flat cap, baggy trousers and one of those shirts with the button-on collar. I bet he was a right lad.

'And it set me on the right track for life.' His eyes softened and a smile crept over his face. Thinking of his wife Celia, more than likely. 'Nowadays kids don't always have someone to show them the way. I reckon it's a good thing this community service. You've got my support.'

He sat back down. Peter looked like he might kiss him.

Charlie cleared his throat. 'I'm with Alf. Everyone deserves a second chance.'

He looked my way and I felt my face heat up. We hadn't spoken much since the day of the show in August.

'Here, here,' said Nigel.

An air of victory settled on the top table and Peter and Nigel began shuffling papers officiously. Most of the plot-holders, however, still had their arms folded tightly.

Dougie stood up. 'Do you think any of these offenders will know how to grow cannabis?'

The room erupted into groans, which more or less signalled the end of the meeting.

Gemma leapt to her feet. She was quite sprightly considering her shape.

'Don't go yet!' she said, waving her arms above her head. 'Helen and I have brought you free drinks to try.'

She and Helen produced two large pump pots and some cups and the atmosphere in the room lifted considerably. The Ivy Lane folk were suckers for a free drink, even one that included beetroot juice.

'Hi, Tilly.'

I turned my gaze from the pop-up juice bar to meet Charlie's smiling face. My glass, which I liked to think of as half-full, slopped a few drips at the sight of him.

Gemma wasn't the only person I'd been dodging throughout late summer. In the grand scheme of things, Charlie entering my fruit and vegetables in the annual show without my permission was nothing. But the rest – the whole him-and-me thing – was not nothing. It was definitely something. Something that I didn't want.

I'd missed him these past few weeks and I did want us to be friends, but the question was, was that do-able if Charlie's feelings ran deeper?

His smile threw me, though. It was as if our August heart-to-heart had never happened. Not that I was complaining.

I took a deep breath. 'Charlie! You look well. Been away?'

He rubbed his suntanned face self-consciously. 'Yeah. Mountain biking in Austria. What an adrenalin rush! I know why you go everywhere by bike now.'

Actually, I was quite adrenalin-averse. I smiled encouragingly anyway.

Off he went, describing in enthusiastic detail with added hand-actions the ravines, the sheer drops, the banked turns, and the thrills and spills of mountain trails.

I drifted off.

James and I had loved our holidays. I would book the flights – just cheapo airlines – and he would sort out the itinerary. That was his forte. Left to me we would have spent two weeks on the beach with maybe a half-day trip round the local market. Not him. We went truffle hunting in Italy, wine tasting in Croatia and sat through a toe-curling erotic show in Amsterdam, which to this day neither set of our parents knows about.

Aidan would be in Peru now. Peru sounded exotic. I wondered what it was like. Would he be thinking of me? I blinked and touched my cheeks to check I wasn't blushing. Warm but not flaming thankfully.

Charlie was grinning at me. He seemed to be waiting for some sort of acknowledgement.

'Great!' I said weakly.

'Really? Great!' His grin widened.

What? What had I agreed to?

'I'll set it up. Peak District, something like that. You'll love it,' he said, gripping my arm. 'Ha. I was convinced you'd say no.' He walked away, shaking his head to himself.

Had I just agreed to go cycling with Charlie? Nooo! Buggeration. Had he *seen* my Little Shopper with its double panniers? It was to off-road riding what Chitty Chitty Bang Bang was to Formula One: big on charm but sadly lacking in the oomph department.

A large hand touched my upper arm.

As my eyes travelled up from its fingertips to its adjoining torso, my stomach disappeared in the opposite direction. Mr Cohen.

'Might I have a word, Mrs Parker?' he murmured. His intense gaze under thick black eyebrows made my body tremble.

'Of course,' I stammered, gesturing towards the door.

Poker face, poker face, poker face.

My heart was thundering so loudly that I doubted I'd be able to hear a word he said. I cast my eye around the room. Everyone was too busy slurping juice and listening to Gemma's sales patter to notice me. Good.

He opened his mouth to speak but I silenced him with a hand.

'Please,' I said, glancing over his shoulder. 'Whatever it is, I'd rather not know.'

He shook his head and smoothed the lapels on his jacket. 'I understand your concerns,' he said in a low voice, 'but this is about the community service clients.'

I blinked at him, dry-mouthed.

'No obligation or anything on your part,' he continued, 'but I wondered whether I could ask a favour?'

I took a deep breath. Too inquisitive for my own good, that was my problem. 'Go on.'

'One of the offenders is female, eighteen, not been set the best example in life so far. All I'm asking is for you to take her under your wing, you know, show her an alternative path. With your background you could make all the difference to her right now. A steadying influence, if you like.'

Me? Steady? I was flakier than a Greggs cheese and onion pasty. She must be desperate.

'I'm not asking you to go out of your way but . . .'

There was something dodgy about this. I treated him to my special owl stare. 'What was her offence? Anything to do with drink-driving?'

And there it was: the slightest dilation in the pupils. I had him. If I ever needed a break from teaching conjunctions, contractions and connectives to small people, I'd be a shoo-in for MI5. How dare he?

I squared my shoulders and tilted my chin. 'Over my dead body.'

Cue lull in conversation, and my words ricocheting around the hall.

There was a communal intake of breath and all eyes were suddenly on me.

I flung back the pavilion door and ran.

Chapter 24

Apparently I had been a bit of a talking point after my dramatic departure. Not that I'd had the guts to go back yet and find that out for myself.

Instead, I sat quivering at home like one of those Japanese dogs that has to wear a coat even when it isn't snowing. I only found out because Gemma sent me a text. She told me that I should be pleased; it was a definite improvement on my original reputation, she informed me, which unbeknownst to me had been an unflattering mix of meek and mild.

In the end my cabbages forced me to return. It was late September and although the weather had cooled, we hadn't had any rain for a while. Those brave little soldiers needed me if they were to survive. Well, if not me specifically, then water and protection from slugs at any rate. And after all the effort I had put in to getting them this far, it would have been a shame to leave them orphaned now.

The fact that I had chosen the start date of the community service group to tend to my cabbages was completely and utterly coincidental.

For someone who claimed to keep herself to herself, I was, I realized, as I dragged my bike out of the hall and on to my front path, incredibly nosy and sneaking a peek at our resident 'crims' was too much of a temptation. It was a misty damp sort of September day, almost mitten weather, and I had purposefully donned my full safety gear of helmet and hi-vis jacket for the occasion.

Oh yes, never let it be said that Tilly Parker was not a sensible, law-abiding citizen.

The gates to Ivy Lane were locked when I got there and I had to fiddle about inside my pocket to find the key – not easy astride a bike. I hardly ever had to wrestle with the padlock these days and it made me wonder: were we keeping people out or certain people in?

Vicky scurried straight over. 'They're here,' she said, nodding up past the pavilion. 'Six of them. Got dropped off in a minibus.'

I scanned the car park for evidence. Nothing.

'Exactly,' said Vicky. 'The supervisor had a chat with Christine, gave some orders and buggered off. Tell you what,' she went on, tapping her nose, 'don't leave anything lying around . . .' She made a whistling noise. 'They'll nick it before you can say *Midsomer Murders*.'

I liked Vicky. She was an unlikely gardener – although to be fair, most of us fitted that category – she smoked thin cigars, wore low-cut tops and kept a hip flask of gin in her shed.

I thanked her for the advice and tried not to stare as I approached them.

My heart sank.

The group was easy to spot as, rather embarrassingly, they all wearing neon jackets. Just like me. The only difference was that theirs had COMMUNITY PAYBACK on the reverse.

They were huddled in a group on the overgrown plot

opposite mine and Gemma's, waist-high in weeds and laughing at something.

Not me, thankfully. Yet.

Bugger. One of them looked over as I was shoving my safety jacket into my rear pannier.

'Coming to join us, miss?' He was taller than the rest, as thin as my rake and had a massive smirk on his face.

I fumbled to undo the straps of my cycle helmet and the huddle unfolded as they all turned to stare at the red-faced nerd on a bike. Alf stood at the centre of the group, his hands full of soil that he was crumbling in front of them.

I softened instantly.

Most of the Ivy Lane community were nowhere to be seen today. So far, other than Vicky, I'd only spotted Nigel and Liz and they were both keeping their heads down. But not Alf. As promised, there he was, in the thick of it, sharing his wisdom, showing them the way.

I loved Alf. I wanted to grab hold of his big whiskery face and kiss him.

'Morning, everyone.' I arranged my features in a welcoming not-at-all-fazed-by-the-fact-you're-here smile and disappeared down the path to plot 16B.

I'd watered the cabbages and removed the bamboo canes from my runner beans by the time Alf ambled towards me, leaning heavily on a walking stick. He had a girl in a hi-vis vest with him. I scanned the rest of the group.

The *only* girl. So she was the one.

Act cool, Tilly, ice-cool, I advised myself, as my nostrils flared in readiness.

Unfortunately, my knees went all wobbly and I inadvertently curtsied before the pair of them.

'Tilly, I've been teaching Hayley about enriching the soil,' said Alf in his gravelly voice.

Well, that would be useful next time she got behind the wheel of a car after a few Barcardi Breezers.

'Really.' I flicked a surreptitious eye over her, ripped a handful of runner bean stems up out of the ground and threw them behind me.

Hayley had thick blonde hair, darting green eyes and barely reached Alf's shoulder. It was doubtful whether she would even be able to see over a steering wheel, let alone reach the pedals.

Alf scooped up my dead beans with a grunt and tottered over to the compost bin.

'You get out what you put in,' he said, giving me a pointed look, 'with gardening.'

'Are these broad beans?' asked Hayley. I couldn't help it; I glared at her and she flushed. Then I felt ashamed. She had sounded genuinely interested.

I coughed. 'Yes,' I mumbled, 'I'm just about to dig them up for the compost too.'

'Mmm,' she said, closing her eyes. 'My absolute favourite vegetable. What did you do with them?'

She didn't sound like a criminal. Not that they were easily identifiable by their voices, of course. Otherwise the police wouldn't have such a tricky job catching them.

'I ate them.'

She blinked at me. 'Well, yeah . . .'

'Oh, I see.' My turn to blush. 'Boiled. With a pork chop.'

She raised an eyebrow and didn't look impressed. 'I like to fry them off with garlic and pancetta. Huh, although you'd be lucky to find as much as a rasher of streaky bacon in our house.'

Well, that put me in my place.

Alf took a knife out of his pocket and stooped to the broad beans.

'Take the stalks off, leave the roots in,' he panted and cut through the first couple of plants. 'Here you go.' He passed the knife to Hayley and straightened up to catch his breath. 'You do the rest.'

There was an offender on my plot. With a knife. Surely this had to contravene at least fifty European health and safety laws?

'What for?' asked Hayley, slicing through the bean stalks with far too much relish for my liking. I could see the top of her thong when she bent down. I glanced at Alf. That would do his blood pressure no good at all.

'Nitrogen,' said Alf as I ushered him to the bench where Hayley's underwear was less visible. 'The roots will add nitrogen to the soil. Next spring, when Tilly plants a new crop, it'll have super powers.'

'Safe,' said Hayley with a solemn nod.

Alf frowned at me.

'It means cool,' I whispered, proud that I knew that. 'Shouldn't you be working with your group, Hayley?'

She shook her head and flicked the blade of the pocket knife in and out. I couldn't take my eyes off it. 'Tea break.'

She stared at me defiantly. 'You want to know what I've done, don't you? I can see it in your face. You don't trust me, do you?'

'Noooo,' I said, trying to laugh off my embarrassment. 'I mean, yeeees.'

Nicely handled. In fact, what did I mean? I wished *I* could see my face. Was this the steadying influence that Mr Cohen had hoped for? I wondered. Unlikely.

'None of our business, is it, Tilly?' said Alf, slapping my knee.

'Well, the answer is, I didn't do nothing.'

I winced internally at the double negative. I almost

corrected her but she did still have the knife.

'What it was was,' she huffed impatiently, 'my mum's idiot boyfriend said we'd taken his car without consent. I hate him, the pervert,' she added under her breath, bending down to hack her way through another clump of my broad beans.

Alf folded his arms, whistled a tuneless tune through his teeth, looked up at the gathering clouds and generally tried to give the impression that he wasn't interested.

I was though. Very.

'And had you?'

'Well . . .' She hesitated with her mouth open and considered her answer, hand on hip. She looked like a little teapot.

Yes, then.

'Technically . . . yes.'

Ha. Guilty as charged.

'Don't look at me like that,' she said haughtily, drawing a circle in the air with her knife.

I swallowed.

'He always let us borrow it—'

'Us?'

'Me and my mate Andrew.'

I nodded slowly.

'He only reported it stolen because we'd had a row that night. I knee'd him in the balls for trying to feel me up. He blamed Mum for him being horny because she was away seeing her sister in London. So to pay him back I lifted the keys from the kitchen drawer and took the car to get to a party instead of going by bus. Only I can't drive so I gave Andrew the keys. What I didn't know was that he'd had a Magners. The police pulled us over and he failed the breathalyser test.'

That entire incident was awful on so many levels that it

was hard for my head to know where to start. Her face had gone all red from screwing it up. Alf, on the other hand, had gone white.

'Anyway,' she sighed, looking down at the broad beans in surprise, as if she couldn't remember what she was doing here, 'it was worth it because Mum dumped him for pressing charges.'

How could she be so blasé about it?

'No.' I stood and descended on her in slow-motion mode until I towered over her. 'No, it wasn't worth it.'

Hayley blinked at me and took a step back as I took the knife from her hand. My pulse had doubled and was throbbing loudly in my ears. I thought for a moment that I might burst out of my clothes like the Incredible Hulk. Perhaps that would help, get rid of some fury, perhaps I should throw in an almighty roar for good measure.

'Now then, Tilly,' said a gruff voice of reason from the bench.

I took a deep breath and exhaled sharply.

'You could have killed someone. Your friend. He could have hit another car or a pedestrian. Would it have been worth it then? Hmm?'

'Well, no.' She blinked at me and paled, as if the thought had just occurred to her. 'Obviously. But he didn't, did he?' She folded her arms and looked at me sideways like I was a lunatic then stomped off to rejoin the rest of her group.

I made short work of the remaining broad beans, bending down, letting my hair cover my face to hide the frustrated tears.

When I stood up, Alf was poking the end of his walking stick at my cabbages.

'Want to talk about it?' he asked.

I rubbed a hand over my face and shook my head.

'I'm glad you're coming back next year,' he said. 'I'll enjoy thinking of you here, learning and growing,' he lowered his voice, 'and healing.'

My throat throbbed and I could do nothing more than nod.

'I shan't be here. I'm packing it in. I know the committee don't believe me. But I am. Come on, my plot next,' he said, offering me his arm.

It had all got too much for him, I could see that now; he hadn't kept on top of it and although he had a wide variety of crops, they were fighting a losing battle with the weeds. The sight of his beloved plot looking less than perfect was upsetting. For me and for him.

'So really,' he said, wheezing after all the effort of bending down, showing me his Heath Robinson irrigation system, the last of his beetroots, his top-notch turnips and ready-to-come-up potatoes, 'everything's ready now and then the plot will be just right for some young blood to take on fresh next year.'

Normally, I would have nudged him and teased him that of course he'd be back next year, but this time I squeezed his hand and placed a kiss on his whiskery cheek.

'Right you are,' I said, leading him to the pair of deck-chairs in the shed.

He unzipped his anorak and rearranged it as he sat down. The pictures of him and Celia that used to be pinned up had gone from the shed wall. I think that made me feel sadder than anything. He'd packed up already, mentally moved out of Ivy Lane.

Anyway. Time to change the subject before I got all miserable.

'That was a brave move back there, Alf,' I laughed, 'giving that girl a knife.'

He flapped a hand at me and chuckled. 'That's the thing with trust. You'll never know if someone's trustworthy until you trust 'em.'

God, I was going to miss him. He was so wise. My chest heaved and I reached out a hand and patted his arm.

'You're such a kind man, Alf. A much better person than me.'

'Codswallop, girl. Besides, we've all got history.' He stared at me for a few seconds and I wondered what was coming. 'I've been inside, you know. Prison.'

I held my breath.

'Broke into a builder's yard with my mates. There was no CCTV then, but there was a vicious Alsatian who took a chunk out of my backside and I had to go to hospital. No sooner had the nurse started to clean the wound than an orderly whipped back the curtain round my bed. Next thing I knew a copper appeared and caught me with my pants down. The orderly was Celia. We always joked that she saw my bare arse before she saw my face. She must have liked what she saw, though.'

Funny how life turned out. If Alf hadn't committed a crime, he'd never have met his Celia. I bet he didn't regret a thing.

'You're full of surprises, you.' I grinned at him and shook my head.

'Well, there you go,' he said, eyeing me apologetically. 'My criminal past. Got three months for that. Nowadays I'd probably get away with community service like this lot.'

I got the message. People could change; sometimes all they needed was a kick up the bum – or a bite in his case.

'Thank you for telling me,' I said, standing up to go. I

placed a kiss on his head, still covered with a thick thatch of silver hair. 'I'd better be off.'

'Come back tomorrow,' he said, grabbing on to my hand with his gnarled fingers. 'Got something for you.'

'I've got school in the morning. Can it wait till the weekend?'

'Pop in early. Before school. I shan't keep you long, I promise.'

He pulled a hopeful face. I rolled my eyes affectionately and tutted.

'Go on then, see you tomorrow, eight o'clock sharp. I'll even bring you some breakfast.'

Chapter 25

What had possessed me to offer to bring Alf breakfast? I rarely ate anything before school unless it was a bland and boring breakfast biscuit. A desperate dredge of the freezer unearthed two battered croissants left over from a recent lazy Sunday morning. Hardly a gourmet feast, but they would have to do.

I shoved them in the microwave for a few seconds and then tucked them in my coat pocket.

I felt odd cycling past school, seeing the already busy staff car park. I had a hectic day ahead too; I hoped Alf was on time, I really couldn't hang around. Our topic at the moment at school was People Who Help Us and we were having a themed fancy dress day (I was already dressed as a nurse, not the ideal outfit for an early-morning rendezvous with an octogenarian, admittedly) and one of the children's mums was coming in this afternoon to talk about her job as a dentist.

Thinking about it, perhaps Charlie would like to bring his fire engine down to school or Karen could visit, a real nurse? Maybe even Nigel could come in in his old army uniform. This topic could run for weeks with any luck.

The gate was locked. Bad sign. Alf obviously hadn't

arrived. I cast a look over my shoulder to see if he was behind me – he wasn't – and let myself in.

Ivy Lane allotments were deserted so I pedalled at full pelt up to Alf's plot, hoping against hope that he'd let himself in and re-padlocked the gate.

His raspberry canes had been cut back since yesterday, I hoped he hadn't overdone it. He had seemed shattered when I left him.

Phew, Alf was here. The shed was open and I could see him inside, the back of his head protruding over the top of his deckchair, exactly where I'd left him yesterday. Good, I would still be able to make it to school on time.

'Morning,' I called in a suitably sing-song voice. 'Nurse Parker here with your breakfast. I hope you haven't been there all night.'

I should have brought a flask of coffee, I realized, looking at the crumbly croissants; it would be like eating a loofah without a drink to wash it down. I slipped off my helmet and coat to better display my uniform and hurried into the shed. Much as I loved Alf, I needed to keep this brief.

He still hadn't moved. He must have nodded off.

'Boo.' I pressed my hands over his eyes.

His face was cold. I whipped round to face him, my heart thumping with fear. His eyes were closed, head slumped to one side, lips slack and dry, hands clasped in front of him.

'Alf?'

I shook his shoulders.

'Alf?'

Goose pimples flashed across my skin, making my whole body shudder and panic rise in my throat. I could hear my own breathing, my own heartbeat, as I registered the signs of a life departed.

Or perhaps it wasn't? Maybe I wasn't too late.

I grabbed his wrist and felt for a pulse. My own hands were trembling so much it was difficult to feel anything. I pressed firmly, softly, in several different places . . . but nothing.

People Who Help Us. People Who Help Us. I dashed back to my bike and fumbled for my phone.

'Emergency Services, which service do you require?'

'Ambulance. Please . . .' I swallowed a sob. 'It's my friend. I think he's gone . . . please hurry.'

Ten minutes, the calm voice at the end of the phone had informed me. The ambulance would be with me as quick as it could. I ran to the gates and opened them wide. Ran back. I had ten minutes to say goodbye.

We had sat like this yesterday. On deckchairs in his shed. Only I hadn't reached for his hand then. I wished I had. How long had it been since someone had held Alf's hand?

I covered the back of his hand with mine and saw something sticking out from his closed palm. I tweaked it and with a bit of tugging managed to pull out a screwed-up photograph. I smoothed it out on the skirt of my nurse's uniform. It was a picture of him with his arm round Celia, the two of them standing outside the shed, beaming at the camera.

My eyes let go of their tears and I sobbed.

The thought of Alf spending his last moments alone were so sad. But I supposed that he hadn't been. Not really. Celia had been with him, smiling up at him from that photograph. In my heart of hearts I knew that that was what he would have wanted. The last face he saw would have been the one he loved more than any other. His last thoughts would have been happy ones. The relief was overwhelming.

By the time the paramedics arrived, I was in a bit of a trance. I let go of Alf's hands and stood aside. Two of them. A man and a woman.

'You, er, his nurse, love?' said the man, kneeling down in front of Alf and unzipping a large nylon bag.

My outfit was from eBay. Most of the nurse's uniforms had not been appropriate for school, but I'd found a blue one that came to the knee, had a mock apron printed on the front and a pretend fob watch pinned to my chest. The crowning glory was a floppy headpiece with a red cross on the front, probably crushed now from the weight of my cycle helmet.

I shook my head. 'A friend.'

The two of them exchanged looks.

At any other time, I'd have been mortified.

I turned away to Alf's workbench to give him his dignity while the paramedics carried out their checks and noticed a spade and fork leaning up against the worktop. Unheard of; every tool in Alf's shed had its own special hook. A place for everything and everything in its place – I'd heard him say it enough times.

Then I saw it: an envelope with my name on it propped up on a box of tomato food. This must have been what he wanted to give me. I recognised Alf's hesitant writing in pencil. He always used a short chubby pencil, sharpened with his pocket knife, to write names on plant labels.

Should I open it? Was I even allowed to touch it?

The paramedics were lifting Alf on to a stretcher and weren't paying me any attention. It *did* have my name on it. I inserted a finger under the flap, it wasn't stuck down and I took the letter out.

He had written it all in uppercase as usual, with the first letter of each sentence bigger than the others.

Tilly,

I'm hanging up my gardening gloves for good at Ivy Lane, but I shall be popping back to check up on you! I'm trusting you with my Celia's tools. They are old but there's plenty of dig in them yet if you look after them like I showed you. You're a grand girl, Tilly, and it's done my old heart good seeing you come out of your shell this year. Keep it up, lass.

Alf

PS No need to thank me, but I'm always partial to a bit of cake!

I brushed the tears away and looked at the spade, wrapping my fingers around the smooth wooden handle, worn thinner in the middle from years and years of digging. Celia's tools. What a lovely gift. From a lovely, lovely man.

The female paramedic put her hand on my shoulder. 'Are you all right, sweetheart?'

I nodded. And in a strange way, I was all right. Because seeing Alf like this, so at peace at the end of his days, had shown me that death didn't have to be violent and bloody and shocking; sometimes it could be peaceful and calm and the perfect way to end a happy life.

By the time Alf's body had been transferred to the back of the ambulance and I had given what details I could to the paramedics, Nigel had arrived.

I filled him in about Alf, adding 'Don't ask,' when I caught him eyeing my nurse's uniform.

It was only eight thirty; it felt like I'd been here hours. I had the whole day ahead of me still. As soon as the thought popped into my head, the breath caught in my throat. Poor, poor Alf.

My chin stiffened, my lip wobbled and my bones turned to jelly.

240

I slumped against Nigel and rubbed my tears against his soft wool jumper. He rubbed my back awkwardly and we both watched the ambulance leave. I could hear his heartbeat. It was hypnotic and reassuring.

'What next?' I mumbled. I should phone school for starters. The bell would be going shortly.

'I'll give Christine a ring. We've got his son's details somewhere.'

He peeled me off him and peered into Alf's shed before gently closing the door.

'Alf did well on his own after Celia died,' he said gruffly. 'Not easy to carry on with your life when half of it's gone.'

I could only nod at that. The lump in my throat was too much of an obstacle to navigate.

He removed a folded handkerchief from his pocket and performed a series of impressive nose-trumpets, dabbing his eyes to finish.

'I'm glad you were here, Tilly.' He patted my arm. 'Well, I'd better do the necessary.'

I watched Nigel stride off to the pavilion, picked up my bike and wheeled it along the road.

I didn't get very far.

'Well, I must say I'm shocked.'

Brenda. She must have spoken to Nigel.

In my dreamlike state of numbness it took me a few seconds to process her body language. Feet planted firmly on the road-end of plot sixteen. She flicked her long red hair over one shoulder. Dressed in black, like always; pinched red lips, twisted to one side; one hand leaning on her fork, the other balled into a fist and wedged on her hip.

She didn't look very happy. Join the club.

'A share,' she snapped. 'That's what we agreed.'

I was confused. Celia's tools? I blinked at her.

'I said you could have some of the crop in return for me borrowing part of your plot. Not half the whole lot.'

Oh. The potatoes.

'I'm sorry, Brenda, but—'

'This way.' She flicked her head towards the end of my plot. I didn't have the wherewithal to argue so I dropped my bike and followed.

'Just nipped in early to dig them up and what do I find? Somebody's beaten me to it!'

She couldn't seriously suspect me? Ordinarily, I might have laughed, but this morning I was barely present, let alone prepared to stand my ground.

But I could see she was right: one of the rows had been dug up and discarded potato plants lay strewn all over the churned-up soil. Most peculiar.

'Oh dear.'

'Is that all you can say?' She stared at me, eyebrows furrowed, and stabbed the fork into the ground. 'That crop was very valuable to me.'

The phrase 'as cheap as chips' popped into my head again, but I kept it to myself. She really did look angry.

All of a sudden I couldn't bear to continue the conversation any longer and began to walk away.

'Excuse me,' she called, all red-faced and indignant. 'Aren't you at least going to apologize?'

I turned back to her and breathed deeply before speaking. 'This really has nothing to do with me, Brenda. And quite honestly, I'm not worried about a few potatoes right now.'

She opened her mouth to protest but I held up a hand. 'Brenda, I'm afraid Alf has passed away.'

Brenda fell instantly silent. I picked up my bike and walked on. I should probably have given her more information rather than just walk away, but my throat was burning.

As I passed the car park by the pavilion, a minibus pulled up and the community service lot climbed out.

'Hello, miss,' called the lanky one from yesterday.

I smiled and ducked my head down.

'Hey, Tilly.'

I lifted my eyes to come face to face with Hayley fastening up the Velcro on her neon jacket.

'You know Alf who you met yesterday,' I said quietly, taking her to one side.

Her face lit up briefly and then fell at the sight of my serious expression. 'Yeah?'

She looked so young and vulnerable that I reached out and touched her arm before speaking. 'He's passed away, I'm afraid.'

'Ahh.' Her shoulders drooped; in fact, her whole body drooped. 'He was so cute.'

My face softened. He would have loved being described as cute.

Hayley gazed at me and to my surprise I saw tears in her eyes. 'He was so nice to me. Like a proper granddad.'

The tone of her voice broke my heart. Was it so uncommon, I wondered, that someone was nice to her?

Shivers ran down my spine as a gravelly voice vibrated in my ear: *You'll never know if someone's trustworthy until you trust 'em.*

I held my arms open, she stepped into them and we hugged silently, with our cheeks pressed together and our tears mingling.

After a long moment she pulled away and we both wiped our tears away.

I smiled at her. 'OK?'

She nodded. 'Don't know why I'm so cut up. But, you know.' She shrugged.

I nodded back. 'Alf had that effect on people. Hey, fancy coming round to my house one day to help me bake a cake?'

A little one-sided smile appeared and she nodded.

I beamed back at her. 'Safe,' I said, raising my hand for a high-five.

Hayley sighed and rolled her eyes. 'Seriously? No one does that any more.'

I couldn't help smiling. Perhaps Mr Cohen was right. If not quite a steadying influence, then certainly pathologically uncool. That would have to do.

Chapter 26

I spent the week following Alf's death in a bit of a daze and by the day of his funeral I was a mess.

The day turned out to be an emotional journey round mood-swinging bends, down plunging ravines of melancholy and up teetering precipices of hysteria. And it *would* have to be on October the fourth. Looking on the bright side, at least it had kept me occupied for most of the day.

I glanced round the crowded pavilion and then down at my watch. Four o'clock. There were still five hours to go before I would allow myself to go to bed. And even then I knew I wouldn't sleep.

The mood in the church had been sombre but pragmatic; Alf had had a good innings, it was what he would have wanted, he'll be with his beloved Celia . . . and yes, that was all very true, but it didn't stop me from feeling incredibly sad. The service had been much as I'd expected until the final song: the body left the church for the cemetery to the tune of 'Spirit in the Sky' by Doctor and the Medics, which had me and Gemma chuckling and sobbing in equal measure.

Most of the allotment crowd had been at the church. I nearly didn't go but I was glad I did in the end. Hayley had begged me to go with her; she said that even though she'd only met Alf once, he'd made a big impression on her. He had that effect on people, I'd told her, remembering all the little stories he'd told me since I'd come to Ivy Lane. Hayley said that other than me and him, no one had been very welcoming. I'd flushed at this point; I had been just as guilty until I'd got to know her. She said the other people from Ivy Lane allotments shot her daggers and made her feel like she wasn't wanted.

Which was another thing.

There had been more thefts at Ivy Lane. Some of Charlie's butternut squashes had gone, Peter's kohlrabi had vanished, stuff had been taken from Nigel's greenhouse, Graham's prize parsnips had all been plucked out and more of Brenda's potatoes were missing, this time from her own plot. In fact, nearly everyone had lost something. It was only Liz and me who hadn't been affected. If I hadn't been quite so preoccupied, I might have taken umbrage at the oversight.

The atmosphere of mistrust had driven me to distraction over the last week. I was almost glad Alf wasn't here to see it; he would have been so disappointed in them all. But at least now that most of us had suffered some sort of loss, everyone had stopped accusing each other. Unfortunately, the finger of suspicion was now firmly directed at the community service team, which was ludicrous. Even if they had wanted to, sneaking basket-loads of fruit and vegetables into the minibus without being spotted would be virtually impossible.

Hayley had slipped away after the burial, not wanting to brave the wake in the pavilion. Who could blame her? Gemma had given her a lift back into Kingsfield; she had a hot stone massage booked in later and wanted to get set up. I was surprised she still had willing clients; I wasn't sure I would find it very relaxing having a beautician who clutched her side every few minutes and squealed, 'Ooh, Braxton Hicks!'

So I was on my own. I took a cup of tea to a quiet corner, sat down and tried to avoid letting maudlin thoughts crowd my head.

A posse of moaning mourners had surrounded Peter by the tea urn. To start with, they had all been sharing happy memories of Alf, but now talk had turned to the future of their precious plots.

'Padlocks,' said Vicky. 'I warned you.' Vicky's plot was nearest to the gate and she had been stolen from twice, the poor thing. No wonder she was agitated. She was looking very glamorous today in a black jersey wrap dress with a glittering purple brooch pinned to her left bosom. Alf would have approved, I felt sure. In her heels she towered over Peter who was smoothing his hair repeatedly in a sweeping motion.

'Nothing has been taken from sheds, though, Vicky. So in theory extra security wouldn't have helped.' He gave her a reassuring smile and sipped at his tea.

'I'm not taking any chances,' said Dougie, shaking his head. 'I've taken my new batch of scrumpy home. Just in case.'

'Well, I think the probation service should be told,' said Brenda. 'That Mr Cohen. Either the committee phones him or I do.' She pressed her red lips together and glared at poor Peter.

I had gone off Brenda a bit. After accusing me of stealing her spuds, she'd tried to lay the blame on Charlie, on the basis that he wanted her crop because he'd lost all his to blight. When that had failed to get a response, she'd harangued the community service supervisor, forcing him to interview the team about the thefts and to check their bags as they left.

Hayley had been really upset about it. 'Made to line up, we were. It was so embarrassing,' she had said. 'And she didn't even apologize when nothing was found in our bags.'

'Why is she so bothered about a few potatoes?' I'd asked.

Hayley had enlightened me. 'She's got a baked potato stall in Kingsfield near my old school. Packed at lunch time, she is. Home-grown, organic potatoes. Really nice, actually.'

So that was her catering business. And that was why she grew so many potatoes! Was it against allotment rules, I wondered, using council land to grow vegetables for commercial use?

'We should never have allowed these people into Ivy Lane,' Brenda was saying now, jabbing a finger in Peter's direction. 'I don't know how they're stealing from us, but we didn't have any of this trouble before they arrived. I can't abide dishonesty.' She tutted and dunked a digestive biscuit into her tea.

I'd heard enough. I banged my cup and saucer down and marched over.

Cool and professional, Tilly.

I filled my lungs with a calming breath. I could actually be quite commanding when I chose.

'Talking of dishonesty, when were you going to tell me that you're using my plot to stock your catering business?' I said, tapping her on the shoulder and staring her squarely in the eyes.

The colour drained from her face and she looked first at

Peter then at me. 'It's not illegal,' she stammered, sliding her eyes back to Peter, 'is it?'

'Er,' said our committee chairman, 'well . . .'

'*These people*, Brenda,' I continued, 'are part of our community for the next few weeks. And quite frankly, I think you owe them and everyone else you have accused an apology.'

Brenda flicked her hair over her shoulder and flared her nostrils indignantly as if she was about to reply, but I hadn't finished.

'Alf made an effort to make friends with them, to trust them. And today of all days . . .' My voice faltered and I swallowed. 'Today of all days, we should perhaps have a bit more respect for others.'

Then I did what I seem to do best when faced with a confrontational situation: I walked away. I almost made it to the door unscathed.

'Thank you for coming.'

I blinked and a tall man in his fifties with a chin-length black bob came into focus. Alf's son, William. He held out a hand.

'He was a lovely man, your dad,' I said, as he clasped my fingers in a firm, dry handshake.

'Very kind of you to say. Tilly, isn't it? Dad talked about you.'

I nodded, flicking a glimpse over to the allotment crew. Brenda was dabbing her face with a tissue. Dougie caught my eye and rolled his eyeballs skywards.

'Really, what did he say?'

He laughed nervously. I sensed he didn't want to tell me, which made me even more curious. 'Go on.'

'He said he couldn't understand why a smashing girl like you was on your own.'

249

Alf said that? My eyes brimmed with tears. William's face dropped and he glanced around him with a grimace.

'I'm so sorry.' He reached towards me and then clearly thought better of it, plunging both his hands into his jacket pockets instead.

I hadn't been to many funerals. I don't think I spoke at all at the last one I went to, but perhaps some people react differently and say things they wouldn't normally dare. Or perhaps William was flirting with me. He had certainly turned pink.

'I spoke out of turn. None of my business,' he stuttered.

'I'm a widow.'

The word seemed to hang in the air and float between us. My mouth went completely dry and I stared at him. What on earth had I said that for?

'I'm sorry.'

'Yes. Well. So am I. For you, I mean.'

'I've never been married.'

'I meant for your loss. For Alf. He really was a lovely man. Excuse me.' I squeezed out a wobbly smile and pushed past him. Suddenly I couldn't bear to think about loss any more. Memories of the last funeral I'd been to came rushing back to me, my legs started to shake and I couldn't breathe.

Open the door. Inhale the fresh autumn air. Walk. Keep walking. Keep breathing. Home.

I reached the safety of my little house in Wellington Street, closed the door behind me and slumped against it.

What time was it? Five o'clock. Was that all? One measly hour since I last checked. Hell.

Still four hours to go.

Cally meowed and wound himself around my legs. I cradled him in my arms and sank down on to the sofa. He purred for a while before springing off my lap haughtily. I didn't blame him, the sobs I had finally allowed to surface weren't exactly restful.

I couldn't cope. I didn't want to be on my own. My constant clock-watching was driving me mad. This time two years ago . . .

I needed Gemma. I had to talk to her. Tonight was the night. And anyway, what if William said something to someone about me being a widow? I'd feel terrible.

I punched her number into my phone and chewed the inside of my cheek while I waited to hear her bubbly voice.

Damn. It clicked through to voicemail and I thought I would expire with misery and frustration. I pressed the button to end the call and simply sat and stared at the screen, hoping that she'd call me back.

Yes! A text message flashed up at me.

Sorry, Tills, can't talk at the mo. Am at Kingsfield General Hospital. Mia has broken three toes and we're getting them strapped up. What did you want?

My chest heaved as I read her message. Good question. What did I want?

I typed a message back: Meet me later?

It would be hours before she was free. I didn't care. I'd wait until midnight if I had to.

My stomach was growling but I didn't want to eat. My body was tired, but I was restless and couldn't bear to watch the TV. I dragged myself upstairs, ran a bath, lit some candles and turned on the radio.

I twisted my hair up into a bun, submerged my body until only my ears were above the waterline and allowed the smooth voice of the radio presenter to wash over me.

There was a talk show on that I'd heard before. The presenter always asked the interviewee when things had changed for them: When had the singer got her lucky break? When had the athlete realized he had Olympic potential? When had the drug addict decided to get help? The answer was invariably, 'It was around the time when . . .' And that always struck me as odd.

'But when *precisely*?' I wanted to ask. 'Surely you must know?'

I knew and I wished with all my heart that I could un-know it.

October the fourth two years ago. That was when my life changed.

I closed my eyes and slowly, gradually, let the memories flood in.

James had taken the afternoon off work to take me to hospital. We'd stared incredulously at the screen while our baby wriggled and waved back at us. We'd gasped at the speed of the 'wow-wow-wow' sound of his or her insistent little heartbeat.

We looked at each other and our happiness was so all-consuming it was almost palpable, and even the radiographer was beaming.

'What do you think?' I whispered to James.

'I think our baby is beautiful,' he said huskily, placing a kiss tenderly on my mouth. 'Just like its mum.'

I had never loved my husband more than I did in that moment. Our future, the three of us, seemed so certain, so idyllic. I was going to be a mum and I was sure I had to be the luckiest woman alive.

It was his idea to drive straight over to his parents with the good news. We hadn't been planning to tell anyone yet, but as we skipped across the hospital car park that afternoon, arms around each other, both of us with a finger and thumb on the scan photograph, we were too impatient to wait, too desperate to share our baby joy.

James's dad wanted to open the champagne, of course. Just a small one, to celebrate, his mum had said. We ended up staying for dinner and at one point, I popped upstairs to a quiet room and phoned my mum. It didn't seem fair to leave her out.

'What shall we call you,' I asked with a giggle, 'next May when the baby comes, Nanny or Grandma?'

'Nana,' she'd replied instantly. 'I'll be Nana like in *Peter Pan*.'

We'd both cried and I didn't remind her that Nana was the big dog. It had been a gloriously happy evening.

By nine o'clock we were in the car. James's mum and dad waited on the doorstep to wave us off. It was pitch black and the windy rural road in Derbyshire where they lived was desperately lacking in street lights. I stuck my hand out of the car window and waved as James began to ease the car off his parents' gravelled drive.

The impact was immediate.

A car, travelling at speed, wrong side of the road on the bend, came from nowhere. It hit us on James's side, mounted our car, crushing my darling man while my hand was still in the air.

The thud, the spin, the airbags, screams, noise. My lungs screeching in terror, the blood racing through my body. And then nothing.

His parents had witnessed their only son's death and when I gained consciousness an hour later everything was gone.

My husband. My baby. Our future. All gone.

My mobile phone rang and I nearly had a heart attack. I propelled myself out of the bath with such force that most of the water joined me on the bathroom floor and I slipped as I grabbed the phone.

'Gemma,' I gasped with relief.

Chapter 27

Gemma had to be the world's best ever best friend. When I said meet me at Ivy Lane allotments she didn't question it. She just said she'd see me there.

I spread out a rug on my bench next to the shed, pulled my scarf tightly around my neck and waited.

The night air was still and incredibly clear.

Somehow, out here in the dark underneath a wide sky and a million glittering stars, James seemed tantalizingly close, his presence like a soft kiss, a warm breath on my face, a gossamer touch around my shoulders.

Love you for always, Tilly.

His voice swirled around me, filling my head, drenching my heart with an exquisite calm and even though I knew it was just the trees whispering their night-time lullabies, it felt wonderful.

I heard the approaching crunch of autumn leaves underfoot and then a blonde head appeared from behind her fruit trees.

'Magical mystery tour dot com!' laughed Gemma, planting a kiss on my cheek. She plonked herself down beside me and looked up at the sky.

Poor Gemma: she was heavily pregnant, she'd spent all

evening in the accident and emergency department (which, I realized, I'd not even asked about on the phone earlier) and was now traipsing through trees at the behest of her crazy friend.

'Is Mia OK?' I asked belatedly.

'Oh, what a palaver.' She shook her head and her curls bounced on her shoulders. Her hair was longer these days, although it seemed to grow outwards more than down. 'My massage client had a hot flush while I was on the loo and cried out to be rescued. Mia dashed in and grabbed the stones off her back. The client sat up, topless. Mia screamed and dropped the stones on her foot. It turned out the client was her old history teacher. She says the sight of that woman's droopy boobs was worse than the pain in her foot.'

We both laughed and I shuffled up closer to her and looped my arm through hers.

'What are we doing out here, then?' she asked shrewdly. 'Not that it isn't totally gorge on a night like this.'

'Sorry,' I said, breathing in her coconutty smell. 'I'm a nuisance, aren't I? But I really needed to talk to you. Just you and me.'

She looked sideways at me and smirked. 'I hope you're not about to reveal you've got a crush on me, Tills. Because I've got to tell you,' she pointed comically to her rounded tummy with both index fingers, 'I'm spoken for.'

I laughed awkwardly and Gemma blinked at me slowly.

'What would you say . . . ?' I faltered and the words caught in my throat.

Tell her, Tilly, trust her.

I exhaled deeply and turned to face my friend. Gemma stared back, all trace of laughter gone, her eyes full of tenderness, waiting for whatever it was I wanted to share.

She squeezed my hand and smiled encouragingly.

And so I began my story.

I leaned my head on her shoulder, she rested her head on mine and we both stared at the stars and I told her how I'd met James at university and how I'd known after one night that I would be his for ever. I told her about our woodland wedding, the tiny house we'd renovated together and how we'd been planning to move to Cornwall for his new job with the National Trust. And then I told her, my voice barely more than a whisper, about the baby, the car crash and the end of my perfect, perfect life.

The guilt was the worst thing. Guilt for being alive, for carrying on without them both. Every time I laughed or lost myself in the moment, seconds later the memory returned and a knife twisted in my heart as a sharp reminder. Each May, when our baby should be celebrating his or her birthday, I pined for the entire month about what might have been and on October the fourth I mourned what I had lost.

Widow. Bereaved. Alone.

And the flipside: guilt at not making the most of the life I had escaped with.

By the time I had run out of words, the moon had risen directly above us, my face was stinging as tears chilled against my skin and Gemma's body was trembling against mine, her grip tight on my fingers.

She took tissues from her pocket and passed me one. We both had a good blow and gazed at each other. I bit my lip and waited for her to speak.

'I'm so sad that you've had to go through that,' she said finally. 'And I'm so very proud of you for the way you've coped. You're such a strong person.'

I laughed softly at that and twisted the tissue into a tight rope. 'Rubbish. I hide from the truth. Look how long it's taken me to tell you all this. I'm too scared to trust, or to give anything of myself in case . . . in case it happens again.' I scanned her face, looking for answers. 'Maybe that was it for me. Maybe I've had my one chance of happy ever after.'

'No way.' Gemma shook her head. 'I don't believe that for a minute. In fact, I think you've done exactly the right thing. You've given yourself time to heal.'

She bent towards me and kissed my cheek.

Nobody had ever said that to me before. The counsellor, my mum, even James's parents – everyone had always been in such a hurry for me to Get Over It. To find a way through the grief and make it out to the other side.

I felt my shoulders sag and realized they'd been tensed up around my ears.

'Life twists and turns in directions that we can't foresee and don't always deserve,' she said. 'Nobody has it completely smooth but you've been through more trauma than most people will suffer in their entire lives. Physically, mentally, emotionally . . . It would have been weird if you hadn't withdrawn from relationships for a while.'

I thought about her life: falling pregnant at eighteen, re-mapping her career around her family and now, just as her life had seemed so settled, pregnant again. Less catastrophic, but no smooth journey either.

'How long, Gemma, how long will it take me to get over it?'

She sighed and took my hand in hers. 'I guess your past will always be with you. But,' she raised her eyebrows and gave me a tentative smile, 'I did notice a new glow to your cheeks when a certain TV director was around. I'd say that you're making excellent progress. When you're ready, you'll love again. I'm sure of it.'

'But what about James? When I move on, it'll be without him.'

'He was lucky enough to have your love for years. He wouldn't want you to put your heart on ice for the rest of your life.'

She wrapped her arms around me then and I leaned against her, returning her hug. We sat in silence for a few minutes while I let her words sink in and I knew she was right.

A brilliant white light appeared from nowhere, blinding my eyes. We both screamed and clung to each other. A second later there was a thud of heavy feet as someone jumped out in front of us. We screamed again.

The torch dipped to the ground revealing a tall man dressed in a dark jacket and a hat pulled down over his eyes.

'Bloody hell, you two!'

It was Charlie.

'For God's sake, Charlie,' I panted, 'you frightened the life out of us. You all right, Gemma?'

She was clutching at her heart, mouth open and gasping for breath. 'Nearly peed my pants, you idiot.'

He crouched down in front of us and flashed the torch from me to Gemma. 'Don't stop on my account,' he said with a grin. 'You've just made one of my fantasies come true.'

'Charlie!' squealed Gemma indignantly.

We both laughed and shoved him against his shoulders playfully and he toppled over on to his back into Brenda's ravaged potato patch.

'Ouch.' He brushed the leaves off his jacket and settled himself on the bench next to me. 'So. Any sign of him, then?'

Gemma and I exchanged blank looks.

'The mysterious vegetable thief,' said Charlie. 'Isn't that why you're here? I thought I'd prowl about in the dark and catch him red-handed. I heard rustling coming from the trees and came across you two doing . . . whatever you were doing.'

He raised his eyebrows hopefully. I ignored the implied question and rolled my eyes at him.

'You've decided to take matters into your own hands then and sort out the mystery once and for all?' I said.

He scratched his head through his hat and sighed. 'To be honest, I'm not that bothered about losing a few veggies, if someone's that desperate for them. But what I can't stand is all the suspicion, the whispering behind hands and finger-pointing. I just want us to all be friends again.'

I caught Gemma's eye and we both pulled 'aww' faces.

'You big softie,' I said, nudging him in the ribs. 'You don't think it's one of the community service lot, then?'

He wrinkled his nose and shook his head. 'Nah. Stands to reason it's someone with a key. And the only way they could get away with it is under cover of darkness.' He shone the torch under his chin to light up his features ghoulishly and gave an evil laugh.

'You're hardly going to surprise them if you keep flashing that thing around,' said Gemma.

'Good point.' He turned it off and laid it on the grass. 'So,' he said slapping his thighs, 'come on, tell Uncle Charlie. You are freezing your butts off in darkness because . . . ?'

I looked at Gemma and she nodded and squeezed my hand. I stared down at our hands, at her wedding ring and my bare fingers and took a deep breath.

'Charlie, there's something I haven't told you about myself. Before I came to Kingsfield, I was married to a man called James. Today is the anniversary of his death. Two years today. I didn't want to be alone.'

I'd said it. Now both of my friends knew. And as painful as it was to see the sadness in their faces, I was so relieved not to be keeping the truth from them any longer.

'Ffff . . .' He dropped his face into his hands, leaned forward until his elbows touched his thighs and groaned. The next instant I found myself crushed to him, his arms tight around my back, his breath in my hair, murmuring how sorry he was, over and over again.

'It's OK, Charlie. I'm OK.'

Gemma cleared her throat and stood up slowly. 'Shall I, er . . . ?'

I struggled my way out of Charlie's embrace. 'No,' I said and pulled her gently back down. I looked at my watch. Nearly nine. 'Please, stay a few minutes longer.'

'Tilly,' Charlie hesitated, 'I hope I haven't been, you know, out of order? Listen, forget about going cycling together. Oh God. If I'd known . . .'

I laid a hand on his chest. 'It's fine, Charlie. Really. But I just need friends right now.'

That wasn't completely true. My face burned and I was glad of the dark. I thought of Aidan and that magical moment in the summer when his lips had met mine. I needed more than friends in my life; I wanted to be loved, to know the happiness of being half of one whole again.

The three of us sat in contemplative silence, lost in our own thoughts, gazing up at the stars, linked by hands and friendship.

Suddenly Charlie's body tensed. 'Shush,' he hissed, reaching in slow motion towards the torch.

There was a rustling coming from Shazza and Karen's plot only a few feet away. I could just about make out a shadowy shape hunched low the other side of a row of bamboo canes.

'They might be dangerous,' whispered Gemma.

'Yes, don't be a hero, Charlie,' I added.

Charlie raised one eyebrow James Bond-style, eased himself off the bench and crept stealthily towards the intruder. Halfway up the path separating our plots, he lunged forward out of sight and shouted, 'Gotcha!'

There was some grunting and scrabbling and I heard a second voice swearing at Charlie to leave him alone.

'Come on,' said Gemma, wriggling to her feet.

Against my better judgement, given her condition, we advanced warily to see a pair of flailing legs pinioned underneath Charlie's bulk and slender fingers wrapped around two freshly dug leeks. I kept my arm through Gemma's to make sure she stayed on the path until we knew what we were dealing with.

'I can't breathe,' gasped a small voice. 'You're cracking all my ribs. I'll sue, you know.'

'He's only a lad,' panted Charlie, shining the torch into his prisoner's face. He hauled himself to his feet, dragging the slight figure up with him. He barely reached Charlie's chest, but he was doing his best to wriggle free.

'Hold on,' said Gemma, shrugging me off. She stepped over the remaining leeks towards the pair of them and peered into the boy's face. 'I know you, don't I? You're Lee, Frank Garton's son. You're in Mia's year at school.'

The Frank Garton? I leapt forward and pulled Gemma back to safety. He didn't look dangerous, but he could have had a knife for all we knew.

'So is it you, then, you little scumbag?' said Charlie, holding him by the hood of his hoody. 'Have you been stealing off everyone's plots?'

'I'll phone the police,' I said, patting my pocket to find my mobile. 'Keep well back, Gemma.'

I was expecting the teenager to duck backwards out of his hoody and do a runner any second. I'd seen that move with boys younger than him many a time in the school playground.

But I'd got it wrong this time. At the sight of my phone, Lee flung his arms round Charlie's torso and burst into noisy tears. 'Please don't tell the police. We'll all be put into care.' His voice was somewhere between a croak and a yodel – the curse of the teenage boy.

We three adults looked at each other and I slid the phone back into my pocket.

'We'd better go and have a chat,' said Charlie, jerking his head towards the pavilion.

Two hours later as I curled around my hot-water bottle in bed I still couldn't get the haunted look on Lee's face out of my head.

Over mugs of illicit tea in the pavilion we had heard the full sorry story.

It seemed that since Frank Garton had been in prison, his wife had taken to her bed with depression, leaving Lee to look after his four younger siblings. With no money coming into the house, things had got to the point where Lee simply didn't know where to turn to feed his family. When he found the spare key his dad had had cut for the allotment, he'd thought it was the answer to his problem.

He'd been missing school to care for his mum, keep the house clean and look after the little ones. His main worry, he told us, was social services getting involved, and the family being split up.

My heart ached for him. What a responsibility at only fifteen.

I had no idea how I was going to help him. But I definitely would.

I stretched an arm out in the darkness to touch the cool space on the empty side of the bed. It was late and I needed to be up early for work in the morning.

Nine o'clock had come and gone.

The earth had kept spinning, I had carried on living and that was exactly as it should be. I had my own place in the world and for the first time in two years, I didn't feel quite so guilty or alone being there.

Chapter 28

It was Friday evening and I had broken up for October half-term. Hurrah! Much as I loved All Saints Nursery and Infants School, I was very much looking forward to having some time to relax.

As soon as I got home, I had a shower, washed my hair and made myself a quick bowl of pasta. Yesterday's leftovers, which I'd intended to have, hadn't looked the least bit appealing. I'd had Gemma and Hayley round, unlikely trio you might think, but we'd bonded splendidly over pizza, a tub of Ben & Jerry's and my wedding album. We'd shed some tears, obviously, especially when Hayley found out about James and that I'd lost my baby, and then cheered ourselves up by watching *Bridesmaids*. Despite the emotional interlude, we had had fun, although I was pretty sure that Hayley would never be flippant about the implications of drinking and driving again.

It had been one of those eventful weeks at home and at school when before I'd had chance to react to one event, another had come along and sent my poor brain spinning off in a new direction.

My job-share colleague had made a sudden decision

to retire at Christmas and I had been summoned to Mrs Burns, the head teacher's office.

'Tilly, you would be doing me a huge service if you would consider applying for the full-time post,' Mrs Burns had said. 'There would be a formal interview, of course, but in all honesty, I can't think of anyone I'd rather have in the job.'

'I'm flattered,' I'd replied. In fact, I was thrilled! And although the prospect was a little bit daunting, the wonderful thing was that I knew I could do it. I enjoyed my job and the thought of having total ownership of a class certainly had its appeal. Mrs Burns had given me the half-term holiday to think it over, which was what I fully intended to do.

I'd had some good news for Lee Garton, too. A spot of discreet digging had unearthed a young people's soup kitchen based in a local church and now Lee and his brothers and sisters were sitting down to a hot meal each night after school. I'd also phoned his school and had a word with his head of year to get him a bit of support from that quarter. It wasn't a complete solution – I knew that – but it was a start.

Then Gemma had told me that she was giving up her half of plot sixteen and the committee wanted to know if I'd take it on. If it hadn't come along at the same time as the job offer, I probably would have taken it. Plot 16B had taken over my life this year, which had been exactly the right thing to do. But I wasn't sure if I wanted the allotment to become an even bigger commitment; I rather thought my social life was the next item on the agenda. I was really going to miss all the fun Gemma and I had had this year at Ivy Lane, though, and had extracted a pledge from her to visit me at least once a week to keep me company.

Since the fruit and vegetable thefts had stopped, Gemma,

Charlie and I had kept our promise and not breathed a word about it to the rest of the Ivy Lane community. The plot holders were still puzzled by what had happened but, by and large, peace and harmony had been restored. Brenda had apologized to everyone who she'd accused and the community service team had finally been welcomed into the fold.

And Aidan was coming back to Ivy Lane. Tonight.

At seven o'clock, every single Ivy Lane plot holder was crammed into the pavilion. A large television screen kindly donated for the evening by *Green Fingers* dominated one end of the room. My stomach was fluttering as I tried to locate my favourite TV director amongst the crowd when Vicky bustled past.

'You look nice, Tilly!' she said.

'Thank you.' I smiled and did a little twirl.

I wished I could say the same for my bedroom; it looked like it had been ransacked by the fashion police. What do you wear to a premiere of your very own episode of *Green Fingers*? It had been a difficult choice. On the one hand, it was only an evening in the pavilion, but on the other, Aidan would be there. Working on the principle that the last time I saw him I'd been wearing a dress and that seemed to have been a roaring success, I'd plumped for a plum-coloured wool dress with high-heeled boots.

My breath caught in my throat as I spotted him. Far side, bottom perched on the edge of a table, arms folded, ankles crossed, head thrown back in laughter, flanked on either side by Peter and Nigel. A sudden memory of our summer kiss popped into my head and my heart performed a perfect somersault.

His hair was a bit longer, his face deeply tanned – and he

had the beginnings of a beard, but apart from that he was every bit as I remembered: totally gorgeous.

Up until this moment, I hadn't been sure what my reaction to seeing him again was going to be and now I had my answer. Goosebumps, quickening pulse and hot cheeks.

Right, Tilly, if you get another chance with Aidan, do not burst into tears and do not turn him down again.

What was I thinking? He'd given me his number and I hadn't got in touch, why on earth would he risk rejection a second time? His card had been tucked into the corner of my mirror since August. But I hadn't phoned him. I'd thought about it – I'd even keyed in his number on one occasion – but something had held me back and I'd invented a million reasons not to call.

I was still chewing my bottom lip, quite possibly wearing my owl face, when he looked across and caught sight of me. I smiled and held my breath, waiting to see what he did next with his face.

He smiled and lifted his eyebrows and then to my absolute relief, murmured something to Nigel and Peter and bounded across.

I let out a long calming breath and smoothed the skirt of my dress.

'Hello,' I said, smiling shyly. My heart thumped, my mouth was dry and my hands floundered around uselessly. I clasped them behind my back. I could barely stop myself from swinging from side to side like a little girl.

'Hi. Nice dress.'

I met his eyes and he grinned at me knowingly. There was an awkward pause and we both giggled.

He cleared his throat and folded his arms. 'So how are you?'

'Good. You?'

So far no prizes for scintillating conversation. I couldn't speak for him, but I was incredibly nervous.

'How was Peru? How were the spectacled bears?' I pressed my lips together. I'd done my research.

He whistled softly. 'Incredible. And Peru was possibly the most amazing place I've ever worked in.'

'Even more amazing than Ivy Lane?' I raised my eyebrows.

'Well, Ivy Lane did have its attractions.'

We locked eyes and my heart absolutely soared.

'I'm sorry I didn't phone,' I said.

He grinned and shrugged. 'That's OK, it wasn't compulsory.'

Oh. My confidence slipped a notch. He didn't seem at all bothered.

Peter stuck his head between us. 'Sorry to interrupt, Aidan, but I think we'll get started if you're ready?'

'Sure.' Aidan touched a hand lightly to my arm. 'Shall we catch up afterwards?'

I nodded and watched him stroll to the front of the room.

Gemma waved to me and I took a seat next to her. 'Well?' she whispered. 'How does it feel, seeing him again?'

I looked at her and sighed. 'He's lovely. But I think I might have ruined my chances. I did harbour a hope that we might pick up where we left off. But now I'm not so sure.' I smiled at her sadly. She pulled a sympathetic face and squeezed my arm.

Shall we catch up afterwards?

A polite way to end our conversation? Or a genuine desire to talk to me again?

I had an entire episode of *Green Fingers* to get through before I'd have an answer to that.

'Evening, everyone,' said Aidan loudly above the babble of voices. He smiled and waited as people settled themselves into chairs.

'It's lovely to be back at Ivy Lane and see you all again. The *Green Fingers* crew had a great time here over the summer. Dougie,' he said, singling him out in the audience, 'Suzanna couldn't make it tonight, but she sends her best.'

'She hasn't forgotten old Dougie!' grinned Dougie, punching the air.

'So.' Aidan threw his arms wide. 'Your TV programme. We wanted to create something special with our allotment episode and we believe we have. I hope you'll be as delighted as we are.'

He crossed his fingers and held both hands up, pretending to be worried.

'The show will go out next Sunday night, but we thought you deserved to see it first. If you like it, please tell all your friends. If not, then I apologize and it can just be our little secret.' His brown eyes sparkled playfully and a rumble of laughter ran around the pavilion.

'So without further ado, as they say. The moment of truth!' He nodded to Christine as he started the DVD and she turned out the lights.

The *Green Fingers* theme tune came on, people wriggled in their seats and then silence fell as the pavilion, looking delightful in all its summer finery, filled the screen. Suzanna stepped into the shot and everyone cheered.

I stole a last furtive glance at Aidan as he found a seat and then focused my attention on the TV and waited for my first on-screen appearance.

I didn't have long to wait.

Only a minute into the show, a slightly frosty girl stomped across her vegetable patch, slopping water from a watering can, which she then upended all over a tiny cour-gette plant.

Gemma grabbed my arm and I had to cover my mouth to stop myself from squealing. There I was, hair tied up with string, mud-splattered trousers and boasting about my carrots. I looked so comical: a scruffy, feisty know-all with blotchy eyebrows. I wondered what on earth Aidan must have thought of me that first day.

I certainly hadn't been overly impressed with him then. I flicked my eyes towards him and studied his handsome profile; he had a gentle smile on his face and was completely absorbed in the show. I took a deep breath and turned back to the screen.

How things had changed.

The next hour flew by. I was totally captivated. The pro-gramme was utterly charming and portrayed Ivy Lane and all its characters in such a heart-warming and friendly way that I felt guilty for ever thinking that Aidan might have had some sort of hidden agenda.

We were a good audience, silent for the most part with only the odd cry of 'That's me!' as individuals saw them-selves on screen for the first time.

Aidan had done a superb job: each little tableau per-fectly captured the personality behind the plot, whether it was Liz waist-high in flowers, Christine explaining how to make bird-scarers or Dougie bottling some of his home-brew, and one particularly poignant moment when Alf ap-peared in his greenhouse. There were a few sniffs in the audience at that point.

Gemma nudged me with her elbow. 'Makes me yearn for the summer already.'

The show was nearly at an end and my face filled the screen yet again. This time I was at the annual show, smiling and laughing as I discovered I'd won second prize for my sweet peas.

'Me too,' I whispered, realizing how much I had blossomed at Ivy Lane this year. I slipped my arm through Gemma's and gave it a squeeze. It had been so good for me, taking on the allotment. So many wonderful memories.

Only hours after that scene had been filmed, I'd kissed Aidan for the first time. Possibly the only time. I looked back over to him; his features were in shadow with just the light from the screen flickering across his face. My fingers itched to stroke his face.

Why hadn't I phoned him? I could kick myself.

My solo life over the past two years had been a series of firsts and that evening had marked a massive turning point for me. The first kiss with someone other than my husband. Major moment for me, but for Aidan, who knows? He had been halfway around the world since then. He would have probably forgotten all about the kiss by now.

I felt sad all of a sudden and let out a weary breath as the credits rolled and everyone clapped.

The lights came back on and Aidan jumped back up to the front.

He held his hands out. 'Did you enjoy it?'

There was a chorus of appreciation. Peter added a formal word on behalf of the committee and Aidan clasped his heart with mock relief.

'Thanks to you my bosses are very pleased with me, so if it's all right with you . . .' He darted to a box at the side of the room and pulled out some bottles of champagne. 'I thought we'd celebrate.'

'You can't take your eyes off him,' whispered Gemma

five minutes later as she put a plastic cup of bubbly in my hand.

'I know you don't drink,' she said as I began to protest. 'Just hold it in case there's a toast.'

I took it from her. I hadn't touched alcohol since the night of James's death. My last drink ironically had also been a tiny glass of champagne. I hadn't thought I would ever stomach it again. I sniffed at it tentatively.

'Evening, girls,' said Charlie, waving a bottle in our direction. Gemma and I both shook our heads and covered our cups.

'What did you think?' I'd spotted him at the back with Roy but hadn't managed to speak to him so far.

He puffed his cheeks out and shifted his gaze to the floor. 'There was a lot of you in it,' he said, bringing his eyes to meet mine. 'Anyone would think the cameraman had a crush on you or something.'

I went bright red, swallowed and tried to come up with a witty retort.

'Ooh, Charlie, you are funny,' giggled Gemma, tapping his arm playfully and taking the spotlight off me.

Phew.

'Jeff was a total sweetheart, but I don't think he was interested in Tilly. No offence, Tills.'

'Could have fooled me,' Charlie muttered, taking a swig of his champagne.

Just as Gemma rolled her eyes at me, I felt a warm hand on my arm.

'Aidan!' I stammered, turning to meet his smile.

He lowered his head to whisper in my ear. 'Can we have that chat?'

So he really had wanted to talk me. Hurrah!

Charlie frowned and I flushed.

On the spur of the moment I took a sip of the champagne. The bubbles exploded exquisitely on my tongue.

I nodded to Aidan, handed my cup to Gemma, who slipped me a wink, and followed him to the door.

Chapter 29

Aidan held the door open and the two of us stepped outside into the cold night air. A thick fog had descended over the allotments, blanking out the world until all that was left was him and me.

I shivered and wrapped my arms around my body.

'I don't fancy driving in this,' he said, zipping up the neck of his jumper.

Invite him back to Wellington Street, then he won't have to.

'Me neither,' I giggled nervously. 'But then I haven't got a car so, er . . .'

Awkward silence. He raised his eyebrows and I had to stop myself from whistling to fill it. Tomorrow morning I was going to buy myself a new book. *How Not to Talk Twaddle in Front of the Opposite Sex*, or something along those lines.

There we were standing in the porch light, like a couple of teenagers after a date, me tongue-tied and nervous and him – well, I wasn't entirely sure, but his feet were fidgeting and he kept clearing his throat.

'Shall we go for a walk?' I gestured towards the road that led to the bottom of the allotments.

'Good idea,' said Aidan, sounding relieved.

Aidan fell into step beside me, our bodies close, but not

quite touching. We walked for a minute or so before either of us spoke. I felt eighteen all over again, nervous and timid, waiting for him to make the first move.

His hand brushed my sleeve, making my skin tingle and I almost gasped.

'Tilly?'

'Yes?'

I whirled round to face him and we stopped under a street lamp.

This was it; he was going to kiss me. I could hear my own heart beating.

The light cast an orangey glow over us and fog particles danced in its spotlight. The allotments were completely silent, as if the fog had wrapped everything in a layer of cotton wool. I wasn't even sure exactly where we were, there were no visible landmarks to give me any clues.

'What happened in August,' he began hesitantly, 'I hope I didn't frighten you off when I asked to see you again?'

Ask me now and I'll say yes.

'No. Well, not exactly. I . . .' Aidan gazed at me under the lamp light, waiting for me to elaborate.

This was my chance to set the record straight. I'd told everyone else, it should have simply been a matter of explaining about James, about all that had happened in my life to bring me to Ivy Lane. A bit of a conversation dampener, though.

I sighed instead and shook my head. 'It's complicated.'

'I see.' He nodded and his brow wrinkled slightly. 'It's just that you were pretty adamant that you didn't want to see me again and when you didn't call, I'd made my mind up to admit defeat. But . . .'

We took a tiny step towards each other.

'Yes?' I breathed.

'I decided to give it one last shot.' He chuckled, stared at the floor and then lifted his beautiful brown eyes to meet mine. 'I'll tell you a secret.' He leaned towards me and whispered conspiratorially, 'We don't normally arrange a special preview of *Green Fingers* prior to the show airing.'

'No?'

He shook his head sheepishly and stuck his hands in his pockets. 'It was an extremely convoluted ploy to see you again.'

'You did that for me?' I whispered. That was possibly one of the sweetest, most elaborate things anyone had done in order to see little old me. I thought I might burst with pride.

'Listen, I know I'm not much of a prospect, always flying off to the next project, never staying in one place for long. That's the nature of my job. Most of my stuff is wildlife.'

'Yes. Alf told me.'

Aidan groaned. 'I'm sorry. I should have said something earlier. I was very upset to hear about Alf. And Nigel said you found him?' He studied my face. 'That must have been awful for you.'

I nodded and swallowed a lump in my throat.

He pulled a hand out of his pocket and laid it gently on my arm.

'But the thing is, overall, I think I'm an all right type of guy,' he murmured softly. 'But if there's someone else in your life, then obviously I'll go my merry way and never darken your door again.' He gave a self-deprecating laugh. 'Look, I have to ask, is it Charlie? Are you and he . . . ?'

'No! Gosh, no!' I laughed and gasped at the same time and Aidan clasped his chest with mock relief.

The fog suddenly swirled and lifted and I realized that we were next to a clump of apple trees at the edge of Dougie's plot.

'Charlie and I are— Oh my goodness!'

Before I could fill Aidan in on the situation between Charlie and me, I spotted something out of the corner of my eye: just a short distance away I could see a pair of feet on the ground, with the worn soles facing upwards. As I stared, the rest of a prone body came into focus.

'Aidan, look!'

I dashed over and dropped to my knees, closely followed by Aidan. It was Dougie, lying face first in the soil, seemingly fast asleep.

'Dougie! It's me, Tilly, wake up!' I shook his shoulders, but he didn't make a sound. The beam of the street lamp didn't stretch this far and I could barely make out Aidan's face.

'I think he's unconscious,' he said.

'Get Karen from the pavilion, she'll know what to do, and see if you can find a torch.'

He jumped to his feet and hesitated. 'You OK?'

I nodded and Aidan sped off up the road.

'Come on, Dougie, wake up,' I pleaded. Still no response. I couldn't bear it if anything were to happen to him, especially coming so soon after Alf. A wasp buzzed low to the ground near his face and I wafted it away. 'You're not supposed to be out at this time of year,' I muttered crossly.

I leaned back to rest on the trunk of a tree. There were still fallen apples on the floor around my knees and I picked one or two up and threw them out of the way.

It seemed so awful leaving him in this position on the cold wet ground, but I didn't dare roll him over until Karen had taken a look. I gingerly reached for his hand and held on to it, hoping that somehow Dougie would know that I was there.

I heard the door to the pavilion bang in the distance and suddenly a herd of footsteps charged towards us, led by Aidan carrying a torch. Another wasp drifted by and I tutted as I flapped a hand at it.

'Over here,' I called.

The entire community had evacuated the pavilion and Karen had to push her way through to Dougie. She crouched down and felt for his pulse.

Charlie appeared and knelt down by my side. 'OK?'

'Fine, thanks,' I murmured.

'Here, I brought your coat. You must be freezing.' He laid it over my shoulders and I wriggled my arms into it.

'You're a star,' I groaned. The sudden layer of warmth was bliss. I hadn't realized just how cold I had been.

I sought Aidan in the crowd, but the beam from the torch blinded my eyes and I couldn't make out specific faces.

'He's probably passed out from too much of that home-brew,' said Vicky with a sigh.

Karen batted a wasp away and shook her head. 'I think he's gone into anaphylactic shock,' she said, rolling Dougie over and going through his pockets. 'Damn, he hasn't got his EpiPen.' She sat back on her heels. 'He's breathing, but it's faint. He needs hospitalization and he needs adrenalin fast.' She pulled her phone out of her pocket and began to punch numbers.

'I'd take him,' said Nigel, 'but I've been drinking.'

'I'll drive!' I blurted. I took hold of Dougie's hand again and squeezed it. I hadn't been able to do anything for Alf, but there was still time to save Dougie.

'You don't drive!' cried Gemma.

'No time,' said Karen, rolling Dougie into the recovery position, 'we need an ambulance.' She stood and turned away as she gave the information to the emergency services.

'I can actually,' I said in a shaky voice. 'I just haven't for a while, that's all.' Gemma locked eyes with me and I could see she understood.

I didn't drive. But I could. Our car had been a write-off and because I'd never replaced it, it had been easy to avoid driving. For a long time I was too traumatized even to be a passenger in a car.

I looked back down at Dougie and made a pledge with myself. It was time to get behind the wheel. What if this happened again? What if Gemma went into labour while she was with me? I owed it to myself and to others to be in a better position to help.

It must have been a quiet night for emergencies that evening because the ambulance reached Ivy Lane in record time. Two paramedics leapt out and within seconds Dougie had been given a shot of adrenalin. Karen had apparently been spot on with her diagnosis. Dougie was lifted on to a stretcher and hoisted into the ambulance. He'd regained consciousness, thank God. According to Christine, he had popped back to his shed to fetch a bottle of scrumpy because he didn't like the champagne. I bet he regretted that now. Christine offered to go in the ambulance with him and we stood back as it performed a three-point turn and sped off into the night.

'How did you know, Karen?' I asked as Shazza wrapped a proud arm around her partner's shoulders.

Karen rubbed a weary hand over her face. 'He once told me he was petrified of wasps because he was allergic to their sting. He normally carries a shot of adrenalin with him, but he must have thought he was safe in October.'

'Wasps are particularly vicious at this time of year,' said Aidan, stepping towards us. 'If Dougie stepped on their nest by accident in the fog, they would have gone berserk.'

'Really?' I said, feeling myself go all fluttery, the nearer

280

he got. 'Why's that? I thought they'd all died or hibernated by now.'

'Their queen will have abandoned them, flown off to start a new nest for next spring leaving the remaining worker wasps bereft and without a hierarchy.' Aidan blew on his hands and tucked them under his armpits.

'They make nests in the ground?' asked Shazza.

'Yup. And when there's rotting fruit lying around, they gorge themselves, get drunk and start looking for a fight.'

'Fascinating.' I gazed at him, wondering how on earth he managed to make the antisocial behaviour of wasps so . . . seductive.

We locked eyes and grinned foolishly at each other. *Now where were we . . . ?*

Our moment had been well and truly ambushed. And it had been going so well. I did a quick mental recap. Oh yes. He'd just done a fantastic job of persuading me that he was an 'all right guy' and I'd successfully – I hoped – convinced him that there was nothing going on between Charlie and me. Now if everyone could kindly leave us alone maybe we could pick up where we left off.

'Sounds like Kingsfield on a Saturday night,' said Charlie with a sniff, joining our little group. 'Well, that was all very dramatic,' he said, grabbing me round the shoulders with one arm and planting a kiss on my cheek. 'Just as well you two were out here, wasn't it?'

I tried to edge away discreetly, but Charlie held firm. He looked from Aidan to me. 'What were you doing out here, by the way?'

I felt my face heat up as Shazza, Karen, Charlie and Aidan all looked at me. Aidan raised his eyebrows, waiting for me to speak. My mouth had gone dry and words escaped me. What could I possibly say to that?

The moment stretched on interminably until Aidan cleared his throat.

'Evidently absolutely nothing,' he said. 'I'd better start packing up to go. Good night.' He nodded curtly, spun on his heels and with head bowed and hands in pockets strode off towards the pavilion.

My eyes brimmed with tears of frustration as I watched him disappear into the fog.

Nicely handled, Tilly.

There were a million things I could have said in answer to Charlie, any one of them better than drying up completely. No wonder Aidan had got the wrong end of the stick. I was an absolute disaster zone when it came to saying the right thing.

A sudden surge of emotion flooded me and I wriggled free from Charlie's grasp. Actually, I wasn't prepared to let this go. 'Aidan!'

I ran as fast as I dared through the blanket of fog. The door to the pavilion was open and light spilled out on to the road. I darted up the steps following the sound of voices. Aidan was dismantling the TV equipment and talking to Peter.

He glanced up briefly as I came in and then turned away.

I'd have preferred to be alone, but maybe this was better, maybe Peter being here would strengthen my case.

'Charlie and me . . .' I said quietly. 'We're just friends.'

Aidan flicked his eyes my way and made a noise somewhere between a grunt and a laugh. 'If you don't mind me saying—'

'I'll, er . . .' Peter pointed towards the kitchenette and made himself scarce.

'I think you're kidding yourself,' continued Aidan. 'I've seen how attentive he is. And the way he looks at me . . .' He shook his head. 'He obviously sees me as a threat.'

I couldn't deny that; I'd spotted Charlie giving Aidan dark looks myself, but I was amazed that Aidan had picked up on it too. A tiny part of me was thrilled, though. Jealousy, although not necessary an attractive trait, had to be a good sign.

'I'm sorry about that,' I said. I took a step closer until we were within touching distance. There were footsteps approaching the pavilion, I had mere seconds to get this right. 'But it's not reciprocated, I promise.'

Aidan took a deep breath and exhaled slowly. 'Then why is it complicated?'

'I—' I broke off as the hordes poured noisily back into the pavilion.

I pleaded with my eyes. *Give me another chance to explain, another time.*

He shrugged sadly and turned as Nigel slapped him on the back.

'It's our Hallowe'en party next Friday. We'd love you to come as our guest of honour, do the judging and what have you. If you're not jetting off somewhere exciting that is?' he said.

'Oh. Er . . .' Aidan looked at me.

My heart started to beat double time.

Say yes. Don't just think it, Tilly, tell him.

'Please come,' I said, holding his gaze.

'In that case, thank you, Nigel,' said Aidan quietly, still looking at me. 'I'd be delighted.'

'It's compulsory fancy dress,' added Nigel.

I grinned at the look of horror on Aidan's face and let out the breath that I hadn't realized I'd been holding.

Hallelujah.

Chapter 30

'Right, let's go through the plan again,' said Gemma, plunging a knife into her pumpkin with surprising force.

I grinned at her. 'OK. I leave a mysterious note on Aidan's windscreen inviting him to a secret love tryst in my shed and then I light the candles and wait for him to come and take me in his arms and, well, we know the rest, hopefully.' I giggled.

'TMI,' Mia interjected with a grimace.

'Sorry,' I laughed as Gemma rolled her eyes.

'Why don't you just drag him to your shed?' said Mia. 'Why all the secrecy?'

'Drag him?' cried Gemma. 'Is that the London Zoo school of romance, by any chance? Unromantic dot com, that's you.'

She tutted and bent back over her pumpkin. Mia responded maturely by sticking her tongue out.

'Well, I think it's sweet that you've got a crush . . .' said Hayley, leaving the rest of the sentence hanging. I narrowed my eyes. *At your age*, she'd been about to say, I knew it. She raised her eyebrows at me innocently.

There was another part to the plan, but we'd decided not to share it with the teenagers so as not to cause any embarrassment. I was aiming to have a quiet word with Charlie tonight; I would even tell him the truth about Aidan and me if necessary. I was dreading it, but despite everything that had happened during the past year, Charlie did seem to act rather over-protectively towards me and I wanted to let him down gently.

I was determined to get it right with Aidan this time. We had been very close, *so close*, to kissing before I'd spotted poor Dougie, who was now completely recovered and embarrassed about causing us all heart attacks. Not that I was getting desperate or anything, but if Aidan didn't kiss me tonight I would probably self-combust with unfulfilled lust.

It was five o'clock in the afternoon and so far today, I had had great fun. I had spent the whole day with Gemma – the first time we had ever done that outside of the allotments. She had picked me up this morning and driven me to Mike's car mechanics' business on the other side of Kingsfield. It was based in an old Victorian building with huge tall garage doors and ornate brick detail around the roofline. That was where the beauty began and ended though. The forecourt was littered with cars, cars and more cars in various states of repair. The brickwork was grimy, the ground was sprinkled with oily blobs and inside the garage the smell of petrol was over-powering.

The welcome, however, was warm and over a cup of builders'-strength tea, Mike told me about 'a little smasher' that had just come into his possession: a sunshine-yellow hatchback, low mileage, one careful lady owner and – though he said so himself – an absolute bargain.

And so with trembling knees, I took it out for a test drive. Mike, bless his heart, came with me. I imagine that he was every bit as nervous as I was given the circumstances, but if so he didn't let on.

I can't say that I was at ease at the wheel, but I had done it, that was the important thing, and after pottering at twenty miles an hour for fifteen minutes, I had delivered us safely back to the garage and the deal was done. All I had to do was sort out the insurance and once Mike had given it a thorough service, fitted new tyres and fiddled about under the bonnet I would have my very own car.

This afternoon had been all about getting ready for to-night's party. Hayley and Mia had joined us back at my house; Hayley, because she said she couldn't walk to the party in her outfit on her own, which was a bit worrying, and Mia because she idolized Hayley.

Thankfully since all that business over the thefts at Ivy Lane had been cleared up, Hayley and the other community service people had been made to feel a lot more welcome. Hayley had made friends in unexpected places and had even been helping Helen with her juice bar business. So far we'd watched Hayley make toffee apples with the last of the apples from my tree, Mia make dead men's fingers from rolled-up bread with almonds for nails and ketchup for blood and now we were carving pumpkins for the Best Carved Pumpkin competition.

I was glad of the company and the distraction; know-ing that I would be seeing Aidan again tonight at the Hallowe'en party had made it one of the longest weeks of my life.

'Wow, Hayley! That's amazing,' cooed Mia as Hayley attached an intricate stencil to her pumpkin and began punching holes through the skin with a screwdriver.

'Cheers,' said Hayley, her brow furrowed in concentration. 'I designed it on the computer. This pumpkin is a winner, I'm telling you. Which just goes to show,' she flashed us a grin, 'five years at secondary school to get two measly GCSEs – one in food technology and one in IT – were not totally wasted.'

'Mine looks pathetic in comparison,' said Mia gloomily. She had carved slanting, menacing eyes and a shark-like mouth full of pointed teeth.

'I think it looks well evil,' said Hayley.

'Really?' Mia glowed with delight.

'I hope I won't be penalized for having a small pumpkin,' I said, frowning at the size of my home-grown one compared to everyone else's shop-bought monsters. It was too small to risk carving a face into it, so I'd settled for an all-round pattern instead. Cute, but not scary.

Gemma shot me a sly smile. 'Seeing as the judge is a certain TV director, I don't think you need worry. There,' she sat up and swivelled her pumpkin towards me, 'what do you think?'

'Very you,' I said, smiling at its happy face.

My phone started to ring and I walked to the far side of the kitchen to answer it still smiling; only my mum used the landline, everyone else I knew rang me on my mobile.

'Hi, Mum!'

Mia and Hayley burst into laughter and I turned to see them trying to balance their pumpkins on their heads. Gemma rolled her eyes at me good-naturedly.

'Tilly, darling! How are you? Goodness, it sounds like you're having a party!'

'Great, thanks! I've got the girls round and actually we're getting ready for a Hallowe'en party at the allotment to-night.'

'Oh, no men then?'

'Mum!' I laughed, shaking my head at the disappointment in her voice. I didn't dare confide in her that with any luck my single days might soon be over; I didn't want to get her hopes up and I didn't want to tempt fate either.

'Anyway, how are you?' I asked in an attempt to steer the conversation away from my love life.

'Fine, fine,' she said dismissively. I could envisage her flapping a free hand at the phone. 'It's just that . . . well.' She paused to clear her throat. 'Women have . . . certain needs, you know.'

Oh God. I closed my eyes. I knew she meant well but I could really do without going into this at this precise moment, particularly with Mia and Hayley in the room.

'It's not healthy to be on your own for too long and sometimes . . .'

I smiled. Hopefully I wouldn't be on my own for too much longer. 'Mum, I appreciate your concern, really.'

Gemma's chair scraped on the kitchen tiles as she pushed herself up. She tapped her watch as she caught my eye. Time was ticking on and we still had to get into our fancy dress outfits.

'And you're right,' I continued. 'But could we talk about this later, do you think?'

'Oh. Of course, if you're too busy . . .' Mum sighed. 'But I really did need a chat.'

My heart sank. Now I felt guilty. 'I'll call you again soon, Mum, I promise.'

'All right, darling. Tonight perhaps?'

'Yes, when I get home, if it's not too late,' I said. *And if I'm alone*, I added mentally. My stomach fluttered with nerves as I told my mum that I loved her and ended the call.

At seven o'clock, two witches, a pumpkin and a vampire made their way to Ivy Lane allotments in Gemma's car. Hayley's sexy witch outfit would definitely turn heads. No wonder she hadn't wanted to walk through the streets on her own. My outfit, everyone agreed, was lovely. Call me vain, but I just couldn't bring myself to look ugly at a fancy dress party, regardless of the theme – not when the man I fancied would be there. I'd opted for a costume entitled 'cute witch', comprising purple and pink over-the-knee socks, a similarly coloured hat and a wench-style satin dress with a criss-cross bodice. My pocket-sized pumpkin completed the look perfectly.

Gemma was already pumpkin-shaped (her words, not mine) and all it had taken was to pull on an orange dress and a green bobble hat and she was ready. Quite frankly, Mia was too scary for my liking; not only had she dressed the part with white face, pointed teeth and a black cape, but she had assumed the sinister demeanour of a vampire too and kept sliding me sidelong glances and baring her fangs. I was glad to get out of the car by the time we got there.

'Thanks for today,' said Hayley, flinging her arms round my neck. 'And don't forget to come and get your juices. Especially you, Mia, you're looking very pale.' She winked and dashed off to help Helen set up the juice bar.

Mia sighed adoringly as she watched Hayley totter off across the car park in her patent leather thigh boots. 'She's so cool.'

'Hmm.' Gemma loaded a large pumpkin into her daughter's arms and placed a hand on the small of her back. 'That's very true, as well as unemployed, with a criminal record and precious few qualifications to her name.'

'She's a good kid,' I said defensively, although I could understand why Hayley might not be Gemma's idea of a role model for her teenager. I collected the bag containing the toffee apples and dead men's fingers from the boot and tucked my pumpkin under my arm. 'She'll turn out all right, I think, she just hasn't found her niche yet.'

'You're a good person, Tilly,' Gemma said, slamming the boot of the car. 'You see the best in everyone.'

I smiled, remembering a very similar conversation I'd had with Alf no more than a month ago.

I'd learned to trust again, that was all.

Mia dashed on ahead and Gemma and I schlepped across the car park weighed down with Hallowe'en goodies.

'So what do you reckon then,' said Gemma, 'ghost, skeleton, zombie?'

'You've lost me,' I said with a frown.

She rolled her eyes. 'Aidan, of course. What do you think he'll dress up as?'

My stomach lurched just thinking about him. After seven long days, the wait was finally over. 'I don't care as long as he's still recognizable,' I giggled. 'Gosh, I don't even know what car he drives. How am I going to pick the right windscreen to leave the note?'

We'd reached the pavilion steps and a sudden bout of cold feet took hold and stopped me in my tracks.

'Gemma,' I groaned, 'what if this plan goes spectacularly wrong? What if I make a mistake?'

She rested her pumpkin on the top step and stood up to catch her breath. 'Relax, Tills. You look gorgeous, you know he likes you, so, you know, just go with your heart.'

I took a deep breath, put on a bright smile and walked up the steps and into the pavilion.

Chapter 31

I arranged our party food contributions at the buffet table, lit a candle in my pumpkin lantern and left it to be judged while I chatted to everyone there, comparing outfits and listening to them moan about Trick or Treaters, but all the while giving only ninety per cent of my attention. The other ten per cent was scanning the room nervously looking for Aidan. But unless his fancy dress costume was exceptionally shape-altering, he hadn't arrived.

My spirits drooped a little and I accepted a glass of witch's brew from Rosemary to cheer myself up.

'No Colin tonight?' I asked, smiling at Rosemary's Catwoman outfit.

She shook her head. 'He's away on a photo-shoot,' she said proudly. 'For men's underwear,' she added, lowering her voice.

'Wow, how exciting!' I said, taking a sip. It tasted sweet and fruity and if there was any alcohol in it, I was sure it was fairly innocuous.

'Although I hope he doesn't bring any of it home with him, there was nothing in the catalogue he showed me that I should be able to hang on the washing line!'

I smiled at her. So Colin had finally trusted his mother

with the truth about his job. 'Any idea what Peter is dressed as?' I said, searching in vain amongst the bats, ghosts and skeletons. 'I need a word.' He would know what had happened to Aidan.

'A gorilla,' she laughed, shaking her head.

I found Peter, glass in hand, talking to Nigel, who was dressed as Frankenstein, and Christine, who was in a black polo neck jumper and jogging bottoms, her black wellies and a bat mask.

I cleared my throat and tapped him on the shoulder. 'Peter, have you heard from Aidan?' I whispered. 'Is he still coming?'

The gorilla's shoulders slumped. 'How did you guess it was me?'

'You're holding your little finger away from your glass.' I grinned. 'I've never seen an ape with such manners. It could only be you.'

'Ah, of course.' The gorilla nodded slowly. He leaned forward and hissed vaguely in the direction of my ear. 'He's running late. Bad traffic, apparently.'

But he was still coming. I exhaled with relief. Hayley caught my eye and waved me over.

She and Helen had set up a table selling freshly made juices. The business idea appeared to have come on in leaps and bounds since September.

'What do you think?' said Helen, extending a hand to her new logo, pinned to the front of the table. *Nature's Nectar*, it read and then in smaller letters underneath, *Organic juices*. 'Hayley designed it for me,' she said, passing me a leaflet, 'and this.'

I gazed at Hayley proudly. She had come a long way since her first day at Ivy Lane. She had finished her community service now and I had to admit, I was going to miss her.

'You, young lady, are a woman of many talents.'

She rubbed her neck and stared at the floor. 'Cheers. It's something to put on my CV, which let's be honest isn't very impressive at the moment.'

'I've got a stall at a farmers' market in a few weeks,' said Helen, tucking her hair behind her ears. She pointed at the leaflet in my hand. 'The address is on here. It was Gemma's idea. I can't believe it, my own business – it's a dream come true!'

'I'll come and support you.' I swallowed. That could be my first outing in my new car. Yikes.

Helen smiled shyly. 'Thank you, Tilly I'd like that. Graham will be there too, but he'll mostly be looking after Honey and it will be lovely to see you.'

I turned back to Hayley. 'So, what about you? What's your dream?'

'I quite fancy being a chef.' She shrugged. 'Any job in food would do. I like helping Helen, but she can't afford staff at the moment.'

A ghost with Brenda's unmistakable red lipstick poking through a hole in its white shroud wafted over. 'Hiya, I'll have banana and strawberry please.' She handed over some money and Helen leapt into action with the blender.

'I might be able to help you out there, Hayley,' said Brenda, adjusting her sheet to get a better look at her. 'Fancy a few hours at the potato oven? Full training provided. Month's trial and then see how we go.'

Hayley and I exchanged looks. That was unexpected.

Brenda cleared her throat. 'You youngsters need a bit of a leg-up to get your careers started,' she said, paraphrasing Alf all those weeks ago, 'and I've noticed you're a hard worker. What do you say?'

I gave Hayley a hug and left her and Brenda to sort out

the details. Hayley would flourish under Brenda's tutelage, I was sure of it. I sighed with satisfaction at another job ticked off my list and checked round the room for Aidan again. Now if I could just manage to sort out my own life, everything would be fine and dandy . . .

And then I spotted him: a tall figure dressed as the grim reaper, edging his way towards me through the crowd, trying not to take anyone's eye out with his scythe. It had to be Aidan. My breath caught in my throat and it was all I could do not to throw my arms around his hooded neck.

No more misunderstandings, Tilly. Be absolutely clear how you feel.

'You made it,' I beamed, 'I've been so looking forward to seeing you.'

He stopped in front of me and extended a long bony finger. 'I've come for you,' he said in a menacing husky voice.

I shivered. 'All right, you can stop now,' I laughed shakily, 'you're scaring me.'

He hooked his scythe playfully round my neck and brought my face to his. He had really gone to town with his outfit, even his eyes had devilish red and black coloured lenses in them.

'You must have been quite a sight, stuck in traffic, dressed like that. I'm surprised you didn't cause any accidents!'

'My shift didn't finish until seven.' He dropped his hood back. It was Charlie. My disappointment was almost crippling. It was obvious, now I looked more closely; he was tall like Aidan but broader. My eyes had simply seen what they'd wanted to see. And what was worse, instead of repeating the 'just friends' conversation, I'd just given Charlie a very warm welcome indeed. So far my plan was going abysmally wrong.

'Who said I was stuck in traffic?' He frowned.

'Er. . . gosh, I . . .' I was saved further embarrassment, momentarily at least, by a tap on the arm. Aidan had materialized by my side.

'Wow! Tilly, you're the most beautiful witch I've ever seen.' He was dressed as a wizard, a very friendly wizard, with snowy-white beard, long purple robe and silver slippers with turned-up toes. 'Sorry I'm late.' He leaned forward and kissed my cheek.

A kiss. On my cheek. As brazen as you like. What if I'd turned my face to him at that precise moment and it had landed on my lips? What if I'd actually had a bona fide, public kiss right then? God, I wish I had.

'I've been stuck in terrible traffic,' he was saying.

My cheek burned where his lips brushed against my skin. In fact, my whole face was burning. It was so good to see him. His eyes were warm like molten chocolate and in spite of the fact that the beard hid most of his face, I think he was pleased to see me. I gave him a breathy smile and turned back to Charlie.

My smile faltered. His jaw was set firm and his eyes unblinking. He looked from me to Aidan and pulled his hood back up. 'I'm off to do some reaping.' And he stalked off.

Aidan pulled a face. 'A bit sinister, that outfit.'

Out of the corner of my eye, I saw Frankenstein advancing towards us. I would lose Aidan to his official duties at any moment. It was already eight o'clock and time was slipping away. The note that I'd written to put on Aidan's car was burning a hole in my bodice and I'd still not had a chance to have a word with Charlie. Although judging by the look on his face as he'd swept away, I might not need to say anything. Still, best to be on the safe side, I couldn't allow for even the slightest margin of error if this crazy plan was to have a chance at working.

'I bought a new car today,' I said, keeping one eye on Nigel.

'Oh . . . good,' replied Aidan, looking surprised by the change of topic. 'What sort is it?'

'A little yellow one.'

'Right.' He grinned. 'I know the sort.'

'What's yours?' I garbled. Nigel already had a hand raised in greeting.

Aidan chuckled softly. 'A medium-sized, silver one.'

'Aidan!' Frankenstein pumped the wizard's hand enthusiastically. 'You made it.'

'Type?' I tugged on his purple robe.

Aidan grinned. 'What's this, *Top Gear*? An Alfa Romeo.'

'Sorry to drag you away,' said Nigel, 'but some of the pumpkins' candles are already starting to flicker. So if you could judge those first while I get you a drink and then you can have a wander round to judge the best fancy dress.'

'No problem,' said Aidan affably. 'Catch you later?'

My heart swelled at the prospect and I nodded. 'Oh!' I grabbed his hand as he moved away. 'One more thing.'

'Engine size?' His lips twitched.

'Take special notice of the large pumpkin with the Moroccan lantern design,' I whispered. 'That one was Hayley's. I would so love her to win; it would be the icing on the cake for her tonight.

He raised his eyebrows. 'Tut tut, Tilly Parker!'

He bent his head down to mine and I felt his warm breath on my mouth. My body lifted towards his on autopilot and for one knee-trembling moment I thought he was going to kiss me again. 'Shame on you for trying to influence the judge's decision,' he murmured against my

296

lips before disappearing after Nigel towards the pumpkins.

I stumbled back, lightheaded after such a sensuous exchange and bumped into Gemma.

'Blimey, look at you with your glittering eyes!' she exclaimed.

I grabbed her hands and squeezed. 'I know!' I said, my voice barely more than a squeak. 'I'm so excited I think I'm going to burst.'

Gemma chuckled. 'Unlike Mia. Apparently we're all half-dead and she's even bored with Hayley now she's gone – and I quote – all *Dragons' Den* with Helen.'

'Where is she now?'

'She had a text off a friend to go trick or treating, so she left. Anyway. Back to you. How is Operation Aidan going?'

'So-so,' I said, drawing her close to me. 'I know what sort of car he's got now. But I've discovered a fatal flaw in the plan. How do I get him to go out to it? I could be sitting out in a candlelit shed for hours on my own. What if he doesn't go back out to his car until it's time to leave?'

'Mmm.' Gemma chewed on her lip thoughtfully. Her blonde curls had escaped from her green bobble hat and curled round her face – she looked like a little cherub in an Anne Geddes photograph. 'I know, you give me the nod when the note is in place and I'll ask him for a business card. He won't have one under his wizard's dress and he'll have to go back to the car. Simple.'

I um'd and ah'd a bit but in the absence of a better idea, I had to agree.

She elbowed me and winked suggestively. 'Hey, I wonder what he's got on under there. You will tell me, won't you? I'll see you later.'

The thought was rather distracting, so much so that I forgot to ask her what reason she could possibly give for wanting Aidan's card. I watched her walk over to the buffet table and made my way to the door.

My witch costume, though indisputably cute, was sadly lacking in pockets and I'd had to tuck the note between the ribbons of my purple bodice. I fished it out as elegantly as I could and gripped it with both hands.

Charlie was propping up the doorway, biting into a sausage roll, looking strangely at ease in his harbinger of doom outfit. I faltered at first, but then pressed on until I was right under his nose, shoving the note hastily back into its hiding place. My news might have been unpleasant to deliver, but deliver it I must.

Staring into the red eyes of the devil did not help matters one bit.

'Charlie?' I thought I'd better check, just to be on the safe side.

'Hi.' That was a mumble. I couldn't be sure if it was a mouthful mumble or a bad mood mumble, but it was at least definitely Charlie.

'Charlie, please can we be completely honest with each other?'

He bowed his head and nodded.

'I really like you,' I began carefully, offering him a smile.

'I really like you, too.' He reached for my hand.

I couldn't help it; I glanced over my shoulder to check whether we were being watched. Aidan was bent over the pumpkins narrowly avoiding setting fire to his beard. I let out a tiny breath of relief and turned my attention back to Charlie.

'I might be barking up the wrong tree here . . .' I hesitated and gazed up at him. He had such lovely expressive eyes normally, all sparkly and blue. I'd never appreciated how important eyes are to a conversation before now. They say so much without saying a word, a window to the heart. What was going on in his head now?

'But I think I may like you differently to the way you like me.' I pulled my bottom lip between my teeth and waited.

To my utter relief, Charlie's face broke into a smile and he lifted one shoulder casually. 'You just want to be friends at the moment, right?'

'Yes,' I almost gasped in relief. 'Just friends.'

'Listen,' he said, leaning down towards me and linking my fingers through his. 'What you've been through – losing your other half – takes a lot of getting over. It stands to reason you aren't ready for another relationship. But I want you to know,' he paused and squeezed my fingers tightly, 'I'm here for you. And I'll wait.'

I gulped and nodded and to my eternal shame, I didn't drive the point home further. I excused myself on the pretext of needing the loo and fled from the pavilion.

Chapter 32

The car park was full but luckily there was only one Alfa Romeo, a sporty looking thing with shiny wheels and brown leather seats. It was a world away from my new yellow baby. I admired the car for a moment, popped the note under the windscreen wiper and nipped off to the loo.

I locked myself in the cubicle and tried to be as quick as I could. The outdoor loos were very handy in summer, but a bit cold for skimpily dressed witches at Hallowe'en.

So. The note was in place.

Meet me in the shed, plot 16B x

Now that I'd deposited the note, I began to worry that I hadn't written the right thing. Was it too forceful? I'd kept it fairly nondescript in case it fell into the wrong hands but maybe I should have written something more seductive, more romantic perhaps? Plus I'd sort of assumed that he'd remember that that was my plot. Which in the cold light of day, or evening, was perhaps a bit presumptuous.

Oh well, too late now. I washed and dried my hands and darted back across the car park, shivering in the chilly night air towards the pavilion. I flicked my eyes quickly towards Aidan's car to reassure myself that it was on the right car. Which was ridiculous, of course it was . . .

I gasped. The note had gone! Aidan must have gone back to his car for something. Now he was possibly there at my shed before me! This was all going wrong!

Hell's bells, I was not cut out for romantic liaisons, I thought as I pegged it up the road towards my plot, hanging on to my witch's hat for dear life. I arrived at the shed, puffed out and sniffing from the cold. There was nobody there. I didn't know whether to be relieved or disappointed. Either way I was freezing.

I unlocked the shed with a key on a string round my neck and escaped out of the cold for a moment while I collected my thoughts.

OK. Deep breaths and panic not. Concentrate on the facts.

Fact One: Aidan has the note. Hurrah! I gave myself a mental round of applause for at least getting something right.

Fact Two: he is not here yet. *Yet* being the operative word. He was probably still busy. In all likelihood, he had just popped to his car for something, a pen maybe, seen my note and had to return to the pavilion to . . . I don't know . . . finish judging the fancy dress or something. But he would come, I was sure of it.

Fact three: no way was I sitting here in the shed, in the dark, for much longer. It was damp, musty, smelled of fertilizer and I was probably surrounded at this very moment by three thousand pairs of spiders' eyes.

I glanced out of the shed window furtively. Nothing. No one. And especially not a tall purple wizard. I locked the shed, scampered back towards the pavilion and re-joined the party, hopefully unobserved.

The stiff point of a purple wizard's hat led me to my quarry. Aidan was circulating with a clipboard and a pen, jotting notes as he walked. Ha. Just as I thought, still busy with the judging. Nothing to be concerned about at all. And now he was in possession of the note it was simply a matter of time.

I tapped his arm and smiled at him coquettishly when he turned to me.

'Have you nearly finished?' I said, batting my eyelashes. My first flirtatious manoeuvre in a very long time. I hoped it passed muster.

'Almost,' he said with a wink. 'No peeking at the judge's notes please.'

'OK,' I giggled. 'How long will you be, five minutes, ten?'

'You're very giddy tonight,' he laughed.

'Well,' I said, fiddling with my ribbons, 'I'm looking forward to later.' I quirked an eyebrow at him.

'I won't be long, just judging the costumes now,' he said, nudging his wizard hat up out of his eyes. 'Then shall I grab us some drinks?'

I nodded happily and let him carry on with his task. Bless him, he was taking his judging role very seriously. Now that Mia had gone, Charlie was the obvious winner as far as I was concerned. Those coloured lenses were the scariest thing I'd ever seen. In fact, I'd be lucky not to have nightmares tonight. Unless of course Aidan gave me something sweet to dream about . . .

I was jolted from my reverie by Christine, who thrust another glass of punch in my hand. Her bat mask was now firmly in place, presumably while the judging took place.

'I love seeing the place packed like this,' she said, clinking her glass against mine. We both took a sip. I gasped and choked.

'Me too,' I wheezed. 'Goodness, I think this stuff has got stronger!' I'd broken my alcohol abstinence recently and had discovered chocolate-flavoured Baileys. I blamed Hayley, she had brought a bottle round. But so far I had only had the odd tipple. This stuff tasted lethal.

Christine tutted. 'That bloomin' husband of mine,' she chuntered. 'Two minutes I left him in charge of the punch-bowl. Take it steady, love, he'll have poured a bottle of Hennessy into it, so he will. Anyway, as I was saying. More events, more chances to get the community together, that's what we need.' She eyed me sideways over the rim of her glass.

'Well,' I said, choosing my words very carefully. I'd fallen foul of her cunning ways before by saying the wrong thing. I was determined not to get talked into anything. 'Put on more events.' Note, I did not say *We could*. It was an instruction, not an offer of help.

It seemed to have worked.

'Go on,' she nodded, her bat mask quivering with enthusiasm.

'Er . . .' I racked my brains. I knew what worked in schools but this was a much older age group. 'A bonfire party, too late for this year, of course, but you could have a Guy Fawkes competition. Or what about a summer garden party? And a Christmas Fayre is a must, I'd say.'

'And you'd like those things, would you?' She was still nodding.

'Oh yes, absolutely!' I confirmed, risking a second sip of the punch.

'Grand!' She threw an arms around my neck and kissed my cheek. 'We were looking for a bit of help on the committee. Someone younger. That's grand!'

My shoulders sagged. She'd done it again. Christine bustled off, presumably to give the good news to Peter. Gemma took her place at my side.

'Did you see what just happened?' I looked at her gloom-ily.

'Yes, but never mind that, have you planted the note?' she hissed.

'Yes and he's picked it up!' I hissed back.

'Has he?' She frowned and then her face cleared and she shrugged. 'Must have been when I was in the kitchen. Well, go on then.' She jerked her head at the door. 'Go and drape yourself over the chaise longue, he can't be much longer.'

'OK.' I knocked back the last of the punch. 'Wish me luck.'

'Don't do anything I wouldn't do,' she whispered.

We both looked at her tummy and then back at each other and laughed.

Suddenly the sight of her bump tugged sharply at my heart strings and my eyes pricked with tears. I felt a vision from my past beginning to form and I threw my arms round Gemma and shut my eyes tight to blink it away.

It's no use worrying about the life you can't have . . .

'You're going to be fine, Tilly,' murmured Gemma close to my ear.

I pulled away, squared my shoulders and gave her a bright smile. 'Right. I'm off. Definitely.'

And with a backward glance at Aidan, I set off into the night for a second time.

Chapter 33

Nerves steered me towards the loos again first and then I skirted the pavilion and walked to the road. This time, without the panic to reach the shed ahead of Aidan, I took the walk at a much more ladylike pace. The downside to this was that my brain had time to take in my surroundings: it was cold and silent, the only sound being the echo of my boots, clip-clopping eerily along the tarmac and the occasional rustle of the trees. I shivered and walked faster. What this outfit lacked, I realized, was a swirling purple cape to keep me warm. The sooner I could light those candles and wrap myself in my picnic blanket the better. I glanced behind me for any sign of Aidan, but the road was empty.

Still chatting, no doubt. I smiled to myself. It was a pity he hadn't noticed me leave really, then he could have made his excuses and escaped immediately. Oh well, he would join me soon, I was sure.

I'd waited so long for this moment and I couldn't wait to feel his arms around me again away from the well-meaning but curious eyes of the Ivy Lane community. I was thrilled with myself for taking the lead and concocting this plan. There was something exciting about a secret rendezvous and no better way to show Aidan that he was special to me. My heart was already fluttering in anticipation.

I stepped off the road and on to the grass path that led along plot sixteen to my shed. The sound of a stick cracking in the trees beyond my plot made me yelp with shock and I pressed a hand to my mouth.

For goodness sake, Tilly, it was probably just a fox.

I forced myself to breathe calmly but then instantly stopped in my tracks and stared ahead. There was an orange glow shining through my shed window. I had definitely not left a candle burning; I distinctly remember being in the dark. Which meant that someone else must have done it.

Oh my God. This was so spooky. My entire body was trembling and bristling with goose pimples. I had the urge to run. But which direction, towards the shed or away?

A nervous laugh bubbled up through me and I shook my head. All this Hallowe'en nonsense was making me overreact. It must be Aidan in the shed! He must have followed me immediately after all and arrived while I was at the toilets.

'Phew,' I said aloud and darted to the shed. The key on its string banged against my chest as I ran. Oh, how had he opened the door? I tutted at myself. I had obviously forgotten to lock it.

I paused at the door to compose myself, dabbed under my eyes to remove any smudged make-up and ran my fingers through the ends of my hair to smooth it over my shoulders. A smile spread across my face as my fingers wrapped around the door handle.

This is it. A new chapter. Go for it, Tilly Parker.

The smile, which was probably more accurately a radiant beam, was still going strong as I pushed my way into the shed with a triumphant, 'Ta dah!'

The shed was empty. My face crumpled in confusion as I turned towards the source of the light. At the far end of the shed three pumpkin lanterns adorned my little table, but the sides facing outwards weren't carved. With a pounding heart I twisted each one round. The first had simply the letter 'I' carved out of it, the second a loveheart and the third the word 'you'.

I love you.

I stared at the message, my brain whirring and my heart thumping. Aidan loved me? This was all moving very fast, surely we weren't at the stage for this sort of declaration? It was an incredibly romantic thing to do, not to mention complicated to organize. And regardless of whether the timing was right or not, I was truly touched by the effort he had gone to.

Maybe I was reading too much into it. Perhaps I wasn't supposed to take it too literally. Perhaps that had just been easier than carving 'would you like to go for dinner?' Of course, that would be it, I chuckled to myself with relief. As my eyes adjusted to the light, I noticed a piece of folded paper. A note. I picked it up. It was the note I'd left for Aidan. But where was he?

I was still holding it between my fingers when the door behind me opened softly.

I whirled round, my pulse racing to see Aidan with a warm smile, his eyes crinkling with humour.

'My hat's too tall to get under the doorframe.' He took off his pointed hat, stepped through the doorway and in two strides was standing right in front of me.

'Thank goodness, I was wondering where you'd got to.'

He chuckled. 'Well, the bad news is, you didn't win the fancy dress competition.'

'Ah,' I pouted. 'Who did?'

'Gemma. She looked so jolly and pumpkin-like, I had to give it to her. But I did choose your pumpkin as the winner. That Moroccan design was incredible.'

'Hayley's. Not mine.' I grinned. 'I wanted her to win.'

'Oh!' His face softened. 'You're all heart.'

We stared at each other and I held my breath, savouring the nearness of him, his delicious smell, his eyes, his rumpled hair. It was all I could do not to jump into his arms.

'Hello, you,' he murmured. His eyes flicked to the pumpkins briefly and then back to me and I almost said something there and then, but the electricity between us was flying and I couldn't bring myself to break the spell.

His brown eyes gazed at me as he lowered his head to mine. Suddenly I couldn't wait any longer and I let the note flutter to the floor. I plunged my hands into his hair and brought his lips to meet mine. I kissed him hard with a newly found confidence and immediately he returned my kiss, looping his arms around the small of my back, lifting me, pulling me into him so that our bodies were practically one. Still wanting to be closer, I guided him backwards, towards the side of the shed until he was leaning against the wall. I pressed myself against him until I heard him groan with pleasure.

Breathless, my body on fire with desire, I pulled back, a smile playing on my lips.

'Don't look now,' I murmured, 'but I think I just made your toes curl!'

We giggled as he wriggled his silver slippers.

'Thank you for that welcome,' he said with a soft laugh.

I think I'd shocked him. I'd shocked myself, come to that.

'Thank you for the message,' I whispered, grazing my

lips against his stubble as I planted a row of kisses along his jawline.

'What message?' He slipped my hat off and brushed my hair off my face with his fingers.

'The pumpkins.' I pressed my lips together in a cheeky smile. 'Rather forward, I thought.'

A cloud passed over his face and his hands slipped from my hair. He straightened up and I stepped back from him. The hairs on the back of my neck tingled and I instinctively knew I'd said the wrong thing.

'Nothing to do with me.' He frowned. 'In fact, I was thinking the same thing. I assumed you had carved them.'

I swallowed. Someone else had been in my shed. Who? Hayley, Mia or Gemma? But they would have told me, besides which they couldn't have brought any extra pumpkins here without me knowing. Which only left . . . My heart sank. It had to be Charlie.

I sighed and rolled my eyes. 'Look, it'll just be Charlie, messing about . . .'

Aidan fixed me with a stare. 'Charlie? That figures.'

'But you got my note. Look!' I picked up the piece of paper from the floor and handed it to him.

'Meet me in the shed, plot sixteen B, kiss,' he read. He frowned at me and shrugged. 'I've never seen this.'

The humour had completely disappeared from his face and the kiss we had shared already seemed like a lifetime ago.

'So why come to the shed?' I asked.

'Gemma sent me. She said you'd get hypothermia if I didn't hurry up. I didn't even know you were waiting for me.'

I placed my hands on his chest tentatively, desperate to

undo the damage of the last few seconds. 'Look,' I said softly, 'there's just been a bit of a mix-up, that's all. We're both here now so—'

'It's always Charlie, isn't it?' he said sadly, peeling my hands from him. Our fingers were loosely entwined but I didn't dare tighten my grasp.

'I told you there's nothing between him and me. Don't you believe me?'

'"It's complicated" – that's what you said to me last time we met.' He sighed and shook his head. 'Maybe if your life is so complicated, there's just no room in it for me.' He folded his arms and looked at his feet.

So this was it. Our love affair, cut short before it even had a chance to grow.

'Few delights can equal the presence of one whom we trust utterly,' I quoted my calendar from weeks ago. His unblinking eyes met mine, desire replaced by disappointment. 'And you don't trust me, do you, Aidan?'

I couldn't bear to hear his response. I darted back out into the night and ran.

My heart didn't stop racing until I was back in the pavilion. I spotted Gemma, chomping her way through a cake-pop decorated to look like an eyeball.

'You look shattered,' I said, pulling her to her feet. 'Let's go home.'

Gemma took one look at my face and marched me to the car. Well, she marched, I stumbled with tears blinding my eyes.

We climbed in and as she put the key in the ignition she turned to face me.

'Not here,' I said, before she could speak. 'Just drive.'

Less than five minutes later we pulled up outside my house in Wellington Street.

She turned off the engine. 'So?'

I gazed at my best friend. Poor Gemma, I bet she was dying to be at home with Mike, putting her feet up in front of the fire. Instead, she was in a car that hadn't been moving long enough to warm up, forced to have a heart-to-heart with the most depressed witch in Kingsfield.

I let out a big shuddering sigh and filled her in. About the 'I love you' pumpkins, the mess-up with the note, the kiss that was so intense that I thought I would faint in his arms, and then the harsh words and the look he gave me that I would never forget.

'I'm so sorry,' said Gemma, reaching for my hand. 'But do you know what? It's his loss.'

She jumped suddenly. 'Ooh, baby's kicking.'

I stared at her bump. 'May I feel it?'

'Of course,' she laughed. 'I'd have suggested it before now,' she said, guiding my hand to her side, 'but I wasn't sure how you'd feel.'

The baby moved under my hand. 'Wow!' I beamed at Gemma. 'That's quite sharp!'

She raised her eyebrows. 'Tell me about it!'

The car windows were beginning to steam up and she turned the engine back on to demist them.

'I'm scared, you know.' She turned her blue eyes to me. 'I'm so much older than I was when I had Mia.'

'You're only in your early thirties, that's young by most people's standards.'

'Suppose. But what if there are complications? What if something goes wrong? Do you know, I haven't even dared buy any baby clothes yet. Me and Mike have been and bought all the equipment, but . . .' She sighed.

I'd been a terrible friend these past few months, I realized. Too wrapped up in my own problems to pick up on her worries. That was going to change, I decided, however painful it would be to be around her when this baby was due, I would support her every step of the way.

'I'll come baby clothes shopping with you,' I said quietly. 'I'd like to.'

'Oh Tilly, thank you. I'd love that!' She beamed at me. 'I wanted to ask but I thought you might not want to.'

I kept my hand where it was as the baby continued to push against me. 'I'm scared too, Gem. Scared it might never happen for me. It seems like a lifetime ago now that I was pregnant. I never got the chance to feel my baby moving like this.'

'Look,' she placed her hand over mine, 'it will happen. You've come so far this year. You've changed so much since I met you.'

'Have I? Have I really?'

I gazed out of the window at my rented house. It was exactly two months until New Year's Eve. Last year, I had just moved in and I spent the night alone, listening to the fireworks and the parties and the celebrations going on around me. Would I have to do that again this year?

The prospect made me shudder.

Gemma squeezed my fingers and I turned to face her. 'Of course you have. You've opened your heart up to people and it's obvious just how much happier you are. You will fall in love again. I promise.'

I thought about Aidan's handsome face, his lips as they grazed mine, the way his arms had held me close. I smiled bravely at her as tears pricked at my eyes.

She was right. I had already fallen in love. Was it asking for too much if I put Aidan Whitby on my Christmas List, I wondered?

'Oh, knickers!' Gemma winced, pulling me back into the moment. 'I'm suddenly absolutely desperate for the loo, do you mind if I come in?'

The two of us scurried along the path and I let her in to the house as quickly as I could.

Gemma waddled upstairs to the bathroom as fast as her pumpkin costume would allow and I went into the kitchen to put the kettle on. The phone began to ring and I smiled to myself. That mother of mine must be psychic, not to mention ultra-keen to talk to me.

'Hello again, Mum.'

'Tilly . . . how do you always know it's me?'

'Just a good guess,' I laughed. I tucked the phone under my chin and took two mugs out of the cupboard. 'What can I do for you?'

'Darling, there's something important I need to tell you. The thing is—'

'Oh my goodness!' I gasped, removing the phone from my ear and pressing it to my chest.

I stared at Gemma who had appeared in the kitchen doorway, her fingers gripping the door frame. She had removed her pumpkin costume and was wearing just a black T-shirt and leggings. But it wasn't her outfit that had caused me to gasp; she looked terrified and all the colour had drained from her face.

'Gemma, what's wrong?'

I watched in horror as my best friend's face crumpled and she began to sob.

'I'm bleeding, Tilly.' She gazed up at me as her whole body began to shake. 'I'm bleeding a lot. What if I'm losing the baby?'

My eyes filled with tears and my mouth had gone totally dry. I licked my lips before putting the phone back to my

313

ear. 'Mum, I'm so sorry, Gemma's ill, I've got to go. I'll call you tomorrow.'

I dropped the phone back into its cradle and lunged towards Gemma just as she collapsed to the floor.

'Call an ambulance, Tills,' she groaned.

'Just hold on, Gemma,' I pleaded, wrapping one arm around her and reaching for my mobile phone with the other. 'Just hold on.'

I was going to have to get her to hospital, and fast. If there was anyone who understood just how precarious life was, it was me. And after all that Gemma had done for me this year, there was no way I was going to let her lose this baby.

Winter

Chapter 34

I love winter.

As of the first of November each year, I enter my official winter mode: thermal underwear, a Thermos of soup for my lunch at school, fleecy pyjamas at night . . . the lot.

Winter is about walks in the snow, it's about snuggling up in front of the fire with mugs of tea and crumpets, indulging in wild and ambitious plans for the following year and dreaming about hot places to visit in summer. Of course, I'd done none of these things for the past two winters, except for the 'sitting in front of the fire' part, but this year would be different. I was sure of that.

And, of course, the very best thing about winter is Christmas. I love everything about Christmas. Some people moan when the shops get full of decorations and presents and food weeks before the big day itself, but not me. The more robins, snow, mistletoe and Christmas lights the better, as far as I'm concerned.

Winter is definitely my favourite season. The only downside is that all the things I love most about winter are, without doubt, more enjoyable when you have someone to share them with.

This first of November, I poked my head out of the

door to check on the weather and the wind nearly took my breath away.

A meow at my feet alerted me to my errant feline's return.

'Well, good morning, CallyCat, you dirty stop-out.' I bent down to stroke his head. 'And where were you all night? Hmm? Come on in out of this wind.'

He meowed again and padded straight past me towards the kitchen where his breakfast was waiting.

I stared at the sky and tried not to dwell on the fact that my cat appeared to have a better social life than I did.

What I really needed was a sunny day to cheer me up. One of those bright, crisp and clear winter mornings that invigorates and energizes. Unfortunately, it was rather grey and extremely blustery today, and the poplar trees along Wellington Street had been well and truly stripped of leaves overnight. Ho hum. Gloves, hat and thick woolly socks weather, I decided. And my bike would have to stay at home in case I got blown off.

It was the start of the weekend. More importantly, it was the morning after the Ivy Lane Hallowe'en party and what an eventful night that had turned out to be!

I shuddered at the memory of how the night had ended. Gemma had really panicked when she'd started to bleed, which had made me panic with her and by the time Mike arrived to take her to the hospital, only ten minutes later, she'd convinced herself that she was definitely in the process of losing the baby.

I'd had a call from Mike shortly after midnight. Gemma had a nasty infection, which had caused her to lose some blood, but she and baby were going to be fine. I had burst into tears of relief and sent them all my love down the phone. Gemma had stayed in hospital overnight so that they could keep an eye on her, but she would be home later this afternoon and I planned to go round to see her if she was up to having visitors.

In the meantime, although the prospect of returning to the scene of last night's disastrous events was about as appealing as a visit to the dentist for root canal treatment, I had to nip back to Ivy Lane and lock up my shed. I'd fled the vicinity having neither turfed Aidan out of it nor secured it for the night. But that was all I was planning to do and with any luck I could be there and back home again in time to see Mary Berry's new baking show on iPlayer as I'd missed the first episode earlier in the week.

Suitably attired, I set off for Ivy Lane allotments and braced myself against the swirling wind. It was a good job I was wearing a woolly hat or my hair would have been all over the place. Looking on the bright side, at least the walk would liven me up a bit. I'd hardly slept all night, what with worrying about Gemma and what might have happened and thinking about Aidan and what *didn't* happen. The lack of sleep might not have done much for my complexion, but it had given me an opportunity for a long hard think.

As I marched along, I ran through my big decisions to see if they still stood the 'cold light of day' test.

Firstly (for the main reason that it had been the easiest one to think about), I was going to accept the full-time teaching position that I'd been offered at school. My career had taken a back seat for two years, but I was ready to go for it again now. And although I loved the allotment, it wasn't enough to fill all of my time – especially now that winter had begun and I didn't have so much to do. I'd been baking a lot recently, which was fun, but I'd be the size of a house by Easter if I didn't watch it. The answer was work and lots of it. I looked up briefly as I passed school, still closed up for the half-term holidays until Monday. The flutter of excitement in my tummy told me that I'd definitely made the right decision.

Secondly, Aidan Whitby.

My heart did that scary elevator thing of zooming up and then plunging back down at the thought of him. I didn't blame him at all for pulling away from me last night. I mean, poor man. He was probably just looking for a nice straightforward relationship with a normal girl. Instead, he happened to choose me, someone with more baggage than Virgin Airlines and a jealous pumpkin-carving, not-so-secret admirer.

I ducked my head down and suppressed a sigh as I rounded the corner into Ivy Lane. All my hopes for the future, all my brave resolutions to move on from James, had been cruelly dashed. What should have been a romantic, candlelit rendezvous in my little shed, marking the start of – I had hoped – a new chapter in my life, had ended up being one rather passionate interlude followed by an equally passionate argument.

The truth was, I really, really liked Aidan. Oh, who was I kidding? I was well past the 'like' phase. In all honesty, I only had the merest scrap of hope that our . . . whatever it was (relationship? dalliance? snogfest?) could bounce back from the battering it had received last night but I was going to let fate decide and keep everything crossed that said fate was on my side.

But one thing I knew: I was ready to share my life with a man again.

Those precious few moments with Aidan had been more than enough to convince me of that. In fact, there was a point – when we were alone in my shed – when I'd thought I might explode with desire. But it hadn't just been his physical presence that was so intoxicating: the maleness of him, his delicious spicy scent, the feel of his arms around my body and how our bodies fitted together, although that had been amazing, obviously . . . It was the feeling of belonging with someone that I really wanted to enjoy again. I wanted someone to come home to, to care for, to create new memories with, to share special moments with. I wanted someone to love.

I had wanted so much for that person to be Aidan.

Because as well as finding him heart-spinningly attractive, intelligent and a genuinely decent man, there was one other major appeal. It might sound a bit odd and I wasn't sure if I'd ever be able to admit it to anyone but . . . well, I had this overwhelming feeling that Aidan and James would have been friends.

I shook my head firmly.

No matter how many times that scenario ran through my brain, it still sounded weird.

And if Aidan and I *weren't* meant to be and nothing came of our . . . whatever it was by, say, the end of November, then, for the first time in ten years, I was going to start dating again. I felt a prickle of cold sweat at the back of my neck just thinking about it.

The allotment gates were open and ahead I could see three cars in the car park: Charlie's and Peter's I recognized, the other I didn't.

Charlie was the subject of my third decision. And as he was here I might as well get it over with now. Or maybe later.

Tilly Parker, stop procrastinating. OK, I would go and see him as soon as I'd checked on my shed.

I hurried up the path along the edge of my plot. Someone, Aidan presumably, had at least shut the shed door. I held my breath and put my hand on the door handle. Imagine if he was still in there. His car has gone, whispered the rational side of my brain. Yes, but imagine . . .

The shed was empty. I exhaled, laughing at myself. Of course it was. What had I expected? Aidan to still be there, dressed as a wizard with that same look of disappointment on his face? Unfortunately, the three offending pumpkin lanterns were still in situ.

'You've had it for starters.' I tucked one under each arm and headed out to the compost bin.

'Hello, there!' Peter waved from the path, accompanied by a middle-aged couple in anoraks.

'Can I introduce Wendy and Richard?' He shouted over the wind. 'Prospective plot-holders.'

We shook hands and Richard, a wiry-looking chap with a pointy chin but a kind smile, explained that since their son had left for university, they suddenly found themselves with less taxiing, washing and food shopping to do and they were looking for something to fill the gap at week-ends. They were debating whether to go for Gemma's half plot by me or one of the newly dug ones.

Wendy had short neat grey hair, a button nose and a healthy glow to her cheeks.

'Classic empty-nesters,' she said with a smile. She pulled her collar up around her chin. 'I've been so busy being a mum for the last eighteen years that I don't know what to do with myself.'

Oh gosh! That reminded me, Mum had called last night with something important to tell me and I still hadn't found out what it was. I would call her from my shed as soon as my visitors had gone.

'Lovely cabbages!' Wendy added, pointing at my only re-maining crop.

'Thank you.' I pulled Alf's knife from my pocket and cut one for her and she beamed with pleasure. 'I wish I'd grown more winter crops now. Some sprouts or something.' I sighed. 'Everywhere looks so bare.'

'You wouldn't say that if you'd seen mine,' chuckled Peter, pointing to his plot next door. 'Blasted pigeons have made a right mess of my sprouts.' He led them away. I waved them off and pulled my mobile from my pocket as I walked into the shed out of the wind.

'Hi, Mum, it's me. Sorry I had to cut you off last night,' I said as soon as she picked up the phone.

'Tilly, darling! What on earth happened?'

'My friend Gemma — you know, from the allotment — started to bleed and we had to get her to hospital. Her baby is due at the end of December and . . .' I felt my throat swell as I relived the fear of last night's events. 'But she'll be fine. Just an infection. Nothing major.'

'Poor thing. Well, I'm glad to hear she'll be all right. Anyway, thank you for ringing me back.'

I detected hesitation in her voice and wondered if I'd called at an inconvenient time.

'Did you have something to tell me, Mum?' I asked.

'Yes. Well, it's nothing really, it's just that . . .' She cleared her throat and my heart began to race. *Please don't tell me you're ill, I couldn't bear it.* 'Oh gosh, Tilly, I feel so awkward saying this . . .'

'Mum, please just spit it out.'

My shoulders were hunched up around my ears and I was holding my breath.

'I've got a boyfriend. There, I've said it.' Mum went quiet and I let out a huge breath of relief.

'Sorry, darling, I didn't mean to worry you. You . . . you don't mind, then?'

My heart ached for her. Always so concerned about me. Suddenly I couldn't wait for Christmas to see her again. There is nothing as comforting as a hug from my mum.

I shook my head. 'Mum, I'm delighted that you've met someone, truly I am. And please don't worry about me. Come on, tell me all about him.'

'Well, his name is Clive and he runs the local history society . . .'

I could hear the happiness in her voice as she confided that they had actually been courting since Easter, but that she had not wanted to tell me earlier in case it upset me.

'He sounds lovely, Mum, and it must be great not to be on your own any more.' My voice cracked a bit and I swallowed. It did seem as if I was the only single person on the planet at this precise moment.

'And what about you, love?' Mum asked softly. 'Is there anyone new in your life?'

I stared at the remaining pumpkin lantern and an image of Aidan in his wizard's outfit filled my mind. I turned to look out of the shed window at the bare trees and wiped a layer of dust from the window sill. 'I did meet someone,' I said, 'but so far things haven't exactly gone smoothly.'

'Well, that's good news,' she said, 'and give it time, a new relationship is bound to be difficult for you at first.'

That was the understatement of the year. I managed a wry smile. We ended the call with promises to sort out Christmas arrangements over the next few weeks and I slipped the phone back in my pocket and peered out of the shed.

The wind had picked up even more, with leaves and twigs blowing everywhere, and I could hear Shazza and Karen's shed door creaking as the wind rattled against it. Apart from me, Peter and the visitors and Charlie, Ivy Lane was deserted. It was as if the Hallowe'en party last night had marked the end of the allotment year. My heart sank as I realized how much I was going to miss the place over the coming months when there was nothing to do and no one to do it with. The Christmas party was the next highlight on the Ivy Lane social calendar but that was weeks away. The conversation I'd had with Christine last night popped into my head about organizing some more events. Perhaps that was the answer.

I dumped the remaining pumpkin in the compost and locked the shed. Now to talk to Charlie. I headed off towards his plot.

I saw him before he saw me. He was in his greenhouse, earphones in, head nodding in time with the music and scooping potting compost into seed trays. I paused at the door and composed myself.

Not to put too fine a point on it, Charlie had completely stuffed up my chances with Aidan last night. And at moments, as I lay in bed during the wee small hours and my feverish brain dissected the evening, I'd been truly livid with him. But if there was anything that the last two years had taught me it was that life is too short to bear grudges.

After all, the carved pumpkins that had to have been left by him spelled out the words 'I love you', and if someone loves you, no matter how unrequited, should you punish them for it?

No. Absolutely not.

Still, a few firm words wouldn't go amiss.

I knocked briskly on the glass so as not to make him jump and went in.

His eyes widened and his face blushed a vivid scarlet. He instantly dropped the seed tray and yanked the earphones from his ears.

325

'Hi.' He folded his arms and did his best to look nonchalant.

'I got your message,' I said quietly, shutting the door behind me to keep out the swirling wind.

'What? Sorry, I don't follow?' He glanced at me nervously.

'Charlie,' I chastised him gently. I squeezed myself next to him, folding my arms and mirroring his stance. 'The one carved in the pumpkins.'

He let out a defeated sigh. 'Oh, right.'

I took a deep breath and felt my face heating up as I spoke. 'The thing is, Aidan and I, we—'

'Why him? Why Aidan?' he muttered.

'Well, it's not him now, you'll no doubt be pleased to know. He got your message too,' I retorted, ignoring the question.

I stared at him and forced myself not to react as a fleeting smile played across his lips.

Count to ten, Tilly.

The blasts of air whistled through the gaps in the greenhouse and I shivered. Several plastic plant pots, carried along by the wind, blew past and it occurred to me for the first time that I really didn't relish being outdoors for much longer.

'I saw you put the note on his car window so I went across and read it. I couldn't believe it.' He lifted his blue eyes to mine and shook his head.

I pulled my bottom lip in between teeth. My face was probably absolutely scarlet by now. I had to admit that some of the blame had to be laid at my door. I hadn't been totally straight with Charlie and I should have done more last night to make it clear that I would never see him as anything other than a friend.

'I've been patient, waiting for the right moment to ask you out, but then last night, I realized I was running out of time.' He puffed out his cheeks and exhaled. 'Christine had got some spare pumpkins in the pavilion so I brought them in here and carved them. I don't know why I did it really; it was a bit of a sad thing to do.'

'How did you get into my shed?' That had been bothering me, I was sure it had been locked.

He shrugged. 'It was open.' He scratched his nose, pulled his phone out of his pocket, squinted at the screen and slipped it away again.

I frowned at him, still unconvinced.

'You ruined my night, Charlie.'

Charlie groaned. 'You and me, we've got so much in common. I know losing your husband like you did is much worse than me and my wife splitting up. She had an affair and threw me out, just like that, and I thought I'd never get over it. I actually think I went a bit mental for a while . . .' He paused and gazed at me hopefully. 'We could be so good for each other, Tilly.'

'I'm sorry, Charlie, I really am.' I reached for his hand and rubbed it gently. 'But I don't feel the same way.'

'Aidan jets off all over the place with his job. You need someone to be here for you. I'm here, Tilly.' He brought my hand to his lips and was about to kiss it before I wriggled it away.

'I can't explain how love works, Charlie,' I said sadly, moving towards the door, 'but I know that Aidan is special to me. He makes me happy and I think I deserve a bit of happiness, don't you?'

He scuffed the toe of his boot against the floor. 'Fine, but just so as you know, I can't just be friends. I'm sorry, Tilly. It's him or me.'

'Charlie, that's not fair!' I exclaimed.

He just shrugged and turned back to his seed trays.

I stared at his back in disbelief for a few seconds before wrenching open the door and flinging myself back out at the mercy of the elements.

What had just happened in there? Charlie's friendship was important to me and I'd hoped he would understand how I felt. Now it looked as if I'd lost both him and Aidan in less than twenty-four hours.

Way to go, Tilly.

The wind was so strong that I could barely breathe. I pulled my hat down round my ears and stomped along the path towards the pavilion, intent on making it home for a restorative hour of Mary Berry before my temper worked itself up into a proper fury.

A movement on the pavilion roof caught my eye; the gable end appeared to be moving. I stopped in my tracks and stared, clamping a gloved hand across my mouth in horror. All of a sudden there was an almighty creak, followed by a tearing sound as the wind lifted the corner of the roof clean away from the walls of the building. An entire panel, almost a third of the roof, splintered off with an ear-splitting crack, flipped over in the air and then came thundering down in the car park, missing the visitors' car by a whisker.

I screamed as a second roof section – smaller this time, thankfully – was wrenched off the building, tossed up by a swirl of wind, and came crashing down to the ground, partially blocking the pavilion doorway.

Where were the visitors? Where was Peter? Oh my God, please say that no one had been hurt.

Heart clattering, I ran towards the pavilion and heard Charlie's footsteps close behind me.

Peter, Wendy and Richard appeared white-faced at the pavilion door. Peter shoved the torn roof panel to one side and I joined them inside. I look up at the huge holes in the roof, it was surreal. The posters on the noticeboards were flapping and a stack of loose papers were blowing around the floor.

'Oh, thank goodness no one was in the car park when that happened,' I panted, clutching a hand to my chest.

'Someone could have been killed,' said Wendy, her voice shaky.

Charlie arrived only seconds behind me. 'Is everyone all right?'

I nodded but noticed that he didn't look at me directly. Richard wrapped an arm around his wife's shoulders. I wondered briefly whether someone would put an arm around me. I could certainly do with it. My knees had turned to jelly.

'The rest of that roof could go at any second,' said Peter, rubbing a hand over his face. 'This is all we need after the fire in the shop in July. I'd better get on the phone to a roofing specialist to secure it.'

'Come on, let's move those roof panels from the car park first,' said Charlie. 'We should be able to lift them between us.'

We bowed our heads against the wind and carried the smashed panels around the back of the pavilion and stowed them safely.

'I shouldn't wonder if this has put you off Ivy Lane somewhat,' shouted Peter as Wendy and Richard said their goodbyes.

'Goodness, not at all!' cried Wendy. 'This is the most excitement we've had in months! Count us in, don't you agree, Richard?'

'Good grief, yes!' said Richard, pumping our hands before dashing out to their car. We waved from the pavilion as the two of them drove off with promises to be back in touch soon.

Trees were almost bending over double in the howling wind and I wasn't looking forward to the walk home one bit.

'Dear, oh dear,' said Peter, shaking his head. I took in the dazed expression on his face and slipped an arm around his waist. Poor man, it looked like this was excitement that the Ivy Lane chairman could well do without.

Chapter 35

Although the pavilion had been given a temporary water-tight covering, it was still out of action for the time being and so I had persuaded the head teacher, Mrs Burns, to let us use the school staff room for the next Ivy Lane allotments committee meeting.

Actually, it suited me anyway. It was Bonfire Night and I was going out with Hayley to the big bonfire party in Kingsfield later. I needed this meeting to be short and sweet so that I could get home and change; and I knew the school caretaker would usher us out in an hour so that he could lock up.

'Tea,' I said, placing a tray with a teapot, mugs, milk, sugar and a plate of homemade chocolate-chip cookies on the table in the centre. 'Help yourselves to cookies, the children and I made them today.'

'This is very kind of you, Tilly,' said Peter, doing as he was told and tucking in.

'The pleasure's mine, really.' I sat down in the chair between him and Nigel and picked up my notebook from the floor.

I meant it too. This was exactly what I needed: to keep busy and stop myself thinking about Aidan. I was driving myself barmy; every time a silver Alfa Romeo flashed past me I found myself peering through the windows to get a glimpse of the driver. I'd heard absolutely nothing from him since Hallowe'en and I suppose as time ticked on, it was getting less likely that I ever would.

I tutted under my breath. This was precisely the problem: every time I had nothing to think about, my thoughts drifted back to him . . .

'And thank you for offering to join the committee,' said Nigel.

I glanced over at Christine and smiled. 'Offer' wasn't quite the word I'd have chosen. As usual, she had talked me into it without me even realizing, but I didn't mind. She and Roy were about to become grandparents again; if I could take some of the weight off her shoulders over the coming months then she would have more time to be with her family.

'Formal nomination, et cetera, can't be done until the next AGM in February,' he continued, 'but I can't see it being a problem; we're desperately short of numbers.'

Christine took control of the teapot and poured tea for us all. 'So, what's the situation with the insurance for the roof, Peter?' she said, handing him a mug.

'Thanks.' He set it down and flicked through his paperwork. 'I've had a letter from the insurance assessors. The good news is that I have permission to go ahead and authorize the repairs. I've spoken to a roofing company and they can start next week.'

'Excellent,' said Nigel.

'And the bad news?' I asked.

'Most of the damage to the roof will be covered by our insurance, but I'm afraid there will be a shortfall that will have to be met from the Ivy Lane bank account.'

'Ah,' said Nigel, smoothing his tie with a frown. 'That is a problem. Coming so soon after the fire in the shop.'

'You've hit the nail on the head, Nigel,' said Peter, nodding.

'Funds are at an all-time low, so they are,' explained Christine glumly, taking a noisy sip of her tea.

'I'm afraid this will wipe out what little is left in the pot,' sighed Peter.

'Oh dear.' I offered round the plate of cookies again in an attempt to cheer them all up. 'And what is it we need funds for exactly?'

'The Christmas party,' they all answered as one.

'Oh no,' I gasped. 'The Christmas party is a must! Please don't say it'll be cancelled?'

The Ivy Lane Christmas party was the next highlight on my social calendar – actually, the only highlight on my social calendar. I'd heard so much about it during the course of the year and I was really looking forward to it. Apparently, it was always a jolly affair, with festive food and drink and the awarding of the prizes from the annual show. Not only that, it would probably be Gemma's last allotment event for ages. Her baby was due at the end of December, she had already given up her plot and for all I knew, she might not come back to allotment gardening for years.

The show *had* to go on.

'No, no,' Peter assured me, 'we won't cancel it. It's just that this is usually the one free event of the year. All food and drink is traditionally provided by the committee. It won't go down well if we have to charge an entry fee or ask people to bring their own.'

'Mmm,' I said, sneaking a glance at my fellow members, 'I can see the problem.'

Secretly, I didn't think that anyone would mind. I

mean, everyone knew about the fire in the shop and the damage to the roof. Surely they would understand and not grumble? But this was my first official committee meeting, far be it from me to contradict anyone. Besides which, I had a sort-of plan forming.

'When will the pavilion be ready for use again, Peter?'

'Two weeks,' he said, consulting his diary. 'Weather permitting.'

'How about we christen the new roof with a fund-raising event?' I said, feeling quite excited at the prospect. 'A cake sale, perhaps?'

This would be perfect. My new-found passion for baking needed an outlet other than feeding myself huge quantities of cake. And my energies needed an outlet, too; I'd foolishly been thinking that I would have a blossoming romance with Aidan to keep me busy this side of Christmas but as that didn't seem to be the case, an event could serve as a substitute, albeit a poor one.

I smiled encouragingly at the three of them. Nigel scratched his head, Peter tapped his cheek with a pen and stared blankly at his papers and Christine lifted her shoulders in a weary sigh. Not quite the reaction I'd been hoping for.

'There's a lot of work involved in these events, you know, Tilly.' Nigel frowned. 'And I'm not really sure that all the effort would pay off financially.'

'I'll organize it all,' I added, pulling my hopeful face.

That seemed to do the trick: they all perked up considerably.

'And we can have a tombola and a raffle. Those sorts of things always raise loads. And you love seeing the pavilion busy,' I reminded Christine.

'True.' She nodded thoughtfully. 'Although I don't know

if selling cakes to the other plot holders will make us much money and there aren't many people around at this time of year.'

'I do love home-baking, though.' Nigel sighed wistfully. 'I remember the cakes my wife used to make. Shop-bought ones aren't the same at all.'

My heart twisted for him. It was easy to forget sometimes that I wasn't the only one who had lost their special someone.

'Well, I think this should be a cake sale with a difference,' I said, patting his arm. 'And to make it more exciting, why not introduce an element of competition? We could make it easy for everyone to enter – even you, Nigel. There can be all sorts of prizes so that it's not all about baking skills. We could have a category just for men, or does that sound sexist? Perhaps a beginners' category, to be fair? How about one for the most unusual flavour? Ooh, I know, we could have a theme . . .'

I was off. All sorts of ideas were popping into my head. We could invite the whole neighbourhood, it needn't just be the Ivy Lane community. This would bring us all together again before Christmas. I felt a shiver of excitement. Oh yes, this was going to be such fun.

Peter chuckled. 'I can see you've got it all worked out, Tilly.' He flicked through his diary and scribbled himself a note. 'What about the last Saturday in November, how does that sound?'

Three weeks from now. I clapped my hands and managed to restrict my excitement to an acceptable small squeak.

'That's perfect.' I grinned. 'We're going to make loads of money, I promise, and then Ivy Lane will have the best Christmas party ever.'

*

The following Saturday I met Gemma for lunch in the café on Shenton Road. The café was a short walk from my house, but I had picked up my new car from Mike's garage a few days before, so I decided to drive. Having my own car was a huge milestone, if a little scary at times, but I'd done it and I was proud of myself. And it felt so good to be able to jump in the car and just drive whenever and wherever I wanted to.

I parked right outside the café and spotted Gemma straightaway through the glass in the prime spot by the window.

I tooted the horn until she noticed me and we waved excitedly at each other.

'Tilly! How's the new set of wheels?' she squealed as I joined her at the table. She struggled to her feet to give me a hug.

'Amazing! It's a bit weird driving again, but oh, the bliss of taking shopping home in a car instead of stuffing everything in the panniers of my bike. I think I bought up half of Tesco's stock in my excitement last night!'

'I'm so pleased for you, babe,' she said softly.

'I'll take you for that baby clothes shopping spree I promised you soon, if you like?'

She nodded and we stared at each other knowingly for a long moment until I felt myself going a bit teary.

'Anyway, you look fantastic,' I said, planting a kiss on her cheek. Gone were the dark circles and pale complexion from a few months ago and in their place: bright eyes, glowing skin and an inner calm that made me feel positively pasty by comparison.

'Don't be daft,' she giggled, flicking her curls off her face as she sat back down. 'I've ordered us both bacon sandwiches and a pot of tea, hope you don't mind?' She pulled a face. 'I'm starving. I was even contemplating eating the ketchup just before you walked in.'

I laughed and shook my head. 'This might not help matters then.' I plonked myself in the chair next to her and pulled a poster from my bag.

Gemma took it out of my hand and read aloud. 'Ivy Lane Great Cake Competition? Now I definitely need food,' she groaned and rubbed her rotund belly with one hand. 'Ooh, thank goodness,' she hissed, looking over my shoulder. 'Here it comes.'

'Bacon sandwiches and tea for two.' The waitress set our order down on the table and smiled at us. She bent low and hissed into Gemma's ear, 'I've put extra bacon in yours.'

'You're literally a life saver,' Gemma beamed and took a giant bite.

'Excuse me, would you mind displaying one of these, please?' I said, pinching the poster from Gemma's fingers.

'Sure.' The waitress was roughly my age with luscious red hair, and a smattering of freckles across her pale cheeks. 'Oh, I'd love an allotment,' she sighed, pushing a strand of hair out of her eyes. 'Is it very hard work?'

'Depends on who you ask.' I smirked at Gemma. 'But no, not really. Come along to the cake event of the year and have a look around for yourself. You could join the waiting list if you like what you see.'

'Thanks, I might do that. Although I'm not much of a cook.' She walked over to the noticeboard and pinned up my poster.

'Look at you, advertising the place!' exclaimed Gemma, squirting a generous amount of ketchup on top of the bacon. 'Mother will be so proud.'

'I'm on the committee now, you know.' I smiled at her haughtily.

'So tell me about this cake thing, then,' she said, taking a large bite of her sandwich.

I poured us both a cup of tea and filled her in. Since coming up with the idea last week the event had snowballed and had taken over my life. With the rest of the committee's rather bewildered consent I had created a cake sale with a difference. Each person would enter their cake to be sold and judged under a certain category: novelty cake shapes, cakes with hidden vegetables, the 'taste better than they look' cakes, the 'unusual flavour' cakes and 'first time ever in the kitchen' cakes.

This list, I rather thought, left no room for anyone at Ivy Lane to try to wriggle out of it.

I had designed posters like the one I'd just given to the waitress and pinned them up everywhere and had leaflets printed which I was hoping Mia might help me deliver. Plus every child at school had gone home with one in their reading folder yesterday. I'd phoned up every plot holder and begged them all to take part and I'd arranged for people to buddy up, so those who didn't bake had someone to call on for help or some moral support if their Victoria sponge failed to rise, or whatever. Liz had offered to help Nigel, and Vicky and Dougie, who both claimed not to be able to cook a thing, were going round to Brenda's for a baking lesson. I'd even phoned Wendy and Richard after Peter had told me they were definitely taking a plot next spring. Wendy had hooted with excitement until she'd realized that the event clashed with their three-week Caribbean cruise, so they couldn't make it. Charlie hadn't picked up his phone so I'd left him a message and everyone else had agreed to come. I was thrilled!

'I've even made a collection of some easy recipes with hidden vegetables, just to give people a few ideas,' I said, taking a copy from my bag and waving it under Gemma's nose.

I bit into my bacon sandwich. 'Yum. Good choice. What?'

Gemma's eyes were twinkling at me and she shook her head innocently.

I sighed and swallowed my mouthful. 'I know what you're thinking. I'm taking it too seriously. But it's my first event and I want—'

'No, 'Tills,' said Gemma softly, covering my hand with hers. 'That was *not* what I was thinking.'

'Oh?' I felt my cheeks colour at her tone.

We eyed each other in silence for a long moment.

'Just ring him,' Gemma said finally.

I took a deep breath with the intention of pretending not to know what she was talking about but I caught her eye and snapped my mouth shut instead. My shoulders drooped and she gripped my hand a bit tighter.

'I know what this is, you know. All this cake competition stuff,' she said primly, dabbing the corners of her mouth with a napkin. 'You're in classic distraction mode: keeping yourself busy to keep your mind off Aidan.'

I kept my mouth shut. She was right, of course, but I hadn't realized how transparent I was.

'So why don't you phone him and explain, once again, that Charlie is just a friend?'

'But don't you think I should wait for him to call me?' I dropped my sandwich back on to the plate. Gemma eyed it up hungrily and I handed my untouched half to her.

'Well, pardon me, Jane Austen.' She rolled her eyes and took a large bite. 'I think we women have moved on a bit since *Pride and Prejudice*, you know.'

'Oh God,' I groaned and squeezed my eyes shut briefly.

'I've thought about phoning him, truly. And I hear what you're saying, but it's been ten years since I've been on the dating scene.'

We both winced at the expression.

'And the thing is, if I contact him, I'll never know whether he would have got in touch with me himself, will I? And I want him to want to get in touch with me.' Very badly, in fact.

Gemma looked a bit confused for a moment and then nodded. 'I see where you're coming from.'

'And I know he's in the country at the moment, so if he wanted to phone, he could,' I added.

'You've been keeping tabs on him, then?' she smirked.

I went bright red and buried my face behind my teacup.

'No, not exactly, your mum happened to mention that he was in London for a few weeks editing his Peru programme, that's all. She's still in touch with the *Green Fingers* team apparently.'

'So what are you going to do?' Gemma craned her neck round to get the waitress's attention. 'All this talk of cake has made me hungry again,' she muttered.

'I am going to run the most profitable cake event Kingsfield has ever seen,' I announced solemnly. 'And you are going to help me.'

'OK.' She nodded. 'I'm on it.'

'Really?' I beamed at her. 'Thanks, Gemma.'

'Yeah. The bun's already in the oven, isn't it? Boom boom!' She elbowed me and guffawed at her own joke.

I cast my eyes heavenwards. 'I hope your cakes are better than your jokes,' I sighed, 'or you will be in trouble.'

Chapter 36

The day of the Ivy Lane Great Cake Competition had arrived. Thankfully all the repairs had been completed on time and the weather couldn't have been more perfect if it had tried. It was cold but the sky was dazzlingly blue. There had been frost on the inside of the pavilion windows when I'd arrived an hour ago. But now the room was cosy and warm.

Sunlight poured through the glass and dust motes danced in the sunbeams as Roy and I and the rest of the allotment committee darted around putting the finishing touches to the display tables. I was beginning to see why Christine always seemed to move at over a hundred miles an hour; there was so much to do!

I shimmied with a mixture of pleasure and fear as I set out a new notebook, several pens and a Quality Street tin to store the money in on a table by the door. The tin was possibly a bit on the large side, but there was no harm in being optimistic.

We'd arranged tables all around the room to display the cakes that I was hoping would arrive imminently to be judged; there were chairs in the centre of the room for people to sit and enjoy our delicious refreshments; and in pride of place at one end of the room was the enormous raffle prize: a wicker basket filled with every chocolatey thing imaginable. All we needed now were customers . . .

'What next?' asked Peter, wiping his forearm across his brow.

'Just these signs to go on the tables please, anywhere will do.' I whipped out the cardboard signs I'd made for each competition category from my bag and handed them over. 'And then I think we're good to go,' I added.

'Perfect timing, love,' said Christine, nodding her head towards the clock. 'Let's open up.'

'Already? Oh my goodness!' I yelped. 'What if there's no one there?'

My heart was clattering like a runaway horse. I'd worked so hard for today and really, really wanted to make a success of my first committee fund-raiser. It would be awful if no one turned up.

She rolled her eyes and chuckled. 'I take it you haven't looked outside recently. Go on, away with you, I need to start pouring cups of tea.'

I scurried to the door to open up but Nigel caught hold of my arm as I passed.

He cleared his throat and shuffled from foot to foot. 'Tilly, before you open the doors, I just wanted to thank you for putting on this event.'

I smiled at him. Nigel had been the most sceptical member of the committee, not that that had stopped him working his socks off for me this morning. But I was delighted to see his change of heart, nonetheless. 'Let's hope you're still saying that at the end of the day, Nigel. We might not make any money if we don't get any entrants!'

'Well, I'm entering a cake, so that's one at least,' he said proudly. 'And anyway, that's not what I wanted to thank you for,' he added, lowering his voice. 'Spending a morning with Liz, in her kitchen . . . Well, let's just say that a bit of female company, not to mention a most informative baking lesson, has done me the power of good.'

Was it my imagination or had his face gone a bit pink?

I threw my arms around his neck and kissed his cheek. 'Thanks, Nigel. Now, battle stations, I need you selling those raffle tickets as if your life depends on it.'

'Roger that,' said Nigel with a salute and he marched off to his position.

I wrapped my fingers around the door handle and took a deep breath. The moment of truth.

I opened the door a sliver and squinted through it with one eye. Oh my word! A queue of people all bearing cake tins, boxes or plastic tubs snaked back as far as the end of the car park.

'I think we're going to need more tables,' I said to the rest of the committee tremulously.

I swallowed an anxious squeal and flung back the door with a flourish.

'Come in, everyone, and welcome to the Ivy Lane Allotments Great Cake Competition,' I cried. 'Only one pound to enter!'

Unless anyone looked very closely, I doubted they would have seen my legs trembling at all.

An hour later, the Quality Street tin was heavy with coins, the pavilion was humming with the sound of people chatting and the tables were positively groaning under the weight of the competition cakes. I had been so busy welcoming everyone in and handing out entry forms that I'd not even moved from my seat at the front door.

'Where on earth are these people coming from?' whispered Roy incredulously as he raided the tin for money. He was off on a second trip to buy more milk for the tea stall. Christine was on permanent duty at the tea urn.

'W-e-ll, Mia and I might have gone a bit overboard on the leafleting,' I admitted sheepishly. 'And at the last minute yesterday, I invited all the staff from my school to take part too, just in case we didn't get enough entries. Which in hindsight . . .' I looked over my shoulder at the packed pavilion and cringed at Roy.

'You're doing grand, girl,' he chuckled and patted my head as he squeezed past my little table to make his way outside. 'Oh and here's all the family!' he cried, holding the door open to let Gemma, Mia and Mike in.

I stood up to hug them, touched that they had all come to support us.

'Pink cheeks suit you,' said Gemma, pretending to burn her fingers on my skin, 'very English rose.'

'Oh no! Do I look hot and sweaty?' I tried to see my reflection in the window but it was too steamed up. I pressed my hands to my cheeks instead.

As well as being flushed with the event's success, my high colour was due in no small part to the fact that I appeared to be semi-famous. 'I recognize you from the *Green Fingers* show!' being the most common observation, with my least favourite being: 'You look much thinner in real life.' Although I supposed looking fatter in real life would be marginally worse.

'You look gorgeous, Tilly, as ever,' said Mike and then chuckled at his wife's mock outrage. 'What do you want us to do with these cakes? I'll warn you, Mia wants to win the unusual flavour competition, so you might want a glass of water handy for judging.'

'They are edible, though,' Mia added, although the glint in her eye did make me wonder.

I peered at her cakes and tried to commit them to memory. I could be in for some fun this afternoon. Thankfully, I wasn't the only judge: Toni, our school cook, was coming to help me out. She might not have Mary Berry's audience-pulling power, but round here her treacle sponge was legendary.

I sent them off to deliver their cakes to the correct tables and sighed happily. We still had another half an hour to go until the judging would commence and already I was sure we had raised enough to put on a spectacular Christmas party next month. And once the cakes had been judged, they would be sold off to make even more money. Every single plot holder had delivered a cake for the refreshment table and entered at least one for the competition.

The door opened again and a little boy poked his head in. He had wavy blond hair, huge blue eyes and the longest eyelashes I had ever seen. He stepped inside and smiled at me shyly, holding out a battered tin in front of him.

I caught my bottom lip between my teeth. He was so absolutely adorable that I thought my heart might melt.

'Hello.' I smiled, fighting the urge to scoop him up in a huge cuddle. I peered around the open door to see if he was being followed by an adult. 'Are you with anyone else?'

He nodded solemnly. 'My dad. But he's a really slow runner.'

'I see,' I said, amused, looking forward to the moment when his 'slow' dad appeared. I wondered how far away the poor man was.

'Is there a prize for boys' cakes, miss?' he said, resting the tin on my desk.

'Er, let me see,' I said, hastily scribbling a new sign under the table. I was breaking all my carefully constructed rules in one fell swoop, but who cares, he had me besotted from the first second I saw him. 'Ah, yes, here it is.' I looked back up, holding the new sign, to see his father standing behind him. The likeness was unmistakable now that I saw them both together.

'Charlie!' I gasped.

Chapter 37

Charlie was the last person I'd expected to see today. He hadn't returned my phone call and his last words to me were pretty final. But putting our situation to one side for a moment, he was spending time with his son, and for that, I was truly delighted for him, for them both.

Charlie rubbed a hand over his cropped hair. 'Hi, Tilly, this is Ollie. Ollie decided to run across the car park without me, didn't you?' He was a bit out of breath and had a panicky look in his eye.

'Sorry, Dad.' Ollie grinned, not looking especially penitent.

'Why don't you go and give your cake and this sign to that man over there, while your dad gets himself a cup of tea?' I pointed Peter out to Ollie and he scampered off to deliver his masterpiece.

I felt at a distinct disadvantage sitting down with Charlie towering over me, so I stood up.

There was an awkward silence and we both cleared our throats.

'Ollie's a lovely boy,' I said eventually.

Charlie nodded. 'He is. I thought about what you said in the summer about having Ollie in my life. About what a privilege it is. You were right, as usual.' He rolled his eyes teasingly. 'Getting access is still tricky, my ex doesn't make anything easy for me, but I'm making the effort to see him as much as I can.'

'I'm very proud of you,' I said, turning to hug him. *He doesn't want to be friends any more, remember?* I dropped my arms instantly. 'Whoops, sorry.'

Now my face was less English Rose and more Blazing Inferno.

'Don't apologize,' Charlie muttered, wrapping his arms round me. He rested his chin on the top of my head. 'That's *my* job. I seem to be a proper idiot where you're concerned. And I'm sorry.'

I sighed and relaxed against him, inhaling his familiar scent, a mixture of wood smoke and earth. Gemma caught my eye across the room and I felt my face heat up an extra notch.

'Apology accepted.' I stared down at my feet as I pulled away. 'Look, Ollie's waving to you from the raffle, you'd better go over.'

It appeared that Nigel was doing his best to explain to Ollie that he needed to have the winning ticket in order to take home the chocolate hamper.

'Never a dull moment,' sighed Charlie, going to Nigel's rescue. I pressed my lips together, hiding my smile. He didn't fool me; his eyes were shining and I'd never seen him look so relaxed. He was enjoying every minute of looking after Ollie, I thought as I sat back down at my table.

The door opened again and the waitress from the café launched herself through it, red hair flying in a swirl behind her.

'Am I too late? I've made banana muffins for the hidden fruit and veg—' She clapped a hand over her mouth and opened her eyes wide. 'Shoot! I shouldn't have said that, should I?'

I giggled and shook my head. 'You could go for another category?' I showed her the list. 'I'm Tilly, by the way.'

'Freya. Otherwise known as Freya the terrible cook.' She showed me the contents of her cake tin and pulled a face.

'Mmm, well, I think you're spoilt for choice as far as competition categories go,' I said. I'd never seen such lumpen, wholesome-looking cakes. But bless her for making the effort. 'Am I right in thinking there's bran in there too?'

Freya nodded and opted for the 'taste better than they look' category and I sent her off in Peter's direction with a suggestion that she also book him for a tour of the allotments later.

I watched her plough her way through the crowds towards Peter. I hoped she would take on an allotment, I liked her. A lot.

'Here you go, love,' said Christine, setting a cup of tea in front of me.

'Ooh, you're a life saver.' I picked it up and took a long slurp.

'I think we should get cracking with the judging, Tilly, we've run out of cakes on the refreshments stall and the sooner we can start selling off the competition cakes, the better.'

Before I had chance to reply, Toni appeared with a blackberry tray-bake that was nearly as big as her.

'Our esteemed judge, hurrah! Just in time!' I said, jumping up to give her a hug.

'Sorry,' she said, 'I only had time to make one cake.'

'Nonsense, that'll keep us going for an hour!' said Christine, whipping it away to serve up to the waiting customers.

I whisked Toni towards the kitchen to explain the competition rules and passed Dougie on the way.

'Dougie, do me a favour and sit in my seat in case anyone new arrives, will you?'

'No problem.' He cupped a hand over his mouth. 'Just watch out for the dark fruit cake, I went a bit wild with the rum.' He winked at me and sauntered off.

'I'm a bit nervous,' said Toni. She was in her thirties, had short black hair, sharp blue eyes and an endless supply of patience. She was also incredibly slim. If I worked in such close proximity to Toni's treacle sponge, I'd be huge.

'There's nothing to be nervous about,' I assured her. Except, of course, the 'unusual flavour' category. I handed her a glass of water (Mary Berry always has a drink on hand when she's judging, I'd noticed) and ushered her towards the cakes.

Thirty minutes later, I was full to bursting and convinced I would never eat another crumb of cake as long as I lived. I had been delighted with the entries; some of the cakes were amazing. My favourite had been a rectangular cake decorated to look like an allotment plot, complete with bamboo canes, tiny pumpkins, perfect little cabbages and even a miniature butterfly. It put my flapjacks to shame! There were one or two less successful entries. One particular fruitcake had been so dry that I could still feel it on the roof of my mouth, but the baker had made the effort and that was what counted.

All the cakes had been judged, prizes awarded and Toni had gone to chat with a friend over a cup of tea. All that was left to do was the clearing up. Officially the event had ended, not that anyone seemed in a hurry to leave.

Ollie, by default, had won the boys' cakes category,

350

although of course he wasn't aware of the lack of competition, and was very pleased with his chocolate selection box prize.

Dougie won the 'tastes better than it looks' category, which wasn't difficult: his offering could hardly have tasted any worse than it looked. Karen won the award for 'best icing' and Shazza took the prize for most unusual flavour with her dark chocolate and bacon cake, beating Mia's marmite and fudge cupcakes by the narrowest of margins. Both of them had a sweet and salty thing going on, which should have been wrong, but they were delicious! There were winners from outside our allotment community, too: the cake with the hidden vegetable that we couldn't fathom to save our lives contained parsnips and came from a neighbour of mine. And the novelty shape award was won by a lady who had fashioned a wellington boot out of sponge cake.

I spotted a seat next to Gemma and made a beeline for her. She only had four weeks to go until the baby was due and while she was absolutely huge, probably uncomfortable and almost certainly nervous about the impending birth, she looked impossibly beautiful and I couldn't help feeling proud and envious all at the same time.

'Call yourself a friend,' she said, pouting at me as I squeezed in beside her. 'I can't believe my ginger cake didn't win.'

'Sorry, Gem, but if it's any consolation, it certainly was the strongest flavour of any of the entries,' I said and sipped gratefully at my water. I had a feeling the memory of her ginger cake, not to mention the heartburn, would stay with me for days.

'Anyway, not to worry,' she grinned and pulled me in for a hug, 'I still think you're amazing. This must be the busiest fund-raiser Ivy Lane has ever seen.'

'Really?'

'Definitely.' She nodded earnestly.

I beamed back at her with delight.

My first event – the busiest ever! I felt a lump-in-the-throat moment coming on as I glanced around at the crowded room. The community had really come together today – not just the plot holders, but people from the neighbouring area too.

And I was part of it. James would be so proud of me. Tears pricked at my eyes and I blinked them away.

James.

I'd hardly thought of him today, and whilst he would always be a part of me, it was comforting to know that I was putting the traumatic end to our marriage behind me. The old Tilly, who couldn't see a way through the pain and sadness, had been replaced by a new Tilly, a girl with friends, a good job and a bright future. My new life was almost complete. Almost.

I sighed happily and leaned my head on Gemma's shoulder.

Chapter 38

I sat up with a start. I was still in the pavilion. Gemma was still here too, but the crowds had gone. I must have dropped off. I was only twenty-nine, what was I doing nodding off to sleep in the middle of the day? In public! How mortifying!

'And she's back in the room,' giggled Gemma. She rolled her shoulders in a circle where I'd been leaning on her and winced. 'Am I that boring that I send you to sleep with my conversation?'

'I'm so sorry; of course you're not boring.' I rubbed my eyes. 'What time is it?'

'Two.' Gemma pointed to my mouth. 'And you're dribbling. Anyway, thank God you're awake, I'm desperate for the loo.' She rubbed her hand on her tummy and pushed herself up to her feet. 'What with you on my shoulder and this one bouncing on my bladder, it hasn't been the most relaxing thirty minutes of my life, believe me.'

She wandered off to the loo, leaving me, still slightly dazed, trying to focus my eyes on all the activity around me.

Nigel was stacking chairs, Roy was ostensibly sweeping the floor, although I noticed he only moved when Christine was in the room as she ran backwards and forwards to the kitchen carrying dirty crockery.

I caught myself suddenly and jumped to my feet. This was my event; I shouldn't just be watching everyone else at work! I strode towards the kitchen to find myself a job as Freya burst into the pavilion followed closely by Peter and a gust of cool fresh air.

'Has Peter given you the tour, Freya?' I asked.

'Yeah, I didn't see as much veg as I thought I would?' She stared at me, wide-eyed, and pulled a face that I interpreted as meaning that she had some reservations. 'I thought it would be all full of colour.'

'I've explained that the allotment is not at its best in winter,' said Peter, looking more than a little exhausted. 'Let me know if you decide to go ahead with a plot and I'll get the necessary forms to you. You'll have to join the waiting list, mind you.'

'I'll think about it, Pete, yeah?' she said, punching his arm.

'Marvellous.' Peter nodded to us both and scampered off.

Freya pulled her phone out of her pocket and tucked her red tresses behind her ears. She stuck her tongue out in concentration as she tapped on the screen.

'Me and some friends are going out for a few drinks next Friday, fancy coming along?' she said with a grin.

'Thank you. Er, Friday night? I'm not sure if I'm free, can I let you know?' I stammered.

Of course I was free. I was always free. And I did like her; she was full of life, just slightly more life than I was used to.

She shrugged. 'Sure. Let's swap numbers.'

'Of course,' I breathed.

She reeled off her number, I stored it straight into my phone and gave her mine.

'I'll give you a ring if I can make it,' I said.

'Great.' She turned to leave and flashed me a big smile, her eyes sparkling wickedly. 'It'll be wild!'

I gulped as I waved her off, trying not to look alarmed. I couldn't remember the last time Tilly Parker went 'wild'.

A pang of guilt stabbed me as I took in the state of the room; it was virtually back to normal and I hadn't as yet lifted a finger to help. My eyes were still looking for a useful task when Liz, pink-cheeked and looking lovely in a pale blue jumper and jeans, tugged on my sleeve.

'I'm glad I caught you,' she said. 'I'm off to spend an hour in the greenhouse before it gets dark. But I wanted you to know how much I enjoyed the cake competition, Tilly. I can honestly say it has been my favourite allotment event ever.'

'Thank you.' I smiled and hugged her.

'Baking is one of life's joys for me and it has been lovely not to have to throw half a cake away, to be able to share my baking with others.' She sighed and clasped her hands under her chin.

An almost buried memory of Liz with half a cake at Easter popped up. That had niggled me at the time.

'Why half a cake?' I asked.

A cloud passed over her face and she swallowed. 'You'll think I'm silly, but I don't have anyone to share a cake with, so I always throw half of it away as soon as I've made it, to avoid eating it all myself.'

I blinked at her. Part of me marvelled at her restraint (I could never throw cake away) and the other part wondered why she didn't just make a smaller cake.

She chuckled as she read my mind. 'I could make a smaller cake, I suppose, but it just doesn't feel right. A slice of cake should be a certain size. A slice cut from a small cake . . .' She shuddered. 'Oh no.'

'I see,' I said, pressing my lips together to suppress a smile. Obviously I was just greedy; cake was cake, as far as I was concerned.

'But baking aside, having a bit of male company in the kitchen . . .' She sighed and her eyes sought out Nigel in the room and then drifted back to me. 'It's been, well, it's been the happiest few days I've had for a very long time, Tilly, and I really mean that.'

Liz and Nigel? Actually, now that I thought about it, they made a lovely couple . . .

'My ex-husband, he . . .' She stared at me for a moment, seeming to weigh up whether I was confidante material or not.

I squeezed her hand encouragingly. 'Go on.'

Liz tucked her hand under my elbow and led me to the comparative privacy of the far corner of the room.

'I'm no oil painting, I know,' she murmured, 'but he used to make jokes about me in front of his friends, about how plain I was and how it was a good job I could cook, because I was useless at everything else. In the end, he left me for a younger woman.' She smiled at me but there was no mistaking the pain in her eyes.

'I'm sorry.' I was touched that she had chosen to confide in me and cross at the same time that she had lived her life under this shadow for so long.

'Don't be. He gave me back my freedom. Well, my own space at least. I'm afraid years of his put-downs made me want to hide away. But spending time with Nigel,' her eyes misted over, 'what a lovely man. Such a gentleman. I've felt valued for the first time in years and years.'

'And now you feel ready to love again?' I said softly.

'Me?' she squeaked. 'Oh goodness me, no!' Liz's fingers fluttered up to her neck, which had gone slightly blotchy all of a sudden. 'That part of my life is over now. I mean who would . . .? It's not as if I'd be a catch for anyone.' She sighed and my heart broke for her; she would be a catch, I was sure of it.

'Anyway,' she continued, 'I'd best get cracking.' And with one final wistful glance at Nigel, she ducked her head and darted from the room.

I popped into the kitchen to fetch a glass of water, thirsty after my impromptu nap, and found Brenda and Christine still in there washing up.

'Isn't that your bag, Tilly?' asked Christine, nodding her head to a large shopping bag on the floor.

'Sorry, Christine, it is, I'll move it out of your way and I do apologize for not helping clear up.'

She waved me away with a hand covered in soap suds. 'You've done enough today. Go home and have a rest.'

I smiled and sighed. 'Thank you. I am shattered, I must admit.'

I scooped up the bag and wandered back into the main room. Just as I was saying my goodbyes, Hayley appeared at the pavilion door and bounded over to me, her arm wrapped round a tall cake tin.

'Have I missed the competition?' she asked, giving me a one-armed hug as she looked round the room. 'I have, haven't I?'

I glanced at her cake tin and my heart sank. It was so kind of her to come and support me and knowing her baking skills, her cake would probably have been a winner. 'Oh, I'm sorry, Hayley, we're just clearing up. Well, everyone else is; I slept through most of the work.'

Hayley grinned and shrugged one shoulder. 'Never

mind. The reason I'm late is because . . . drum roll please . . . I passed my driving test this morning!'

'Yay!' I flung my arms round her and kissed her cheek. 'That's fantastic! You are such a dark horse, I only saw you a couple of weeks ago and you didn't mention a thing, I didn't even know you were learning to drive.'

She blushed and lowered her eyes, bouncing the toe of her Converses against the floor. 'Didn't know how you'd feel, worrying about another nutter on the roads.'

'Oh Hayley,' I whispered, swallowing a lump in my throat. 'I'm really proud of you.'

She coughed and held out her cake tin. 'Anyway, have a look at this. I don't normally do fancy stuff, but I saw this on Pinterest and thought I'd have a go myself.'

She pulled the lid off the tin and I peered inside. There sat a large, exquisitely decorated cake, covered in pastel fondant icing.

'That is fabulous!' I said, meaning it.

Hayley shrugged modestly. 'It's a multi-layered almond-flavoured sponge cake. When you cut into it each layer of sponge is a different colour. It came out all right, I suppose. Anyway, seeing as I made it for Ivy Lane, you might as well take it.'

She thrust the tin into my hands before I had chance to argue. 'Right,' she said, turning to go, 'I'm off. I'm sup-posed to be meeting Ben in half an hour to go Christmas shopping.'

I noticed the flush of young love spring to her cheeks. I'd heard all about Ben at the bonfire party. Hayley had started catering college as well as working for Brenda. Ben was a fellow student and he sounded like he was a good influence on her.

I kissed her goodbye and placed the cake tin in my bag. I

certainly wouldn't be able to face any of that today after all the cake I'd eaten during the judging. I collected the rest of my things and made my way to the door. Perhaps I should cut it in two and give half away. But no, that wouldn't do at all. A cake like that deserved a special occasion, to be nibbled on daintily, to be shared, and preferably accompanied by Earl Grey tea served in delicate china cups.

Half a cake. Someone to share it with. Liz and Nigel. Nigel and Liz.

My breath caught in my throat as a crazy idea formed. Nigel was still here. I looked at the clock. Two thirty. Possibly an hour, maybe a bit more before it went dark.

'Are you around all afternoon, Nigel?' I called nonchalantly.

Nigel scratched his head. 'Not too long, another cup of tea perhaps, then I'll pull up some leeks and head home.'

I beamed at him. 'Good, great, see you then. Bye.'

I dashed to my car, flung my bags in the boot, and set the cake tin carefully on the passenger seat. My heart was racing and my hands were wobbly as I wrote two identical notes.

Please come to tea at the stone bench in the woods behind plot 16 at 3.30 this afternoon.

I chewed my lip while I deliberated and finally added a kiss at the end of each note.

OK. I exhaled shakily. Now to plant the notes.

I hurried along the road towards their plots. Nigel's would be easy: he was still in the pavilion. But Liz was on her plot somewhere. I wedged one of the notes in the gap around Nigel's shed door and tiptoed silently towards the plot opposite. Liz was in her polytunnel, humming softly to herself, completely absorbed in watering some seedlings. I snaked my hand through the open door and dropped the note on top of her bag. Slowly, being ultra-careful not to touch anything or make a noise, I withdrew my arm, creeping backwards. As soon as I was far enough away I broke into a sprint and headed for my car. I was going to have to move fast if this plan was to work.

Back at home, I set the kettle to boil while I unwound the fairy lights from around the mirror in the living room and sent up a silent prayer a) that the batteries wouldn't conk out and b) that they were, in fact, suitable for use outdoors.

I made a flask of tea – Earl Grey, of course – and ferreted about in the back of the kitchen cupboard until I found my best china. I paused, swallowing the lump in my throat as I stroked a finger along the delicate cups and saucers, the dainty plates. The tea set had been a wedding present. Pink and red and beautiful, decorated with tiny birds. Arguably the allotment wasn't the best place for its first airing in two years, but then again, hiding it in a cupboard wasn't doing it justice either. I took a deep breath, wrapped the china carefully in towels and stowed everything in my shopping bag.

Nigel and Liz deserved this, I told myself as I drove back to the allotment in my little yellow car. They were two lovely, lonely people and they deserved a second chance at happiness, at love. I was meddling, I knew, but something told me to do it anyway.

I hopped out of the car and darted along the road, past my plot and into the woods. I checked the time. Three fifteen. My breath was coming in short sharp spurts as I threaded the fairy lights through the branches to accentuate the arch above the stone bench. I spread out a blanket, placed the cake on a plate and set out tea for two.

Finally, with two minutes to spare, I stepped back to check that everything looked OK.

Oh my word.

I held a hand to my mouth to stop myself from making a sound. It was every bit as magical as I'd imagined. The sky had turned a purple-grey as the sun began to fade and the tiny lights twinkled above the bench.

It was the perfect setting to fall in love.

I sighed happily, shrank backwards into the shadows and hid behind a tree a few feet away. I held my breath as I heard the sound of footsteps crunching through the undergrowth from the other side of the archway — two sets — accompanied by low voices.

The footsteps stopped. I heard Liz gasp and Nigel chuckle.

I let my breath out slowly. So far so good.

I should go now. I should creep away and leave them alone, I had done my bit, the rest was up to them. And I would go . . . soon. I squinted through the trees to see what they were up to.

Oh, hurrah! My heart surged with happiness for them. They were sitting on the bench, side by side, Nigel with his arm around Liz's waist, her head resting on his shoulder, tea and cake forgotten for the moment.

I was thrilled for them, truly I was. I wrapped my arms around myself and tiptoed away, intent on keeping a brave smile on my face. *Tilly Parker, you are a match-making genius.*

Why was it that everyone else's love life seemed so much simpler to sort out than my own?

Chapter 39

The following Friday, I convinced myself that my body needed some TLC more than it needed a night at the pub with Freya and her friends. So it was pamper night *chez moi*. I'd had a steaming hot bath, given myself a pedicure, massaged a hot oil treatment into my hair and was about to apply a face mask that promised to 're-moisturize, replenish and rehydrate'.

The cold weather had been playing havoc with my skin recently and being on playground duty every lunchtime this week had been the last straw. I had chapped lips, flaky patches on my cheeks and red nostrils from excessive nose blowing. My hair wasn't much better either. An aversion to the hairdresser's combined with a fondness for my hair straighteners meant that I had a serious case of the longest split ends in the western hemisphere.

Normally I would have roped Gemma in to sort me out with a few beauty treatments, but her tummy was so round and taut these days, that even brushing her own hair left her breathless. So I'd carted home half the contents of Boots' 'emergency repair' counter and was going it alone.

Besides, Gemma was having an early night tonight. I knew this because she had been here earlier and we had spent an expensive hour shopping online for all her baby needs. In the end, she hadn't fancied 'real shopping'. She declared herself too big to waddle around sweltering shops that were packed with too many Christmas shoppers and too few loos, and so we had opted for some virtual shopping instead. In all honesty, this had suited me better. I probably wouldn't have been the only non-pregnant woman in the baby department of John Lewis, but I would have felt like I was.

I snipped off the corner of a sachet of blueberry face mask, squeezed the contents into the palm of my hand and applied it in a gentle massaging motion, avoiding the 'delicate eye area' as per the instructions. I studied my reflection as I washed my hands. I certainly looked like a blueberry anyway.

My phone rang and I answered it, trying to keep the guilt out of my voice when I saw who the caller was.

'Hello, Freya!'

'So are you up for it tonight? We're already in The Feathers – you know, the pub on Shenton Road – then we're going into Kingsfield later.'

I'd thought about joining her and her friends for drinks tonight but the truth was I wasn't 'up for it', whatever 'it' might be. I still felt awkward in social occasions on my own, I still didn't drink much and I still had . . . I glanced at the clock . . . five hours left of November.

'Can I take a rain check, Freya? Only I'm a bit tired and . . .' My voice petered out. It was only seven o'clock and I'd been about to admit that I was already in my dressing gown and pyjamas. I was pathetic, certainly, but there was no need to advertise it.

'No worries. Oh, by the way, you don't happen to know if that gorgeous bloke at your allotment is single, do you?'

I grinned. 'The tall, muscly, good-looking one?'

She sighed longingly. 'The very same.'

'That's Charlie and yes he is. Do you want me to put in a good word?'

I held the phone away from my ear as Freya squealed her answer.

I was still smiling as I ended the call. I'd got out of that one nicely and to top it off I might have made another romantic match. I was getting to be quite the expert at this! Now I could look forward to a relaxing evening in front of the TV while my beauty treatments worked their magic.

Unfortunately, just as I was lowering my bottom on to the sofa, remote control in one hand, steaming hot chocolate in the other, there was a sudden thunderous knock at my front door. I yelped in surprise, tried to stand back up too quickly and tipped scalding hot liquid down the lapel of my white dressing gown.

The downside of a terraced house, I'd come to realize, as I dithered on the spot deciding what to do first, is that there's no option of pretending to be out. The living room was at the front of the house; whoever had decided to call round at this particularly inconvenient moment would have seen the light on and probably even heard the TV.

There was nothing else for it, I sighed, catching my blueberry-tinted reflection in the mirror above the fireplace, I would have to answer the door.

'Bear with me!' I shouted in the direction of the front door and dashed into the kitchen to remove the worst of the mess.

'Nobody ever knocks on my door when I'm looking my best,' I muttered to myself as I rummaged in my bag for my door keys. Why didn't I get unexpected visitors when my hair was softly styled, my make-up immaculate and my outfit flattering? I rolled my eyes. I never looked like that.

Finally I unlocked the door, trying not to twitch as the face mask started to peel away from my upper lip.

'Sorry to keep you waiting . . . oh! Hello.'

I don't know who I'd been expecting; I'd been too concerned with my appearance to think that far ahead. Someone from school maybe, or the allotment or perhaps Hayley, she popped round occasionally to fill me in on her news . . . but not this stranger.

My visitor was a young woman with wiry black hair wearing a Minnie Mouse sweatshirt, a floral corduroy skirt and brogues. It was an unusual outfit by anyone's standards, but particularly for someone in her twenties. Even more surprising was that she was holding Cally in her arms. My Cally! He sprang out of her grasp and slunk past me.

The girl gave me a nervous smile and twisted her hands together.

'I've been knocking for ages, quietly at first, but you didn't answer so I gave it one last knock. I hope I didn't frighten you?'

I shook my head and tried to cover up the wet patch on my dressing gown.

'Would you like to come in?'

'Oh, no. I just wanted to let you know that your cat has been spending a lot of time in my house recently.'

I raised my eyebrows. 'So that's where he's been. He hardly comes home at night these days. I'm sorry about that.'

'I live directly behind this house, our gardens back on to each other. So he hasn't been far away.'

'Oh right; well, thank you very much, then.' I put my hand on the door, a gentle signal to end the conversation.

After all, it was cold, she didn't want to come in and my face was getting really itchy.

'I, um . . . this is a bit difficult,' she said, turning the toe of her shoe inwards awkwardly.

I looked at her foot and then up at her face, my expression questioning and waiting.

'It's just that I've got a cat called Pebbles.' She blushed, pushed her thumb up to her mouth and began to chew on the nail. 'She's expecting kittens and I think your cat is the father.'

I gasped. 'Cally? But he's only a kitten himself! He's not even one yet!' My brain was whirring: what were my responsibilities, how would we know for sure if they were his kittens, would I have to keep some of the litter?

'I believe male cats are,' she cleared her throat, 'sexually active from as young as six months old.'

'Oh.' I was momentarily glad that my face was coated in a purple layer as it probably went some way to hiding my mortification.

Slightly bewildered, I fetched my phone and we swapped numbers and she promised to get in touch when the kittens were born. I waved her off, shut the door and leaned against it heavily.

Great. Even my cat has got a girlfriend.

I turned my phone over and over in my hand and felt my heart thump against my chest.

It was the last day in November. Tonight I was officially going to give up on the idea of Aidan and me ever getting together.

I had neither heard from him nor been brave enough to contact him myself. And that meant, according to my self-imposed ultimatum, that as of tomorrow I was declaring myself on the market. I shuddered at the expression, it made me sound like a house, or a second-hand car, or worse, downright desperate. Perhaps 'open to amorous advances' would be more appropriate. A bit Jane Austen, though.

Well, pardon me, Jane Austen.

Gemma's words when I'd said I was waiting for Aidan to phone me.

I still had his number.

He didn't have mine.

Oh my word. Aidan didn't have my number! Why on earth had that not occurred to me before?

My heart ached suddenly and I hauled myself back up-stairs to the bathroom. My fingers were shaking as I rinsed the oil from my hair and peeled the rubbery mask from my face.

Was this it, then? The end of the line for Aidan and me? What if I was throwing away something special out of pride or propriety or fear? I pressed my fingers to my lips and stared at my pink face in the bathroom mirror while my heart debated the matter in hand with my head.

Heart: I've come so far this year, building a new life for myself, a new career, a new town, why shouldn't I be the one to make the call? What's the worst that could happen?

Head: He could turn you down and then you'd be devas-tated.

Heart: But that kiss – kisses, in fact – I haven't been imagining it, I'm sure; there was chemistry between us, a connection.

Head: True . . .

Before my head had completely made its mind up my heart had decided on behalf of both of them and my entire body was already quivering.

I swallowed, scrolled through my contacts to where I

had saved his number, as yet undialled but already stored under 'favourites'.

My finger hovered over his name. And I pressed the call button.

The number began to ring. An English dial tone. Phew. At least he was still in the country, in the same time zone as me, it would have been awful if he was somewhere else and it was the middle of the night . . .

'Hello, Aidan's phone?'

It was a woman. I could hear the smile in her voice, she sounded breathless and distracted, as if I'd interrupted something . . .

Perhaps I *had* interrupted something. Something of a personal nature. My mouth went dry and my heart hammered in my ears. 'I . . . I . . . sorry, wrong number.'

I cut off the call and dropped the phone into the sink.

Why, why, why had I listened to my heart instead of my head? Of course he would have found someone else by now – he was talented, handsome, entertaining, kind-hearted . . . Of course he wouldn't still be single.

Arrghhh!

A sudden picture of Aidan and a woman lying in bed, languid and lazy from love-making made my stomach flip over and I clutched my throat. I shut my eyes tight to banish the image.

So that was that.

I needed a drink.

I pulled on my jeans, applied a layer of mascara, a slick of lipgloss and waved the hairdryer around until my hair was just dry enough not to give me pneumonia, and thirty minutes later I was marching to The Feathers.

As pubs go, The Feathers was nothing special; it didn't do food, or have a play area or tables on the pavement, it was simply a place to drink. Which meant that at this precise moment it was exactly where I wanted to be.

Unfortunately, as soon as I pushed open the door I knew I'd made a mistake. The pub was packed, noisy and for a stay-at-home girl like me, totally intimidating.

There was a live band playing on a raised stage at the far end. I didn't recognize the song but whatever it was I didn't like it and it was too loud. I spotted Freya with her friends near the stage. There were six girls, all in full-on party mode: the table was cluttered with empty glasses, they were animated and happy, flicking their hair back and giggling, and trying to catch the eyes of the group of men on the next table.

I couldn't do it. I didn't belong here with them. Freya hadn't noticed me, thankfully. A huge lump appeared in my throat and I turned around and walked out before tears gave me away.

What on earth had I been thinking? It was one thing to make new friends and have a couple of drinks when you were on top form, but quite another to go out with the sole intention of drinking yourself to oblivion in the company of strangers. At least I had come to my senses before ending up in some dodgy club in Kingsfield, I thought as I stomped back along Shenton Road.

I pulled my scarf up over my mouth and wrapped my collar tight around my throat against the icy winds and walked as fast as I could in the direction of home. The sooner I could get tonight over with the better. Tomorrow was another day. Tomorrow was December, in fact, almost Christmas. Perhaps I could go Christmas tree shopping?

I was so busy debating the merits of a real tree versus an artificial one that I paid little attention to a fire engine that rumbled silently past.

Its lights hadn't been flashing I realized belatedly, which meant that it must be on its way back to the station. Whatever catastrophe had arisen in Kingsfield tonight, it had obviously been dealt with. Shame there wasn't an emergency service for broken hearts . . .

As I turned into Wellington Street the fire engine reappeared and pulled to a halt beside me with a hiss of brakes. A door opened and Charlie jumped out and slammed the door behind him. The faces of four firefighters pressed up against the windows and stared at me.

I'd never seen him in his uniform before. He was every bit as handsome as usual, but more so. I felt a flutter of pride.

'I thought it was you.' He stood with his hands on his hips and looked around as if he was expecting someone else to jump out from the behind a lamp-post. 'What are you doing out on your own?'

'For the record, I'm not actually twelve, but thank you for your concern,' I laughed and wrapped my arms around myself.

He raised his eyebrows. 'Sooo?'

I rolled my eyes and flapped a hand. 'Oh, I was going to the pub with Freya from the café, but I changed my mind. I'm on my way home.'

'I'll walk you back.' He turned to the driver of the fire engine and shouted through the window, 'See you later.'

There were a couple of shouts of approval, which was a bit embarrassing, and then the fire engine tooted its horn and drove away. For some reason, I waved too and then felt silly.

'Is that allowed, bunking off?' I said before he asked me any more details about my disastrous night out.

He shrugged. 'My shift finishes in a few minutes anyway. Come on.'

'I'm absolutely fine on my own, but if you insist.' I smiled and shrugged, feigning indifference, although secretly I was pleased to have company.

We began to walk, my clip-cloppy heels echoing along the pavement while his black boots didn't make a sound.

'Freya's very nice,' I said.

'Hmm,' he replied in a non-committal sort of way that I couldn't interpret.

'She asked me to put in a good word for her with you.'

He laughed softly and shook his head. 'Nah, not my type.'

I watched the breath swirl around his face in the cold air and bit back the words on my tongue. I had a pretty good idea what his type was. I shivered and he held out his elbow for me to take. I looped my arm through his and leaned against him, savouring his warmth. We walked along in companionable silence for a few minutes, with me contemplating how on earth I'd managed to go from a pamper evening in front of the TV to a cold walk home with a fireman.

Charlie and me.

It would be so easy.

Me and Charlie.

I could ask him to come in with me and he would. I could ask him to stay the night so that I wouldn't have to be alone and he probably would.

But that wouldn't be fair. I wished I was in love with Charlie but I wasn't. He was, and always would be, the big brother I'd never had.

We were nearly at my house and I reached into my bag to get my keys. His next question nearly made me choke on my own breath. 'So what's the story with you and the TV guy, any news?'

'Who? Aidan? Oh, gosh no,' I laughed, shook my head and rolled my eyes. 'No, that's all ancient history, water under the bridge. Gosh no!'

It was a good job it was dark, even if my words convinced him, which I doubted, my blazing cheeks would certainly have betrayed me.

Charlie sighed, whirled round to face me and rubbed his hands over his face. I heard the rasp of stubble against his fingers. I jingled the keys in my hand and stared at my feet.

'I am so sorry for what I did, Tilly. If I'd known what a mess I would make of everything . . . He's a nice bloke and I had no right to come between you. If there's anything I can do to help, you know, put in a good word . . .' His face softened into a smile and I smiled back sadly.

I remembered the girl who had answered Aidan's phone earlier and shook my head.

'You're not to blame. I'm the only one who made a mess of things.' I sighed. 'It's too late for Aidan and me, Charlie, but thank you for the offer and thank you for walking me home. Goodnight.' I stood on my tiptoes, kissed his cheek and let myself into the house, leaving him standing there in the moonlight with his hand still rubbing his face.

Chapter 40

Next morning after a rather restless night's sleep I made myself a cup of tea, perched myself on a kitchen stool and called Gemma, thinking as I dialled that I probably wouldn't be able to do this for much longer; she would be far too busy with a new baby in the family to deal with my dating dilemmas. But at least at the moment she was fully recovered and hopefully would have time to talk to her single friend.

'Ah, sad face,' Gemma said with a sigh, after I'd regaled her with the events of the previous evening, from Cally's impending fatherhood to Aidan's new woman. I left out the bit about how Charlie leapt from his fire engine to chaperone me home. I wanted sympathy, not speculation.

'To be honest, you don't know how lucky you are, being single,' she added.

She must have heard me gulp.

'I'm sorry, Tills, I know that probably sounds insensitive.'

It did rather. I made a polite soothing noise all the same.

'But last night, I swear, Mike snored from the second he turned out the lights until the birds started twittering this morning while I lay there propped up on three thousand pillows, trying to ignore him and my flippin' heartburn. At one point I found myself looming over him holding one of my pillows inches from his face. I was tempted, I can tell you.'

'Poor Mike!' I couldn't help giggling at the image of an exasperated Gemma being driven to suffocate her mild-mannered husband for the rather innocent crime of snoring.

'Poor me, more like!' I could hear the pout in her voice. 'What I wouldn't give to have a double bed all to myself for one night.'

I'd had a double bed all to myself for over two years and frankly enough was enough.

'Oh God,' I groaned, 'what I *wouldn't* give to be kept awake all night by someone in bed with me. I need some loving. Does that sound desperate?'

'A bit.' She giggled. 'Ooh, I know, Date Me dot com!' she exclaimed.

'Er, I'm not sure I follow you.'

'The internet dating site, you know?'

'Oh right.' I sighed with relief. 'For a moment there . . . oh, never mind. But no. Thanks for the suggestion, but definitely not.'

Internet dating had 'dodgy men' written all over it and I think I'd suffered enough failures in the romance department this year already.

'It's quite safe, Tilly, my hairdresser has been on loads of dates that way.'

My point exactly.

'Mmm. Thing is I don't want "loads of dates". I just want one really nice one.'

Preferably with a man with intelligent brown eyes and a broad nose and thick wavy hair . . .

I snapped my eyes shut.

Forget about Aidan like he's forgotten about you.

'Actually, Marcia, one of the teachers at school, keeps trying to set me up with her brother,' I said brightly.

'A blind date!' Gemma squealed down the phone. 'That was how me and Mike got together and look how that turned out!'

I pressed my lips together and decided not to mention last night's near miss with the pillow.

'You should go for it, what have you got to lose?' she added.

'Apart from my dignity in the staff room, you mean?' I sighed. 'Marcia showed me a picture and he didn't look too bad until she admitted that he still lived at home with their parents, sleeps in a single bed and kisses his Kylie Minogue posters before going to sleep each night.'

'Oh dear,' she sniggered. 'Sounds like that film, *Failure to Launch.*'

We both fell silent, thinking about Matthew McConaughey's tousled hair.

I cleared my throat. 'Anyway. What are you up to for the rest of the day?'

I heard her shuffle in her seat. 'Well, Mike and I are doing some planning for next year.' She sounded all excited and happy.

I smiled, glad she was over her desire to strangle him.

'Me too,' I said. 'I've ordered some seed catalogues and I'm going to pop down to the allotment later and make a list of everything I think I should grow next year. I'm toying with the idea of setting up a gardening club at school, too. I thought I might ask your mum for some advice. I think the children would love growing their own vegetables.'

'Ah, that's a terrific idea and I'm sure she'd love to help. We're planning on knocking through the kitchen into the dining room, to make the downstairs more open. It'll make it easier to keep an eye on the baby when I'm in the kitchen if we've got one big room. And then Mia can be in the living room watching telly or revising. Hmmph, although I'll believe that when I see it.'

My smile slipped away and I swallowed. 'Sounds perfect,' I said, forcing a lightness that I didn't feel.

My plans sounded like the plans of a single lonely person. Hers sounded like the plans of a growing family. Which was true, of course.

I rang off with promises to see her soon as I needed to get on. I had an appointment with a hoe and some errant weeds at Ivy Lane. Besides which, I wanted to see who was around. Funny how I'd taken on the allotment to give myself some peace and quiet and now I made it my destination whenever I needed company.

But that was the thing about life, I mused; no matter how diligent you are, it never does quite go to plan.

Two weeks later, we were halfway through December and I was still relying on Ivy Lane for my fix of social contact. Our numbers were rather depleted, though, I thought sadly as I looked across the allotment. Shazza was here, but no Karen. I'd spotted Christine in the pavilion office and Liz was in her polytunnel. But that was it. Roll on summer when Ivy Lane was teeming with colour and people and life . . .

I pushed the spade into the soil, rested my foot on it and took a breather. Despite the temperature, which was barely above freezing, I was hot and out of breath.

Today I was digging the area that Brenda had had her potatoes in. I hadn't really done much digging on my plot all year. Since Charlie had ploughed it all up with the rotavator in March, I'd managed to keep it ticking over with a fork and a hoe. But now that I was virtually a gardening expert, I knew about leaving clods of earth for the winter frosts to break down to give me a good start next spring. The next job would be to cover all the bare earth over with manure. I was in no rush to do that bit.

It was back-breaking work but fairly mindless, which was just as well because my head was crammed full with all the things I still had left to do before Christmas.

'Tilly!' I looked across to the road to see Christine bustling towards me waving a piece of paper in her hand. 'Are you busy next week?' she called.

I bit my lip and smiled. Ask any teacher if they are busy in the run-up to Christmas and they are likely to stare at you, gimlet-eyed, before either bursting into hysterical tears or charging at you with the nearest blunt instrument.

'Why?' I asked as she got closer. I'd learned my lesson with Christine. She would have to reveal her hand before I revealed mine.

She hugged me, smiled from underneath her bobble hat, and held out a mocked-up poster for the Ivy Lane Christmas party.

'I need some ideas for the party and as you did so well with the cake sale . . . ?' She beamed at me hopefully.

I took a deep breath.

Before the end of term, which was less than two weeks away, I had the Christmas disco to supervise and the staff Christmas lunch to attend (think soggy sprouts, dry pre-sliced turkey and not even a sniff of sweet sherry to wash it down). My class had been chosen to sing carols at a local old people's home, which I was assured was an honour, but the exchange of relieved looks between the deputy head and the reception teacher didn't go unnoticed, and there were three performances of the whole school nativity to be organized and endured. And our 'Mary', a little girl in my class, had informed me two days ago that she wouldn't be there for the show, because she was going to Tenerife with her whole family for Christmas.

All of this would be hard enough to cope with at any time of year, but now, with thirty children in full Christmas party mode in my charge, I was exhausted.

Nonetheless, I took the piece of paper from her.

The poster promised mulled wine, mince pies and the presentation of the prizes won at the annual show back in August. But apart from the refreshments, it lacked a certain 'festiveness'.

'Hmm, it doesn't seem very Christmassy.'

Christine sighed. 'Exactly. That's just what I was thinking.'

She shoved her hands in her anorak pockets, rolled her lips inwards and frowned. I stifled a smile; with her red cheeks, bobble hat and earnest expression she looked like a little elf.

'I think we need a bit more Christmas spirit,' I said. 'How about a Secret Santa? We pick names out of a hat and buy each other a present? And what about collecting a gift from each plot holder for the children that go to the soup kitchen? That would be a nice touch. And decorations . . .' I twinkled my eyes at her. 'Leave the decorations to me.'

'Oh Tilly, I'll leave it all to you if you don't mind.' Christine threw her arms around my neck and kissed my cheek.

I swallowed anxiously. I did mind really.

'What with the baby coming soon, me helping Gemma out with the cooking and cleaning and trying to sort everything out at Ivy Lane . . . it's all getting on top of me.'

I scanned her face. She did look tired and, if I wasn't mistaken, a bit tearful too.

'Of course,' I said, squeezing her arm. 'Anything I can do, just ask.'

'Thanks, Tilly, love. I'm sorry it didn't work out with you and Aidan, but his loss is our gain. You'd be too busy to help me out if you were courting.'

I watched her go, glanced down at the poster and exhaled.

Great.

At least my single status was useful to someone. I would probably end up alone, with no one but Cally's offspring for company, but as long as there was someone to fiddle about with allotment posters, all was well with the world.

Which reminded me, I really should make an appointment at the vet's for him. I'd bottled out of taking him to have the snip so far because I'd felt sorry for him, but he'd had his fun and I needed to be sensible about it before he impregnated any more fertile felines.

Poor Cally. I winced at the thought on his behalf. A life of celibacy probably wasn't top of his Christmas list. I sighed and put the poster in my pocket.

Quite frankly, it wasn't at the top of mine either.

Chapter 41

It was beginning to look a lot like Christmas. And despite being on my tiptoes on the top rung of a ladder on the porch of the pavilion, I had that warm tingling sensation in my stomach confirming that it was beginning to feel a lot like Christmas too. Tomorrow was Christmas Eve, I had broken up from school for a fortnight and put all the frenetic activity of the end of term behind me. All I had to do now was finish off the pavilion decorations for to-night's party and then I would switch to relaxation mode for a whole two weeks. Hurrah!

I hummed happily to myself as I wound the last set of fairy lights along the edge of the porch. The pavilion was covered with the lights, which was as it should be. There's no such thing as too many Christmas lights, as far as I'm concerned. I just hoped Nigel didn't notice anything amiss with the electricity bill next month.

'Right then . . .' Right on cue Nigel appeared from the pavilion and tied a smart knot in his checked woollen scarf. His eyes lifted to all the fairy lights and I held my breath, wondering if he'd read my mind. 'Oh, Tilly,' he beamed, 'this is going to be a marvellous Christmas party. I've never seen the place look so wonderful.'

And I'd never seen him look so happy. 'Thank you,' I said, smiling as Liz joined us on the porch.

'We're all set inside,' she said. 'The mulled wine is in the urn on low, the glasses are all laid out and I think everything's ready.'

'We'll get off then, Tilly, unless you'd like us to help you with the lights.' Nigel slipped a proud arm around Liz's shoulders and the pair of them grinned goofily at each other.

Oh, that first flush of love. I remember it well. I blinked rapidly as unbidden tears popped into my eyes. Here we go again. That was possibly the only downside of Christmas; I lived on a permanent knife edge of emotional outpourings. Christmas carols were my absolute weakness; I'd yet to make it to the second verse of 'Silent Night' without my voice going all wobbly.

I shook my head and smiled. 'I'll be fine, Nigel. You two go and get ready. Besides, I don't want to turn the lights on until you've gone. Then it will be a surprise when you come back later.'

I waved them off and reminded them to drive carefully on the snowy roads.

We had had our first snowfall during the night and when I'd woken up this morning I'd been quite alarmed by the muffled silence in Wellington Street until delightful realization had dawned. I'd bounced out of bed to get my first glimpse of the Christmas-card beauty of my street and I'd been ridiculously excited ever since.

The daylight had already faded and I had almost finished. Good job really, as I still had to dash home, change into something stunning and be back here for the festivities in little more than an hour.

I wrapped the end of the cable around the final wooden

upright on the porch, climbed down from the stepladder and held my breath as I tried the electrics.

Ta dah! At the flick of a switch the pavilion was transformed from a damp and dreary hut to a fairy-tale house. I stood back to admire the sight and pressed a hand to my mouth to stop myself from squealing. It was absolutely breathtaking.

'Sterling work, Tilly,' I murmured to myself as I moved the ladder to the centre of the porch.

There was just one more thing to do.

I tied a big red satin ribbon around the huge bunch of mistletoe that I'd bought from Kingsfield market, climbed back up the ladder and fixed it just above the front door.

I smiled to myself; this would put a twinkle in many a person's eye this evening. Kissing under the mistletoe was de rigueur at all the best Christmas parties. And this was definitely going to be *the* best Christmas party, if I had anything to do with it. My friends at Ivy Lane had done so much for me over the year and this was my way of thanking them. For bringing me back to life.

Inside the pavilion I checked that the mulled wine was simmering nicely before switching off all the lights except those on the Christmas tree. I paused and looked around the room before locking the door, my heart swelling with pride. Nigel was right, everywhere did look wonderful. We'd set up a small Christmas tree adorned with red baubles and strings of silver beads as well as hundreds of tiny fairy lights, of course. The entire room was festooned with garlands of ivy and holly picked from the allotment and dozens of little candles were dotted about the room ready to light at the start of the evening.

As I drove away, I glanced at the magical picture behind

me, the pavilion twinkling in the darkness and the bunch of mistletoe hanging like a big question mark above the door.

I looked away and concentrated on the road ahead.

Chapter 42

My party outfit for this evening consisted of a short-sleeved teal satin mini dress, which floated elegantly around my legs and gathered softly around the scooped neck. It was very flattering and, worn with a tiny black cardigan, black tights and heels, it was verging on the sexy side for the Ivy Lane pavilion, but for once, I decided to throw caution to the wind. It was Christmas after all and if I couldn't let my hair down at Christmas, when could I?

I ruined the effect slightly by setting off from home in wellingtons with my heels tucked into my handbag, but it couldn't be helped. Better to arrive in wellies than with a broken ankle. I'd hoped to be one of the first to arrive in order to witness everyone's gasps of wonder when they saw all the fairy lights, but shuffling along the icy pavements had taken longer than I'd anticipated and I could already see people inside as I approached the steps.

As I paused on the porch under the mistletoe to change my shoes, Gemma and Mike arrived.

'Christmassy dot com, Tilly! Everywhere looks amazing!' she cried as she waddled up the steps towards me like a side-stepping penguin. Mike was following closely behind, carrying an assortment of bags in one hand and supporting his wife's bottom with the other.

I helped her up the last step and laughed as I pulled her into my arms. 'Hello, you! I knew you wouldn't let me down with your appreciation of my efforts.'

I was so relieved to see her. Part of me had been worried that the baby would come before the night of the party and whilst I was sure she would rather be propped up in bed with a new baby in her arms, selfishly, I was delighted that she had made it.

And she looked absolutely radiant. She wore a long black dress with tiny crystals around the low neckline with a long black coat over the top and her hair sparkled with little diamantés. The baby was due in a matter of days and I had a sudden prickle of tears as I realized that this would probably be the last time we'd see her at Ivy Lane for months.

'Promise me we'll still be BFFs when the baby comes,' I whispered as she returned my hug.

'Promise,' she said, kissing my cheek. 'And I don't think we'll have long to wait for that to happen,' she added in a faint whisper close to my ear.

Which didn't sound at all worrying . . .

I glanced at her sharply but she gave me a don't-say-a-word look.

'How are you feeling, father-to-be?' I said, releasing Gemma to kiss Mike.

'Excited, nervous and scared witless.' He shot a smile of pure adoration at Gemma.

'Aww,' said Gemma and I at the same time.

'You go in, love, I just want a quick word with Tilly,' said Gemma, nudging her husband towards the door.

'A quick word,' said Mike with a frown, 'it's too cold out here for you.'

She rolled her eyes and he reluctantly left us to it.

'He's right,' I said. My lips had started to go numb and as Christmassy as it was on the porch, standing under the mistletoe might actually be construed as looking a teeny bit desperate. 'Let's go in.'

'Oof!' Gemma bent forward, leaning her hand on the porch railings, and started to pant.

'Gemma?'

She held her hand up to silence me. I shut up and stared.

As soon as she was able to talk again she glanced over her shoulder to check we were still alone. 'Tilly, don't say a word, but I'm in labour,' she hissed.

Only Gemma could come up with a sentence like that.

'Well, yes, I gathered that much,' I hissed back. I began to breathe rapidly with her. I had a woman in labour right here. It was all I could do not to scream for Mike, for help, for anyone, but she'd asked me not to. 'Are you completely mad?'

'Oh, I'll be ages yet,' she said airily now that the contraction had passed. 'There's no need to panic and if I'd mentioned it to Mike, there's no way he'd have let me come to the party.'

'Well, no and rightly so, I'd say.'

'Tilly, you are sweet,' she smiled breathlessly, 'but this is my only Christmas party and I bought this maternity tent-dress especially for it and if I'd gone into hospital I'd have missed out on wearing it. But don't worry. I've organized for Mia to spend the night at a friend's and I've got my hospital bag in the car. We'll just go straight there from here. It'll be a doddle!'

'And very lovely you look too,' I said. 'But I'm really not sure this is the best place for you.'

'Oh it is,' she said, widening her eyes. 'At home I'd just be

386

pacing around worrying. The party will take my mind off it for the next couple of hours.'

She scrunched up her face and bent over again as another contraction hit her. She reached into a pocket in her coat and brought out a little controller.

'Full blast this time, I think,' she muttered.

I recognized the white square in her hand from research into my own pregnancy, it was a TENS machine, designed to give gentle pain relief. I frowned. I hoped it was up to the job of disguising full-on labour from everyone including her husband at the party.

'Are you sure about this?' I said as soon as the pain passed.

She nodded and took my arm.

'Merry Christmas, everyone!' she yelled as we walked into the pavilion together. She turned to me and tapped her nose. 'Mum's the word.' She winked at me, sucked in her breath and went over to join Mike.

Thirty minutes later I was on my second mulled wine and had really started to enjoy myself. I'd had several compliments about my dress and many more about the party itself.

'I love the Secret Santa idea, Tilly,' said Vicky, clinking her wine glass against mine. 'Cheers!'

'Cheers,' I responded and took a warming sip. Vicky was looking ravishing tonight in a red velvet blazer, black trousers and spiky heels.

'It's always a bit awkward trying to second guess who on the allotment will give you a Christmas present and who won't,' she added. 'This is a much neater way of doing it.'

'Thanks, Vicky. I'm glad you think so. And the soup kitchen will be delighted with all the gifts for their Christmas party tomorrow too.'

The Secret Santa idea had gone down really well. I'd put everyone's names into a hat and we'd all pulled one out and bought our recipient a present costing no more than ten pounds. I'd had to buy a present for Graham, Helen's husband, and had found a little solar-powered radio that I thought suited his green ethos and would be perfect to bring to the allotment with him next summer. We'd all put our Secret Santa gifts on the table, clearly labelled for the recipient. There didn't seem to be one for me yet. Not that I'd been checking, obviously.

At a nod from Peter, Nigel turned down the volume to gentle background level and Peter asked us all to find a seat. Nigel had done an amazing job with the music. I'd been a bit sceptical at first when he'd offered to take charge of the party tunes, assuming we'd have nothing but Bing Crosby and Frank Sinatra's Christmas medley, but I'd been way off the mark. He had set up his iPad and wireless speakers and was blasting out a mix of everything from Beyoncé to Michael Bublé.

Peter joined Christine in front of a table, which was groaning with trophies and shields, and cleared his throat. 'Now for the formal bit of the evening: the presentation of the Annual Show prizes. And then we'll all open our Christmas presents.'

'Keep it short, Pete,' cried Dougie, 'I've got a lot of ladies to kiss under that mistletoe.'

'Ladies, if you could kindly control yourselves, we'll be as quick as we can,' said Peter, tongue firmly in his cheek.

'But before we present the prizes, we have some exciting news,' announced Christine, clapping her hands together.

I looked over at Gemma anxiously, wondering if the impending birth of her next grandchild was 'the news'. Gemma waved back. She looked a bit flushed and fidgety but otherwise fairly calm. I gave her a thumbs-up, turned back to Christine and sipped my drink.

'We've had an email from Aidan Whitby from the *Green Fingers* show.'

My heart thumped wildly against my ribcage as I swallowed. The spiciness and heat of the mulled wine hit the back of my throat and the liquid somehow missed its target. I choked and coughed, turned puce and then I gasped for breath.

I hadn't been expecting to hear his name again. And if I'd been under the impression that I was over him, I now knew unequivocally that I wasn't.

'Sorry,' I croaked to the thirty or so pairs of eyes that stared at me full of concern.

Christine raised her eyebrows at me warily and I gestured for her to continue. 'Our episode of *Green Fingers* has been nominated for an award for best TV documentary!'

Everyone clapped. So I clapped too. They all smiled and I smiled too, so hard, in fact, that my cheeks ached. That was amazing news. I was pleased for Aidan, delighted even. And he deserved it, he was brilliant at his job, the whole team was brilliant. I felt proud to have been part of it.

But my eyes were burning and my stomach was flipping over repeatedly like a performing seal. Aidan had emailed Christine. He was still in touch with Ivy Lane, but just not with me. Had he asked Christine about me? I wondered. Did he know I'd phoned him? Why, why, why had that girl answered? And why had I left it a whole month to call him?

Suddenly I'd had enough of this party. I didn't feel Christmassy any more. I felt cross and sad and fed up.

Christine was still talking. The awards evening was a big posh do in London in the spring and Aidan had sent invitations for two people to attend.

Please don't expect me to go to that.

I knew without looking that Gemma was sending me sympathetic vibes, but I didn't meet her gaze. I stared at my toes and concentrated on not looking as miserable as I felt.

'So to the prizes . . .' Peter began the presentation of the awards and my shoulders slumped with relief. True to his word, he and Christine handed out the various trophies, cups and shields with efficiency and speed and even I got a mention for my prize-winning apples. The apples I hadn't even entered.

Before long there were just two prizes left on the table. A large shield and a small silver cup.

Christine picked up the shield, opened her mouth and paused before speaking.

'The Ivy Lane Committee trophy, as most of you know, goes to the plot holder with the most points awarded overall at the annual show. And this year . . . this year—' Christine's voice broke and she pressed a hand to her mouth.

I felt a lump in my throat. I was pretty sure who had won.

Peter stepped forward and placed a comforting hand on Christine's shoulder. 'This year's winner is Alf,' he finished for her. 'Would you all please raise your glasses to absent friends? Alf, we miss you dearly. Merry Christmas, old chum.'

My eyes sparkled with tears as I and my fellow gardeners drank a toast to the lovely Alf.

Christine dabbed her eyes with a tissue and took a deep breath. 'We've decided that it's only fair that Alf is crowned our winner and we'll leave the trophy in the pavilion until someone else wins it next year.'

'Hear, hear!' said Nigel, sparking off another round of applause.

'Which leaves us with just this one prize left,' said Peter, collecting the silver cup from the table. 'The committee has decided that in remembrance of Alf, we would like to establish a new award. The Alf Jackson award for outstanding contribution to Ivy Lane life.'

This was news to me. Not that anyone needed my say-so to hand out awards, of course; I was very much the junior member of the committee. Even so . . . I sniffed and tried to maintain a neutral expression.

'This prize will be awarded annually,' continued Peter, 'and from next year, each plot holder will vote for who they think deserves the title. But this year the committee has nominated a winner.'

I folded my arms. Make that *most* of the committee.

'This person has thrown herself into Ivy Lane life with gusto.'

So it was a woman. Probably Christine. I couldn't think of another woman more full of gusto than her.

'She was instrumental in the success of the *Green Fingers* show and took one of the community service youngsters under her wing.'

Christine again, although I was less sure about the community service bit. Not that I was one to boast, but I was fairly sure I'd made more of an effort with Hayley than anyone else after Alf died.

'She has supported every Ivy Lane event this year and even organized our most successful one single-handedly, despite being new to our community and new to gardening.'

Now that definitely sounded like . . .

'Congratulations to Tilly!'

Me?

Tears filled my eyes as everyone clapped and I stood

there for a few seconds stunned. Then I leapt up to the front, threw my arms around Christine and Peter's necks and hugged them until they begged for mercy.

'I'm not sure that I deserve it, but thank you, thank you,' I squealed, as Peter handed me the cup. 'Oh, this has made my night. Thank you so much!'

'Now if you'd all like to re-charge your glasses, we'll be doing our Secret Santa in a few minutes,' announced Peter.

Nigel turned the music back up and everyone started milling around again.

'Thank you again,' I said to Christine, pulling her back towards me for another hug. 'Truly. I'm overwhelmed.'

She smiled indulgently at me. 'You deserve it, love, now away with you and enjoy yourself.'

I whirled round to share the moment with Gemma, but she was staring at her feet. The smile fell from my face and I pushed past assorted chairs, people and obstacles to get to her side.

'Gemma?'

The tone of my voice must have startled Mike. He turned to his wife and followed her gaze to the floor. 'You all right, Gem? Oh look, clumsy, you've spilt your drink!' he laughed. 'Has anyone got a cloth?'

Gemma puffed her cheeks out, gripped on to Mike's arm and gave a low guttural moan.

Mike winced as her grip tightened. 'Hey, I was only joking.'

Her drink sat untouched on the table next to her, which meant the water had to have come from somewhere else. I crouched down beside her and looked into her eyes.

'Have your waters broken, Gemma?' I whispered.

She nodded but didn't meet my eye.

'I think it's time to get you to hospital,' I said.

Mike's eyes lit up. 'Trust you to go into labour now, Gem! This is it then, babe, the big moment. How long do you think we've got – a couple of hours?'

I shook my head. 'Mike, she's been this way for some time. She didn't want to miss the party.'

Gemma panted and flashed her eyes at me. I ignored her. Party time was over.

'As soon as this contraction finishes, I think we should get her to the car,' I added in as calm a voice as I could muster.

Mike stood up and frowned at me. 'You knew about this?'

I nodded. Gemma tried to say something but I couldn't make out what it was between the grunts.

I gulped. 'She made me promise . . .'

Mike narrowed his eyes. 'I have to say, Tilly, that was bloody irresponsible of you. What if it had snowed again? The roads are already treacherous.'

His voice was low and controlled but there was no mistaking the anger in it. I felt terrible for keeping quiet, but I'd been so excited to see Gemma and she had seemed fine, not to mention adamant that she wanted to come to the party. I could kick myself now, though. But the main priority was to get Gemma to hospital as soon as possible.

'Phew, that was a strong one!' She blew her cheeks out and looked from me to Mike sheepishly.

'Shall I fetch Karen?' I asked, feeling the need to redeem myself and do something sensible.

Karen was dancing with Shazza and so far hadn't realized what was going on.

Gemma shook her head. 'I don't want to draw attention to myself.'

All three of us looked at each other and laughed and the tension between Mike and I eased a little.

Mike rolled his eyes and kissed her forehead. 'What are you like?'

'Don't blame Tilly,' she said, leaning her head against his arm.

I chewed my lip anxiously. 'Gemma, your contractions are coming faster now, we should get you to the car before the next one comes.'

She squeezed my hand and nodded. 'You're right. Come on, Mikey, let's go,' she said, getting to her feet. 'Tilly, hold my arm.'

Between the two of us, with her parents fussing behind, carrying bags and coats, we half-carried her the short distance across the icy car park, which thankfully had been sprinkled with grit, and into the passenger seat of the car.

'You take care, now,' said Christine, hugging her daughter. 'And phone us as soon as you have news.'

'And don't worry about Mia, we'll make sure she knows what's happening,' said Roy, wrapping an arm around his wife's shoulders.

I bent down and kissed Gemma's cheek. I placed a hand gently on her tummy.

Safe journey, little one, see you very soon.

'I'll come with you, if you like,' I said hopefully.

'It's OK,' said Mike, giving me a smile. 'I'll take it from here.'

'Sure. Well, good luck.' I shut Gemma's door and tried to organize my wobbling features into an encouraging smile.

'Bye!' Christine, Roy and I shouted together.

What had I said that for? Obviously they wouldn't want me there. This was their moment. Their baby. I knew that.

But did that not stop tears springing to my eyes as I watched them drive out of the car park?

No, of course not.

I swallowed the large lump that had wedged itself firmly in my throat and followed Christine and Roy back to the party.

Chapter 43

Charlie was waiting on the steps of the porch. He was directly under the mistletoe but he looked so fidgety and distracted that I don't think he'd even realized.

'Come back inside,' he said, beckoning us in with an impatient arm wave. 'Hurry up!'

'All right, all right, where's the fire?' tutted Roy, helping his wife up the steps chivalrously.

Charlie was peering over my shoulder, his brow furrowed.

'They've gone,' I said, following his gaze. 'I hope they get there without Gemma having too many more contractions. Or giving birth in the car.' I gulped at the thought.

'But we're all waiting to do Secret Santa,' he said.

'For goodness' sake, Charlie, you're a grown man,' said Christine, giving his arm a chastising tap. 'Anyone would think you'd never had a Christmas present before.'

Charlie grinned sheepishly. 'I know. I'm a bit excited, that's all. And anyway, it's better to give than receive.'

He winked at me as he held the door open for us all. I let Roy and Christine go in first and caught Charlie glancing around the car park again.

'I hope you're not expecting a visit from the real Santa,'

I said, cupping my hand to my mouth in a stage whisper, 'because if so I've got some bad news.'

He rolled his eyes and gave me a gentle nudge back inside.

Just in time. The music had been lowered again and Peter's eyes sought me out in the crowd.

'After that dramatic interlude, I think we'll do Secret Santa. Tilly, over to you.'

Goodness, from delivering babies (well, almost – thank heavens her waters had broken when they did) to delivering presents, tonight was fast becoming one of the most eventful parties I'd ever been to, I thought as I took my place in front of a table heaped with gifts.

'Hello, everyone. Well, firstly thank you all for the gifts for the children's soup kitchen, they're having their party tomorrow complete with a visit from Santa. And thank you for indulging me in the Ivy Lane Secret Santa. Now then . . .' I stared at the pile of presents, unsure how to proceed. Should I just make it a free-for-all or should I hand each present out separately? And what if someone ended up without a present? Decisions, decisions.

Shazza was standing next to me. I looked at her and pulled a help-me-out face. She beamed at me, picked up the parcel nearest to her and read the label. 'Dougie,' she called and threw the package in his direction.

Within seconds parcels were flying all over the place and grown adults were ripping off paper and whooping with delight at their new gardening gloves or watering cans or kneelers or bird feeders (most of us had gone with allotment-themed gifts, it seemed) with unadulterated excitement.

'Smell this,' said Brenda, holding the back of her hand up to my nose.

I sniffed obediently. 'Lovely.' Which was the truth, luckily.

'Crabtree and Evelyn gardeners' hand cream. What a treat! What have you had?'

My hands were clasped behind my back and she tried to look over my shoulder.

'Don't know; I haven't opened it yet. It's still on the table.' Which could possibly be the truth, although as far as I could tell, there was only one unopened present and I distinctly remember seeing Gemma's name on that. I'd take it home for her and put it under my tree.

I felt a bit conspicuous standing near the present table, present-less, so I went over to the makeshift bar and poured myself a glass of wine with a dash of lemonade and told myself I didn't mind not having a present. Not one bit. I gulped at my drink.

Graham was really chuffed with his little radio, so that was the main thing, and as Charlie had said, it was better to give than to receive. I sank down, resting my bottom on the edge of the table and sighed. All the same, I thought, taking another large restorative sip of alcohol, I couldn't help but wonder why I hadn't got a gift.

Unless, of course, I'd forgotten to add my own name to the hat. That was bound to be it! No one would have pulled my name out of the hat and *not* bought me a present, would they? So that had to be the answer. Everyone here was my friend. I smiled with relief and decided to keep my error to myself. If anyone asked about my gift, I would make something up. Easy peasy.

I giggled to myself as I took another sip of wine. The alcohol was going down extremely well. Anyway, what was one more present? I was a primary school teacher and primary school teachers never went short of presents at

Christmas, did they? In fact, I had thirty small gifts under the tree at home ready to be opened on Christmas morning.

Mum was coming to stay with me for Christmas. Or should I say Mum and Clive! They would be arriving tomorrow afternoon and I was really looking forward to it. Nervous too. It had been just Mum and me for the last two Christmases and we hadn't had much to celebrate. I'd decided to make a big fuss this year, though, and it was obvious that Mum was head over heels with Clive and wanted to spend Christmas with him, so it seemed the right thing to do. It would be different, but in a good way, I hoped. And when they left on Boxing Day, I would give Mum half of all the body lotions and chocolates and diaries and mugs that my class had given me.

So really, one more present was neither here nor there . . .

'Merry Christmas, Tilly.' I blinked myself out of my reverie to find Charlie in front of me holding my coat out.

'Oh, is the party over?' I said, jumping to my feet and skidding slightly in my heels.

His eyes twinkled at me and he took the glass out of my hand. 'No,' he chuckled, 'but I think you should perhaps slow down on the wine.'

'The floor's slippy,' I protested. Although he might have had a point. The glass was empty. Which was odd. It had been full a minute ago. The wine was beginning to make me feel all warm and fuzzy and I realized that I'd already drunk two glasses of mulled wine earlier and the last thing I'd had to eat was . . . I couldn't remember. Which couldn't be good.

'Coat on,' he murmured, still grinning at me.

'Why? Where are we going?' I said, sliding my arms into the sleeves obediently.

'Outside, come on.'

He turned and headed for the door and I had no choice other than to follow him. Well, I did, I suppose, but I was nosy and a bit tipsy and so going out on to the porch with Charlie seemed like the logical thing to do.

The freezing air assaulted my nostrils and sobered me up instantly, which was just as well because Charlie was standing directly under the mistletoe.

'Do you like the lights, Charlie?' I said, waving my arm along the porch to distract him as I slipped past and leaned on the wooden railings. 'I did them. Aren't they Christmassy?'

'Very,' he replied. He snorted with laughter and shook his head. 'You're quite safe,' he said. 'Look, I'll move away from the mistletoe if it makes you happy.'

'Most considerate,' I said, nodding earnestly. I was beginning to feel the cold creep its way into my bones and I wrapped my arms across my body. 'Now, can you please tell me what we're doing outside before my extremities drop off with frostbite.'

He took a deep breath, squared his shoulders and took a step towards me. 'I picked you in the Secret Santa.'

Oh goodie, I do get a present after all.

'Charlie! You're not supposed to tell me. The clue's in the name, you know,' I giggled.

He shrugged self-consciously. 'Most of us swapped. Well, the men anyway. Nigel started it.'

I shook my head. There was I, tearing up strips of paper diligently to make everything completely fair . . . honestly, they were no better than children.

'He wanted to surprise Liz. Dougie wanted Vicky.' He swallowed and directed his blue eyes at me. 'And I wanted you.'

Oh. This was beginning to have an all too familiar ring

to it. The wine had made my mouth dry. I licked my lips nervously.

'But, Charlie—'

He held a hand up and I pressed my lips together and dug my hands into my pockets for warmth.

'Let's sit down.' He gestured towards a bench further along the porch. I took a seat and he sat down heavily beside me.

He exhaled, a long shaky breath, and for the life of me I couldn't work out what was coming next.

'So?' I said eventually. 'Where's my Secret Santa present?'

'I'm coming to that.' He looked at me and laughed awkwardly. 'I've got a confession to make first. I'm getting the worst bit over with in the hope that you'll like your present so much that you'll forgive me.'

I groaned. 'Oh, Charlie, why does everything have to be so complicated with you?'

'Please don't give me that scary teacher look but . . . God, this is hard . . . I've got something of yours.' He hesitated and rubbed a hand over his cropped hair. He was sitting with his knees apart and bouncing on the toes of his right leg, jiggling his thigh; a man in perpetual motion.

'Look, I might as well just tell you, you already have a pretty low opinion of me anyway.'

'Charlie, that's not true . . .' My voice faded away as I stared at the object he'd pulled out of his pocket.

'A key?' I frowned at him. 'Is that my Secret Santa?'

He bit down on his bottom lip, stared at me with unblinking eyes and shook his head. He reminded me of the little boys in my class when they own up to their latest misdemeanour; in fact, in that moment he reminded me of Ollie, with his big blue eyes and irresistible face.

He looked up to the sky and let out a long breath.

'It's the key to your shed.'

I took the long silver key from his hand and as I turned it over in my hand, I simultaneously turned this new fact over in my brain. Charlie had a key to my shed. It didn't make sense.

'I had a copy cut just before Easter when you ran off crying because all your seedlings had died.'

I nodded slowly. 'I remember. You locked my shed for me and gave me the key back on Seedling Swap Sunday. But why make a copy?'

He didn't answer straight away but delved into his pocket again. Another key appeared.

'The shop,' he said in answer to my confused expression.

I shivered, slipped the shed key into my pocket and pulled my coat tighter around my neck.

'I'm sorry,' he said. 'You're freezing. Let me make this quick. But please, Tilly, hear me out and believe me when I say I'm so sorry for everything I'm about to tell you.'

He was really scaring me now and I could feel the blood pulsing through my veins. I was on the verge of making my escape, but he took hold of both of my hands and squeezed them gently.

'Please?' he said.

'OK,' I whispered hoarsely.

'Back in the summer, I don't how it happened but I became a bit . . . obsessed with you.' He pulled a comical face to lessen the impact of his words and I tried to smile back. I'd more or less guessed that anyway. 'I'm over it now, though.'

My lips twitched at that.

'I thought you were perfect, with your beautiful face and cheerful personality. You're kind and thoughtful and sensitive and,' he laughed softly, 'you look so funny on that bike in your helmet and neon safety jacket.'

My eyebrows shot up in indignation. I love that bike.

'I thought you were the one.' He sighed. 'I thought if only you would love me back, I'd be able to move on and finally get over my ex-wife. But when you weren't interested it sent me a bit crazy.'

He paused and stared at the floor and his thigh started jiggling again. He lowered his voice and I had to strain to hear the next bit.

'I decided to get your attention. Oh, God.' He let go of one of my hands and pinched the bridge of his nose and squinted at me with one eye shut. 'I set that fire in the allotment shop.'

'Charlie!' I gasped.

'I know, I know.' He hung his head low. 'I wanted to show you what a hero I was. And I'm ashamed to admit, I wanted to sabotage Aidan's work. I thought if I ruined the programme he might just go away. What a total idiot. The bloody thing is up for an award now.'

I was speechless. Now I thought about it, he had been running from the shop when I'd seen him. But what an irresponsible thing to do. What if someone had been hurt?

'Why steal the keys in the first place?' I croaked.

'My ex changed the locks after I found out about her affair. I couldn't get into my own house, or see my own son. I felt helpless, locked out of my own life. So for the last couple of years I've had a fixation with keys. If I came across a key, I made a copy. Just in case.' He shrugged helplessly. 'It was a control thing. I'm over that, too.'

I swallowed, unsure how to respond. 'Well, that's good,' I muttered.

He stood up and pulled me to my feet. 'Anyway, you'll

probably never want to speak to me again, let alone want us to be friends. But I had to tell you. And I hope that one day you'll forgive me for all the stupid things I've done. But I'm going to be a better person from now on. To set Ollie a good example. I'm determined to do that. Actually, I was thinking of a sponsored bike ride to raise money for the pavilion or something.'

We stared at each other for a long moment. My teeth started chattering and I shuddered as a sudden cold shiver ran down my back.

'Look, Charlie, I can't pretend that I'm comfortable with what you've told me. But I'm glad you did. And organizing a fund-raiser is very generous of you.' I gave him a lopsided smile and held my arms out. He stepped into them and we gave each other a hug.

'Does that mean we *are* friends?' he asked.

We rocked from side to side for a few seconds together before I tilted my head back and grinned up at him.

'If I say yes can I have my present?'

He pulled a torch out of his jacket pocket and handed it to me. 'Here, take this. Your present is in your shed, it was too big for the table in there.' He flicked his head towards the pavilion steps.

'My shed? How big is it exactly?' I narrowed my eyes. 'I hope you didn't go over the ten-pound budget?'

He smiled, leaned forward and pressed his lips softly to my forehead. 'It cost me a lot more than that, Tilly. Now shush,' he said, noticing me about to argue. 'Off you go.'

Chapter 44

Had I been thinking clearly, I'd have nipped back and changed these ridiculous high heels for my wellies, I thought belatedly as I picked my way gingerly across the icy tarmac towards plot 16.

Thinking clearly – hah! Chance would be a fine thing. I mean, exactly how many surprises can a person take in one evening? First the shock of hearing Aidan's name again, then Gemma's waters breaking, followed closely by Charlie's confession. This was one Christmas party I was never, ever going to forget.

Lost in my thoughts, I savoured the night-time silence, unbroken except for my crunching footsteps and a solitary 'hoo-hoo' as an owl hooted in the distance. I breathed in the frosty air and shoved the torch into my pocket. I didn't need it; the night was bright enough. I lifted my eyes up to the sky and gasped. Wow! How amazing was that?

No matter how spectacular my display of fairy lights was around the pavilion, it couldn't begin to compete with the glamour of Mother Nature. The inky night sky stretched out above me, twinkling with stars like chunky diamonds around a slender crescent moon. It was as if the whole galaxy sparkled with Christmas magic.

I sighed happily. I love Christmas. And I was getting a Secret Santa present after all!

Walking on frozen snow whilst gazing heavenwards wasn't so wonderful, though, and a second later I was brought back down to earth with a bump, almost literally, when I tripped over a large lump of snow at the roadside. I flailed my arms to stop myself from falling and decided to concentrate on the ground instead of the sky.

I wondered what Charlie had bought me?

It was probably something gardening-related like everyone else's presents, so he'd left it in the shed. I hoped it wasn't a new spade or fork; I was more than happy with the ones Alf had given to me, the ones Celia had used for so many years. It could be anything, knowing Charlie. I smiled wryly to myself. After what he'd revealed about himself tonight, nothing would shock me any more.

But what I would really love, I thought, as I turned off the road in front of Gemma's plot and on to the snow-topped grassy path towards my own, although I doubted it would occur to a man to buy them, was some solar-powered fairy lights. Then I could decorate the outside of my shed and have Christmas sparkle all year round.

Now that would be really lovely . . . oh! My thoughts tailed off into oblivion as the shed came into view. There was light coming from inside.

At first, I frowned in confusion and then I clapped my hands with delight. Well, I take that back, Charlie! How amazing, he obviously had bought me lights and what's more he had even strung them up and switched them on.

What a lovely surprise!

I picked up my pace and hurried towards the shed only to freeze a second later as a figure appeared at the window. I stood, dazed, my heart in my mouth, hardly daring to believe what my eyes were telling me. Even though his face was in shadow, I would recognize him anywhere.

The shed door opened and I held my breath as the world according to Tilly Parker tilted on its axis and everything – everything – changed. There in the doorway, illuminated by the golden glow from within, was the man who had wrapped himself irreversibly around my heart.

'Aidan?' I whispered, my feet riveted to the spot. My shoes had sunk down into the snow and I was vaguely aware of the cold biting into my toes. But the spark of hope that flickered back to life in my heart sent a rush of warmth around my body, more than making up for the cold.

Aidan's handsome face broke into a smile and he held his arms out to me. 'Merry Christmas, Tilly.'

I hesitated, just for a second, aware on some cosmic level that this moment was one of such importance that it shouldn't be rushed. I gazed at his silhouette framed in the doorway, at the ice crystals on the grass, which sparkled and danced in the moonlight, a carpet of diamonds, perfectly mirroring the stars above. It would only take me a few steps to reach him, but it was possibly the start of a whole new journey.

And then I was laughing and yelling 'Merry Christmas' and running straight into those warm strong arms and he was laughing too as he gathered me up and spun me round until I squealed for him to put me down.

My mind was full of questions that were tripping over each other to get to the front of the queue, but for now it was enough that I was in his arms, that the brown eyes that gazed back at me were full of an emotion that I didn't dare put a name to. Because none of this made any sense.

I've missed you, Aidan.

'I am so happy to see you.' He buried his face in my hair and hugged me tight, his voice husky and low.

'What are you doing here?' I asked, leaning away from him so that I could read his expression.

'Well, at this precise moment, turning to a block of ice.' He grinned. 'But speaking in more general terms, I'm your Secret Santa gift, apparently. Come on inside.'

Still holding me tight, he shuffled backwards until we were inside and then closed the door behind me.

My eyes roamed the shed in disbelief. The light wasn't coming from fairy lights at all, but candles, dotted around the shelves and on the table. And despite being surrounded by gardening tools and stacks of empty plant pots and half-full bags of compost, there was something intimate and romantic about the setting. In fact, the shed was exactly as I had planned for it to look for my rendezvous with Aidan at Hallowe'en, before Charlie sabotaged my plans.

And now, in a scene that could have come straight from my wildest dreams, we were here again. My heart was beating so wildly that Aidan could probably feel it through his jacket.

I looked up at him. 'Did you do this?'

He shook his head and laughed self-consciously. 'All Charlie's work.'

Charlie had done this? For me? That explained why he'd said it had cost him dearly.

'He phoned me. Told me the whole story.'

I swallowed and loosened my arms around his neck. 'When you say the whole story . . .'

I blinked up at him, my voice shaky with fear. Did he know about James? Was that why he had come, to humour Charlie? If Aidan had come back out of pity, then my heart could quite easily crumble into a million pieces and I would be right back to where I was last year: broken and lonely.

He exhaled slowly, lifted a hand from my waist and traced a line down my face with the tip of his finger.

'About you and him being nothing more than mates.' He laughed softly. 'Although he did admit that it wasn't for want of trying.'

I nodded and felt my face flush. 'I tried to tell you that.'

He squeezed his eyes shut and shook his head. 'And to my eternal shame I didn't listen. I suppose I just thought it was too good to be true that someone like you would be unattached.'

The corners of my mouth lifted. That was exactly how I'd felt about him.

He shrugged apologetically. 'Ever since Hallowe'en, even though I suspected that there was something going on between you and Charlie, you've been in here.' He took one of my hands and placed it on his chest inside his jacket and I felt the insistent beat of his heart.

'Then why not call?' I thought back to the nights I'd sat at home, hoping that he would somehow get in touch. Even though he didn't have my number, if he'd really wanted to he could have found a way, surely?

'I wanted to call you. But I felt as if I'd been too pushy, that I'd misread the signals. And I was pretty ashamed about the way I'd acted at Hallowe'en. I should have called straight away after that to say that even if you were spoken for, I'd still like us to be friends.'

So that was why he was here. To be friends.

I smiled sadly. 'And now you've met someone else. You've moved on . . .'

He frowned and shook his head. 'There's been no one else. Since meeting you, I . . .'

I folded my arms and looked away. 'I know you've met someone else because I phoned you and she answered.'

'Wait? You called me? When was this?' He placed his hands on my shoulders and scanned my face.

I didn't hesitate with my answer. 'Friday the thirtieth of November at seven forty-five.'

'Approximately?' He tried to keep a straight face but his eyes gave him away. 'Actually I remember that night very clearly.'

So much for playing it cool. I blushed furiously. 'Now you'll probably think I'm a bunny boiler or something.'

'No.' He stepped towards me, his eyes boring into mine. 'I'm thinking how overjoyed I am that you did call, I'm thinking that we've wasted a whole month. Two, in fact. More if you count back to the allotment show.'

'So . . .' I swallowed, determined to get the answer I needed. 'Who is she?'

'My sister,' he said simply.

'Your sister? But she was all breathless and I thought . . . well, never mind,' I groaned. We both seemed to be expert at jumping to the wrong conclusion.

'I was babysitting for my niece and nephew for the first time. My sister was in a complete flap, running late and convinced that I'd take a work call, forget about her children and something awful would happen. So I left my phone in the spare room where I was sleeping. My sister and her husband were running late, she must have answered it before she went out and then forgotten to mention it. She certainly never passed the message on. I'm so sorry. To be honest, my phone rings all the time, I don't ever think to check my call history.'

That was true. I'd seen it for myself this summer; he'd had a phone clamped to his ear semi-permanently. And of course I hadn't left a message; I'd panicked and ended the call immediately.

I smiled shyly at him. 'In that case, we're both single.'

He nodded and I gazed into his eyes and took a step closer, weaving my arms round him, desire for him intensifying as all the things that had stood in our path melted away. I could hardly wait to feel his body against mine, to taste his kisses. There was just one last thing to say . . .

'I told you my life was complicated and it is . . . was . . .' I hesitated, my mind searching for the right words.

Tell him, Tilly, open your heart.

I wanted to tell him, but the lump in my throat got in the way and I lowered my forehead to his chest.

Aidan gently lifted my chin and the look he gave me was so tender that tears pricked at my eyes.

'Charlie told me about James, about the car accident and losing the baby,' he murmured.

Words failed me suddenly so I simply nodded.

'Tilly, knowing what you've been through only makes me . . .' He took a deep breath and brushed the tip of his thumb across my lips. 'It makes me love you more. And I promise you that from now on, I will do everything – anything – to make you the happiest girl in the world. I can only imagine . . .'

I placed a finger lightly to his lips.

'Thank you,' I whispered, my mind racing as I processed his words.

He loves me.

'Aidan, sometimes terrible things happen and you wish with all your heart that you could turn the clock back, do things differently, and you tell yourself that if only this had happened, or that had happened it could have all worked out perfectly.'

411

I swallowed and stroked his beautiful face with my fingertips.

'But that's not how life works. It's taken me a long time to come to terms with that since losing James. And an even longer time to look on the bright side, to find the silver lining in my life. But the thing is . . .' I tilted my chin until I could feel his breath on my face. 'I think that you just might be my silver lining.'

He laced his hands through tendrils of my hair and kissed me. The feel of his lips against mine was so sweet, so exquisite, that it was almost too much to bear. And as I kissed him back, with every atom of my body rising to meet his, I felt a lightness, as if I was floating on air. My heart was lifting too and the last traces of grief that had been with me since losing James finally dissolved and melted in to the past.

As the kiss ended, I pulled away and cradled his face in my hands, committing the feel of his cheekbones, the scent of his skin, every contour, every detail to memory. From now on I realized I would be making new memories and, whilst James would be forever part of me, I had a new life to look forward to.

My new life with Aidan.

As we gazed at each other for a long moment, a feeling of peace washed over me and I knew unequivocally that this man was my future.

I glanced up to the ceiling and noticed a small sprig of mistletoe, nailed roughly to the ceiling in the middle of the shed.

All Charlie's work.

What a sweet thing to do. My heart swelled with warmth for Charlie for bringing Aidan and I together so selflessly.

'I'm so sorry,' I said, pulling him playfully by the lapels of his jacket until we were directly underneath the mistletoe. I lifted my eyes upwards and he followed my gaze. 'But I'm afraid we are going to have to do that all over again.'

I smiled into the eyes of the man who had brought me back to life, back to love, and saw my own happiness reflected back at me.

He lowered his mouth to mine. 'With my absolute pleasure.'

Four months later

I finally located my mobile on approximately the twelfth ring after a frantic search through the trail of abandoned clothes on the living-room floor and blushed at the memory of our 'quiet night in'.

Whoever it was, calling at this time in the morning, was certainly persistent. I peered at the screen and grinned: Gemma – who else?

'Take your time dot com!' she huffed down the line.

'Sorry,' I panted, 'couldn't find my mobile.'

I grabbed a blanket from the end of the sofa and wrapped it sarong-style around me. Conversations with my best friend were rarely brief and despite the sun glinting through the – thankfully – closed curtains, the morning was still chilly.

'OK, so what are you wearing?' she asked briskly.

'Um, at the moment? Just a blanket,' I laughed.

'A bl . . . ? Ooh, Tilly Parker, you little minx! Well, lucky you, that's all I can say. His Lordship woke me up a full three hours ago. Anyway,' she sighed, 'I dread to think when I'll be brave enough to let Mike see me naked again. My body is strictly for my eyes only at the moment.'

'Nonsense,' I retorted. 'Your husband worships the

ground you walk on. Even more so now you've given him a baby boy. Talking of whom, how is my godson today?'

'Adorable. And he's so clever. Do you know what he did this morning . . . ?'

I clamped the phone between my ear and shoulder and made appropriate noises while I boiled the kettle for tea. Gemma and Mike, rightly so, were besotted with their three-month-old son and liked to keep me updated with his miraculous progress in minute detail. I didn't mind one bit; I was completely smitten with him myself.

'Anyway, what I called to say was that he's wearing a purple velvet suit to his christening, so can you just bear that in mind when you're picking your outfit out for today, please. I don't want you two to clash on the photographs.'

'OK,' I said, rather bewildered. 'I thought babies traditionally wore white?'

'Oh no.' I heard her shudder down the phone. 'White completely drains him. Actually, we're all wearing purple; we thought it would be nice to be fully colour-coordinated.'

'*We?*' I chuckled, imagining the look of resignation on poor Mike's face.

I promised to dress appropriately and rang off. I carried two mugs along the hall, past Aidan's suitcase – a sight that gave me butterflies every time I saw it – and trotted up the stairs as quickly as I could without spilling the tea.

I paused in the doorway to give my heart the chance for a proper flutter. Aidan was still asleep, his swirl of thick dark hair the only thing visible above the duvet. I sighed. A big happy, contented sigh. I didn't think I would ever tire of looking at him.

Four months. Just four months together and he had totally transformed my world. And not gradually either! Aidan had appeared on Christmas Day after lunch with

415

presents for all of us, including Mum's new boyfriend Clive (who is one of the sweetest men I've ever met) and had even accompanied me to James's parents' Boxing Day buffet. I sighed again, remembering what an emotional day it had been for all of us, but James's mum had taken me to one side before we left and given me her blessing. We would always be welcome in their home, she had promised, both me and Aidan.

Setting a mug down next to his side of the bed, I moved to the window to open the curtains. There was still so much to do before the christening, especially now I'd have to rethink my outfit. The red flowery dress I planned on wearing certainly wouldn't do.

I pulled back the curtains and peered outside. A beautiful morning, perfect for such a special day. Aidan stirred as the sun bathed the room in a pinky orange light.

'Good morning, sleepy head.'

I dropped a kiss on his lips and he stretched languorously and rubbed his eyes.

'Hello, gorgeous.' He pulled me towards him, but I slipped out of his grasp. Much as I'd rather climb back into bed and while away the morning wrapped in his arms, I had too much to do. I knew I couldn't get away without washing my hair (I did not want to suffer the wrath of Gemma if I turned up to my godson's christening looking anything less than immaculate). Then I needed to get dressed in purple – which wasn't going to be easy – not to mention finish packing and drop off Cally at the cattery. After that we would pack the car, arrive at the church for noon and drive straight from there to the airport . . . Heavens! All of that in less than two hours!

'What sort of day is it?' Aidan asked.

'Weather-wise, glorious. Activity-wise, extremely busy,

so time to get up, I'm afraid. We're already behind schedule. You might have packed your suitcase, but I've still got heaps to do.'

I opened my wardrobe doors and looked for something purple.

'What can I say, you wore me out last night, I need my sleep.' He sat up, sipped his tea.

I giggled and peered at him over my shoulder. 'Are you complaining?'

He pulled the corner of the duvet back and patted the mattress. 'Come on, get back in.' He stared at me with those beautiful eyes and gave me his cutest grin.

My whole body tingled with love for him. How could I resist? He was simply irresistible. I sighed and looked at the clock.

'Please? I won't be here for another six weeks.'

There was a handsome man in my bed and I was wittering on about schedules. What was I even hesitating for? I dived back under the covers and kissed him. Another fifteen minutes wouldn't hurt . . .

We made it to the church in plenty of time, although I was convinced I'd forgotten to pack something. But I had the tickets and my passport and Aidan and really, nothing else mattered.

'Here you go.' Mia handed us a pamphlet each. 'All the prayers and stuff are in it. You've got words to say, Tilly.'

'Have I?' I bit my lip and followed Aidan into the church.

'Parker *Elton*?' he sniggered with an amused frown as he read the Order of Service.

I giggled. I was honoured that Gemma and Mike had named their son after me, but no matter how often I heard his middle name, it still made me smile.

'Elton John,' I whispered. 'Gemma's guilty pleasure. Ooh look, it's the proud grandparents!'

I linked my arm through Aidan's and led him to the side of the church where Christine was flicking invisible specks from Roy's jacket while he tugged at his collar.

'Well, don't you scrub up well!' I said, placing a kiss on Roy's cheek and giving Christine a hug.

'I could say the same about you, Tilly,' said Christine, beaming at Aidan and me. 'Being in love suits you. Put some colour in your cheeks, so it has.'

'She's beautiful, isn't she?' agreed Aidan, reaching an arm around my waist. 'A fairy godmother, I'd say.'

I certainly had colour now. 'Stop it, you lot. You're making me blush!'

'Congratulations on your TV award, Aidan,' said Roy, shaking his hand.

'Thank you.' Aidan bowed his head modestly. 'Couldn't have done it without the Ivy Lane community, of course.'

'Oh yes!' exclaimed Christine, turning to me. 'Was it very exciting? Did you see lots of celebs?'

I laughed. She sounded just like her daughter had when I'd phoned her after the red carpet event. 'It was amazing,' I confirmed. 'I've never been so nervous in my life. Nor so proud, seeing Aidan and Suzanna accepting the award.'

Aidan and I exchanged glances. I felt his arm tighten around my waist and thought my heart would burst with love.

'Tilly!' I turned to see who had called my name and spotted Liz waving at me, hanging on to Nigel's arm. I left Aidan to save me a space in a pew and went over to say hello. They were tanned and relaxed and clearly more in love than ever.

'How was Madeira? You look well,' I said, kissing them both.

Tickets to see the flower festival in Madeira had been Nigel's Secret Santa present to Liz. Hardly within the ten-pound budget, but the two of them looked so happy that I was sure it had been worth every penny.

'Wonderful,' breathed Liz. 'Wasn't it, Nigel?'

'Absolutely,' said Nigel, 'and er, quite eventful as it turned out.'

Liz flushed and waggled her left hand. An elegant solitaire diamond ring sparkled from her third finger.

'Congratulations! I'm so pleased for you.' I gave them a hug and excused myself to join Gemma, who was on the altar testing the temperature of the water in the baptismal font.

'Freezing!' she hissed. 'Parker's going to do his nut when the vicar splashes him with this.'

'He looks like Little Lord Fauntleroy in this outfit,' I giggled, planting a kiss on Gemma's cheek and taking Parker from her. I nuzzled his soft velvety skin and inhaled his delicious baby scent.

'I'm going to miss you,' I murmured, pressing my lips to his cheeks.

'More to the point, aren't you going to miss Aidan?' Gemma touched my arm gently and frowned.

I shrugged helplessly. 'We'll have two weeks together in the Galápagos Islands before I have to come back to school, so he'll only be there for four weeks without me. And his next job after that is producing a programme about woodland habitats back here so it won't be too bad. Anyway, I'll be busy on the allotment in May, you know how it is.'

Besides which, we had the rest of our lives together. There was no rush.

The church was filling up and virtually everyone from Ivy Lane allotments was here. It was nearly time for the christening to start and I saw Mike trying to catch Gemma's eye to come and sit down.

'I met Aidan's family yesterday,' I whispered out of the corner of my mouth.

'And?' Her blue eyes widened with curiosity.

'Perfectly lovely, of course.' I grinned and lifted one eyebrow. 'You'd love his sister, completely barmy, didn't shut up for a second . . .'

'Cheek!' she tutted, pretending to be affronted but then her eyes softened and she hugged me, planting an indulgent kiss on Parker's cheeks as she did so. 'Seriously though, Tills, he's just right for you and I'm delighted to see you looking so happy.'

The vicar appeared from a door at the side of the church and asked us all to take our seats. Gemma took baby Parker from my arms and joined Mike and Mia in the front row and I squeezed into the row behind next to Aidan, catching sight of Hayley as I did so, clamped to her boyfriend Ben in the back row. She winked and did a double thumbs-up and I grinned back.

The church's double doors clattered as they opened and shut and Charlie dashed in, pulling Freya behind him, the pair of them breathless and windswept. I pressed my lips together in a secret smile. So much for her not being his type.

Gemma turned round in her seat and twinkled her eyes at the pair of us. 'Ah, look at you two! Happy ending dot com.'

Aidan leaned forward and dotted Parker's nose affectionately with his finger. 'Who says it's the end?' he whispered to Gemma with a grin.

At that moment the vicar cleared his throat and gestured for us all to stand. 'We are gathered here today to celebrate a new life . . .'

I turned to Aidan and gazed into his loving brown eyes. He laced his fingers through mine and we shared a knowing smile.

I couldn't have put it better myself.

The Thank Yous

There are two people without whom this book simply would not have been written. Firstly, thank you to my mum, Sue Cope, whose dedication to her allotment and vegetable knowledge know no bounds (she's met Monty Don, you know). Mum, your contribution was completely priceless; I couldn't have done it without you. This is probably the closest we will ever get to working on an allotment together: you doing the growing and me writing about it!

Secondly, Harriet Bourton, my editor. Of all the writers you could have chosen to work with this year, you chose me and I will be eternally grateful. Working with you is an absolute joy and if Charlie were real, he would be very glad of your intervention in his life, I'm sure.

Thank you to Julie Mernick for your medical input and once again, may I apologize for sending you a text at seven a.m. asking what you knew about anaphylactic shock. If I'd known you'd turn up ten minutes later prepared to give CPR I'd have worded it very differently . . .

Thanking Dickie Hallam for his severe allergy to wasps feels a bit wrong, but if he hadn't once ended up face first in his potato patch, I wouldn't have thought of my own Ivy Lane version, so thanks Dickie!

Thank you to Susanna Zakarian and Marie Saunders for allowing me to raid your memories for Tilly's and Gemma's stories.

Many thanks to Trevor Ward for your help with the criminal element to Ivy Lane, your input made a big difference to Hayley and the crew and thanks to Andy Peet for showing me around your allotment one cold Sunday in January – I pinched the idea for white onions from you!

And not forgetting a massive thank you to the readers and bloggers whose generosity and support have enabled me to get this far. Your tireless cheering and flag-waving has kept a smile on my face during some of my trickier moments. I hope you enjoy Ivy Lane!

Thank you to Hannah Ferguson, my agent, for being the best Christmas present ever, it is lovely to know I have you on my side.

And finally thank you to my family, Tony, Phoebe and Isabel for joining in with everything from naming characters to critiquing covers to making book trailers and testing recipes, I love you very much.

#IvyLaneLove

Thank you to each and every fan that has supported
Ivy Lane on its journey over the last year!

A special thank you goes to all those who got in touch
to tell us about their #IvyLaneLove . . .

Carole Coupe
Karen de Ronde
Angie Gilbert
Jill Stratton
Gill Corbitt
Linda Chambers
Chris Grew
Sheerie Franks
Jo @Cometbabe
Rebecca @BeccasBoooks
Agi @Agi_mybookshelf
Louise Wykes @jaustenrulesok
Megan in the Sunshine @MeganIntheSun
rosie @kohsamuirosie
That Thing She Reads @joanne2913
Evelyn @ChickLitterEve
Paris Baker @PBscribbles
Sharon @ShazsBookBlog
Holly @BookaholicHolly
jooleysbooks @fluffychicko
Jo-Anne Wright @JoAnneW73792535
Sue Watson @suewatsonwriter
Holidays to Europe @holidays2europe
Haeddre77 @Haeddre77
Dawn @dawnlcrooks
Janet Harness @harness_janet
lolla2_uk @lolla2_uk
Sarah Baverstock @baversthebrave
Ellie Campbell Books @ecampbellbooks
Sonya @destinylover09
Marie Webdale @marieteapot22
Mummyreadsbookstoo @MrsHills126
Samantha Tonge @SamTongeWriters
Laura McGilley @lolla2_uk
Shaz Goodwin @shazjera

Helen @helenredders
Jayne Morley @JaneyMorley
Kay Shaw @Kessy26
Leonie Upson
Christine Caple
Samantha Pepper
Jane McDonough
Jean Lees
Jo Pollard
Shirley Giles
Dawn Williams
Lisa Day
Zarina de Ruiter
Doe Evans
Rosie Dharamsi
Tricia Clark
Cassie Cooper
Joanna Louise Williams
Dominique Ayliffe
Leila Benhamida
Becks Dawe
Linda Chambers
Liz Lawton
Carol Pack
Georgia Hinton
Lyn Abbott
Rachel Bustin
Gill Bow
Sharon Moore
Amy Jane Beckett
Nancy Hart
Jane @JanieDiver
Alison Page @aalisonpage
Andy @slacky109
Missie Watts @fupixepugom

A Note From Cathy

Dear readers,

So we come to the end of a year at Ivy Lane and what a year it has been for Tilly and Co.! Even though there is a happy ending for the lovely Tilly Parker, I don't know about you, but I miss her already.

I just want to say a huge Heart-Felt THANK YOU to everyone for reading *Ivy Lane*. The story was launched as a four-part series in 2014 and you may have seen the many Twitter and Facebook conversations which have appeared as readers finished each part and began speculating how the story would conclude. It has been absolute torture keeping schtum about the ending, but I managed it. I didn't even confide in my mum, the allotment aficionado, as to what happened to Tilly in the end!

Almost as soon as I had finished writing *Ivy Lane*, I immediately began to miss my fictional friends. Luckily, Harriet Bourton, my wonderful editor, who seems to know exactly what I should do next, planted a little seed in my mind for a new ebook series to follow on from *Ivy Lane*. The more I thought about it, the more I realized that the waitress who'd only popped up in *Winter* seemed to have a lot more to say than I'd given her chance to so far.

After a few days of walking around with a glazed expression, muttering to myself, looking straight through my poor family, Freya Moorcroft had her own story to tell. And now you can read all about her and some other familiar characters in my second ebook series called *Appleby Farm*.

Thank you all so much for your lovely messages, emails and Tweets. Please keep them coming, they really do mean the world to me. Writing fiction is ninety-nine per cent sitting alone with my computer, and receiving encouragement from my readers really does help me to keep on going.

Warmest wishes,

Cathy Bramley ✗

You can also enjoy the charming and funny four-part ebook series from Cathy Bramley . . .

Part One – A Blessing in Disguise
Part Two – A Family Affair
Part Three – Where The Heart Is
Part Four – Love Is In The Air

Read on for a sneak peek at the opening chapters of the first part!

Appleby Farm

Freya Moorcroft has wild red hair, mischievous
green eyes, a warm smile and a heart of gold.
She's been happy working at the café round the corner
from Ivy Lane allotments and her romance with her new
boyfriend is going well, she thinks, but a part of
her still misses the beautiful rolling hills of her
Cumbrian childhood home: Appleby Farm.

Then a phone call out of the blue and a desperate
plea for help change everything . . .

The farm is in financial trouble, and it's taking its
toll on the aunt and uncle who raised Freya. Heading
home to lend a hand, Freya quickly learns that things are
worse than she first thought. As she summons up
all her creativity and determination to turn things
around, Freya is surprised as her own dreams
for the future begin to take shape.

Love makes the world go round, according to Freya.
Not money. But will saving Appleby Farm and
following her heart come at a price?

An extract from

A Blessing In Disguise

Chapter 1

The door opened with a ding of the bell, letting in a welcome blast of fresh air as a group of teenaged girls left the café.

'Adios amigos!' I called. 'Ciao bellas!'

It was the Thursday before the Easter weekend, children were off school and the spring sunshine had brought us a steady stream of customers all day long. Now, at four o'clock, we were having a quiet spell, which was just as well because the service side of the counter, where I stood, looked like a scene out of *Titanic*.

I had spent the last hour training Amy, our new recruit, in the art of making espressos, cappuccinos and lattes. The work area was awash with her efforts; we were marooned in a sea of brown liquid, puddles of spilt milk and numerous abandoned mugs, spoons and jugs. The pair of us were looking a bit worse for the experience too: my red hair had turned to frizz after repeated exposure to random gusts of steam and Amy had a streak of coffee across her forehead like a third eyebrow.

On the plus side, despite the steamy atmosphere, there was a heavenly aroma of fresh coffee and I'd had enormous satisfaction from seeing her get the hang of the equipment – eventually. I watched over her shoulder, a bit close actually seeing as her short ponytail was tickling my nose, as she poured steamed milk from a stainless steel jug into a tall glass.

'Yay! Perfect. That's it, nice and slow so you don't spoil the foamy bit on top,' I cheered from behind. *Phewsha!* I thought she was never going to get there.

Amy placed the jug down with a shaky hand and exhaled. We both examined her first latte.

'What do you think?' She pulled her bottom lip between her teeth and wrinkled her smeared brow.

'I think you've cracked it,' I grinned.

Which was just as well because I was hanging up my apron any second, leaving early, and then she would be on her own behind the counter. I flung an arm round her shoulders and gave the sixteen-year-old a squeeze. 'But now you've got to pass the boss's taste test.'

I nodded towards the far corner of the café. Shirley, head down over a pile of invoices, sat at a small table with one foot raised on the chair beside her. Her ankle was completely better now; it was simply a habit she'd fallen into after being told to keep it raised when she broke it last autumn.

That foot was the reason I was here. Shirley's daughter, Anna, is a friend of mine and when Shirley had her accident, Anna begged me to come and help out in the café for a few months until her mum was back on her feet. At the time I was working in promotions, handing out free samples and money-off coupons in supermarkets around Manchester – a job which, to be quite honest, had lost its sparkle early on. So I moved to Kingsfield, a small town on the outskirts of Derbyshire, and into Anna's spare room – and I'd been working at the café ever since.

I watched Amy creep towards Shirley, the tall glass rattling in its saucer as she placed one foot cautiously in front of the other. I held my breath; it was like witnessing a tight-rope walker crossing the Niagara Falls.

'Delicious. Well done, both of you,' Shirley declared, lifting her latte in approval. 'Amy, you're now officially allowed to use the coffee machine and, FYI, I like three sugars in mine.'

'Go Amy, go Amy,' I hollered, waving my fist in the air as my student smiled bashfully, dipped her head and twisted one foot behind her other leg, looking far less than sixteen all of a sudden.

I also dropped into a curtsey, holding imaginary skirts out with my fingertips. 'And my work here is done.'

Shirley chuckled, shook her head and went back to her paperwork.

Is it?

As soon as the words were out of my mouth a fluttering sensation worked its way from my head to my heart. *Was* my work here actually done? Was it time to move on? Again. Eek! I stared at the top of Shirley's bowed head until it dawned on me that Amy was looking at me rather oddly.

I gave myself a shake, pointed Amy in the direction of the floor mop and, leaving her to soak up the spillages, went to clear the table vacated by the teenagers.

Yikes. My face felt scarlet now after that unbidden thought, which, seeing as I almost qualified for official albino status in the pale skin department, was pretty hard to hide.

Freya Moorcroft, you are up to your old tricks. Can't you stick at a job for more than five minutes? And anyway, what about you-know-who? Aren't you in L.O.V.E.?

I puffed out my cheeks and began to stack plates loudly to crowd out my snarky inner-thoughts.

Shirley's café was booming. And without being big-headed about it, the boom had something to do with me. When I arrived six months ago the coffee had been instant, the menu consisted almost entirely of jacket potatoes and barely any customers bothered coming to the café after two o'clock.

Now we had a fancy chrome coffee machine hissing like a contemptuous goose on the counter, a panini grill permanently making posh toasties, and we did a roaring business in afternoon tea. The free Wifi, which I'd suggested we install, had also proved a hit, especially with teenagers. The café was heaving with youthful hormones for an hour after school, earning us the reputation of being *the* place to hang out and doubling our sales of hot chocolate and smoothies. A win-win as far as I was concerned.

It had been a whirlwind few months, which was exactly how I liked my life to be. The whirlier the better, in fact. Shirley had pretty much let me have free rein once I'd convinced her to pimp the place up a bit and I'd had a ball. And, outside of work, my life was good too. I loved living with Anna, I'd made loads of new friends and most importantly, I'd met Charlie, my boyfriend of four months.

Charlie.

You know those ads for yogurt where the actors go all dreamy when the spoon goes into their mouth? Well, that's what happens to me just thinking about him. Tall, fit, amazing blue eyes, the cheekiest smile in the universe and to top it all, he was a fireman. I mean, hello?

So yep, my life in Kingsfield was pretty good.

But now – I paused from swiping cake crumbs into my hand and glanced out of the window at the row of shops, the pub on the corner, the parked cars, the total lack of greenery . . . the same view I'd been looking at since November – I could do the job standing on my head. Blindfolded. One hand tied behind my back.

Unlike Amy, I noticed out of the corner of my eye, who was making hard work of clearing up the kitchen.

I took the dirty crockery over to the counter and handed it to her. 'So how has your first day been?' I asked. 'Can you see yourself as a waitress? Or have I scared you off with caffeine-options overload?'

'It's OK,' she replied, nodding earnestly. 'As a part-time job. Till I go to uni.'

'Great.' I suppressed a smile but I must have raised my eyebrows higher than I'd intended because Amy blushed. Nothing like being told by a teenager your career choice was only someone else's stepping stone to greater things.

'Sorry,' she muttered, plunging her arms into the sink. 'That came out wrong. Not that there's anything wrong . . . Oh god.' She bent low over the sink so I couldn't see her face.

'Hey, no worries,' I laughed. 'Good on you for knowing what you want to do with your life. I got the grades at A-level to go to uni, but had no idea what to study.' I shrugged. 'So I opted for a gap year instead.'

Eight gap years as it turned out . . .

Auntie Sue referred to my decision to go travelling after sixth form as studying at the university of life. My mother called it a waste of a private education.

Amy glanced over her shoulder at Shirley and then looked back at me. 'I can only work here until I leave sixth form. I'm going to study architecture and it takes seven years to qualify then I want to move to London, so I really need to save up.'

'Right. Well, good luck!' I swallowed, smiled and shuffled off.

Flippin' 'eck. Sixteen and she'd got a ten-year plan. I thought I was being organized if I had a ten-*day* plan.

A career butterfly, that was me. I couldn't seem to help it. I'd start a job full of enthusiasm, throw myself into it, loving the whole 'new challenge' thing. Then as soon as I'd mastered it and put my own spin on the role, for some reason I sprouted wings and an urge to fly off somewhere new.

Uncle Arthur reckoned that one day I'd find my niche and my career would take off. My father, on the other hand, put my transient tendencies down to lack of ambition and commitment. I hoped Uncle Arthur was right because I couldn't bear it if Dad was.

The edited highlights of my career included: apple picker in New Zealand, stable hand in Dubai, chalet girl in Austria, bar maid in Cornwall (eighteen months – a personal record for me, largely down to a lifeguard called Ivan), a short-lived stint as a tour guide at a pencil museum and now here, waitress in the Shenton Road café in Kingsfield.

I was sure all the random experience I'd gained was preparing me for something, I just wished I knew what. I dropped down into the empty chair opposite to my boss and pondered whether to tell her that it might be time for me to move on. Or whether I should perhaps, for once, keep my ponderings to myself.

'You're wasted here, you know that, don't you?' Shirley said without looking up. Which was just as well because my face was now as red as my hair.

I shifted in my seat. Shirley Maxwell should never, ever be underestimated. She had an uncanny knack of reading

438

minds. Not that I'd been thinking that I was wasted, just a bit . . . unchallenged.

'Meaning?' I asked, playing for time. I pulled the sugar bowl towards me and started mashing the crystals against the side of the bowl.

Shirley dropped her pen on the table, looked at me and exhaled in a 'what are we going to do with you' sort of way. She moved the sugar bowl out of my reach and I folded my arms.

'Bright girl like you. You could be running your own business like my Anna. Or managing your own branch of Starbucks or . . .'

'Trying to get rid of me, are you?' I said, giving her my fake haughty eyebrow raise.

'Oh, Freya.' She swiped a hand at me. 'You've revamped the menu, helped organize the dreaded paperwork and now you're even training new staff. I'm grateful for all your hard work at my café.'

She pronounced it caff, which always made me smile. She leaned forward and mouthed with exaggerated facial expressions, 'But I can't pay you what you're worth and that upsets me.' She pressed a hand to her bosom. 'You might want to buy a house, settle down—'

'I'm not money-orientated, Shirley,' I said. 'I know people who are. People who put pursuit of wealth before happiness and believe me, I have no desire to go down that route.' I shuddered. My parents, for instance. 'No, as the saying goes, "all you need is love" as far as I'm concerned.' I grinned at her as she rolled her eyes.

'And as the other saying goes, "every little helps",' she retorted and we both laughed.

'You're a case, Freya Moorcroft, you really are,' Shirley sighed.

I reached out and squeezed her hand, the one that wasn't nestled on her cleavage. 'Thank you. It's nice to be appreciated.'

'Be honest with yourself, Freya. Waitressing isn't your future.'

The doorbell dinged and we both turned to see who it was. A familiar pink velour-clad bottom backed into the café pulling a complicated-looking pushchair.

Saved by the bell before I talked myself out of a job.

'Gemma!' I cried, breathing an inward sigh of relief. I jumped up to help my friend and one of our regulars negotiate the door and the step.

'Nightmare dot com,' grunted Gemma, as she attempted a three-point turn with the pushchair. 'You need a blooming HGV licence to drive this thing.'

'Oh dear. Let me make you something healthy, herbal and foul-smelling in a mug.' I heard Shirley huff at my alternative approach to hospitality as I kissed Gemma's cheek. I stood back to let her manoeuvre herself and the baby past me and peered in at him. Parker was wide awake (yay, I could have a cuddle!) and aiming a determined swipe at the toys suspended across his pushchair.

'Actually, sorry to take liberties,' said Gemma, making a beeline for the loos, 'but I only came in to use the facilities. His Lordship's nappy is beyond bearable and I say that as a mother with a very high threshold to bad smells.'

'TMI, love, thank you very much,' said Shirley with a wince. By comparison, Shirley had a low threshold to many things: smells, pain, loud music, most yellow foods . . . once I saw her nearly faint at the sight of mashed banana. Even a jacket potato gave her the shivers if it dared to err on the yellowy side.

'Not even a quick herbal brew?' I offered. I was due to

meet Charlie at his allotment in half an hour and then I had the whole of the Easter weekend off, but I hadn't seen Gemma since the baby's christening at the weekend and I wanted to hear her news. And get my mitts on Parker, obviously.

Gemma paused and then flapped a beautifully manicured hand, which made me tuck my own scruffy nails into my jeans pockets. 'Go on then. Camomile if you've got it, please.'

Five minutes later I was sitting down with a freshly changed baby boy on my knee, watching Gemma squashing and swirling her tea bag round in her white mug.

I couldn't abide those mugs.

Shirley and I had only clashed on a couple of things since I'd been here. I was Team vintage china, she was Team cheap-practical-and-dishwasher-proof. I'd envisaged pretty mismatched cups and saucers, stacked on shelves in pastel shades of pink, yellow and blue. But Shirley had gone pale at the thought of crockery not matching and had put her foot down.

Parker was concentrating on scrunching up a fabric toy between his fingers, which made a rustling noise when it moved. Gemma and I exchanged smiles as he babbled away quietly to himself.

'There's one scone left, do you fancy sharing it?' I said.

I made the café's scones using my Auntie Sue's recipe. The secret was in the mixing; over mix and you've got yourself a batch of primitive weapons. Mine, though I said so myself, were sultana-stuffed clouds of deliciousness.

Gemma shook her blonde curls and patted her stomach which, given that Parker was only about five months old, was in pretty good shape. 'I shouldn't really . . . unless . . . does it come with clotted cream?'

I shook my head. 'Whipped cream,' I said, adding more loudly, 'see, Shirley, someone else thinks it should be clotted cream.'

This, believe it or not, was the other thing we had disagreed on.

'No. Not having clotted cream in my café. That yellow crusty bit . . . eurghh.' Shirley shuddered.

'I'll leave it then, thanks. Probably for the best,' Gemma said, wrinkling her nose. 'Anyway, what are you up to for Easter?'

Tomorrow was Good Friday and the café was closed, plus it was my weekend off, double-plus I'd tagged on an extra couple of days next week – my first proper break since working here.

'Nothing much,' I shrugged, wishing I'd bothered to organize an adventure or two. 'Just chilling out with Charlie, hopefully.'

'Bliss,' sighed Gemma, her blue eyes going all dreamy for a second. 'What I'd give to chill out. But with a fifteen-year-old daughter hell bent on making us suffer because *she's* got exams and a husband who's decided to dismantle a lawnmower in our back garden, I doubt very much that I'll be doing much of that this weekend.'

I tightened my grip round Parker's tummy with one hand and tucked a wayward strand of hair behind my ear with the other. 'Just give me a shout if you want a babysitter for a few hours.'

Her face softened as she leant forward to hand Parker back the toy he had just dropped.

'Aww, thanks, Freya. Are you getting broody by any chance?'

I thought about it for a moment.

'Yes and no,' I replied honestly. 'I'm not ready to do the

whole settling-down thing yet. But at some point, yes. I can see myself with a couple of munchkins, cottage in the country, a horse and a dog . . . But for now, I'm happy to borrow Parker now and then.'

No idea why I'd suddenly blurted all that out. I felt my face redden. I'd never been conscious of this plan before. I did want to be a mother at some point though. And at the risk of sounding a bit 1950s, I wanted to be the sort of mother who was there when my children got in from school, with a kiss and a cake straight out of the oven. Like my Auntie Sue. I'd have to work on the cakes bit; I had a repertoire of one thing – scones.

'Does Charlie know how you feel?' asked Gemma, gazing at me wide-eyed.

The only problem with Kingsfield was that everyone else had been here for donkey's years. I might only have met Charlie a few months ago, but Gemma had known him for ages from Ivy Lane allotments. Unlikely as it seemed looking at those nails, Gemma had had her own allotment plot until Parker had come along.

'Whoa! Steady on, Gem, we've only been together five minutes!' I bent to brush my lips against Parker's head to hide my hot cheeks. 'I'm sure we'll broach the subject when the time comes.'

'It's just that . . . Oh, nothing,' mumbled Gemma. She lifted the mug to her lips and sipped at her tea.

My stomach lurched. Just that what? But before I had chance to ask, Gemma squealed and reached into her bag.

'I nearly forgot to show you this!' She handed me a postcard with a picture of a turtle on a deserted beach on it. 'Came this morning, from Tilly and Aidan. Sounds like they're having an amazing time in the Galloping-wotist Islands. Aww,' she sighed, lifting Parker from me and arranging him back in his pushchair. 'They are such a perfect match, those two.'

My friend, the lovely Tilly Parker, the baby's namesake, was another of the Ivy Lane allotment posse. She was the girl I credited with getting me and Charlie together and she met *her* fella, Aidan, when he came to Kingsfield last year as part of a film crew making a documentary about the allotment. He was filming something else now, in the Galapagos Islands, and Tilly had joined him for a holiday.

A perfect match. The words ran rhythmically through my head while I read Tilly's postcard and Gemma prepared to depart.

I waved her and Parker off with a smile. I didn't feel overly smiley on the inside; I felt a bit churned up. Gemma hadn't uttered the exact words and I might have been putting two and two together and making a fuss about nothing but it felt as though she thought that in some way Charlie and me *weren't* a perfect match. And as Shirley had pointed out only a few minutes ago, Shenton Road Café wasn't my future.

My stomach flipped queasily; when I woke up this morning my life had been quite straightforward, but now . . . well, I wasn't sure of anything.

The first part of *Appleby Farm*

A BLESSING IN DISGUISE

is available as an ebook now.

Ivy Lane recipes

Cathy's Comforting Spring Recipes

Leek and Potato Soup

This is an allotment staple! Early in spring before the growing season is under way, there are always leeks, potatoes and onions to be found. And what could be more warming after a morning on the allotment than returning home to a delicious bowl of homemade soup?

You will need ...

4 large leeks, washed and chopped

1 onion, chopped

A generous knob of butter for frying

2 medium-sized potatoes, peeled and diced

1.1 litres of vegetable stock*

Single cream for swirling (optional)

Black pepper

Chives to decorate the top

*substitute 225ml of the stock for milk if you prefer a creamier soup

Fry leeks and onions in the butter in a large pan very gently for 5 minutes. Add the potato and cook for a further 10 minutes until the potato is soft. Add the stock and simmer for 20 minutes. If you are using milk, add it in the last 5 minutes. Grind in some black pepper and taste. It shouldn't need any extra salt. Skim the top of the soup if necessary. Allow to cool slightly and blitz in a liquidiser. Re-heat and then serve in warmed bowls with a swirl of cream and a sprinkling of chopped chives. A hunk of soda bread would be the perfect accompaniment.

Peanut Flapjacks

Do delicious, sweet, irresistible flapjacks need any introduction? Enjoy . . .

You will need . . .

130g golden syrup

75g unsalted butter

100g soft brown sugar

75g smooth peanut butter

145g rolled oats

30g peanuts

Preheat the oven to 150°C, 300°F, gas mark 2. Grease a square baking tin (around 20–23cm). Put the golden syrup, butter, sugar and peanut butter in a small saucepan and heat gently until it has all melted. Take off the heat and add the oats and the peanuts. Tip the mixture into the baking tin. Don't worry too much about trying to spread it evenly, it will sort itself out in the oven. Bake for

25 minutes or until golden. Leave for 3 minutes before marking it into squares and remove from the tin when completely cool. It's quite floppy when it's warm!

Chocolate Easter Nests

Kids love making these, but I find adults love eating them! They are just so more-ish. For a grown-up serving, you could use Green & Black's chocolate and decorate the nests with truffles.

You will need . . .

225g milk chocolate, broken into squares

50g butter

2 tablespoons of golden syrup

100g cornflakes

1 packet of chocolate mini eggs

10 cake cases

Arrange ten cake cases in a muffin tray. Melt the chocolate, butter and golden syrup together in a large pan over a gentle heat. Stir thoroughly and remove from the heat. Add the cornflakes very carefully so that you don't crush them. Spoon the mixture into the cake cases and decorate with 2 or 3 mini eggs per nest. Make sure that you add the eggs before the chocolate sets or your eggs will roll out of their nests! Place the whole muffin tray in the fridge for 1 hour. After an hour, remove the cakes from the tray, place them into an airtight box and put the box back in the fridge.

Cathy's Favourite Summertime Recipes

Risotto Primavera
(serves 2)

This is quite simply a bowl of summer! If you do grow your own summer vegetables this recipe is a great way of enjoying them at their best. Risotto is easy to make although it does require your constant attention. That said, I have been known to pour half the stock in in one go and it didn't seem to make a bit of difference!

You will need . . .

600ml vegetable stock

1 onion

1 clove garlic

A little olive oil for frying

1 small courgette

4 baby sweetcorn

50g sugarsnap peas or mange tout

Pinch of dried mixed herbs

200g Arborio rice

50ml white wine (plus extra for sipping while you're waiting)

6 asparagus tips

A handful of spinach leaves (chard or callaloo will also do)

1 tablespoon of freshly grated parmesan

Salt and black pepper to taste

Preheat the oven to 180°C, 350°F, gas mark 4. Heat the vegetable stock in a small pan. Finely chop the onion and crush the garlic and add to a large heavy-based saucepan with a slug of olive oil. Heat very gently until soft. Slice the courgette into circles, chop the baby sweetcorn into chunks and put them on a non-stick baking tray along with the sugarsnap peas. Drizzle with a little olive oil and sprinkle over the mixed herbs. Put into the oven to roast for 10–12 minutes then set to one side.

When the onion is soft, add the rice to the pan. As soon as the rice begins to sizzle add the wine and stir until the liquid evaporates. Add a ladleful of stock to the rice and let it simmer. Once the stock has been absorbed repeat with another ladleful and keep repeating, stirring occasionally to make sure that the rice doesn't stick to the bottom of the pan.

After the rice has been cooking for 10 minutes add the diced vegetables and stir. Put the asparagus tips on the baking tray and roast for 8 minutes.

Check the rice after 20 minutes: it should have a bit of bite to it but not be too chalky. Add the spinach leaves and parmesan and season with black pepper and salt if required. Stir and remove from the heat. Allow the risotto to rest for a minute or two. Serve with the asparagus tips on top.

Summer Pudding

The first time I ever had Summer Pudding I was at my mum's cousin Mary's. It was summer – obviously – and I remember holding my breath as Mary cut into this ruby-red dessert and a tumble of delicious fruit cascaded out. It seemed an impossibly glamorous pudding to my ten-year-old self, a fact which was compounded in my memory banks when Mary and her family moved to California only days later!

You will need . . .

175g golden caster sugar

1.25 kilos of summer fruit (a mix of strawberries, raspberries, blackberries, redcurrants and blackcurrants works well)

7 slices of one-day-old white bread, preferably from a square loaf

Gently heat the sugar with 3 tablespoons of water in a pan until the sugar dissolves. Allow to boil for one minute before adding all the fruit except the strawberries to the pan. Let the fruit cook over a very low heat for three minutes. Try to avoid stirring too much as the fruit will break up and it is much nicer to keep it whole. Put a sieve over a bowl and tip the fruit in. You will need all that lovely juice later!

Line a 1.25 litre pudding basin with cling film. You may find it easier to use two sheets overlapping in the centre. Leave a decent overhang so that it is easy to remove later. Remove all the crusts from the bread and save them for the birds. Cut four of the slices into lopsided rectangles by cutting across at an angle and cut two slices into four triangles. Leave the remaining slice whole.

Now the fun bit! First dip the whole slice of bread into the juice to coat it and place into the bottom of the basin.

Then dip the lopsided rectangles in to the juice one at a time and press around the sides of the basin, alternately placing wide and narrow ends together to help them fit. If there isn't enough room for the last slice trim it to fit. Gently spoon in the softened fruit to the basin, adding a strawberry or two after every spoonful. Finally add the remaining bread triangles to form a lid and trim off any excess. Pour any extra juice into a jug and refrigerate until serving.

Bring the edges of the cling film together and loosely seal. Now you need to find something heavy like a couple of tins of baked beans. Place a small plate within the bowl over the pudding. Stand the tins on top and put the whole lot in the fridge overnight (or at least 6 hours if you can't wait that long).

To serve, remove the weights, peel back the cling film and place a serving plate upside down on the pudding. Turn the whole thing over, take the cling film off and serve with double cream and the extra juice.

Moroccan Chickpea Salad

I am a big fan of tabbouleh, a summery salad made with bulgar wheat. But when a friend of mine found she was no longer able to tolerate gluten, I came up with this alternative using chickpeas as an accompaniment to our barbeque menu.

You will need . . .

2 large ripe tomatoes
1 tin of chickpeas, drained

Roughly a 10cm piece of cucumber, finely diced
1 small red onion, peeled and finely chopped
A handful of washed, chopped coriander leaves
A handful of washed, chopped mint leaves
A tablespoon of olive oil
Juice of half a lemon
Salt and black pepper to taste

Cut a small cross in the base of the tomatoes, place them in a bowl and cover them with boiling water. Leave them submerged for 45 seconds then pour away the water. As soon as the tomatoes are cool enough to handle remove the skins, cut into quarters, discard the seeds and chop the tomato flesh finely.

Add the tomato to a large bowl, add all the other ingredients, leaving the olive oil and lemon juice until last. Stir thoroughly to combine the flavours and finally, season to taste.

Cathy's Autumn Recipes

Cinnamon Apple Cake

This cake never fails to deliver: it looks delicious, tastes heavenly and is so simple to make that I (almost) feel guilty accepting praise for it! Eat it warm with thick double cream, or at room temperature on its own. It keeps very well although you won't have to worry about that!

You will need . . .

225g cooking apples* (weight after peeling and coring)

Juice of half a lemon

225g plain flour

1.5 tsps baking powder

115g butter

2 tsps cinnamon

165g soft brown sugar

1 beaten egg

30–45ml milk

*my mum likes to grate half of the apple, but I chop mine.

Preheat oven to 180°C, 350°F or gas mark 4. Grease an 18cm round cake tin and line with baking parchment.

Peel, core and finely chop the apples, then toss with the lemon juice and set aside. Sift flour and baking powder then rub in butter until it resembles breadcrumbs. Sprinkle in 1 teaspoon of cinnamon. Stir in 115g of the brown sugar (keeping 50g aside), then the apple and egg and mix well, adding enough milk to form a soft dropping consistency.

Pour the batter into the tin. Mix the remaining 50g sugar with cinnamon and sprinkle this over the cake mixture. Bake for 45–50 minutes until golden. Leave to cool for 10 minutes in the tin before transferring to wire rack. By now the kitchen will be full of people all waiting eagerly for a slice!

Autumn Roast Vegetables

You can serve this on its own as a warming supper dish on a chilly night, as an accompaniment to a roast dinner, or even nestle some good quality sausages amongst the veg to turn it into a one-pot family feast! To ensure your veggies behave nicely, use a good non-stick roasting tray, which is not too deep.

You will need . . .

   1kg of vegetables, peeled, such as pumpkin, butternut squash, carrots, parsnips, sweet potatoes, shallots
   3 tbsps olive oil
   Handful of fresh herbs (sage, thyme and rosemary work well), washed but kept whole
   ¼ tsp of dried chilli flakes (optional)
   5–6 cloves of garlic, unpeeled
   Salt and black pepper

Preheat the oven to 200°C, 400°F or gas mark 6.

Chop all the vegetables (except the shallots – they can stay whole) into chunks, keeping the carrots slightly smaller as they take longer to cook.

Tip all the vegetables into a large plastic freezer bag, add the oil, herbs, garlic cloves, salt and black pepper to taste and squelch it around to mix in all the flavours. Leave to marinate for 2 hours.

Pour into a non-stick roasting tray and roast for 40 minutes in the pre-heated oven. Adjust the seasoning before serving piping hot.

Chocolate Chip Cookies

When my daughters have had a tough day at school (e.g. cross country running or French tests!), I make a batch of these for them to tuck straight into as soon as they come home. These really are better if you can chill the cookie dough overnight, although you can get away without in an emergency!

You will need . . .

120g salted butter (preferably at room temperature)

75g light brown sugar

75g caster sugar

½ tsp vanilla extract

1 egg

240g plain flour

½ tsp bicarbonate of soda

150g chocolate, roughly chopped (your choice of milk, dark or white)

Preheat the oven to 180°C, 350°F or gas mark 4.

Beat together the butter and sugars until just combined using an electric hand mixer or wooden spoon. First add the vanilla extract, then the egg, and beat well. Sift together the flour and bicarbonate of soda, then add to the mixture, stirring until it just comes together into a dough. Fold in the chocolate pieces, then chill overnight, or for at least an hour if you're pressed for time.

Lightly grease two baking sheets, form the dough into 15 golf-ball sized pieces and space them well apart. Bake for about 13–15 minutes, until golden, but not browned.

Let the cookies cool on the tray for a couple of minutes, before moving to a wire rack to cool completely. Feed to those who need immediate cheering up.

Cathy's Winter Recipes

Stir-fried Cabbage and Bacon

All I am saying is give cabbage a chance. Seriously, if you think you don't like cabbage, give this recipe a go and prepare to change your mind. I served this as part of a Sunday lunch for my family and fully expected them to give me their special 'you have gotta be kidding' looks, but they loved it.

You will need . . .

    4 rashers of streaky bacon, chopped into small pieces

    1 clove garlic or, if you're like me, 2 cloves

    A little olive oil for frying

    450g Savoy cabbage, shredded

    Black pepper and maybe a little salt

Fry the bacon and finely sliced garlic in olive oil, in a large frying pan until the bacon is cooked but not crispy and the garlic is soft.

Steam the shredded cabbage over a large pan of boiling water for two minutes. (If you don't have a steamer, simply boil it in a large pan for one and a half minutes instead.)

Remove the cabbage from the heat and allow any residual water to drain away.

Add the cabbage to the frying pan, mix well and stir fry
for 2 to 3 minutes until it picks up a golden colour and the
flavours are nicely blended. Serve immediately.

Blackberry Traybake

This is the recipe I had in mind for the cake that Toni
brings to the Ivy Lane Great Cake Competition. If you
haven't got the right tin, you can buy disposable tinfoil
trays from most supermarkets which are the perfect size
for this recipe.

You will need . . .

- 275g butter plus extra to grease the tin
- 275g golden caster sugar
- 400g self-raising flour
- 1½ level tsps baking powder
- 5 medium eggs
- Zest of 1 large orange, finely grated
- 1 tsp of vanilla extract
- 4–5 tbsps milk
- 250g blackberries
- 40g flaked almonds
- Icing sugar for decoration

Preheat the oven to 190°C, 375°F, gas mark 5. Grease and
line a shallow 30.5 x 20.5cm (12 x 8in) baking tin with
greaseproof paper.

Cream the butter and sugar together in a large mixing bowl. Sift in the flour and baking powder, stir to combine, then add the eggs, orange zest, vanilla and milk and beat together until light and fluffy.

Gently fold in half the blackberries using a metal spoon. Pour the batter into the tin and dot over remaining blackberries, then sprinkle the almonds on top.

Bake for 40–45 minutes until springy to the touch. Cool in the tin for 5 minutes, then turn out and cool on a wire rack.

Dust the top of the cake with icing sugar and serve.

Chocolate Orange Shortbread Biscuits

I used to work for Mary Berry, years ago, when my company did the PR for her range of salad dressings. We had working lunches on two occasions in Mary's kitchen. She was just as delightful to work for as you'd imagine and the food was delicious too! Anyway, this recipe pays homage to one of Mary's recipes which uses Terry's chocolate orange. I adapted it through necessity i.e. I didn't have any Terry's chocolate orange to hand!

You will need . . .

175g butter
75g golden caster sugar
175g plain flour
75g cornflour
85g milk chocolate, chopped into small chunks
Zest of one orange

Preheat the oven to 190°C, 375°F, gas mark 5. Cream the butter and sugar until soft. Stir in the flour and cornflour and mix until it becomes a smooth paste. This is much easier to do in a food processor if you have one. Stir in the chocolate chunks and orange zest.

Shape the dough into eighteen even-sized balls and space out on to two greased baking sheets. Press the top of each ball with a fork: this will leave a nice pattern when it cooks.

Bake for about 15–20 minutes until the biscuits are golden brown. Leave to cool on the tray for a few minutes before removing to a wire rack to cool fully.

Cathy Bramley is the author of the best-selling romantic comedies *Ivy Lane*, *Appleby Farm* (which were both first published as four-part serialised novels) and *Conditional Love*. She lives in a Nottinghamshire village with her husband, two daughters and a dog.

Her recent career as a full-time writer of light-hearted, romantic fiction has come as somewhat of a lovely surprise after spending the last eighteen years running her own marketing agency. However, she has always been an avid reader, hiding her book under the duvet and reading by torchlight. Luckily her husband has now bought her a Kindle with a light, so that's the end of that palaver.

Cathy loves to hear from her readers. You can get in touch via her website www.CathyBramley.co.uk, Facebook page Facebook.com/CathyBramleyAuthor or on Twitter twitter.com/CathyBramley

TRANSWORLD

Do you love talking about your favourite books?

From big tearjerkers to unforgettable love stories, to family dramas and feel-good chick lit, to something clever and thought-provoking, discover the very best **new fiction** around – and find your **next favourite read**.

See **new covers** before anyone else, and read **exclusive extracts** from the books everybody's talking about.

With plenty of **chat, gossip and news** about **the authors and stories you love**, you'll never be stuck for what to read next.

And with our **weekly giveaways**, you can **win** the latest laugh-out-loud romantic comedy or heart-breaking book club read before they hit the shops.

Curl up with another good book today.